MURDER ON THE MENU

Smithers is my name. I'm what you might call a small man in a small way of business. I travel for Num-numo, a relish for meats and savouries. Well, about the story I have to tell. And you mightn't think that a little man like me could make you shudder.

One day there was that ghastly murder at Unge. Steeger had gone down to live with a girl in a bungalow on the North Downs. The girl had £200, and he got every penny of it, and she utterly disappeared. And Scotland Yard couldn't find her.

Well, I'd happened to read that Steeger had bought two bottles of Num-numo; for the Otherthorpe police had found out everything about him, except what he did with the girl; and that of course attracted my attention. So one day I said to my friend Linley, "I wonder with all the knack you have for seeing through a chess problem that you don't have a go at that Otherthorpe mystery. It's beaten Scotland Yard."

Other Avon Books edited by
Carol-Lynn Rössel Waugh,
Martin Harry Greenberg, and Isaac Asimov

MURDER

✕ ON THE ✕

MENU

EDITED BY
CAROL-LYNN RÖSSEL WAUGH,
MARTIN HARRY GREENBERG
AND ISAAC ASIMOV
WITH AN INTRODUCTION BY
ISAAC ASIMOV

AVON
PUBLISHERS OF BARD, CAMELOT, DISCUS AND FLARE BOOKS

MURDER ON THE MENU is an original publication of
Avon Books. This work has never before appeared in book
form.

AVON BOOKS
A division of
The Hearst Corporation
1790 Broadway
New York, New York 10019

Copyright © 1984 by Nightfall, Inc., Carol-Lynn Rössel
Waugh, and Martin Harry Greenberg
Published by arrangement with the editors
Library of Congress Catalog Card Number: 84-90794
ISBN: 0-380-86918-7

First Avon Printing, April, 1984

AVON TRADEMARK REG. U. S. PAT. OFF. AND IN
OTHER COUNTRIES, MARCA REGISTRADA, HECHO EN
U. S. A.

Printed in the U. S. A.

WFH 10 9 8 7 6 5 4 3 2 1

ACKNOWLEDGMENTS

For Carl Gregory Raymond Rössel

MENU

Introduction: POISON!

by Isaac Asimov

Life is the end result of thousands of interlocking chemical reactions, most of them controlled by specific enzymes. The enzymes are "catalysts," substances capable of speeding chemical reactions without themselves being changed in the process.

Enzymes do their work by offering a surface that is just suited for the proper positioning of the molecules undergoing the reaction. The enzymes are protein molecules built up of hundreds or even thousands of atoms and each is so designed that it will catalyze only *one particular* reaction. There is a separate enzyme for each reaction, and by modifying the enzymes—activating, deactivating and reactivating them—the overall nature of the reactions characteristic of life are controlled.

It is because of the differences in enzyme content that a liver cell is different from a muscle cell or a brain cell. It is because of the differences in enzyme content that the trillions of cells making up a human being produce an organism different from the trillions of cells making up a giraffe or an ostrich—or a tree.

Any substance that will stick to an enzyme and distort its surface so that it can no longer perform its function will, obviously, disrupt the working of the cells of an organism. The distorting substance is a "poison." Since enzymes are present in tiny quantities, it takes but a small amount of poison to knock out enough of them to produce serious illness, or even death.

A number of organisms, in the course of evolution, have developed the ability to form poisons of one sort or another either in attack or defense. Where attack is concerned, snakes, scorpions, toads, etc., have venoms, and bacteria produce their toxins. In defense, plants which are eaten by myriads of animal organisms, from insects to human beings, and must endure this helplessly, sometimes develop complex molecules that are

1

most efficient poisons. Animals either evolve the ability to
avoid these poisons, by finding them noxious to the taste
—or die. The result is that poisonous plants avoid being
eaten, at least to some degree.

Human beings in prehistoric times, driven by hunger or
curiosity, are bound to have tasted everything. They undoubtedly encountered items that, when eaten, made them
drunk, or produced hallucinations (a mild form of poisoning), and such things were sometimes enjoyed and sought
out deliberately. On the other hand there were also some
items that killed. From desperate individual disaster, people learned to stay away from certain mushrooms, for instance, or berries, or leaves.

On the other hand, it must have occurred to human
beings on many separate occasions that poisons could be
useful. A poisonous plant might be mashed up and an arrow point might be smeared with the mess which might
then be allowed to dry there. If an enemy is wounded by
such an arrow, he might die even if the wound is a superfi-
cial one. This was such a convenient practice that the word
"toxic," meaning "poisonous," comes from the Greek word
"toxon" meaning "arrow."

Death in organized conflict is accepted as a sad visita-
tion by those suffering the casualties and as the result
of heroic behavior by those inflicting the casualties, but
what if someone's death is desired, and achieved, over a
private quarrel. Then it is considered murder and any
reasonably advanced society views inflicted death with
sufficient concern to want to visit punishment upon the
murderer.

Any sensible murderer would, therefore, find himself com-
pelled to devise a plan of murder that would enable him to
avoid punishment. He would lie in ambush for his victim,
and then, in secret and unseen, smash him with a blunt instrument or stick him with a knife. He will then sneak
away and hope that no one will find out who did it. However, the murderer usually has a motive that is known to
the community, and he will be suspected even if the murder is unwitnessed. It would be better, then, if the death
did not seem to be murder in the first place.

Suppose a poison mushroom is chopped up fine and added to otherwise harmless food that the victim intends to eat. The victim will enjoy his meal and then, sometime afterward, when the murderer is nowhere in the vicinity, he will die. There will be no obvious sign that murder was done; no cut, no smash, no blood, no break. It will be the kind of death that might have resulted from disease or from some internal stroke or seizure. Prior to the days of modern medicine, there were numerous fatal diseases that weren't understood at all, and no one could differentiate between a disease and a deliberately administered poison.

For that reason, poison became a favorite means of killing, and it was so common that the situation was reversed. Instead of poison being considered mere disease, disease was often considered deliberate poisoning. Right up through modern times, any public figure who died suddenly, especially while not yet aged, was supposed to have been poisoned by his enemies. Even if he died as the result of a lingering disease, he was frequently supposed to have suffered the result of slow poisoning.

So while history has its poisonings, the amount was rather exaggerated than otherwise. Perhaps that is why we have the history of the Borgias (a famous Spanish-Italian family, one of whom was Pope Alexander VI) who were popularly supposed to have poisoned half the people who dined with them. In 1679, in France, there was a sensational investigation of a murder-by-poison organization in Paris, which was apparently patronized by important people including Madame de Montespan, mistress of King Louis XIV.

Nowadays, however, thanks to modern science, things have changed considerably. Medical pathologists know how to detect traces of poisons in a most delicate and unmistakable manner so that it is very unlikely that a victim of poisoning is going to be mistaken for a victim of disease, if a careful autopsy is performed. On the other hand, poisons far more deadly than those of earlier ages are now obtainable. Perhaps 1/15,000 of an ounce of botulinus toxin will be enough to kill a person.

So "murder on the menu" is still something to be considered and here we present you with a score of stories with which murder and food are associated and, mind you, not always through poisoning.

THE CHICKEN SOUP KID

by R. L. Stevens

R. L. Stevens's name was inspired by Robert Louis Stevenson. He first appeared in Ellery Queen's Mystery Magazine *in 1971, and two of his stories have been reprinted in* Best Detective Stories of the Year. *He resides in upstate New York and is active in the Mystery Writers of America.*

As soon as he heard the footsteps, Quinlin knew they meant to kill him.

He'd made too many trips to the casinos in Atlantic City, lost too many spins of the wheel, welshed on too many gambling debts. Now, turning to face the dark shapes closing in on him across the deserted parking lot, he knew his time had come. As they drew closer, his only surprise was that Hagger himself was one of the men.

"Doing your own killing these days?" he asked.

Hagger gave a humorless laugh. "I'm not a barbarian, Quinlin. I'm willing to listen to reason. Perhaps you have something to offer in return for your life."

Quinlin's mouth was dry. "What would you suggest?"

"Oh, something worth roughly two hundred and eight thousand dollars. I believe that's what you owed my friends and me at last count."

"I couldn't raise that sort of money," Quinlin said, his voice barely a whisper.

"Think about it, Quinlin. Think about it real hard. I'll give you a minute or two."

"I don't know—"

"You interview lots of sports figures. There's big money in sports. How about the race next Saturday?"

"The Magnolia?"

"Sure. It could be worth lots of money to know the winning horse in advance. Or even the losing horse."

"How could you know that?" Quinlin asked, his mind racing to keep ahead of Hagger.

"You've interviewed Sid Engle a couple of times, haven't you?"

"The Chicken Soup Kid? Sure, he's good copy."

"And he's riding Overbridge, the favorite, on Saturday. Is it true that when he's at his home track his mother sends over a jar of her chicken soup for him to drink before the race?"

"Well, not right before. He usually has it for lunch. What are you getting at, anyway?"

"We want Overbridge to lose that race Saturday. If you could arrange it, you'd be off the hook."

"How could I do that?"

Hagger sighed in exasperation. "With the soup, dummy! We put something in the soup and Engle gets sick just at race time. Overbridge loses and we win."

Quinlin shook his head. "First of all, the soup comes from his mother. How're you going to slip something into it? And second, he has the soup for lunch, a good five hours before the Magnolia is run. He gets sick at two in the afternoon, the owner has plenty of time to mount a substitute jockey."

"You let us worry about that," Hagger said. "Meet us here tomorrow night, same time. Okay?"

"I guess so."

"If you're not here, you don't get a second chance."

Quinlin had been a sportswriter for most of his adult life, but it wasn't until after his divorce that he started to gamble heavily. He tried to blame it on loneliness, but maybe a spark of it had always been there inside him. At first it was merely sports betting—a day at the track or a sawbuck on the big game. But then he graduated to other things. Atlantic City was too close to Philadelphia for him to ignore, and after the first trip to the casinos he was hooked.

He had a good job with a Philadelphia newspaper, and for a time the casinos extended credit. Once he even managed to get even, and that was when he should have quit cold. He remembered calling it quits and going up to his hotel room one night, but he'd been unable to sleep, and at two in the morning he went downstairs and started all over again.

Hagger loaned him more money and ended up buying some of his IOUs from other places. Thinking about it now, he wondered if the gambler always had thought he could use him for something big when the time came. This Saturday the time was coming, and Quinlin could see no way out for himself.

He met them in the parking lot again the following night.

"That's good," Hagger said with a slight smile. "You follow orders."

"Do I have a choice?"

"Not really." Hagger took a small bottle of clear liquid from his pocket. "Here—this is for Engle's chicken soup."

"What is it?"

"Something to make him a little sick at the proper time. I have a chemist friend who made it up. The active ingredient is encased in tiny timed-release droplets, like they use in some cough medicines. It'll take effect five hours after he drinks the soup. You just make sure he gets it at noon."

"How do I arrange that?"

Hagger merely smiled. "I'm sure you'll think of something. Don't let us down. I've got a great deal of money riding on the Magnolia."

Quinlin placed the bottle carefully in his pocket and walked back to the car. He was about to do something he never would have considered possible only a few months earlier. He drove home to his little apartment trying not to think about it.

On Friday he telephoned Sid Engle's mother and reminded her that they'd once met at the track. "Oh, yes," she said. "Mr. Quinlin. You're the one who wrote about my chicken soup."

"That's right, Mrs. Engle. How've you been?"

"Can't complain."

"Tomorrow's Sid's big day, riding Overbridge in the Magnolia. Will you be at the track?"

"I can't! My niece is getting married and I'll be at the reception. But they said I could watch it on TV."

"What about your chicken soup?"

"I have to get someone to take it to him at the track. I think a neighbor of ours is going."

"Look, Mrs. Engle, I've been thinking I'd like to do an interview with you. It would make a nice Saturday feature, especially if Sid wins the Magnolia tomorrow."

"Oh, he'll win. I'm sure of it!"

"Suppose I come by and talk to you in the morning. I'll be going to the track right after that, and I can take a jar of your soup to Sid."

"Oh, would you, Mr. Quinlin? That would be a big load off my mind."

"I'd be happy to," he assured her.

It was Quinlin who'd first called Sid Engle "The Chicken Soup Kid," after discovering his mother's habit of sending her soup to the track if he was racing at Green Meadow. Engle himself scoffed at the name and tried to ignore it, but his mother thought it was great.

"I really think that soup helps him to win his races," she declared, leading Quinlin into her modest three-room apartment. "He's certainly ridden more winners at Green Meadow than any other track."

"Well, I suppose he just might be more familiar with it," Quinlin murmured, but she was not to be put down. It was the soup, and before the interview ended he had to sample a small bowl of it himself.

"There! What have you got to say to that?"

"It's very good chicken soup," he admitted.

"I'll just fill this jar and you can take it to Sid at the track. They have a hot plate to warm it in the jockeys' quarters. Make sure he gets it, now!"

"Don't you worry. I wouldn't want him riding Overbridge this afternoon without it."

They all knew Quinlin at the track, and he had no trouble getting in to see Sid Engle. The twenty-two-year-old jockey was polishing his riding boots as Quinlin entered, just before noon.

"Your mother sent some of her chicken soup," he said,

holding out the jar. He'd added Hagger's ingredient on the way to the track.

"Thanks, Quinlin. I'll warm it up for lunch."

"You going to be eating now?"

"In a few minutes."

"Feel good about the race?"

Engle grinned. "I always feel good about them. Put your money on Overbridge."

"Riding anything else today?"

"Scott's Tempest in the second race, but he's a dog. Save your money for the Magnolia."

"I had a nice visit with your mother. I'll do a little feature on her tomorrow."

"Great! She'll love that." He opened the jar and took a whiff of the soup. "It smells as good as ever. I don't know how she does it."

Quinlin left him as he was warming the soup and went upstairs to the press box. On the way he saw Hagger lounging against a railing near the refreshment stand. The gates had just opened and the place was already beginning to fill up.

"Hi there, Quinlin," the gambler said.

"Hello."

"Any trouble?"

"No." He dropped his voice. "He's having the soup now."

"Good. You want a tip on the race?"

"No," Quinlin said. What he had done was bad enough without trying to profit from it.

He went on to the press box and tried to write up his interview with Mrs. Engle, but the words had trouble coming. He kept wondering exactly what he'd poured into that jar of chicken soup. Would it harm the kid? Might it even kill him?

Shortly after one o'clock he went downstairs to search for Hagger, but the gambler had moved on to some other section of the grandstand. The daily-double window closed, and the first race went off as scheduled at two o'clock. He stood near the rail for the second race, watching Sid Engle ride by astride a big bay named Scott's Tempest. He seemed in fine shape, and surprised everyone by finishing second.

"It looks like Engle's day," a familiar voice said in Quinlin's ear. He turned to see Hagger behind him at the rail.

"I've been trying to find you," he said. "What was that stuff you gave me? Will it harm him?"

Hagger shrugged. "It'll hit him hard. We had to have something that would take him out fast. There's no margin for error in our timing."

"It won't—kill him, will it?"

"Maybe, maybe not. What difference does it make to you? Are you willing to trade your life for his?"

"No," Quinlin admitted.

"Don't worry so much. No one will connect what happens with the soup. You're in the clear."

Quinlin left him and then went back to the press box. He didn't want to be seen with Hagger, or with Engle, until it was over. He sat at his typewriter through the next three races, staring at the blank sheet of paper. What had he done? What had brought him to this?

"Sixth race," someone said. "The big one's coming up soon."

The Magnolia was traditionally the eighth race on the card, going off just at five o'clock or a few minutes after. That final hour seemed like an eternity to Quinlin, and when the horses finally paraded to the post just before five he took his place at the long press table overlooking the track, focusing his powerful binoculars on Sid Engle's face.

The kid looked all right. He smiled and waved toward the stands.

Hagger had said it would hit all at once, and it had probably been a bit after noon when he got to the chicken soup.

The horses were at the post. . . .

"They're off!" someone shouted.

There was a roar from the crowd as a long shot took the early lead. He wondered if that was Hagger's horse.

Overbridge was way back, trapped between other horses. Quinlin tried to focus on the jockey but couldn't get a fix on him. Now, he thought. It's happening now.

He dropped the binoculars and closed his eyes for a moment as the roar of the crowd increased.

"Look at Overbridge!" someone said. "Quinlin, did you see that?"

He tried to control his thumping heart. "What? What is it?"

"That damned horse just broke from the pack like a shot and took the lead. I think he's got it won!"

The jockey rooms were in turmoil after the last race, but someone told him Engle was still with the owner and trainer in the winner's circle, posing for television and still photographers. By the time Quinlin found him, someone had opened a bottle of champagne and poured it over his head.

"Greatest race I ever ran!" he shouted at Quinlin. "Give me a good story tomorrow."

"Was it your mother's chicken soup? Did that do it for you?"

Sid Engle grinned and hoisted the bottle of champagne. "Tell you a secret, Quinlin, but don't print it! I can't stand that chicken soup—I pour it down the drain! But don't print that. I'm still the Chicken Soup Kid."

Quinlin nodded. He wouldn't print it.

He stayed late in the press box, tidying up. By the time he left it was growing dark and the parking lot was almost deserted. . . .

THE CASE OF THE SHAGGY CAPS

by Ruth Rendell

Author of more than twenty novels, Ruth Rendell is the recipient of numerous prizes for her mysteries. Among them are the Current Crime Silver Cup Award for the Best Crime Novel of 1976, the Mystery Writers of America's Edgar for best short story of 1974, and the Crime Writers' Association Gold Dagger for best crime novel of 1975. Her stories regularly appear in Ellery Queen's Mystery Magazine.

"Blewits," said Inspector Burden, "Parasols, Horns of Plenty, Morels, and Boletus. Mean anything to you?"

Chief Inspector Wexford shrugged. "Sounds like one of those magazine quizzes. What have these in common? I'll make a guess and say they're *crustacea.* Or sea anemones. How about that?"

"They are edible fungi," said Burden.

"Are they now? And what have edible fungi to do with Mrs. Hannah Kingman throwing herself off, or being pushed off, a balcony?"

The two men were sitting in Wexford's office at the police station, Kingsmarkham, in the County of Sussex. The month was November, but Wexford had only just returned from his holiday. And while he had been away, enjoying two weeks of Italian autumn, Hannah Kingman had committed suicide. Or so Burden had thought at first. Now he was in a dilemma, and as soon as Wexford had walked in that Monday morning, Burden had begun to tell the whole story to his chief.

Wexford, getting on for sixty, was a tall, ungainly, rather ugly man who had once been fat to the point of obesity but had slimmed to gauntness for reasons of health. Nearly twenty years his junior, Burden had the slenderness of a man who has always been thin. His face was ascetic, handsome in a frosty way. The older man, who had a good wife who looked after him devotedly, nevertheless always looked as if his clothes came off the peg from the War on Want shop, while the younger, a widower, was sartorially immaculate. A tramp and a Beau Brummell, they seemed to be, but the dandy relied on the tramp, trusted him, understood his powers and his perception. In secret he almost worshiped him.

Without his chief he had felt a little at sea in this case. Everything had pointed at first to Hannah Kingman's having killed herself. She had been a manic-depressive, with a strong sense of her own inadequacy; apparently her marriage, though not of long duration, had been unhappy, and her previous marriage had failed. Even in the absence of a suicide note or suicide threats, Burden would have taken her death for self-destruction—if her brother hadn't come along and told him about the edible fungi. And Wexford hadn't been there to do what he always could do—sort out sheep from goats and wheat from chaff.

"The thing is," Burden said across the desk, "we're not looking for proof of murder so much as proof of *attempted* murder. Axel Kingman could have pushed his wife off that balcony—he has no alibi for the time in question—but I had no reason to think he had done so until I was told of an attempt to murder her some two weeks before."

"Which attempt has something to do with edible fungi?"

Burden nodded. "Say with administering to her some noxious substance in a stew made from edible fungi. Though if he did it, God knows how he did it, because three other people, including himself, ate the stew without ill effects. I think I'd better tell you about it from the beginning."

"I think you had," said Wexford.

"The facts," Burden began, very like a prosecuting counsel, "are as follows. Axel Kingman is thirty-five years old and he keeps a health-food shop here in the High Street called Harvest Home. Know it?" When Wexford signified by a nod that he did, Burden went on, "He used to be a teacher in Myringham, and for about seven years before he came here he'd been living with a woman named Corinne Last. He left her, gave up his job, put all the capital he had into his shop, and married a Mrs. Hannah Nicholson."

"He's some sort of food freak, I take it," said Wexford.

Burden wrinkled his nose. "Lot of affected nonsense," he said. "Have you ever noticed what thin pale weeds these health-food people are? While the folks who live on roast beef and suet and whiskey and plum cake are full of beans and rarin' to go."

"Is Kingman a thin pale weed?"

"A feeble—what's the word?—aesthete, if you ask me. Anyway, he and Hannah opened this shop and took a flat in the high-rise tower our planning geniuses have been pleased to raise over the top of it. The fifth floor. Corinne Last, according to her and according to Kingman, accepted it after a while and they all remained friends.

"Tell me about them," Wexford said. "Leave the facts for a bit and tell me about them."

Burden never found this easy. He was inclined to describe people as "just ordinary" or "just like anyone else," a negative attitude, which exasperated Wexford. So he made an effort. "Kingman looks the sort who wouldn't hurt a fly. The fact is, I'd apply the word *gentle* to him if I wasn't coming round to thinking he's a cold-blooded wife killer. He's a total abstainer with a bee in his bonnet about drink. His father went bankrupt and finally died of a coronary as a result of alcoholism, and our Kingman is an anti-booze fanatic.

"The dead woman was twenty-nine. Her first husband left her after six months of marriage and went off with some girlfriend of hers. Hannah went back to live with her parents and had a part-time job helping out with the meals at the school where Kingman was a teacher. That was where they met."

"And the other woman?" said Wexford.

Burden's face took on a repressive expression. Sex outside marriage, however sanctioned by custom and general approval, was always distasteful to him. That, in the course of his work, he almost daily came across illicit sex had done nothing to mitigate his disapproval. As Wexford sometimes derisively put it, you would think that in Burden's eyes all the suffering in the world, and certainly all the crime, somehow derived from men and women going to

bed together outside the bonds of wedlock. "God knows
why he didn't marry her," Burden now said. "Personally I
think things were a lot better in the days when education
authorities put their foot down about immorality among
teachers."

"Let's not have your views on that now, Mike," said
Wexford. "Presumably Hannah Kingman didn't die because her husband didn't come to her a pure virgin."

Burden flushed slightly. "I'll tell you about this Corinne
Last. She's very good-looking, if you like the dark sort of
intense type. Her father left her some money and the
house where she and Kingman lived, and she still lives in
it. She's one of those women who seem to be good at everything they put their hands to. She paints and sells her
paintings. She makes her own clothes, she's more or less
the star in the local dramatic society, she's a violinist and
plays in some string trio. Also she writes for health magazines and she's the author of a cookbook."

"It would look then," Wexford put in, "as if Kingman
split up with her because all this was more than he could
take. And hence he took up with the dull little school-
meals lady. No competition from her, I fancy."

"I daresay you're right. As a matter of fact, that theory
has already been put to me."

"By whom?" said Wexford. "Just where did you get all
this information, Mike?"

"From an angry young man, the fourth member of the
quartet, who happens to be Hannah's brother. His name is
John Hood, and I think he's got a lot more to tell. But it's
time I left off describing the people and got on with the
story.

"No one saw Hannah fall from the balcony. It happened
last Thursday afternoon at about four. According to her
husband, he was in a sort of office behind the shop doing
what he always did on early closing day—stock-taking and
sticking labels on various bottles and packets.

"She fell onto a hard-top parking area at the back of the
flats, and her body was found by a neighbor a couple of
hours later between two parked cars. We were sent for,
and Kingman seemed to be distraught. I asked him if he

had had any idea that his wife would have wished to take her own life, and he said she had never threatened to do so but had lately been very depressed and there had been quarrels, principally about money. Her doctor had put her on tranquilizers—of which, by the way, Kingman disapproved—and the doctor himself, old Dr. Castle, told me Mrs. Kingman had been to him for depression and because she felt her life wasn't worth living and she was a drag on her husband. He wasn't surprised that she had killed herself and neither, by that time, was I. We were all set for an inquest verdict of suicide while the balance of the mind was disturbed when John Hood walked in here and told me Kingman had attempted to murder his wife on a previous occasion."

"He told you just like that?"

"Pretty well. It's plain he doesn't like Kingman, and no doubt he was fond of his sister. He also seems to like and admire Corinne Last. He told me that on a Saturday night at the end of October the four of them had a meal together in the Kingmans' flat. It was a lot of vegetarian stuff cooked by Kingman—he always did the cooking—and one of the dishes was made out of what I'm old-fashioned enough, or maybe narrow-minded enough, to call toadstools. They all ate it and they were all okay but for Hannah, who got up from the table, vomited for hours, and apparently was quite seriously ill."

Wexford's eyebrows went up. "Elucidate, please," he said.

Burden sat back, put his elbows on the arms of the chair, and pressed the tips of his fingers together. "A few days before this meal was eaten, Kingman and Hood met at the squash club of which they are both members. Kingman told Hood that Corinne Last had promised to get him some edible fungi called Shaggy Caps from her own garden, the garden of the house which they had at one time shared. A crop of these things show themselves every autumn under a tree in this garden. I've seen them myself, but we'll come to that in a minute.

"Kingman's got a thing about using weeds and whatnot for cooking, makes salads out of dandelions and sorrel, and he swears by this fungi rubbish, says they've got far more flavor than mushrooms. Give me something that comes in a plastic bag from the supermarket every time, but no doubt it takes all sorts to make a world. By the way, this cookbook of Corinne Last's is called *Cooking for Nothing,* and all the recipes are for making dishes out of stuff you pull up by the wayside or pluck from the hedgerow."

"These Warty Blobs or Spotted Puffets or whatever, had he cooked them before?"

"Shaggy Caps," said Burden, grinning, "or *Coprinus comatus.* Oh, yes, every year, and every year he and Corinne had eaten the resulting stew. He told Hood he was going to cook them again this time, and Hood says he seemed very grateful to Corinne for being so—well, magnanimous."

"Yes, I can see it would have been a wrench for her. Like hearing 'our tune' in the company of your ex-lover and your supplanter." Wexford put on a vibrant growl. " 'Can you bear the sight of me eating our toadstools with another'?"

"As a matter of fact," said Burden seriously, "it could have been just like that. Anyway, the upshot of it was that Hood was invited round for the following Saturday to taste these delicacies and was told that Corinne would be there. Perhaps it was that fact which made him accept. Well, the day came. Hood looked in on his sister at lunchtime. She showed him the pot containing the stew, which Kingman had already made, and she said *she had tasted it* and it was delicious. She also showed Hood half a dozen specimens of Shaggy Caps which she said Kingman hadn't needed and which they would fry for their breakfast. This is what she showed him."

Burden opened a drawer in the desk and produced one of those plastic bags which he had said so inspired him with confidence. But the contents of this one hadn't come from a supermarket. He removed the wire fastener and tipped out four whitish scaly objects. They were egg-shaped, or rather elongated ovals, each with a short fleshy stalk.

"I picked them myself this morning," he said, "from Corinne Last's garden. When they get bigger, the egg-shaped bit opens like an umbrella, or a pagoda really, and there are sort of black gills underneath. You're supposed to eat them when they're in the stage these are."

"I suppose you've got a book on fungi?" said Wexford.

"Here." This also was produced from the drawer. *British Fungi, Edible and Poisonous.* "And here we are—Shaggy Caps."

Burden opened it at the "Edible" section and at a line and wash drawing of the species he held in his hand. He handed it to the chief inspector.

" '*Coprinus comatus,*' " Wexford read aloud. " 'A common species, attaining when full-grown a height of nine inches. The fungus is frequently to be found, during late summer and autumn, growing in fields, hedgerows, and often in gardens. It should be eaten before the cap opens and disgorges its inky fluid, but is at all times quite harmless.' " He put the book down but didn't close it. "Go on, please, Mike," he said.

"Hood called for Corinne and they arrived together. They got there just after eight. At about eight fifteen they all sat down to table and began the meal with avocado *vinaigrette.* The next course was to be the stew, followed by nut cutlets with a salad and then an applecake. Very obviously, there was no wine or any liquor on account of Kingman's prejudices. They drank grape juice from the shop.

"The kitchen opens directly out of the living-dining room. Kingman brought in the stew in a large tureen and served it himself at the table, beginning, of course, with Corinne. Each one of those Shaggy Caps had been sliced in half lengthwise, and the pieces were floating in a thickish gravy to which carrots, onions, and other vegetables had been added. Now, ever since he had been invited to this meal, Hood had been feeling uneasy about eating fungi, but Corinne had reassured him, and once he began to eat it and saw the others were eating it quite happily, he stopped worrying for the time being. In fact, he had a second helping.

"Kingman took the plates out and the empty tureen and immediately *rinsed them under the tap.* Both Hood and Corinne Last have told me this, though Kingman says it was something he always did, being fastidious about things of that sort."

"Surely his ex-girlfriend could confirm or deny that," Wexford put in, "since they lived together for so long."

"We must ask her. All traces of the stew were rinsed away. Kingman then brought in the nut concoction and the salad, but before he could begin to serve them Hannah jumped up, covered her mouth with her napkin, and rushed to the bathroom.

"After a while Corinne went to her. Hood could hear a violent vomiting from the bathroom. He remained in the living room while Kingman and Corinne were both in the bathroom with Hannah. No one ate any more. Kingman eventually came back, said that Hannah must have picked up some 'bug' and that he had put her to bed. Hood went into the bedroom where Hannah was lying on the bed with Corinne sitting beside her. Her face was greenish and covered with sweat and she was evidently in great pain, because while he was there she doubled up and groaned. She had to go to the bathroom again and that time Kingman had to carry her back.

"Hood suggested Dr. Castle should be sent for, but this was strenuously opposed by Kingman, who dislikes doctors and is one of those people who go in for herbal remedies—raspberry-leaf tablets and camomile tea and that sort of thing. Also he told Hood, rather absurdly, that Hannah had had quite enough to do with doctors and that if this wasn't some gastric germ it was the result of her taking 'dangerous' tranquilizers.

"Hood thought Hannah was seriously ill and the argument got heated, with Hood trying to make Kingman either call a doctor or take her to a hospital. Kingman wouldn't do it, and Corinne took his part. Hood is one of those angry but weak people who are all bluster, and although he might have called a doctor himself, he didn't. The effect on him of Corinne again, I suppose. What he did do was tell Kingman he was a fool to mess about cooking things everyone knew weren't safe, to which Kingman replied that if the Shaggy Caps were dangerous, how was it they weren't all ill? Eventually, at about midnight, Han-

nah stopped retching, seemed to have no more pain, and
fell asleep. Hood drove Corinne home, returned to the
Kingmans, and remained there for the rest of the night,
sleeping on their sofa.

"In the morning Hannah seemed perfectly well, though
weak, which rather upset Kingman's theory about the
gastric bug. Relations between the brothers-in-law were
strained. Kingman said he hadn't liked Hood's suggestions and that when he wanted to see his sister he, Kingman, would rather he came there when he was out or in
the shop. Hood went off home, and since that day he hasn't
seen Kingman.

"The day after his sister's death he stormed in here, told
me what I've told you, and accused Kingman of trying to
poison Hannah. He was wild and nearly hysterical, but I
felt I couldn't dismiss this allegation as—well, the ravings
of a bereaved person. There were too many peculiar circumstances—the unhappiness of the marriage, the fact of
Kingman rinsing those plates, his refusal to call a doctor.
Was I right?"

Burden stopped and sat waiting for approval. It came in
the form of a not very enthusiastic nod.

After a moment Wexford spoke. "Could Kingman have
pushed her off that balcony, Mike?"

"She was a small fragile woman. It was physically possible. The back of the flats isn't overlooked. There's nothing
behind but the parking area and then open fields. Kingman could have gone up by the stairs instead of using the
lift and come down by the stairs. Two of the flats on the
lower floors are empty. Below the Kingmans lives a bed-
ridden woman whose husband was at work. Below that the
tenant, a young married woman, was in but she saw and
heard nothing. The invalid says she thinks she heard a
scream during the afternoon but she did nothing about it,
and if she did hear it, so what? It seems to me that a suicide, in those circumstances, is as likely to cry out as a
murder victim."

"Okay," said Wexford. "Now to return to the curious
business of this meal. The idea would presumably be that
Kingman intended to kill her that night but that his

plan misfired because whatever he gave her wasn't toxic enough. She was very ill but she didn't die. He chose those means and that company so that he would have witnesses to his innocence. They all ate the stew out of the same tureen, but only Hannah was affected by it. How then are you suggesting he gave her whatever poison he did give her?"

"I'm not," said Burden, frankly, "but others are making suggestions. Hood's a bit of a fool, and first of all he would only keep on about all fungi being dangerous and the whole dish being poisonous. When I pointed out that this was obviously not so, he said Kingman must have slipped something into Hannah's plate, or else it was the salt."

"What salt?"

"He remembered that no one but Hannah took salt with the stew. But that's absurd because Kingman couldn't have known that would happen. He wouldn't have dared put, say, arsenic in the saltcellar on the thin chance that only she would take salt. Besides, she recovered far too quickly for it to have been arsenic. Corinne Last, however, has a more feasible suggestion.

"Not that she goes along with Hood. She refuses to consider the possibility that Kingman might be guilty. But when I pressed her she said she was not actually sitting at the table while the stew was served. She had got up and gone into the hall to fetch her handbag. So she didn't see Kingman serve Hannah." Burden reached across and picked up the book Wexford had left open at the description and drawing of the Shaggy Caps. He flicked over to the "Poisonous" section and pushed the book back to the chief inspector. "Have a look at some of these."

"Ah, yes," said Wexford. "Our old friend, the Fly Agaric. A nice-looking little red job with white spots, much favored by illustrators of children's books. They usually stick a frog on top of it and a gnome underneath. I see that when ingested it causes nausea, vomiting, tetanic convulsions, coma, and death. Lots of these Agarics, aren't there? Purple, Crested, Warty, Verdigris—all more or less lethal. Aha! The Death Cap, *Amanita phalloides.* How very unpleasant. The most dangerous fungus known, it says here.

Very small quantities will cause intense suffering and often death. So where does all that get us?"

"Corinne Last says that the Death Cap is quite common round here. What she doesn't say, but what I infer, is that Kingman could have got hold of it easily. Now suppose he cooked just one specimen separately and dropped it into the stew just before he brought it in from the kitchen? When he comes to serve Hannah he spoons up for her this specimen, or the pieces of it, in the same way as someone might select a special piece of chicken for someone out of a casserole. The gravy was thick, it wasn't like a thin soup."

Wexford looked dubious. "Well, we won't dismiss it as a theory. If he had contaminated the rest of the stew and others had been ill, that would have made it look even more like an accident, which was presumably what he wanted. But there's one drawback to that, Mike. If he meant Hannah to die, and was unscrupulous enough not to mind about Corinne and Hood being made ill, why did he rinse the plates? To *prove* that it was an accident, he would have wanted above all to keep some of that stew for analysis when the time came, for analysis would have shown the presence of poisonous as well as non-poisonous fungi, and it would have seemed that he had merely been careless.

"But let's go and talk to these people, shall we?"

The shop called Harvest Home was closed. Wexford and Burden went down an alley at the side of the block, passed the glass-doored main entrance, and went to the back to a door that was labeled "Stairs and Emergency Exit." They entered a small tiled vestibule and began to mount a steepish flight of stairs.

On each floor was a front door and a door to the lift. There was no one about. If there had been and they had had no wish to be seen, it would only have been necessary to wait behind the bend in the stairs until whoever it was had got into the lift. The bell by the front door on the fifth floor was marked "A. and H. Kingman." Wexford rang it.

The man who admitted them was smallish and mild-looking, and he looked sad. He showed Wexford the balcony from which his wife had fallen. It was one of two in the flat, the other being larger and extending outside the living-room windows. This one was outside a glazed kitchen door, a place for hanging washing and for gardening of the window-box variety. Herbs grew in pots, and in a long trough there still remained frostbitten tomato vines. The wall surrounding the balcony was about three feet high, the drop sheer to the hard-top below.

"Were you surprised that your wife committed suicide, Mr. Kingman?" said Wexford.

Kingman didn't answer directly. "My wife set a very low valuation on herself. When we got married I thought she was like me, a simple sort of person who doesn't ask much from life but has quite a capacity for contentment. It wasn't like that. She expected more support and more comfort and encouragement than I could give. That was especially so for the first three months of our marriage. Then she seemed to turn against me. She was very moody, always up and down. My business isn't doing very well, and she was spending more money than we could afford. I don't know where all the money was going, and we quarreled about it. Then she'd become depressed and say she was no use to me, she'd be better dead."

He had given, Wexford thought, rather a long explanation, for which he hadn't been asked. But it could be that these thoughts, defensive yet self-reproachful, were at the moment uppermost in his mind. "Mr. Kingman," he said, "we have reason to believe, as you know, that foul play may have been involved here. I should like to ask you a few questions about a meal you cooked on October 29, after which your wife was ill."

"I can guess who's been telling you about that."

Wexford took no notice. "When did Miss Last bring you these—er, Shaggy Caps?"

"On the evening of the twenty-eighth. I made the stew from them in the morning, according to Miss Last's own recipe."

"Was there any other type of fungus in the flat at the time?"

"Mushrooms, probably."

"Did you at any time add any noxious object or substance to that stew, Mr. Kingman?"

Kingman said quietly, wearily, "Of course not. My brother-in-law has a lot of ignorant prejudices. He refused to understand that that stew, which I have made dozens of times before in exactly the same way, was as wholesome as, say, a chicken casserole. More wholesome, in my view."

"Very well. Nevertheless, your wife was very ill. Why didn't you call a doctor?"

"Because my wife was not 'very' ill. She had pains and diarrhea, that's all. Perhaps you aren't aware of what the symptoms of fungus poisoning are. The victim doesn't just have pain and sickness. His vision is impaired, he very likely blacks out or has convulsions of the kind associated with tetanus. There was nothing like that with Hannah."

"It was unfortunate that you rinsed those plates. Had you not done so and called a doctor, the remains of that stew would almost certainly have been sent for analysis, and if it was as harmless as you say, all this investigation could have been avoided."

"It was harmless," Kingman said stonily.

Out in the car Wexford said, "I'm inclined to believe him, Mike. And unless Hood or Corinne Last has something really positive to tell us, I'd let it rest. Shall we go and see her next?"

The cottage she had shared with Axel Kingman was on a lonely stretch of road outside the village of Myfleet. It was a stone cottage with a slate roof, surrounded by a well-tended pretty garden. A green Ford Escort stood on the drive in front of a weatherboard garage. Under a big old apple tree, from which the yellow leaves were falling, the Shaggy Caps, immediately recognizable, grew in three thick clumps.

She was a tall woman, the owner of this house, with a beautiful square-jawed, high-cheekboned face and a mass of dark hair. Wexford was at once reminded of the Klimt painting of a languorous red-lipped woman, gold-neckleted, half covered in gold draperies, though Corinne Last wore a sweater and a denim smock. Her voice was low and measured. He had the impression she could never be flustered or caught off her guard.

"You're the author of a cookbook, I believe?" he said.

She made no answer but handed him a paperback which she took down from a bookshelf. *Cooking for Nothing: Dishes from Hedgerow and Pasture* by Corinne Last. He looked through the index and found the recipe he wanted. Opposite it was a colored photograph of six people eating what looked like brown soup. The recipe included carrots, onions, herbs, cream, and a number of other harmless ingredients. The last lines read: "Stewed Shaggy Caps are best served piping hot with whole-wheat bread. For drinkables, see page 171." He glanced at page 171, then handed the book to Burden.

"This was the dish Mr. Kingman made that night?"

"Yes." She had a way of leaning back when she spoke and of half lowering her heavy, glossy eyelids. It was serpentine and a little repellent. "I picked the Shaggy Caps myself out of this garden. I don't understand how they could have made Hannah ill, but they must have, because she was fine when we first arrived. She hadn't got any sort of gastric infection, that's nonsense. And there was nothing wrong with the avocados or the dressing."

Burden put the book aside. "But you were all served stew out of the same tureen."

"I didn't see Axel actually serve Hannah. I was out of the room." The eyelids flickered and almost closed.

"Was it usual for Mr. Kingman to rinse plates as soon as they were removed?"

"Don't ask me." She moved her shoulders. "I don't know. I do know that Hannah was very ill just after eating that stew. Axel doesn't like doctors, of course, and perhaps it would have—well, embarrassed him to call Dr. Castle in the circumstances. Hannah had black spots in front of her eyes, she was getting double vision. I was extremely concerned for her."

"But you didn't take it on yourself to get a doctor, Miss Last? Or even support Mr. Hood in his allegations?"

"Whatever John Hood said, I knew it couldn't be the Shaggy Caps." There was a note of scorn when she spoke

Hood's name. "And I was rather frightened. I couldn't help thinking it would be terrible if Axel got into some sort of trouble, if there was an inquiry or something."

"There's an inquiry now, Miss Last."

"Well, it's different now, isn't it? Hannah's dead. I mean, it's not just suspicion or conjecture anymore."

She saw them out and closed the front door before they had reached the garden gate. Farther along the roadside and under the hedges more Shaggy Caps could be seen as well as other kinds of fungi that Wexford couldn't identify—little mushroom-like things with pinkish gills, a cluster of small yellow umbrellas, and from the trunk of an oak tree, bulbous smoke-colored swellings that Burden said were Oyster Mushrooms.

"That woman," said Wexford, "is a mistress of the artless insinuation. She damned Kingman with almost every word, but she never came out with a direct insinuation." He shook his head. "I suppose Hood will be at work?"

"Presumably," said Burden, but Hood was not at work. He was waiting for them at the police station, fuming at the delay, and threatening "if something wasn't done at once" to take his grievances to the chief constable, even to the Home Office.

"Something is being done," said Wexford quietly. "I'm glad you've come here, Mr. Hood. But try to keep calm, will you, please?"

It was apparent to Wexford from the first that John Hood was in a different category of intelligence from that of Kingman and Corinne Last. He was a thickset man of perhaps no more than twenty-seven or twenty-eight, with bewildered resentful blue eyes in a puffy flushed face. A man, Wexford thought, who would fling out rash accusations he couldn't substantiate, who would be driven to bombast and bluster in the company of the ex-teacher and that clever, subtle woman.

He began to talk now, not wildly, but still without restraint, repeating what he had said to Burden, reiterating, without putting forward any real evidence, that his brother-in-law had meant to kill his sister that night. It was only by luck that she had survived. Kingman was a ruthless man who would have stopped at nothing to be rid of her. He, Hood, would never forgive himself that he hadn't made a stand and called the doctor.

"Yes, yes, Mr. Hood, but what exactly were your sister's symptoms?"

"Vomiting and stomach pains, violent pains," said Hood.

"She complained of nothing else?"

"Wasn't that enough? That's what you get when someone feeds you poisonous rubbish."

Wexford merely raised his eyebrows. Abruptly he left the events of that evening and said, "What had gone wrong with your sister's marriage?"

Before Hood replied, Wexford could sense he was keeping something back. A wariness came into his eyes and then was gone. "Axel wasn't the right person for her," he began. "She had problems, she needed understanding, she wasn't . . ." His voice trailed away.

"Wasn't what, Mr. Hood? What problems?"

"It's got nothing to do with all this," Hood muttered.

"I'll be the judge of that. You made this accusation, you started this business off. It's not for you now to keep anything back." On a sudden inspiration Wexford said, "Had these problems anything to do with the money she was spending?"

Hood was silent and sullen. Wexford thought rapidly over the things he had been told—Axel Kingman's fanaticism on one particular subject, Hannah's desperate need of an unspecified kind of support during the early days of her marriage, and later on, her alternating moods, then the money, the weekly sums of money spent and unaccounted for.

He looked up and said baldly, "Was your sister an alcoholic, Mr. Hood?"

Hood hadn't liked his directness. He flushed and looked affronted. He skirted round a frank answer. Well, yes, she drank. She was at pains to conceal her drinking. It had been going on more or less consistently since her first marriage broke up.

"In fact, she was an alcoholic," said Wexford.

"I suppose so."

"Your brother-in-law didn't know?"

"Good God, no. Axel would have killed her!" He realized what he had said. "Maybe that's why, maybe he found out."

"I don't think so, Mr. Hood. Now I imagine that in the first few months of her marriage she made an effort to give up drinking. She needed a good deal of support during this time, but she couldn't or wouldn't tell Mr. Kingman why she needed it. Her efforts failed, and slowly, because she couldn't manage without it, she began drinking again."

"She wasn't as bad as she used to be," Hood said with pathetic eagerness. "And only in the evenings. She told me she never had a drink before six, and then she'd have a few more, gulping them down on the quiet so Axel wouldn't know."

Burden said suddenly, "Had your sister been drinking that evening?"

"I expect so. She wouldn't have been able to face company, not even just Corinne and me, without a drink."

"Did anyone besides yourself know that your sister drank?"

"My mother did. My mother and I had a sort of pact to keep it dark from everyone so that Axel wouldn't find out." He hesitated, then said rather defiantly, "I did tell Corinne. She's a wonderful person, she's very clever. I was worried about it and I didn't know what I ought to do. She promised she wouldn't tell Axel."

"I see." Wexford had his own reasons for thinking that hadn't happened. Deep in thought, he got up and walked to the other end of the room, where he stood gazing out the window. Burden's continuing questions, Hood's answers, reached him only as a confused murmur of voices. Then he heard Burden say more loudly, "That's all for now, Mr. Hood, unless the chief inspector has anything more to ask you."

"No, no," said Wexford abstractedly, and when Hood had somewhat truculently departed, "Time for lunch. It's past two. Personally I shall avoid any dishes containing fungi, even *Psalliota campestris.*"

After Burden had looked that one up and identified it as the Common Mushroom, they lunched and then made a round of such wineshops in Kingsmarkham as were open at that hour. At the Wine Basket they drew a blank, but the assistant in the Vineyard told them that a woman answering Hannah Kingman's description had been a regular customer, and that on the previous Wednesday, the day before her death, she had called in and bought a bottle of Courvoisier cognac.

"There was no liquor of any kind in Kingman's flat," said Burden. "Might have been an empty bottle in the rubbish, I suppose." He made a rueful face. "We didn't look, didn't think we had any reason to. But she couldn't have drunk a whole bottleful on the Wednesday, could she?"

"Why are you so interested in this drinking business, Mike? You don't seriously see it as a motive for murder, do you? That Kingman killed her because he'd found out, or been told, that she was a secret drinker?"

"It was a means, not a motive," said Burden. "I know how it was done. I know how Kingman tried to kill her that first time." He grinned. "Makes a change for me to find the answer before you, doesn't it? I'm going to follow in your footsteps and make a mystery of it for the time being, if you don't mind. With your permission we'll go back to the station, pick up those Shaggy Caps, and conduct a little experiment."

Michael Burden lived in a neat bungalow in Tabard Road, Kingsmarkham. He had lived there with his wife until her untimely and tragic death and continued to live there still with his sixteen-year-old daughter, his son being away at a university. But that evening Pat Burden was out with her boyfriend, and there was a note left for her father on the refrigerator. "Dad, I ate the cold beef from yesterday. Can you open a tin for yourself? Back by eleven. Love, P."

"I'm glad she hasn't cooked anything," said Burden with what Wexford called his sloppy look, the expression that came over his face whenever he thought his children might be inconvenienced or made to lift a finger on his account. "I shouldn't be able to eat it, and I'd hate her to take it as criticism."

Wexford made the sound that used to be written "Pshaw!" "You've got sensible kids and you treat them like paranoiacs. While you're deciding just how much I'm to be told about this experiment of yours, d'you mind if I phone my wife?"

"Be my guest."

It was nearly six. Wexford came back to find Burden peeling carrots and onions. The four specimens of *Coprinus comatus*, beginning now to look a little wizened, lay on a chopping board. On the stove a saucepanful of bone stock was heating up.

"What the hell are you doing?"

"Making Shaggy Cap stew. My theory is that the stew is harmless when eaten by non-drinkers, and toxic, or toxic to some extent, when taken by those with alcohol in the stomach. How about that? In a minute, when this lot's cooking, I'm going to take a moderate quantity of alcohol, then I'm going to eat the stew. Now say I'm a damned fool if you like."

Wexford shrugged. He grinned. "I'm overcome by so much courage and selfless devotion to the duty you owe the taxpayers. But wait a minute. Are you sure only Hannah had been drinking that night? We know Kingman hadn't. What about those other two?"

"I asked Hood that while you were off in your daydream. He called for Corinne Last at six, at her request. They picked some apples for his mother, then she made him coffee. He did suggest they call in at a pub for a drink on their way to the Kingmans, but apparently she took so long getting ready that they didn't have time."

"Okay. Go ahead then. But wouldn't it be easier to call in an expert? There must be such people. Very likely someone holds a chair of fungology at the University of the South."

"Very likely. We can do that after I've tried it. I want to know for sure *now*. Are you willing too?"

"Certainly not. I'm not your guest to that extent. Since I've told my wife I won't be home for dinner, I'll take it as a kindness if you'll make me some innocent scrambled eggs."

He followed Burden into the living room, where the inspector opened a door in the sideboard. "What'll you drink?"

"White wine, if you've got any, or vermouth if you haven't. You know how abstemious I have to be."

Burden poured vermouth and soda. "Ice?"

"No, thanks. What are you going to have? Brandy? That was Hannah Kingman's favorite, apparently."

"Haven't got any," said Burden. "It'll have to be whiskey. I think we can reckon she had two double brandies before that meal, don't you? I'm not so brave I want to be as ill as she was." He caught Wexford's eye. "You don't think some people could be more sensitive to it than others, do you?"

"Bound to be," said Wexford breezily. "Cheers!"

Burden sipped his heavily watered whiskey, then tossed it down. "I'll just have a look at my stew. You sit down. Put the television on."

Wexford obeyed him. The big colored picture was of a wood in autumn, pale blue sky, golden beech leaves. Then the camera closed in on a cluster of red-and-white-spotted Fly Agaric. Chuckling, Wexford turned it off as Burden put his head round the door.

"I think it's more or less ready."

"Better have another whiskey."

"I suppose I had." Burden came in and refilled his glass. "That ought to do it."

"Oh, God, I forgot. I'm not much of a cook, you know. Don't know how women manage to get a whole lot of different things brewing and make them synchronize."

"It is a mystery, isn't it? I'll get myself some bread and cheese, if I may."

The brownish mixture was in a soup bowl. In the gravy floated four Shaggy Caps, cut lengthwise. Burden finished his whiskey at a gulp.

"What was it the Christians in the arena used to say to the Roman emperor before they went to the lions?"

"Morituri te salutamus," said Wexford. " 'We who are about to die salute thee.' "

"Well . . ." Burden made an effort with the Latin he had culled from his son's homework. *"Moriturus te saluto.* Would that be right?"

"I daresay. You won't die, though."

Burden made no answer. He picked up his spoon and began to eat. "Can I have some more soda?" said Wexford.

There are perhaps few stabs harder to bear than derision directed at one's heroism. Burden gave him a sour look. "Help yourself. I'm busy."

The chief inspector did so. "What's it like?" he said.

"All right. It's quite nice, like mushrooms."

Doggedly he ate. He didn't once gag on it. He finished the lot and wiped the bowl round with a piece of bread. Then he sat up, holding himself rather tensely.

"May as well have your telly on now," said Wexford. "Pass the time." He switched it on again. No Fly Agaric this time, but a dog fox moving across a meadow with Vivaldi playing. "How d'you feel?"

"Fine," said Burden gloomily.

"Cheer up. It may not last."

But it did. After fifteen minutes had passed, Burden still felt perfectly well. He looked bewildered. "I was so damned positive. I *knew* I was going to be retching and vomiting by now. I didn't put the car away because I was certain you'd have to run me down to the hospital."

Wexford only raised his eyebrows.

"You were pretty casual about it, I must say. Didn't say a word to stop me, did you? Didn't it occur to you it might have been a bit awkward for you if anything had happened to me?"

"I knew it wouldn't. I said to get a fungologist." And then Wexford, faced by Burden's aggrieved stare, burst out laughing. "Dear old Mike, you'll have to forgive me. But you know me, d'you honestly think I'd have let you risk your life eating that stuff? I knew you were safe."

"May one ask how?"

"One may. And you'd have known too if you'd bothered to take a proper look at that book of Corinne Last's. Under the recipe for Shaggy Cap stew it said, 'For drinkables, see page 171.' Well, I looked at page 171, and there Miss Last gave a recipe for cowslip wine and another for sloe gin, both highly intoxicating drinks. Would she have recommended a wine and a spirit to drink with those fungi if there'd been the slightest risk? Not if she wanted to sell her book, she wouldn't. Not unless she was risking hundreds of furious letters and expensive lawsuits from her readers."

Burden had flushed a little. Then he too began to roar with laughter.

After a little while Burden made coffee.

"A little logical thinking would be in order, I fancy," said Wexford. "You said this morning that we were not so much seeking to prove murder as attempted murder. Axel Kingman could have pushed her off that balcony, but no one saw her fall and no one heard him or anyone else go up to that flat during the afternoon. If, however, an attempt was made to murder her two weeks before, the presumption that she was eventually murdered is enormously strengthened."

Burden said impatiently, "We've been through all that. We know that."

"Wait a minute. The attempt failed. Now just how seriously ill was she? According to Kingman and Hood, she had severe stomach pains and she vomited. By midnight she was peacefully sleeping, and by the following day she was all right."

"I don't see where this is getting us."

"To a point which is very important and which may be the crux of the whole case. You say that Axel Kingman attempted to murder her. In order to do so he must have made very elaborate plans—the arranging of the meal, the inviting of two witnesses, the insuring that his wife tasted the stew earlier in the day, and preparing for some very nifty sleight of hand at the time the meal was served. Isn't it odd that the actual method used should so signally have failed? That Hannah's *life* never seems to have been in danger? And what if the method had succeeded? At postmortem some noxious agent would have been found in her body, or the effects of such. How could he have hoped to get away with that, since, as we know, neither of his witnesses actually watched him serve Hannah and one of them was even out of the room?

"So what I am postulating is that no one attempted to murder her, but someone *attempted* to make her ill so that, taken in conjunction with the sinister reputation of non-mushroom fungi and Hood's admitted suspicion of them, taken in conjunction with the known unhappiness of the marriage, it *would look as if there had been a murder attempt.*"

Burden stared at him. "Kingman would never have done that. He would either have wanted his attempt to succeed or not to have looked like an attempt at all."

"Exactly. And where does that get us?"

Instead of answering him Burden said on a note of triumph, his humiliation still rankling, "You're wrong about one thing. She *was* seriously ill, she didn't just have nausea and vomiting. Kingman and Hood may not have mentioned it, but Corinne Last said she had double vision and black spots before her eyes and . . ." His voice faltered. "My God, you mean—?"

Wexford nodded. "Corinne Last *only* of the three says she had those symptoms. Only Corinne Last is in a position to say, because she lived with him, if Kingman was in the habit of rinsing plates as soon as he removed them from the table. What does she say? That she doesn't know. Isn't that rather odd? Isn't it rather odd too that she chose that precise moment to leave the table and go out into the hall for her handbag?

"She knew that Hannah drank, because Hood had told her so. On the evening that meal was eaten, you say Hood called for her at her own request. Why? She has her own car, and I don't for a moment believe a woman like her would feel anything much but contempt for Hood."

"She told him there was something wrong with her car."

"I see. She asked him to come at six, although they were not due at the Kingmans till eight. She gave him *coffee.* A funny thing to drink at that hour, wasn't it, and before a meal? So what happens when he suggests calling in at a pub on the way? She doesn't say no or say it isn't a good idea to drink and drive. She takes so long getting ready that they don't have time.

"She didn't want Hood to drink any alcohol, Mike, and she was determined to prevent it. She, of course, would take no alcohol, and she knew Kingman never drank. But she also knew Hannah's habit of having her first drink of the day at about six.

"Now look at her motive, far stronger than Kingman's. She strikes me as a violent, passionate, and determined woman. Hannah had taken Kingman away from her. Kingman had rejected her. Why not revenge herself on both of them by killing Hannah and seeing to it that Kingman was convicted of the crime? If she simply killed Hannah, she had no way of insuring that Kingman would come under suspicion. But if she made it look as if he had previously attempted her life, the case against him would become very strong indeed.

"Where was she last Thursday afternoon? She could just as easily have gone up those stairs as Kingman could. Hannah would have admitted her to the flat. If she, known to be interested in gardening, had suggested that Hannah take her onto that balcony and show her the pot herbs, Hannah would willingly have done so. And then we have the mystery of the missing brandy bottle with some of its contents surely remaining. If Kingman had killed her, he would have left that there, as it would greatly have strengthened the case for suicide. Imagine how he might have used it. 'Heavy drinking made my wife ill that night. She knew I had lost respect for her because of her drinking. She killed herself because her mind was unbalanced by drink.'

"Corinne Last took that bottle away because she didn't want it known that Hannah drank, and she was banking on Hood's keeping it dark from us as he had kept it from so many people in the past. And she didn't want it known because the fake murder attempt that *she* staged depended on her victim having alcohol present in her body."

Burden sighed, poured the last dregs of coffee into Wexford's cup. "But we tried that out," he said. "Or I tried it out, and it doesn't work. You knew it wouldn't work from her book. True, she brought the Shaggy Caps from her own garden, but she couldn't have mixed up poisonous fungi with them because Axel Kingman would have realized at once. Or if he hadn't, they'd all have been ill, alcohol or no alcohol. She was never alone with Hannah before the meal, and while the stew was served she was out of the room."

"I know. But we'll see her in the morning and ask her a few sharp questions. I'm going home now, Mike. It's been a long day."

"Shall I run you home?"

"I'll walk," said Wexford. "Don't forget to put your car away, will you? You won't be making any emergency trips to hospital tonight."

With a shamefaced grin Burden saw him out.

They were unable to puncture her self-possession. The languorous Klimt face was carefully painted this morning, and she was dressed as befitted the violinist or the actress or the author. She had been forewarned of their coming, and the gardener image had been laid aside. Her long smooth hands looked as if they had never touched the earth or pulled up a weed.

Where had she been on the afternoon of Hannah Kingman's death? Her thick shapely eyebrows went up. At home, indoors, painting. Alone?

"Painters don't work with an audience," she said rather insolently, and she leaned back, dropping her eyelids in that way of hers. She lit a cigarette and flicked her fingers at Burden for an ashtray as if he were a waiter.

Wexford said, "On Saturday, October 29, Miss Last, I believe you had something wrong with your car?"

She nodded lazily.

In asking what was wrong with it, he thought he might catch her. He didn't.

"The glass in the offside front headlight was broken while the car was parked," she said, and although he thought how easily she could have broken that glass herself, he could hardly say so. In the same smooth voice she added, "Would you like to see the bill I had from the garage for repairing it?"

"That won't be necessary." She wouldn't have offered to show it to him if she hadn't possessed it, he thought. "You asked Mr. Hood to call for you here at six, I understand."

"Yes. He's not my idea of the best company in the world, but I'd promised him some apples for his mother, and we had to pick them before it got dark."

"You gave him coffee but no alcohol. You had no drinks on the way to Mr. and Mrs. Kingman's flat. Weren't you a little disconcerted at the idea of going out to dinner at a place where there wouldn't even be a glass of wine?"

"I was used to Mr. Kingman's ways." But not so used, thought Wexford, that you can tell me whether it was normal or abnormal for him to have rinsed those plates. Her mouth curled a little, betraying her a little. "It didn't bother me. I'm not a slave to liquor."

"I should like to return to these—er, Shaggy Caps. You picked them from here on October 28 and took them to Mr. Kingman that evening. I think you said that?"

"I did. I picked them from this garden."

She enunciated the words precisely, her eyes wide open and gazing sincerely at him. The words, or perhaps her unusual straightforwardness, stirred in him a glimmer of an idea. But if she had said nothing more, that idea might have died as quickly as it had been born.

"If you want to have them analyzed or examined or whatever, you're getting a bit late. Their season's practically over." She looked at Burden and gave him a gracious smile. "But you took the last of them yesterday, didn't you? So that's all right."

Wexford, of course, said nothing about Burden's experiment. "We'll have a look in your garden, if you don't mind."

She didn't seem to mind, but she had been wrong. Most of the fungi had grown into black-gilled pagodas in the twenty-four hours that had elapsed. Two new ones, however, had thrust their white oval caps up through the wet grass. Wexford picked them, and still she didn't seem to mind. Why, then had she seemed to want their season to be

over? He thanked her, and she went back into the cottage.
The door closed. Wexford and Burden went out into the
road.

The fungus season was far from over. From the abun-
dant array on the roadside it looked as if the season would
last weeks longer. Shaggy Caps were everywhere, some of
them smaller and grayer than the clump that grew out of
Corinne Last's well-fed lawn; green and purple Agarics,
horn-shaped toadstools, and tiny mushrooms growing in
fairy rings.

"She doesn't exactly mind us having them analyzed,"
Wexford said thoughtfully, "but it seems she'd prefer the
analysis to be done on the ones you picked yesterday than
on those I picked today. Can that be so or am I just imagining it?"

"If you're imagining it, I'm imagining it too. But it's no
good, that line of reasoning. We know they're not potenti-
ated—or whatever the word is—by alcohol."

"I shall pick some more all the same," said Wexford.
"Haven't got a paper bag, have you?"

"I've got a clean handkerchief. Will that do?"

"Have to," said Wexford who never had a clean one. He
picked a dozen more young Shaggy Caps, big and small,
white and gray, immature and fully grown. They got back
into the car, and Wexford told the driver to stop at the Public Library. He went in and emerged a few minutes later
with three books under his arm.

"When we get back, " he said to Burden, "I want you to
get on to the university and see what they can offer us in
the way of an expert in fungology."

He closeted himself in his office with the three books and
a pot of coffee. When it was nearly lunchtime, Burden
knocked on the door.

"Come in," said Wexford. "How did you get on?"

"They don't have a fungologist. But there's a man on the
faculty who's a toxicologist and who's just published one of
those popular science books. This one's about poisoning by
wild plants and fungi."

Wexford grinned. "What's it called? *Killing for Nothing*? He sounds as if he'd do fine."

"I said we'd see him at six. Let's hope something will come of it."

"No doubt it will." Wexford slammed shut the thickest of his books. "We need confirmation," he said, "but I've found the answer."

"For God's sake! Why didn't you say?"

"You didn't ask. Sit down." Wexford motioned him to the chair on the other side of the desk. "I said you'd done your homework, Mike, and so you had, only your textbook wasn't quite comprehensive enough. It's got a section on edible fungi and a section on poisonous fungi—*but nothing in between.* What I mean by that is, there's nothing in your book about fungi which aren't wholesome yet which don't cause death or intense suffering. There's nothing about the kind which can make a person ill under certain circumstances."

"But we know they ate Shaggy Caps," Burden protested. "And if by 'circumstances' you mean the intake of alcohol, we know Shaggy Caps aren't affected by alcohol."

"Mike," said Wexford quietly, *"do* we know they ate Shaggy Caps?" He spread out on the desk the haul he had made from the roadside and from Corinne Last's garden. "Look closely at these, will you?"

Quite bewildered now, Burden looked at and fingered the dozen or so specimens of fungi. "What am I to look *for?*"

"Differences," said Wexford laconically.

"Some of them are smaller than the others, and the smaller ones are grayish. Is that what you mean? But, look here, think of the differences between mushrooms. You get big flat ones and small button ones and—"

"Nevertheless, in this case it is that small difference that makes all the difference." Wexford sorted the fungi into two groups. "All the small grayer ones," he said, "came from the roadside. Some of the larger white ones came from Corinne Last's garden and some from the roadside."

He picked up between forefinger and thumb a specimen of the former. "This is not a Shaggy Cap, it is an Ink Cap. Now listen." The thick book fell open where he had placed a marker. Slowly and clearly he read: " 'The Ink Cap, *Coprinus atramentarius,* is not to be confused with the Shaggy Cap, *Coprinus comatus.* It is smaller and grayer in color, but otherwise the resemblance between them is strong. While *Coprinus atramentarius* is usually harmless when cooked, it contains, however, a chemical similar to the active principle in Antabuse, a drug used in the treatment of alcoholics, and if eaten in conjunction with alcohol would cause nausea and vomiting.' "

"We'll never prove it," Burden gasped.

"I don't know about that," said Wexford. "We can begin by concentrating on the *one lie* we know Corinne Last told when she said she picked the fungi she gave Axel Kingman from *her own garden.*"

POISON À LA CARTE

by Rex Stout

Rex Stout's brainchild, Nero Wolfe, is one of America's best-known (and probably most rotund) detectives. When it comes to passions, gourmet food is probably uppermost on Wolfe's mind, followed by orchids. He only follows his creator's predilections, although Stout was never as food-fussy as Wolfe.

In his long literary career, Stout wrote about other detectives, but always returned with relish to the Nero Wolfe-Archie Goodwin relationship, depicting it with precision and wit.

I slanted my eyes down to meet her big brown ones, which were slanted up. "No," I said, "I'm neither a producer nor an agent. My name's Archie Goodwin, and I'm here because I'm a friend of the cook. My reason for wanting it is purely personal."

"I know," she said, "it's my dimples. Men often swoon."

I shook my head. "It's your earrings. They remind me of a girl I once loved in vain. Perhaps if I get to know you well enough—who can tell?"

"Not me," she declared. "Leave me alone. I'm nervous, and I don't want to spill the soup. The name is Nora Jaret, without an 'h,' and the number is Stanhope five, six-six-two-one. The earrings were a present from Sir Laurence Olivier. I was sitting on his knee."

I wrote the number down in my notebook, thanked her, and looked around. Most of the collection of attractive young females were gathered in an alcove between two cupboards, but one was over by a table watching Felix stir something in a bowl. Her profile was fine and her hair was the color of corn silk just before it starts to turn. I crossed to her, and when she turned her head I spoke. "Good evening, Miss—Miss?"

"Annis," she said. "Carol Annis."

41

I wrote it down, and told her my name. "I am not blunt by nature," I said, "but you're busy, or soon will be, and there isn't time to talk up to it. I was standing watching you and all of a sudden I had an impulse to ask you for your phone number, and I'm no good at fighting impulses. Now that you're close up it's even stronger, and I guess we'll have to humor it."

But I may be giving a wrong impression. Actually I had no special hankering that Tuesday evening for new telephone numbers; I was doing it for Fritz. But that could give a wrong impression, too, so I'll have to explain.

One day in February, Lewis Hewitt, the millionaire orchid fancier for whom Nero Wolfe had once handled a tough problem, had told Wolfe that the Ten for Aristology wanted Fritz Brenner to cook their annual dinner, to be given as usual on April 1, Brillat-Savarin's birthday. When Wolfe said he had never heard of the Ten for Aristology, Hewitt explained that it was a group of ten men pursuing the ideal of perfection in food and drink, and he was one of them. Wolfe had swiveled to the dictionary on its stand at a corner of his desk, and after consulting it had declared that "aristology" meant the science of dining, and therefore the Ten were witlings, since dining was not a science but an art. After a long argument, Hewitt had admitted he was licked and had agreed that the name should be changed, and Wolfe had given him permission to ask Fritz to cook the dinner.

In fact, Wolfe was pleased, though of course he wouldn't say so. It took a big slice of his income as a private detective to pay Fritz Brenner, chef and housekeeper in the old brownstone on West Thirty-fifth Street—about the same as the slice that came to me as his assistant detective and man Friday, Saturday, Sunday, Monday, Tuesday, Wednesday, and Thursday—not to mention what it took to supply the kitchen with the raw materials of Fritz's productions. Since I am also the bookkeeper, I can certify that for the year 1957 the kitchen and Fritz cost only slightly less than the plant rooms on the roof bulging with orchids.

So when Hewitt made it clear that the Ten, though they might be dubs at picking names, were true and trustworthy gourmets, that the dinner would be at the home of Benjamin Schriver, the shipping magnate, who wrote a letter to the *Times* every year on September 1 denouncing the use of horseradish on oysters, and that the cook would have a free hand on the menu and the Ten would furnish whatever he desired, Wolfe pushed a button to summon Fritz. There was a little hitch when Fritz refused to commit himself until he had seen the Schriver kitchen, but Hewitt settled that by escorting him out front to his Heron town car and driving him down to Eleventh Street to inspect the kitchen.

That's where I was that Tuesday evening, April 1, collecting phone numbers—in the kitchen of the four-story Schriver house on Eleventh Street west of Fifth Avenue. Wolfe and I had been invited by Schriver, and though Wolfe dislikes eating with strangers and thinks that more than six at table spoils a meal, he knew Fritz's feelings would be hurt if he didn't go; and besides, if he stayed home who would cook his dinner? Even so, he would probably have balked if he had learned of one detail which Fritz and I knew about but had carefully kept from him: that the table was to be served by twelve young women, one for each guest.

When Hewitt told me that, I had protested that I wouldn't be responsible for Wolfe's conduct when the orgy got under way, that he would certainly stamp out of the house when the girls started to squeal. Good Lord, Hewitt said, nothing like that; that wasn't the idea at all. It was merely that the Ten had gone to ancient Greece not only for their name but also for other precedents. Hebe, the goddess of youth, had been cupbearer to the gods, so it was the custom of the Ten for Aristology to be waited on by maidens in appropriate dress. When I asked where they got the maidens he said through a theatrical agency, and added that at that time of year there were always hundreds of young actresses out of a job glad to grab at a chance to make fifty bucks, with a good meal thrown in, by spending an evening carrying food, one plate at a time. Originally they had hired experienced waitresses from an agency, but they had tripped on their stolas.

Wolfe and I had arrived at seven on the dot, and after we had met our host and the rest of the Ten, and had sampled oysters and our choice of five white wines, I had made my way to the kitchen to see how Fritz was making out. He was tasting from a pot on the range, with no more sign of fluster than if he had been at home getting dinner for Wolfe and me. Felix and Zoltan, from Rusterman's, were there to help, so I didn't ask if I was needed.

And there were the Hebes, cupbearers to the gods, twelve of them, in their stolas, deep rich purple flowing garments to their ankles. Very nice. It gave me an idea. Fritz likes to pretend that he has reason to believe that no damsel is safe within a mile of me, which doesn't make sense, since you can't tell much about them a mile off, and I thought it would do him good to see me operate at close quarters. Also, it was a challenge and an interesting sociological experiment. The first two had been a cinch: one named Fern Faber, so she said, a tall blonde with a wide lazy mouth, and Nora Jaret with the big brown eyes and dimples. Now I was after the Carol Annis with hair like corn silk.

"I have no sense of humor," she said and turned back to watch Felix.

I stuck. "That's a different kind of humor, and an impulse like mine isn't funny. It hurts. Maybe I can guess it. Is it Hebe one, oh-oh-oh-oh?"

No reply.

"Apparently not. Plato two, three-four-five-six?"

She said, without turning her head, "It's listed. Gorham eight, three-two-one-seven." Her head jerked to me. "Please?" It jerked back again.

It rather sounded as if she meant please go away, not please ring her as soon as possible, but I wrote it down anyway, for the record, and moved off. The rest of them were still grouped in the alcove, and I crossed over. The deep purple of the stolas was a good contrast for their pretty young faces topped by nine different colors and styles of hairdos. As I came up the chatter stopped and the faces turned to me.

"At ease," I told them. "I have no official standing. I am

merely one of the guests, invited because I'm a friend of
the cook, and I have a personal problem. I would prefer to
discuss it with each of you separately and privately, but
since there isn't time for that—"

"I know who you are," one declared. "You're a detective
and you work for Nero Wolfe. You're Archie Goodwin."

She was a redhead with milky skin. "I don't deny it," I
told her, "but I'm not here professionally. I don't ask if I've
met you because if I had I wouldn't have forgot—"

"You haven't met me. I've seen you and I've seen your
picture. You like yourself. Don't you?"

"Certainly. I string along with the majority. We'll take
a vote. How many of you like yourselves? Raise your
hands."

A hand went up with a bare arm shooting out of the purple folds, then two more, then the rest of them, including
the redhead.

"Okay," I said, "that's settled. Unanimous. My problem
is that I decided to look you over and ask the most absolutely irresistibly beautiful and fascinating one of the
bunch for her phone number, and I'm stalled. You are all
it. In beauty and fascination you are all far beyond the
wildest dreams of any poet, and I'm not a poet. So obviously I'm in a fix. How can I possibly pick on one of you,
any one, when—"

"Nuts." It was the redhead. "Me, of course. Peggy
Choate. Argyle two, three-three-four-eight. Don't call before noon."

"That's not fair," a throaty voice objected. It came from
one who looked a little too old for Hebe, and just a shade
too plump. It went on, "Do I call you Archie?"

"Sure, that's my name."

"All right, Archie, have your eyes examined." She lifted
an arm, baring it, to touch the shoulder of one beside her.
"We admit we're all beautiful, but we're not in the same
class as Helen Iacono. Look at her!"

I was doing so, and I must say that the throaty voice had
a point. Helen Iacono, with deep dark eyes, dark velvet
skin, and wavy silky hair darker than either skin or eyes,
was unquestionably rare and special. Her lips were parted

enough to show the gleam of white teeth, but she wasn't
laughing. She wasn't reacting at all, which was remarkable for an actress.

"It may be," I conceded, "that I am so dazzled by the col-
lective radiance that I am blind to the glory of any single
star. Perhaps I'm a poet after all. I sound like one. My feeling that I must have the phone numbers of *all* of you is certainly no reflection on Helen Iacono. I admit that that will
not completely solve the problem, for tomorrow I must face
the question which one to call first. If I feel as I do right
now I would have to dial all the numbers simultaneously,
and that's impossible. I hope to heaven it doesn't end in a
stalemate. What if I can never decide which one to call
first? What if it drives me mad? Or what if I gradually
sink—"

I turned to see who was tugging at my sleeve. It was
Benjamin Schriver, the host, with a grin on his ruddy
round face. He said, "I hate to interrupt your speech, but
perhaps you can finish it later. We're ready to sit. Will you
join us?"

The dining room, on the same floor as the kitchen, three
feet or so below street level, would have been too gloomy
for my taste if most of the dark wood paneling hadn't been
covered with pictures of geese, pheasants, fish, fruit, vegetables, and other assorted edible objects; and also it helped
that the tablecloth was white as snow, the wineglasses,
seven of them at each place, glistened in the soft light from
above, and the polished silver shone. In the center was a
low gilt bowl, or maybe gold, two feet long, filled with clus-
ters of Phalaenopsis Aphrodite, donated by Wolfe, cut by
him that afternoon from some of his most treasured plants.

As he sat he was scowling at them, but the scowl was not
for the orchids; it was for the chair, which, though a little
fancy, was perfectly okay for you or me but not for his sev-
enth of a ton. His fundament lapped over at both sides. He
erased the scowl when Schriver, at the end of the table,
complimented him on the flowers, and Hewitt across from
him, said he had never seen Phalaenopsis better grown,
and the others joined in the chorus, all but the aristologist

who sat between Wolfe and me. He was a Wall Street character and a well-known theatrical angel named Vincent Pyle, and was living up to his reputation as an original by wearing a dinner jacket, with tie to match, which looked black until you had the light at a certain slant and then you saw that it was green. He eyed the orchids with his head cocked and his mouth puckered, and said, "I don't care for flowers with spots and streaks. They're messy."

I thought, but didn't say, Okay, drop dead. If I had known that that was what he was going to do in about three hours I might not even have thought it. He got a rise, not from Wolfe or me, or Schriver or Hewitt, but from three others who thought flowers with spots and streaks were wonderful: Adrian Dart, the actor who had turned down an offer of a million a week, more or less, from Hollywood; Emil Kreis, chairman of the board of Codex Press, book publishers; and Harvey M. Leacraft, corporation lawyer.

Actually, cupbearers was what the Hebes were not. The wines, beginning with the Montrachet with the first course, were poured by Felix; but the girls delivered the food, with different routines for different items. The first course, put on individual plates in the kitchen, with each girl bringing in a plate for her aristologist, was small blinis sprinkled with chopped chives, piled with caviar, and topped with sour cream—the point, as far as Fritz was concerned, being that he had made the blinis, starting on them at eleven that morning, and also the sour cream, starting on that Sunday evening. Fritz's sour cream is very special, but Vincent Pyle had to get in a crack. After he had downed all his blinis he remarked, loud enough to carry around the table, "A new idea, putting sand in. Clever. Good for chickens, since they need grit."

The man on my left, Emil Kreis, the publisher, muttered at my ear, "Ignore him. He backed three flops this season."

The girls, who had been coached by Fritz and Felix that afternoon, handled the green turtle soup without a splash. When they had brought in the soup plates Felix brought the bowl, and each girl ladled from it as Felix held it by the plate. I asked Pyle cordially, "Any sand?" but he said no, it was delicious, and cleaned it up.

I was relieved when I saw that the girls wouldn't dish the fish—flounders poached in dry white wine, with a mussel-and-mushroom sauce that was one of Fritz's specialties. Felix did the dishing at a side table, and the girls merely carried. With the first taste of the sauce there were murmurs of appreciation, and Adrian Dart, the actor, across from Wolfe, sang out, "Superb!" They were making various noises of satisfaction, and Leacraft, the lawyer, was asking Wolfe if Fritz would be willing to give him the recipe, when Pyle, on my right, made a face and dropped his fork on his plate with a clatter.

I thought he was putting on an act, and still thought so when his head dropped and I heard him gnash his teeth, but then his shoulders sagged and he clapped a hand to his mouth, and that seemed to be overdoing it. Two or three of them said something, and he pushed his chair back, got to his feet, said, "You must excuse me, I'm sorry," and headed for the door to the hall. Schriver arose and followed him out. The others exchanged words and glances.

Hewitt said, "A damn shame, but I'm going to finish this," and used his fork. Someone asked if Pyle had a bad heart, and someone else said no. They all resumed with the flounder and the conversation, but the spirit wasn't the same.

When, at a signal from Felix, the maidens started removing the plates, Lewis Hewitt got up and left the room, came back in a couple of minutes, sat, and raised his voice. "Vincent is in considerable pain. There is nothing we can do, and Ben wishes us to proceed. He will rejoin us—when he can."

"What is it?" someone asked.

Hewitt said the doctor didn't know. Zoltan entered bearing an enormous covered platter, and the Hebes gathered at the side table, and Felix lifted the cover and began serving the roast pheasant, which had been larded with strips of pork soaked for twenty hours in Tokay, and then—but no. What's the use? The annual dinner for the Ten of Aristology was a flop. Since for years I have been eating three

meals a day cooked by Fritz Brenner I would like to show
my appreciation by getting in print some idea of what he
can do in the way of victuals, but it won't do here. Sure, the
pheasant was good enough for gods if there had been any
around, and so was the suckling pig, and the salad, with a
dressing which Fritz calls Devil's Rain, and the chestnut
croquettes, and the cheese—only the one kind, made in
New Jersey by a man named Bill Thompson under Fritz's
supervision; and they were all eaten, more or less. But
Hewitt left the room three more times, and the last time
was gone a good ten minutes, and Schriver didn't rejoin
the party at all, and while the salad was being served Emil
Kreis went out and didn't come back.

When, as coffee and brandy were being poured and cigars and cigarettes passed, Hewitt left his chair for the
fifth time, Nero Wolfe got up and followed him out. I lit a
cigar just to be doing something, and tried to be sociable by
giving an ear to a story Adrian Dart was telling, but by the
time I finished my coffee I was getting fidgety. By the
glower that had been deepening on Wolfe's face for the
past hour I knew he was boiling, and when he's like that,
especially away from home, there's no telling about him.
He might even have had the idea of aiming the glower at
Vincent Pyle for ruining Fritz's meal. So I put what was
left of the cigar in a tray, arose, and headed for the door,
and was halfway to it when here he came, still glowering.

"Come with me," he snapped, and kept going.

The way to the kitchen from the dining room was
through a pantry, twenty feet long, with counters and
shelves and cupboards on both sides. Wolfe marched
through with me behind. In the kitchen the twelve maidens were scattered around on chairs and stools at tables
and counters, eating. A woman was busy at a sink. Zoltan
was busy at a refrigerator. Fritz, who was pouring a glass
of wine, presumably for himself, turned as Wolfe entered
and put the bottle down.

Wolfe went to him, stood, and spoke. "Fritz, I offer my
apologies. I permitted Mr. Hewitt to cajole you. I should
have known better. I beg your pardon."

Fritz gestured with his free hand, the wineglass steady

in the other. "But it is not to pardon, only to regret. The man got sick, that's a pity, only not from my cooking, I assure you."

"You don't need to. Not from your cooking as it left you, but as it reached him. I repeat that I am culpable, but I won't dwell on that now; it can wait. There is an aspect that is exigent." Wolfe turned. "Archie. Are those women all here?"

I had to cover more than half a circle to count them, scattered as they were. "Yes, sir, all present. Twelve."

"Collect them. They can stand"—he pointed to the alcove—"over there. And bring Felix."

It was hard to believe. They were eating; and for him to interrupt a man, or even a woman, at a meal was unheard-of. Not even me. Only in an extreme emergency had he ever asked me to quit food before I was through. Boiling was no name for it. Without even bothering to raise a brow, I turned and called out, "I'm sorry, ladies, but if Mr. Wolfe says it's urgent that settles it. Over there, please? All of you."

Then I went through the pantry corridor, pushed the two-way door, caught Felix's eye, and wiggled a beckoning finger at him, and he came. By the time we got to the kitchen the girls had left the chairs and stools and were gathering at the alcove, but not with enthusiasm. There were mutterings, and some dirty looks for me as I approached with Felix. Wolfe came with Zoltan and stood, tight-lipped, surveying them.

"I remind you," he said, "that the first course you brought to the table was caviar on blinis topped with sour cream. The portion served to Mr. Vincent Pyle, and eaten by him, contained arsenic. Mr. Pyle is in bed upstairs, attended by three doctors, and will probably die within an hour. I am speaking—"

He stopped to glare at them. They were reacting, or acting, no matter which. There were gasps and exclamations, and one of them clutched her throat, and another, baring her arms, clapped her palms to her ears. When the glare had restored order Wolfe went on, "You will please keep quiet and listen. I am speaking of conclusions formed by me. My conclusion that Mr. Pyle ate arsenic is based on the symptoms—burning throat, faintness, intense burning pain in the stomach, dry mouth, cool skin, vomiting. My conclusion that the arsenic was in the first course is based, first, on the amount of time it takes arsenic to act; second, on the fact that it is highly unlikely it could have been put in the soup or the fish; and third, that Mr. Pyle complained of sand in the cream or caviar. I admit the possibility that one or both of my conclusions will be proven wrong, but I regard it as remote and I am acting on them." His head turned. "Fritz. Tell me about the caviar from the moment it was put on the individual plates. Who did that?"

I had once told Fritz that I could imagine no circumstances in which he would look really unhappy, but now I wouldn't have to try. He was biting his lips, first the lower and then the upper. He began, "I must assure you—"

"I need no assurance from you, Fritz. Who put it on the plates?"

"Zoltan and I did." He pointed. "At that table."

"And left them there? They were taken from that table by the women?"

"Yes, sir."

"Each woman took one plate?"

"Yes, sir. I mean, they were told to. I was at the range."

Zoltan spoke up. "I watched them, Mr. Wolfe. They each took one plate. And believe me, nobody put any arsenic—"

"Please, Zoltan. I add another conclusion: that no one put arsenic in one of the portions and then left to chance which one of the guests would get it. Surely, the poisoner intended it to reach a certain one—either Mr. Pyle or, as an alternative, some other one, and it went to Mr. Pyle by mishap. In any case, it was the portion that Pyle ate that was poisoned, and whether he got it by design or by mischance is for the moment irrelevant." His eyes were at the girls. "Which one of you took that plate to Mr. Pyle?"

No reply. No sound, no movement.

Wolfe grunted. "Pfui. If you didn't know his name, you do now. The man who left during the fish course and who is now dying. Who served him?"

No reply; and I had to hand it to them that no pair of

eyes left Wolfe to fasten on Peggy Choate, the redhead.
Mine did. "What the heck," I said. "Speak up, Miss
Choate."

"I didn't!" she cried.

"That's silly. Of course you did. Twenty people can
swear to it. I looked right at you while you were dishing his
soup. And when you brought the fish—"

"But I didn't take him that first thing! He already had
some!"

Wolfe took over. "Your name is Choate?"

"Yes." Her chin was up. "Peggy Choate."

"You deny that you served the plate of caviar, the first
course, to Mr. Pyle?"

"I certainly do."

"But you were supposed to? You were assigned to him?"

"Yes. I took the plate from the table there and went in
with it, and started to him, and then I saw that he had
some, and I thought I had made a mistake. We hadn't seen
the guests. That man"—she pointed to Felix—"had shown
us which chair our guest would sit in, and mine was the
second from the right on this side as I went in, but that one
had already been served, and I thought someone else had
made a mistake or I was mixed up. Anyway, I saw that the
man next to him, on his right, hadn't been served, and I
gave it to him. That was you. I gave it to you."

"Indeed." Wolfe was frowning at her. "Who was assigned to me?"

That wasn't put on. He actually didn't know. He had
never looked at her. He had been irritated that females
were serving, and besides, he hates to twist his neck. Of
course I could have told him, but Helen Iacono said, "I
was."

"Your name, please?"

"Helen Iacono." She had a rich contralto that went fine
with the deep dark eyes and dark velvet skin and wavy
silky hair.

"Did you bring me the first course?"

"No. When I went in I saw Peggy serving you, and a man
on the left next to the end didn't have any, so I gave it to
him."

"Do you know his name?"

"I do," Nora Jaret said. "From the card. He was mine."
Her big brown eyes were straight at Wolfe. "His name is
Kreis. He had his when I got there. I was going to take it
back to the kitchen, but then I thought, someone has stage
fright and I haven't, and I gave it to the man at the end."

"Which end?"

"The left end. Mr. Schriver. He came and spoke to us
this afternoon."

She was corroborated by Carol Annis, the one with hair
like corn silk who had no sense of humor. "That's right,"
she said. "I saw her. I was going to stop her, but she had
already put the plate down, so I went around to the other
side of the table with it when I saw that Adrian Dart didn't
have any. I didn't mind because it was him."

"You were assigned to Mr. Schriver?"

"Yes. I served him the other courses, until he left."

It was turning into a ring-around-a-rosy, but the squat
was bound to come. All Wolfe had to do was get to one who
couldn't claim a delivery, and that would tag her. I was
rather hoping it wouldn't be the next one, for the girl with
the throaty voice had been Adrian Dart's, and she had
called me Archie and had given Helen Iacono a nice trib-
ute. Would she claim she had served Dart herself?

No. She answered without being asked. "My name is
Lucy Morgan," she said, "and I had Adrian Dart, and
Carol got to him before I did. There was only one place that
didn't have one, on Dart's left, the next but one, and I took
it there. I don't know his name."

I supplied it. "Hewitt. Mr. Lewis Hewitt." A better
name for it than ring-around-a-rosy would have been
passing-the-buck. I looked at Fern Faber, the tall blonde
with a wide lazy mouth who had been my first stop on my
phone-number tour. "It's your turn, Miss Faber," I told
her. "You had Mr. Hewitt. Yes?"

"I sure did." Her voice was pitched so high it threatened
to squeak.

"But you didn't take him his caviar?"

"I sure didn't."

"Then who did you take it to?"

"Nobody."

I looked at Wolfe. His eyes were narrowed at her. "What did you do with it, Miss Faber?"

"I didn't do anything with it. There wasn't any."

"Nonsense. There are twelve of you, and there were twelve at the table, and each got a portion. How can you say there wasn't any?"

"Because there wasn't. I was in the john fixing my hair, and when I came back in she was taking the last one from the table, and when I asked where mine was he said he didn't know, and I went to the dining room and they all had some."

"Who was taking the last one from the table?"

She pointed to Lucy Morgan.

"Whom did you ask where yours was?"

She pointed to Zoltan. "Him."

Wolfe turned. "Zoltan?"

"Yes, sir. I mean, yes, sir, she asked me where hers was. I had turned away when the last one was taken. I don't mean I know where she had been, just that she asked me that. I asked Fritz if I should go in and see if they were one short and he said no, Felix was there and would see to it."

Wolfe went back to Fern Faber. "Where is that room where you were fixing your hair?"

She pointed toward the pantry. "In there."

"The door's around the corner," Felix said.

"How long were you in there?"

"My God, I don't know, do you think I timed it? When Archie Goodwin was talking to us, and Mr. Schriver came and said they were going to start, I went pretty soon after that."

Wolfe's head jerked to me. "So that's where you were. I might have known there were young women around. Supposing that Miss Faber went to fix her hair shortly after you left—say three minutes—how long was she at it, if the last plate had been taken from the table when she returned to the kitchen?"

I gave it a thought. "Fifteen to twenty minutes."

He growled at her, "What was wrong with your hair?"

"I didn't say anything was wrong with it." She was getting riled. "Look, mister, do you want all the details?"

"No." Wolfe surveyed them for a moment, not amiably, took in enough air to fill all his middle—say two bushels— let it out again, turned his back on them, saw the glass of wine Fritz had left on the table, went and picked it up, smelled it, and stood gazing at it. The girls started to make noises, and, hearing them, he put the glass down and came back.

"You're in a pickle," he said. "So am I. You heard me apologize to Mr. Brenner and avow my responsibility for his undertaking to cook that meal. When, upstairs, I saw that Mr. Pyle would die, and reached the conclusions I told you of, I felt myself under compulsion to expose the culprit. I am committed. When I came down here I thought it would be a simple matter to learn who had served poisoned food to Mr. Pyle, but I was wrong.

"It's obvious now that I have to deal with one who is not only resourceful and ingenious, but also quick-witted and audacious. While I was closing in on her just now, as I thought, inexorably approaching the point where she would either have to contradict one of you or deny that she had served the first course to anyone, she was fleering at me inwardly, and with reason, for her coup had worked. She had slipped through my fingers, and—"

"But she didn't!" It came from one of them whose name I didn't have. "She said she didn't serve anybody!"

Wolfe shook his head. "No. Not Miss Faber. She is the only one who is eliminated. She says she was absent from this room during the entire period when the plates were being taken from the table, and she wouldn't dare to say that if she had in fact been here and taken a plate and carried it in to Mr. Pyle. She would certainly have been seen by some of you."

He shook his head again. "Not her. But it could have been any other one of you. You—I speak now to that one, still to be identified—you must have extraordinary faith in your attendant godling, even allowing for your craft. For you took great risks. You took a plate from the table—not the first probably, but one of the first—and on your way to the dining room you put arsenic in the cream. That wasn't difficult; you might even have done it without stopping if you had the arsenic in a paper spill. You could get rid of the spill later, perhaps in the room which Miss Faber calls a john. You took the plate to Mr. Pyle, came back here immediately, got another plate, took it to the dining room, and gave it to one who had not been served. I am not guessing; it had to be like that. It was a remarkably adroit stratagem, but you can't possibly be impregnable."

He turned to Zoltan. "You say you watched as the plates were taken, and each of them took only one. Did one of them come back and take another?"

Zoltan looked fully as unhappy as Fritz. "I'm thinking, Mr. Wolfe. I can try to think, but I'm afraid it won't help. I didn't look at their faces, and they're all dressed alike. I guess I didn't watch very close."

"Fritz?"

"No, sir. I was at the range."

"Then try this, Zoltan. Who were the first ones to take plates—the first three or four?"

Zoltan slowly shook his head. "I'm afraid it's no good, Mr. Wolfe. I could try to think, but I couldn't be sure." He moved his eyes right to left and back again, at the girls. "I tell you, I wasn't looking at their faces." He extended his hands, palms up. "You will consider, Mr. Wolfe, I was not thinking of poison. I was only seeing that the plates were carried properly. Was I thinking which one has got arsenic? No."

"I took the first plate," a girl blurted—another whose name I didn't know. "I took it in and gave it to the man in my chair, the one at the left corner at the other side of the table, and I stayed there. I never left the dining room."

"Your name, please?"

"Marjorie Quinn."

"Thank you. Now the second plate. Who took it?"

Apparently nobody. Wolfe gave them ten seconds, his eyes moving to take them all in, his lips tight. "I advise you," he said, "to jog your memories, in case it becomes necessary to establish the order in which you took the plates by dragging it out of you. I hope it won't come to that." His head turned. "Felix, I have neglected you purposely, to give you time to reflect. You were in the dining room. My expectation was that after I had learned who had served the first course to Mr. Pyle you would corroborate it, but now that there is nothing for you to corroborate I must look to you for the fact itself. I must ask you to point her out."

In a way Wolfe was Felix's boss. When Wolfe's oldest and dearest friend, Marko Vukcic, who had owned Rusterman's restaurant, had died, his will had left the restaurant to members of the staff in trust, with Wolfe as the trustee, and Felix was the maître d'hôtel. With that job at the best restaurant in New York, naturally Felix was both bland and commanding, but now he was neither. If he felt the way he looked, he was miserable.

"I can't," he said.

"Pfui! You, trained as you are to see everything?"

"That is true, Mr. Wolfe. I knew you would ask me this, but I can't. I can only explain. The young woman who just spoke, Marjorie Quinn, was the first one in with a plate, as she said. She did not say that as she served it one of the blinis slid off onto the table, but it did. As I sprang toward her she was actually about to pick it up with her fingers, and I jerked her away and put it back on the plate with a fork, and I gave her a look. Anyway, I was not myself. Having women as waiters was bad enough, and not only that, they were without experience. When I recovered command of myself I saw the redheaded one, Choate, standing back of Mr. Pyle, to whom she had been assigned, with a plate in her hands, and I saw that he had already been served. As I moved forward she stepped to the right and served the plate to you. The operation was completely upset, and I was helpless. The dark-skinned one, Iacono, who was assigned to you, served Mr. Kreis, and the—"

"If you please." Wolfe was curt. "I have heard them, and so have you. I have always found you worthy of trust, but it's possible that in your exalted position, maître d'hôtel at Rusterman's, you would rather dodge than get involved in a poisoning. Are you dodging, Felix?"

"Good God, Mr. Wolfe, I *am* involved!"

"Very well. I saw that woman spill the blini and start her fingers for it, and I saw you retrieve it. Yes, you're involved, but not as I am." He turned to me. "Archie. You are commonly my first resort, but now you are my last. You sat next to Mr. Pyle. Who put that plate before him?"

Of course I knew that was coming, but I hadn't been beating my brain because there was no use. I said merely but positively, "No." He glared at me and I added, "That's all, just no, but like Felix, I can explain. First, I would have had to turn around to see her face, and that's bad table manners. Second, I was watching Felix rescue the blini. Third, there was an argument going on about flowers with spots and streaks, and I was listening to it and so were you. I didn't even see her arm."

Wolfe stood and breathed. He shut his eyes and opened them again, and breathed some more. "Incredible," he muttered. "The wretch had incredible luck."

"I'm going home," Fern Faber said. "I'm tired."

"So am I," another one said, and was moving, but Wolfe's eyes pinned her. "I advise you not to," he said. "It is true that Miss Faber is eliminated as the culprit, and also Miss Quinn, since she was under surveillance by Felix while Mr. Pyle was being served, but I advise even them to stay. When Mr. Pyle dies the doctors will certainly summon the police, and it would be well for all of you to be here when they arrive. I had hoped to be able to present them with an exposed murderer. Confound it! There is still a chance. Archie, come with me. Fritz, Felix, Zoltan, remain with these women. If one or more of them insist on leaving do not detain them by force, but have the names and the times of departure. If they want to eat, feed them. I'll be—"

"I'm going home," Fern Faber said stubbornly.

"Very well, go. You'll be got out of bed by a policeman before the night's out. I'll be in the dining room, Fritz. Come, Archie."

He went and I followed, along the pantry corridor and through the two-way door. On the way I glanced at my wrist watch: ten past eleven. I rather expected to find the dining room empty, but it wasn't. Eight of them were still there, the only ones missing being Schriver and Hewitt, who were probably upstairs. The air was heavy with cigar smoke. All of them but Adrian Dart were at the table with their chairs pushed back at various angles, with brandy glasses and cigars. Dart was standing with his back to a picture of honkers on the wing, holding forth. As we entered he stopped and heads turned.

Emil Kreis spoke. "Oh, there you are. I was coming to the kitchen but didn't want to butt in. Schriver asked me to apologize to Fritz Brenner. Our custom is to ask the chef to join us with champagne, which is barbarous but gay, but of course in the circumstances . . ." He let it hang, and added, "Shall I explain to him? Or will you?"

"I will." Wolfe went to the end of the table and sat. He had been on his feet for nearly two hours—all very well for his twice-a-day sessions in the plant rooms, but not elsewhere. He looked around. "Mr. Pyle is still alive?"

"We hope so," one said. "We sincerely hope so."

"I ought to be home in bed," another one said. "I have a hard day tomorrow. But it doesn't seem . . ." He took a puff on his cigar.

Emil Kreis reached for the brandy bottle. "There's been no word since I came down." He looked at his wrist. "Nearly an hour ago. I suppose I should go up. It's so damned unpleasant." He poured brandy.

"Terrible," one said. "Absolutely terrible. I understand you were asking which one of the girls brought him the caviar. Kreis says you asked him."

Wolfe nodded. "I also asked Mr. Schriver and Mr. Hewitt. And Mr. Goodwin and Mr. Brenner, and the two men who came to help at my request. And the women themselves. After more than an hour with them I am still at fault. I have discovered the artifice the culprit used, but not her identity."

"Aren't you a bit premature?" Leacraft, the lawyer, asked. "There may be no culprit. An acute and severe gastric disturbance may be caused—"

"Nonsense. I am too provoked for civility, Mr. Leacraft. The symptoms are typical of arsenic, and you heard Mr. Pyle complain of sand, but that's not all. I said I have discovered the artifice. None of them will admit serving him the first course. The one assigned to him found he had already been served and served me instead. There is indeed a culprit. She put arsenic in the cream *en passant,* served it to Mr. Pyle, returned to the kitchen for another portion, and came and served it to someone else. That is established."

"But then," the lawyer objected, "one of them served no one. How could that be?"

"I am not a tyro at inquiry, Mr. Leacraft. I'll ravel it for you later if you want, but now I want to get on. It is no conjecture that poison was given to Mr. Pyle by the woman who brought him the caviar; it is a fact. By a remarkable combination of cunning and luck she has so far eluded identification, and I am appealing to you. All of you. I ask you to close your eyes and recall the scene. We are here at table, discussing the orchids—the spots and streaks. The woman serving that place"—he pointed—"lets a blini slip from the plate and Felix retrieves it. It helps to close your eyes. Just about then a woman enters with a plate, goes to Mr. Pyle, and puts it before him. I appeal to you: which one?"

Emil Kreis shook his head. "I told you upstairs, I don't know. I didn't see her. Or if I did, it didn't register."

Adrian Dart, the actor, stood with his eyes closed, his chin up, and his arms folded, a fine pose for concentration. The others, even Leacraft, had their eyes closed too, but of course they couldn't hold a candle to Dart. After a long moment the eyes began to open and heads to shake.

"It's gone," Dart said in his rich musical baritone. "I must have seen it, since I sat across from him, but it's gone. Utterly."

"I didn't see it," another said. "I simply didn't see it."

They made it unanimous.

Wolfe put his palms on the table. "Then I'm in for it," he said grimly. "I am your guest, gentlemen, and would not be offensive, but I am to blame that Fritz Brenner was enticed to this deplorable fiasco. If Mr. Pyle dies, as he surely will—"

The door opened and Benjamin Schriver entered. Then

Lewis Hewitt, and then the familiar burly frame of Sergeant Purley Stebbins of Manhattan Homicide West.

Schriver crossed to the table and spoke. "Vincent is dead. Half an hour ago. Doctor Jameson called the police. He thinks that it is practically certain—"

"Hold it," Purley growled at his elbow. "I'll handle it if you don't mind."

"My God," Adrian Dart groaned, and shuddered magnificently.

That was the last I heard of the affair from an aristologist.

"I did not!" Inspector Cramer roared. "Quit twisting my words around! I didn't charge you with complicity! I merely said you're concealing something, and what the hell is that to scrape your neck? You always do!"

It was a quarter to two Wednesday afternoon. We were in the office on the first floor of the old brownstone on West Thirty-fifth Street—Wolfe in his oversize chair. The daily schedule was messed beyond repair. When we had finally got home, at five o'clock in the morning, Wolfe had told Fritz to forget about breakfast until further notice, and had sent me up to the plant rooms to leave a note for Theodore saying that he would not appear at nine in the morning and perhaps not at all. It had been not at all. At half past eleven he had buzzed on the house phone to tell Fritz to bring up the breakfast tray with four eggs and ten slices of bacon instead of two and five, and it was past one o'clock when the sounds came of his elevator and then his footsteps in the hall, heading for the office.

If you think a problem child is tough, try handling a problem elephant. He is plenty knotty even when he is himself, and that day he was really special. After looking through the mail, glancing at his desk calendar, and signing three checks I had put on his desk, he snapped at me, "A fine prospect. Dealing with them singly would be interminable. Will you have them all here at six o'clock?"

I kept calm. I merely asked, "All of whom?"

"You know quite well. Those women."

I still kept calm. "I should think ten of them would be

enough. You said yourself that two of them can be crossed off."

"I need them all. Those two can help establish the order in which the plates were taken."

I held on. I too was short on sleep, shorter even than he, and I didn't feel up to a fracas. "I have a suggestion," I said. "I suggest that you postpone operations until your wires are connected again. Counting up to five hundred might help. You know damn well that all twelve of them will spend the afternoon either at the district attorney's office or receiving official callers at their homes—probably most of them at the D.A.'s office. And probably they'll spend the evening there, too. Do you want some aspirin?"

"I want *them,*" he growled.

I could have left him to grope back to normal on his own and gone up to my room for a nap, but after all, he pays my salary. So I picked up a sheet of paper I had typed and handed it to him. It read:

	Assigned to	*Served*
Peggy Choate	Pyle	Wolfe
Helen Iacono	Wolfe	Kreis
Nora Jaret	Kreis	Schriver
Carol Annis	Schriver	Dart
Lucy Morgan	Dart	Hewitt
Fern Faber	Hewitt	No one

"Fern Faber's out," I said, "and I realize it doesn't have to be one of those five, even though Lucy Morgan took the last plate. Possibly one or two others took plates after Peggy Choate did, and served the men they were assigned to. But it seems—"

I stopped because he had crumpled it and dropped it in the wastebasket. "I heard them," he growled. "My faculties, including my memory, are not impaired. I am merely ruffled beyond the bounds of tolerance."

For him that was an abject apology, and a sign that he was beginning to regain control. But a few minutes later, when the bell rang, and after a look through the one-way glass panel of the front door I told him it was Cramer, and he said to admit him, and Cramer marched in and planted his fanny on the red leather chair and opened up with an impolite remark about concealing facts connected with a murder, Wolfe had cut loose; and Cramer asked him what the hell was that to scrape his neck, which was a new one to me but sounded somewhat vulgar for an inspector. He had probably picked it up from some hoodlum.

Ruffling Cramer beyond the bounds of tolerance did Wolfe good. He leaned back in his chair. "Everyone conceals something," he said placidly. "Or at least omits something, if only because to include everything is impossible. During those wearisome hours, nearly six of them, I answered all questions, and so did Mr. Goodwin. Indeed, I thought we were helpful. I thought we had cleared away some rubble."

"Yeah." Cramer wasn't grateful. His big pink face was always a little pinker than normal, not with pleasure, when he was tackling Wolfe. "You had witnessed the commission of a murder, and you didn't notify—"

"It wasn't a murder until he died."

"All right, a felony. You not only failed to report it, you—"

"That a felony had been committed was my conclusion. Others present disagreed with me. Only a few minutes before Mr. Stebbins entered the room, Mr. Leacraft, a member of the bar and therefore himself an officer of the law, challenged my conclusion."

"You should have reported it. You're a licensed detective. Also you started an investigation, questioning the suspects—"

"Only to test my conclusion. I would have been a ninny to report it before learning—"

"Damn it," Cramer barked, "will you let me finish a sentence? Just one?"

Wolfe's shoulders went up an eighth of an inch and down again. "Certainly, if it has import. I am not baiting you, Mr. Cramer. But I have already replied to these imputations, to you and Mr. Stebbins and an assistant district attorney. I did not wrongly delay reporting a crime, and I did not usurp the function of the police. Very well, finish a sentence."

"You knew Pyle was dying. You said so."

"Also my own conclusion. The doctors were trying to save him."

Cramer took a breath. He looked at me, saw nothing inspiring, and returned to Wolfe. "I'll tell you why I'm here. Those three men—the cook, the man that helped him, and the man in the dining room—Fritz Brenner, Felix Courbet, and Zoltan Mahany—were all supplied by you. All close to you. I want to know about them, or at least two of them. I might as well leave Fritz out of it. In the first place, it's hard to believe that Zoltan doesn't know who took the first two or three plates or whether one of them came back for a second one, and it's also hard to believe that Felix doesn't know who served Pyle."

"It is indeed," Wolfe agreed. "They are highly trained men. But they have been questioned."

"They sure have. It's also hard to believe that Goodwin didn't see who served Pyle. He sees everything."

"Mr. Goodwin is present. Discuss it with him."

"I have. Now I want to ask your opinion of a theory. I know yours, and I don't reject it, but there are alternatives. First, a fact. In a metal trash container in the kitchen—not a garbage pail—we found a small roll of paper, ordinary white paper that had been rolled into a tube, held with tape, smaller at one end. The laboratory has found particles of arsenic inside. The only two fingerprints on it that are any good are Zoltan's. He says he saw it on the kitchen floor under a table some time after the meal had started, he can't say exactly when, and he picked it up and dropped it in the container, and his prints are on it because he pinched it to see if there was anything in it."

Wolfe nodded. "As I surmised. A paper spill."

"Yeah. I don't say it kills your theory. She could have shaken it into the cream without leaving prints, and she certainly wouldn't have dropped it on the floor if there was any chance it had her prints. But it *has* got Zoltan's. What's wrong with the theory that Zoltan poisoned one of the portions and saw that it was taken by a certain one? I'll answer that myself. There are two things wrong with it. First, Zoltan claims he didn't know which guest any of the girls were assigned to. But Felix knew, and they could have been in collusion. Second, the girls all deny that Zoltan indicated which plate they were to take, but you know how that is. He could have done it without her knowing it. What else is wrong with it?"

"It's not only untenable, it's egregious," Wolfe declared. "Why, in that case, did one of them come back for another plate?"

"She was confused. Nervous. Dumb."

"Bosh. Why doesn't she admit it?"

"Scared."

"I don't believe it. I questioned them before you did." Wolfe waved it away. "Tommyrot, and you know it. My theory is not a theory; it is a reasoned conviction. I hope it is being acted on. I suggested to Mr. Stebbins that he examine their garments to see if some kind of pocket had been made in one of them. She had to have it readily available."

"He did. They all had pockets. The laboratory has found no trace of arsenic." Cramer uncrossed his legs. "But I wanted to ask you about those men. You know them."

"I do, yes. But I do not answer for them. They may have a dozen murders on their souls, but they had nothing to do with the death of Mr. Pyle. If you are following up my theory—my conviction, rather—I suppose you have learned the order in which the women took the plates."

Cramer shook his head. "We have not, and I doubt if we will. All we have is a bunch of contradictions. You had them good and scared before we got to them. We do have the last five, starting with Peggy Choate, who found that Pyle had been served and gave it to you, and then—but you got that yourself."

"No, I got those five, but not that they were the last. There might have been others in between."

"There weren't. It's pretty well settled that these five were the last. After Peggy Choate the last four plates were taken by Helen Iacono, Nora Jaret, Carol Annis, and Lucy Morgan. Then that Fern Faber, who had been in the can, but there was no plate for her. It's the order in which they took them before that, the first seven, that we can't pry out of them—except the first one, that Marjorie Quinn. You couldn't either."

Wolfe turned a palm up. "I was interrupted."

"You were not. You left them there in a huddle, scared stiff, and went to the dining room to start in on the men. Your own private murder investigation, and to hell with the law. I was surprised to see Goodwin here when I rang the bell just now. I supposed you'd have him out running errands, like calling at the agency they got the girls from. Or getting a line on Pyle to find a connection between him and one of them. Unless you're no longer interested?"

"I'm interested willy-nilly," Wolfe declared. "As I told the assistant district attorney, it is on my score that a man was poisoned in food prepared by Fritz Brenner. But I do not send Mr. Goodwin on fruitless errands. He is one and you have dozens, and if anything is to be learned at the agency or by inquiry into Mr. Pyle's associations your army will dig it up. They're already at it, of course, but if they had started a trail you wouldn't be here. If I send Mr. Goodwin—"

The doorbell rang and I got up and went to the hall. At the rear the door to the kitchen swung open partway and Fritz poked his head through, saw me, and withdrew. Turning to the front for a look through the panel, I saw that I had exaggerated when I told Wolfe that all twelve of them would be otherwise engaged. At least one wasn't. There on the stoop was Helen Iacono.

It had sounded to me as if Cramer had about said his say and would soon be moving along, and if he bumped into Helen Iacono in the hall she might be too embarrassed to give me her phone number, if that was what she had come for; so as I opened the door I pressed a finger to my lips and *sshhed* at her, and then crooked the finger to motion her in. Her deep dark eyes looked a little startled, but she stepped across the sill, and I shut the door, turned, opened the first door on the left, to the front room, motioned to her to enter, followed, and closed the door.

"What's the matter?" she whispered.

"Nothing now," I told her. "This is soundproofed. There's a police inspector in the office with Mr. Wolfe and I thought you might have had enough of cops for now. But if you want to meet him—"

"I don't. I want to see Nero Wolfe."

"Okay, I'll tell him as soon as the cop goes. Have a seat. It shouldn't be long."

There is a connecting door between the front room and the office, but I went around through the hall, and here came Cramer. He was marching by without even the courtesy of a grunt, but I stepped to the front to let him out, and then went to the office and told Wolfe, "I've got one of them in the front room. Helen Iacono, the tawny-skinned Hebe who had you but gave her caviar to Kreis. Shall I keep her while I get the rest of them?"

He made a face. "What does she want?"

"To see you."

He took a breath. "Confound it. Bring her in."

I went and opened the connecting door, told her to come, and escorted her across to the red leather chair. She was more ornamental in it than Cramer, but not nearly as impressive as she had been at first sight. She was puffy around the eyes and her skin had lost some glow. She told Wolfe she hadn't had any sleep. She said she had just left the district attorney's office, and if she went home her mother would be at her again, and her brothers and sisters would come home from school and make noise, and anyway she had decided to see Wolfe. Her mother was old-fashioned and didn't want her to be an actress. It was beginning to sound as if what she was after was a place to take a nap, but then Wolfe got a word in.

He said dryly, "I didn't suppose, Miss Iacono, you came to consult me about your career."

"Oh, no. I came because you're a detective and you're very clever and I'm afraid. I'm afraid they'll find out something I did, and if they do I won't have any career. My parents won't let me even if I'm still alive. I nearly gave it away already when they were asking me questions. So I decided to tell you about it and then if you'd help me I'll help you. If you promise to keep my secret."

"I can't promise to keep a secret if it is a guilty one—if it is a confession of a crime or knowledge of one."

"It isn't."

"Then you have my promise, and Mr. Goodwin's. We have kept many secrets."

"All right. I stabbed Vincent Pyle with a knife and got blood on me."

I stared. For half a second I thought she meant that he hadn't died of poison at all, that she had sneaked upstairs and stuck a knife in him, which seemed unlikely, since the doctors would probably have found the hole.

Apparently she wasn't going on, and Wolfe spoke. "Ordinarily, Miss Iacono, stabbing a man is considered a crime. When and where did this happen?"

"It wasn't a crime, because it was in self-defense." Her rich contralto was as composed as if she had been telling us the multiplication table. Evidently she saved the inflections for her career. She was continuing. "It happened in January, about three months ago. Of course I knew about him—everybody in show business does. I don't know if it's true that he backs shows just so he can get girls, but it might as well be. There's a lot of talk about the girls he gets, but nobody really knows because he was always very careful about it. Some of the girls have talked but he never did. I don't mean just taking them out, I mean the last ditch. We say that on Broadway. You know what I mean?"

"I can surmise."

"Sometimes we say the last stitch, but it means the same thing. Early last winter he began on me. Of course I knew about his reputation, but he was backing *Jack in the Pulpit* and they were about to start casting, and I didn't know it was going to be a flop, and if a girl expects to have a career she has to be sociable. I went out with him a few times, dinner and dancing and so forth, and then he asked me to his apartment and I went. He cooked the dinner himself—I said he was very careful. Didn't I?"

"Yes."

"Well, he was. It's a penthouse on Madison Avenue, but

no one else was there. I let him kiss me. I figured it like
this, an actress gets kissed all the time on the stage and
the screen and TV, and what's the difference? I went to his
apartment three times and there was no real trouble, but
the fourth time—that was in January—he turned into a
beast right before my eyes, and I had to do something, and
I grabbed a knife from the table and stabbed him with it. I
got blood on my dress, and when I got home I tried to get it
out but it left a stain. It cost forty-six dollars."

"But Mr. Pyle recovered."

"Oh, yes. I saw him a few times after that, I mean just by
accident, but he barely spoke and so did I. I don't think he
ever told anyone about it, but what if he did? What if the
police find out about it?"

Wolfe grunted. "That would be regrettable, certainly.
You would be pestered even more than you are now. But if
you have been candid with me you are not in mortal jeop-
ardy. The police are not simpletons. You wouldn't be arrested for murdering Mr. Pyle last night, let alone
convicted, merely because you stabbed him in self-defense
last January."

"Of course I wouldn't," she agreed. "That's not it. It's
my mother and father. They'd find out about it because
they would ask them questions, and if I'm going to have a
career I would have to leave home and my family, and I
don't want to. Don't you see?" She came forward in the
chair. "But if they find out right away who did it, who
poisoned him, that would end it and I'd be all right. Only
I'm afraid they won't find out right away, but I think you
could if I help you, and you said last night that you're committed. I can't offer to help the police because they'd wonder why."

"I see." Wolfe's eyes were narrowed at her. "How do you
propose to help me?"

"Well, I figure it like this." She was on the edge of the
chair. "The way you explained it last night, one of the girls
poisoned him. She was one of the first ones to take plates
in, and then she came back and got another one. I don't
quite understand why she did that, but you do, so all right.
But if she came back for another plate, that took a little

time, and she must have been one of the last ones, and the police have got it worked out who were the last five. I know that because of the questions they asked this last time. So it was Peggy Choate or Nora Jaret or Carol Annis or Lucy Morgan."

"Or you."

"No, it wasn't me." Just matter-of-fact. "So it was one of them. And she didn't poison him just for nothing, did she? You'd have to have a very good reason to poison a man, I know I would. So all we have to do is find out which one had a good reason, and that's where I can help. I don't know Lucy Morgan, but I know Carol a little, and I know Nora and Peggy even better. And now we're in this together, and I can pretend to them I want to talk about it. I can talk about him because I had to tell the police I went out with him a few times, because I was seen with him and they'd find out, so I thought I'd better tell them. Dozens of girls went out with him, but he was so careful that nobody knows which ones went to the last ditch except the ones that talked. And I can find out which one of those four girls had a reason, and tell you, and that will end it."

I was congratulating myself that I hadn't got her phone number; and if I had got it, I would have crossed it off without a pang. I don't say that a girl must have true nobility of character before I'll buy her a lunch, but you have to draw the line somewhere. Thinking that Wolfe might be disgusted enough to put into words the way I felt, I horned in. "I have a suggestion, Miss Iacono. You could bring them here, all four of them, and let Mr. Wolfe talk it over with them. As you say, he's very clever."

She looked doubtful. "I don't believe that's a good idea. I think they'd be more apt to say things to me, just one at a time. Don't you think so, Mr. Wolfe?"

"You know them better than I do," he muttered. He was controlling himself.

"And then," she said, "when we find out which one had a reason, and we tell the police, I can say that I saw her going back to the kitchen for another plate. Of course just where I saw her, where she was and where I was, that will depend on who she is. I saw you, Mr. Wolfe, when I said

you could if I helped you, I saw the look on your face. You
didn't think a twenty-year-old girl could help, did you?"

He had my sympathy. Of course what he would have
liked to say was that it might well be that a twenty-year-
old hellcat could help, but that wouldn't have been tactful.

"I may have been a little skeptical," he conceded. "And
it's possible that you're oversimplifying the problem. We
have to consider all the factors. Take one: her plan must
have been not only premeditated but also thoroughly
rigged, since she had the poison ready. So she must have
known that Mr. Pyle would be one of the guests. Did she?"

"Oh, yes. We all did. Mr. Buchman at the agency showed
us a list of them and told us who they were, only of course
he didn't have to tell us who Vincent Pyle was. That was
about a month ago, so she had plenty of time to get the
poison. Is arsenic very hard to get?"

"Not at all. It is in common use for many purposes. That
is of course one of the police lines of inquiry, but she knew
it would be and she is no bungler. Another point: when Mr.
Pyle saw her there, serving food, wouldn't he have been on
his guard?"

"But he didn't see her. They didn't see any of us before.
She came up behind him and gave him that plate. Of
course he saw her afterward, but he had already eaten it."

Wolfe persisted. "But then? He was in agony, but he was
conscious and could speak. Why didn't he denounce her?"

She gestured impatiently. "I guess you're not as clever
as you're supposed to be. He didn't know she had done it.
When he saw her she was serving another man, and—"

"What other man?"

"How do I know? Only it wasn't you, because I served
you. And anyway, maybe he didn't know she wanted to kill
him. Of course she had a good reason, I know that, but
maybe he didn't know she felt like that. A man doesn't
know how a girl feels—anyhow, some girls. Look at me. He
didn't know I would never dream of going to the last ditch.
He thought I would give up my honor and my virtue just to
get a part in that play he was backing, and anyhow it was
a flop." She gestured again. "I thought you wanted to get
her. All you do is make objections."

Wolfe rubbed the side of his nose. "I do want to get her, Miss Iacono. I intend to. But like Mr. Pyle, though from a different motive, I am very careful. I can't afford to botch it. I fully appreciate your offer to help. You didn't like Mr. Goodwin's suggestion that you get them here in a body for discussion with me, and you may be right. But I don't like your plan, for you to approach them singly and try to pump them. Our quarry is a malign and crafty harpy, and I will not be a party to your peril. I propose an alternative. Arrange for Mr. Goodwin to see them, together with you. Being a trained investigator, he knows how to beguile, and the peril, if any, will be his. If they are not available at the moment, arrange it for this evening—but not here. Perhaps one of them has a suitable apartment, or if not, a private room at some restaurant would do. At my expense, of course. Will you?"

It was her turn to make objections, and she had several. But when Wolfe met them, and made it plain that he would accept her as a colleague only if she accepted his alternative, she finally gave in. She would phone to let me know how she was making out with the arrangements. From her manner, when she got up to go, you might have thought she had been shopping for some little item, say a handbag, and had graciously deferred to the opinion of the clerk. After I graciously escorted her out and saw her descend the seven steps to the sidewalk, I returned to the office and found Wolfe sitting with his eyes closed and his fists planted on the chair arms.

"Even money," I said.

"On what?" he growled.

"On her against the field. She knows damn well who had a good reason and exactly what it was. It was getting too hot for comfort and she decided that the best way to duck was to wish it on some dear friend."

His eyes opened. "She would, certainly. A woman whose conscience has no sting will stop at nothing. But why come to me? Why didn't she cook her own stew and serve it to the police?"

"I don't know, but for a guess she was afraid the cops would get too curious and find out how she had saved her

honor and her virtue and tell her mother and father, and
Father would spank her. Shall I also guess why you pro-
posed your alternative instead of having her bring them
here for you?"

"She wouldn't. She said so."

"Of course she would, if you had insisted. That's your
guess. Mine is that you're not desperate enough yet to take
on five females in a bunch. When you told me to bring the
whole dozen you knew darned well it couldn't be done, not
even by me. Okay, I want instructions."

"Later," he muttered, and closed his eyes.

It was on the fourth floor of an old walk-up in the West
Nineties near Amsterdam Avenue. I don't know what it
had in the way of a kitchen or bedroom—or bedrooms—
because the only room I saw was the one we were sitting
in. It was medium-size, and the couch and chairs and rugs
had a homey look, the kind of homeyness that furniture
gets by being used by a lot of different people for fifty or
sixty years. The chair I was on had a wobbly leg, but that's
no problem if you keep it in mind and make no sudden
shifts. I was more concerned about the spidery little stand
at my elbow on which my glass of milk was perched. I can
always drink milk and had preferred it to Bubble-Pagne,
registered trademark, a dime a bottle, which they were
having. It was ten o'clock Wednesday evening.

The hostesses were the redhead with milky skin, Peggy
Choate, and the one with big brown eyes and dimples,
Nora Jaret, who shared the apartment. Carol Annis, with
the fine profile and the corn-silk hair, had been there when
Helen Iacono and I arrived, bringing Lucy Morgan and her
throaty voice after detouring our taxi to pick her up at a
street corner. They were a very attractive collection,
though of course not as decorative as they had been in
their ankle-length purple stolas. Girls always look better
in uniforms or costumes. Take nurses or elevator girls or
Miss Honeydew at a melon festival.

I was now calling her Helen, not that I felt like it, but in
the detective business you have to be sociable, of course
preserving your honor and virtue. In the taxi, before pick-

ing up Lucy Morgan, she told me she had been thinking it
over and she doubted if it would be possible to find out
which one of them had a good reason to kill Pyle, or
thought she had, because Pyle had been so very careful
when he had a girl come to his penthouse. The only way
would be to get one of them to open up, and Helen doubted
if she could get her to, since she would be practically con-
fessing murder. So the best way would be for Helen and
me, after spending an evening with them, to talk it over
and decide which one was the most likely, and then she
would tell Wolfe she had seen her going back to the
kitchen and bringing another plate, and Wolfe would tell
the police, and that would do it.

No, I didn't feel like calling her Helen. I would just as
soon have been too far away from her to call her at all.

Helen's declared object in arranging the party—declared
to them—was to find out from me what Nero Wolfe and the
cops had done and were doing, so they would know where
they stood. Helen was sure I would loosen up, she had told
them, because she had been to see me and found me very
nice and sympathetic. So the hostesses were making it sort
of festive and intimate by serving Bubble-Pagne, though I
preferred milk. I had a suspicion that at least one of them,
Lucy Morgan, would have preferred whiskey or gin or rum
or vodka, and maybe they all would, but that might have
made me suspect that they were not just a bunch of wholesome, hardworking artists.

They didn't look festive. I wouldn't say they were hag-
gard, but much of the bloom was off. And they hadn't
bought Helen's plug for me that I was nice and sympathetic. They were absolutely skeptical, sizing me up with
sidewise looks, especially Carol Annis, who sat cross-
legged on the couch with her head cocked. It was she who
asked me, after a few remarks had been made about how
awful it had been and still was, how well I knew the chef
and the other man in the kitchen. I told her she could forget Fritz. He was completely above suspicion, and anyway
he had been at the range while the plates were taken. As
for Zoltan, I said that though I had known him a long while
we were not intimate, but that was irrelevant because,

granting that he had known which guest each girl would
serve, if he poisoned one of the portions and saw that a certain girl got it, why did she or some other girl come back
for another plate?

"There's no proof that she did," Carol declared. "Nobody
saw her."

"Nobody *noticed* her." I wasn't aggressive; I was supposed to be nice and sympathetic. "She wouldn't have been
noticed leaving the dining room because the attention of
the girls who were in there was on Felix and Marjorie
Quinn, who had spilled a blini, and the men wouldn't notice her. The only place she would have been noticed was
in the corridor through the pantry, and if she met another
girl there she could have stopped and been patting her hair
or something. Anyhow, one of you must have gone back for
a second plate, because when Fern Faber went for hers
there wasn't any."

"Why do you say one of us?" Nora demanded. "If you
mean one of us here. There were twelve."

"I do mean one of you here, but I'm not saying it, I'm just
quoting the police. They think it was one of you here because you were the last five."

"How do you know what they think?"

"I'm not at liberty to say. But I do."

"I know what I think," Carol asserted. She had uncrossed her legs and slid forward on the couch to get her
toes on the floor. "I think it was Zoltan. I read in the *Ga-
zette* that he's a chef at Rusterman's, and Nero Wolfe is
the trustee and so he's the boss there, and I think Zoltan
hated him for some reason and tried to poison him, but he
gave the poisoned plate to the wrong girl. Nero Wolfe sat
right next to Pyle."

There was no point in telling her that she was simply
ignoring the fact that one of them had gone back for a second helping, so I just said, "Nobody can stop you thinking.
But I doubt very much if the police would buy that."

"What would they buy?" Peggy asked.

My personal feelings about Peggy were mixed. For: she
had recognized and named me. Against: she had accused
me of liking myself. "Anything that would fit," I told her.

"As I said, they think it was one of you five that went back for more, and therefore they have to think that one of you gave the poison to Pyle, because what other possible reason could you have had for serving another portion? They wouldn't buy anything that didn't fit into that. That's what rules out everybody else, including Zoltan." I looked at Carol. "I'm sorry, Miss Annis, but that's how it is."

"They're a bunch of dopes," Lucy Morgan stated. "They get an idea and then they haven't got room for another one." She was on the floor with her legs stretched out, her back against the couch. "I agree with Carol, there's no proof that any of us went back for another plate. That Zoltan said he didn't see anyone come back. Didn't he?"

"He did. He still does."

"Then he's a dope, too. And he said no one took two plates. Didn't he?"

"Right. He still does."

"Then how do they know which one he's wrong about? We were all nervous, you know that. Maybe one of us took two plates instead of one, and when she got to the dining room there she was with an extra, and she got rid of it by giving it to some guest that didn't have any."

"Then why didn't she say so?" I asked.

"Because she was scared. The way Nero Wolfe came at us was enough to scare anybody. And now she won't say so because she signed a statement and she's even more scared."

I shook my head. "I'm sorry, but if you analyze that you'll see that it won't do. It's very tricky. You can do it the way I did this afternoon. Take twenty-four little pieces of paper, on twelve of them write the names of the guests, and arrange them as they sat at the table. On the other twelve pieces write the names of the twelve girls. Then try to manipulate the twelve girl pieces so that one of them either took in two plates at once, and did not give either of them to Pyle, or went back for a second plate, and did not give either the first one or the second one to Pyle. It can't be done. For if either of those things happened there wouldn't have been one mix-up, there would have been two. Since there was only one mix-up, Pyle couldn't possibly have been served by a girl who neither brought in two plates at once nor went back for a second one. So the idea that a girl *innocently* brought in two plates is out."

"I don't believe it," Nora said flatly.

"It's not a question of believing." I was still sympathetic. "You might as well say you don't believe two plus two is four. I'll show you. May I have some paper? Any old kind."

She went to a table and brought some, and I took my pen and wrote the twenty-four names, spacing them, and tore the paper into twenty-four pieces. Then I knelt on a rug and arranged the twelve guest pieces in a rectangle as they had sat at table—not that that mattered, since they could have been in a straight line or a circle, but it was plainer that way. The girls gathered around.

"Okay," I said, "show me." I took *Quinn* and put it back of *Leacraft*. "There's no argument about that, Marjorie Quinn brought the first plate and gave it to Leacraft. Remember there was just one mix-up, started by Peggy when she saw Pyle had been served and gave hers to Nero Wolfe. Try having any girl bring in a second plate—or bring in two at once if you still think that might have happened—without either serving Pyle or starting a second mix-up."

My memory has had a long stiff training under the strains and pressures Wolfe has put on it, but I wouldn't undertake to report all the combinations they tried, huddled around me on the floor. They stuck to it for half an hour or more. The most persistent was Peggy Choate, the redhead. After the others had given up she stayed with it, frowning and biting her lip, propped first on one hand and then the other. Finally she said, "Nuts," stretched an arm to make a jumble of all the pieces of paper, guests and girls, got up, and returned to her chair.

"It's just a trick," said Carol Annis, perched on the couch again.

"I still don't believe it," Nora Jaret declared. "I do not believe that one of us deliberately poisoned a man—one of us sitting here." Her big brown eyes were at me. "Good Lord, look at us! Point at her! Point her out! I dare you to!"

That, of course, was what I was there for—not exactly to

point her out, but at least to get a hint. I had had a vague idea that one might come from watching them maneuver the pieces of paper but it hadn't. Nor from anything any of them had said. I had been expecting Helen Iacono to introduce the subject of Vincent Pyle's *modus operandi* with girls, but apparently she had decided it was up to me. She hadn't spoken more than twenty words since we arrived.

"If I could point her out," I said, "I wouldn't be bothering the rest of you. Neither would the cops if *they* could point her out. Sooner or later, of course, they will, but it begins to look as if they'll have to get at it from the other end. Motive. They'll have to find out which one of you had a motive, and they will—sooner or later—and on that maybe I can help. I don't mean help them, I mean help you—not the one who killed him, the rest of you. That thought occurred to me after I learned that Helen Iacono had admitted that she had gone out with Pyle a few times last winter. What if she had said she hadn't? When the police found out she had lied, and they would have, she would have been in for it. It wouldn't have proved she had killed him, but the going would have been mighty rough. I understand that the rest of you have all denied that you ever had anything to do with Pyle. Is that right? Miss Annis?"

"Certainly." Her chin was up. "Of course I had met him. Everybody in show business has. Once when he came backstage at the Coronet, and once at a party somewhere, and one other time but I don't remember where."

"Miss Morgan?"

She was smiling at me, a crooked smile. "Do you call this helping us?" she demanded.

"It might lead to that after I know how you stand. After all, the cops have your statement."

She shrugged. "I've been around longer than Carol, so I had seen him to speak to more than she had. Once I danced with him at the Flamingo, two years ago. That was the closest I had ever been to him."

"Miss Choate?"

"I never had the honor. I only came to New York last fall. From Montana. He had been pointed out to me from a distance, but he never chased me."

"Miss Jaret?"

"He was Broadway," she said. "I'm TV."

"Don't the twain ever meet?"

"Oh, sure. All the time at Sardi's. That's the only place I ever saw the great Pyle, and I wasn't with him."

"So there you are," I said, "you're all committed. If one of you poisoned him, and though I hate to say it I don't see any way out of that, that one is lying. But if any of the others are lying, if you saw more of him than you admit, you had better get from under quick. If you don't want to tell the cops, tell me, tell me now, and I'll pass it on and say I wormed it out of you. Believe me, you'll regret it if you don't."

"Archie Goodwin, a girl's best friend," Lucy said. "My bosom pal."

No one else said anything.

"Actually," I asserted, "I *am* your friend, all of you but one. I have a friendly feeling for all pretty girls, especially those who work, and I admire and respect you for being willing to make an honest fifty bucks by coming there yesterday to carry plates of grub to a bunch of finickers. I *am* your friend, Lucy, if you're not the murderer."

I leaned forward, forgetting the wobbly chair leg, but it didn't object. It was about time to put a crimp in Helen's personal project. "Another thing. It's quite possible that one of you *did* see her returning to the kitchen for another plate, and you don't want to squeal on her. If so, spill it now. The longer this hangs on, the hotter it will get. When it gets so the pressure is too much for you and you decide you have got to tell it, it will be too late. If you go to the cops with it tomorrow they probably won't believe you; they'll figure that you did it yourself and you're trying to squirm out. If you don't want to tell me here and now, in front of her, come with me down to Nero Wolfe's office and we'll talk it over."

They were exchanging glances, and they were not friendly glances. When I had arrived probably not one of them, excluding the murderer, had believed that a poisoner was present, but now they all did, or at least they thought she might be; and when that feeling takes hold it's goodby to friendliness. It would have been convenient if I could have detected fear in one of the glances, but fear and suspicion and uneasiness are too much alike on faces to tell them apart.

"You *are* a help," Carol Annis said bitterly. "Now you've got us hating each other. Now everybody suspects everybody."

I had quit being nice and sympathetic. "It's about time," I told her. I glanced at my wrist. "It's not midnight yet. If I've made you all realize that this is no Broadway production, or TV either, and the longer the payoff is postponed the tougher it will be for everybody, I *have* helped." I stood up. "Let's go. I don't say Mr. Wolfe can do it by just snapping his fingers, but he might surprise you. He has often surprised me."

"All right," Nora said. She arose. "Come on. This is getting too damn painful. Come on."

I don't pretend that that was what I had been heading for. I admit that I had just been carried along by my tongue. If I arrived with the gang at midnight and Wolfe had gone to bed, he would almost certainly refuse to play. Even if he were still up, he might refuse to work, just to teach me a lesson, since I had not stuck to my instructions. Those thoughts were at me as Peggy Choate bounced up and Carol Annis started to leave the couch.

But they were wasted. That tussle with Wolfe never came off. A door at the end of the room which had been standing ajar suddenly swung open, and there in its frame was a two-legged figure with shoulders almost as broad as the doorway, and I was squinting at Sergeant Purley Stebbins of Manhattan Homicide West. He moved forward, croaking, "I'm surprised at you, Goodwin. These ladies ought to get some sleep."

Of course I was a monkey. If it had been Stebbins who had made a monkey of me I suppose I would have leaped for a window and dived through. Hitting the pavement from a fourth-story window should be enough to finish a monkey, and life wouldn't be worth living if I had been bamboozled by Purley Stebbins. But obviously it hadn't been him; it had been Peggy Choate or Nora Jaret, or both;

Purley had merely accepted an invitation to come and listen in.

So I kept my face. To say I was jaunty would be stretching it, but I didn't scream or tear my hair. "Greetings," I said heartily. "And welcome. I've been wondering why you didn't join us instead of skulking in there in the dark."

"I'll bet you have." He had come to arm's length and stopped. He turned. "You can relax, ladies." Back to me: "You're under arrest for obstructing justice. Come along."

"In a minute. You've got all night." I moved my head. "Of course Peggy and Nora knew this hero was in there, but I'd—"

"I said come along!" he barked.

"And I said in a minute. I intend to ask a couple of questions. I wouldn't dream of resisting arrest, but I've got leg cramp from kneeling too long and if you're in a hurry you'll have to carry me." I moved my eyes. "I'd like to know if you all knew. Did you, Miss Iacono?"

"Of course not."

"Miss Morgan?"

"No."

"Miss Annis?"

"No, I didn't, but I think you did." She tossed her head and the corn silk fluttered. "That was contemptible. Saying you wanted to help us so we would talk, with a policeman listening."

"And then he arrests me?"

"That's just an act."

"I wish it were. Ask your friends, Peggy and Nora if I knew—only I suppose you wouldn't believe them. *They* knew, and they didn't tell you. You'd better all think over everything you said. Okay, Sergeant, the leg cramp's gone."

He actually started a hand for my elbow, but I was moving and it wasn't there. I opened the door to the hall. Of course he had me go first down the three flights; no cop in his senses would descend stairs in front of a dangerous criminal in custody. When we emerged to the sidewalk and he told me to turn left I asked him, "Why not cuffs?"

"Clown if you want to," he croaked.

He flagged a taxi on Amsterdam Avenue, and when we were in and rolling I spoke. "I've been thinking, about laws and liberties and so on. Take false arrest, for instance. And take obstructing justice. If a man is arrested for obstructing justice and it turns out that he didn't obstruct any justice, does that make the arrest false? I wish I knew more about law. I guess I'll have to ask a lawyer. Nathaniel Parker would know."

It was the mention of Parker, the lawyer Wolfe uses when the occasion calls for one, that got him. He had seen Parker in action.

"They heard you," he said, "and I heard you, and I took some notes. You interfered in a homicide investigation. You quoted the police to them. You told them what the police think, and what they're doing and are going to do. You played a game with them with those pieces of paper to show them exactly how it figures. You tried to get them to tell you things instead of telling the police, and you were going to take them to Nero Wolfe so he could pry it out of them. And you haven't even got the excuse that Wolfe is representing a client. He hasn't got a client."

"Wrong. He has."

"Like hell he has. Name her."

"Not her, him. Fritz Brenner. He is seeing red because food cooked by him was poisoned and killed a man. It's convenient to have the client living right in the house. You admit that a licensed detective has a right to investigate on behalf of a client."

"I admit nothing."

"That's sensible," I said approvingly. "You shouldn't. When you're on the stand being sued for false arrest, it would be bad to have it thrown up to you, and it would be two against one because the hackie could testify. Can you hear us, driver?"

"Sure I can hear you," he sang out. "It's very interesting."

"So watch your tongue," I told Purley. "You could get hooked for a year's pay. As for quoting the police, I merely said that they think it was one of those five, and when Cramer told Mr. Wolfe that he didn't say it was confidential. As for telling them what the police think, same comment. As for playing that game with them, why not? As for trying to get them to tell me things, I won't comment on that at all because I don't want to be rude. That must have been a slip of the tongue. If you ask me why I didn't balk there at the apartment and bring up these points then and there, what was the use? You had spoiled the party. They wouldn't have come downtown with me. Also I am saving a buck of Mr. Wolfe's money, since you had arrested me and therefore the taxi fare is on the city of New York. Am I still under arrest?"

"You're damn right you are."

"That may be ill-advised. You heard him, driver?"

"Sure I heard him."

"Good. Try to remember it."

We were on Ninth Avenue, stopped at Forty-second Street for a light. When the light changed and we moved, Purley told the hackie to pull over to the curb, and he obeyed. At that time of night there were plenty of gaps. Purley took something from a pocket and showed it to the hackie, and said, "Go get yourself a Coke and come back in ten minutes," and he climbed out and went. Purley turned his head to glare at me.

"I'll pay for the Coke," I offered.

He ignored it. "Lieutenant Rowcliff," he said, "is expecting us at Twentieth Street."

"Fine. Even under arrest, one will get you five that I can make him start stuttering in ten minutes."

"You're not under arrest."

I leaned forward to look at the meter. "Ninety cents. From here on we'll split it."

"Damn it, quit clowning! If you think I'm crawling you're wrong. I just don't see any percentage in it. If I deliver you in custody I know damn well what you'll do. You'll clam up. We won't get a peep out of you, and in the morning you'll make a phone call and Parker will come. What will that get us?"

I could have said, "A suit for false arrest," but I made it, "Only the pleasure of my company."

There was one point of resemblance between Purley and

Carol Annis, just one: no sense of humor. "But," he said,
"Lieutenant Rowcliff is expecting you, and you're a material witness in a homicide case, and you were up there
working on the suspects."

"You could arrest me as a material witness," I suggested.

He uttered a word that I was glad the hackie wasn't
there to hear, and added, "You'd clam up and in the morning you'd be out on bail. I know it's after midnight, but the
lieutenant is expecting you."

He's a proud man, Purley is, and I wouldn't go so far as
to say that he has nothing to be proud of. He's not a bad
cop, as cops go. It was a temptation to keep him dangling
for a while, to see how long it would take him to bring himself to the point of coming right out and asking for it, but it
was late and I needed some sleep.

"You realize," I said, "that it's a waste of time and energy. You can tell him everything we said, and if he tried
to go into other aspects with me I'll only start making
cracks and he'll start stuttering. It's useless."

"Yeah, I know, but—"

"But the lieutenant expects me."

He nodded. "It was him Nora Jaret told about it, and he
sent me. The inspector wasn't around."

"Okay. In the interest of justice I'll give him an hour.
That's understood? Exactly one hour."

"It's not understood with me." He was emphatic. "When
we get there you're his and he's welcome to you. I don't
know if he can stand you for an hour."

At noon the next day, Thursday, Fritz stood at the end of
Wolfe's desk, consulting with him on a major point of
policy: whether to switch to another source of supply for
watercress. The quality had been below par, which for
them means perfection, for nearly a week. I was at my
desk, yawning. It had been after two o'clock when I got
home from my chat with Lieutenant Rowcliff, and with
nine hours' sleep in two nights I was way behind.

The hour since Wolfe had come down at eleven o'clock
from his morning session with the orchids had been spent,

most of it, by me reporting and Wolfe listening. My visit
with Rowcliff needed only a couple of sentences, since the
only detail of any import was that it had taken me eight
minutes to get him stuttering, but Wolfe wanted my conversation with the girls verbatim, and also my impres-
sions and conclusions. I told him my basic conclusion was
that the only way she could be nailed, barring a stroke of
luck, would be by a few dozen men sticking to the routine—
her getting the poison and her connection with Pyle.

"And," I added, "her connection with Pyle may be hope-
less. In fact, it probably is. If it's Helen Iacono, what she
told us is no help. If what she told us is true she had no reason to kill him, and if it isn't true how are you going to
prove it? If it's one of the others she is certainly no half-wit,
and there may be absolutely nothing to link her up. Being
very careful with visitors to your penthouse is fine as long
as you're alive, but it has its drawbacks if one of them
feeds you arsenic."

He was regarding me without enthusiasm. "You are
saying in effect that it must be left to the police. I don't
have a few dozen men. I can expose her only by a stroke of
luck."

"Right. Or a stroke of genius. That's your department. I
make no conclusions about genius."

"Then why the devil were you going to bring them to me
at midnight? Don't answer. I know. To badger me."

"No, sir. I told you. I had got nowhere with them. I had
got them looking at each other out of the corners of their
eyes, but that was all. I kept on talking, and suddenly I
heard myself inviting them to come home with me. I was
giving them the excuse that I wanted them to discuss it
with you, but that may have been just a cover for certain
instincts that a man is entitled to. They are very attractive
girls—all but one."

"Which one?"

"That's what we're working on."

He probably would have harped on it if Fritz hadn't entered to present the watercress problem. As they wrestled
with it, dealing with it from all angles, I swiveled my back
to them so I could do my yawning in private. Finally they

got it settled, deciding to give the present source one more week and then switch if the quality didn't improve; and then I heard Fritz say, "There's another matter, sir. Felix phoned me this morning. He and Zoltan would like an appointment with you after lunch, and I would like to be present. They suggested half past two."

"What is it?" Wolfe demanded. "Something wrong at the restaurant?"

"No, sir. Concerning the misfortune of Tuesday evening."

"What about it?"

"It would be better for them to tell you. It is their concern."

I swiveled for a view of Fritz's face. Had Felix and Zoltan been holding out on us? Fritz's expression didn't tell me, but it did tell Wolfe something: that it would be unwise for him to insist on knowing the nature of Felix's and Zoltan's concern because Fritz had said all he intended to. There is no one more obliging than Fritz, but also there is no one more immovable when he has taken a stand. So Wolfe merely said that half past two would be convenient. When Fritz had left I offered to go to the kitchen and see if I could pry it out of him, but Wolfe said no, apparently it wasn't urgent.

As it turned out, it wasn't. Wolfe and I were still in the dining room, with coffee, when the doorbell rang at 2:25 and Fritz answered it, and when we crossed the hall to the office Felix was in the red leather chair, Zoltan was in one of the yellow ones, and Fritz was standing. Fritz had removed his apron and put on a jacket, which was quite proper. People do not attend business conferences in aprons.

When we had exchanged greetings, and Fritz had been told to sit down and had done so, and Wolfe and I had gone to our desks, Felix spoke. "You won't mind, Mr. Wolfe, if I ask a question? Before I say why we requested an appointment?"

Wolfe told him no, go ahead.

"Because," Felix said, "we would like to know this first. We are under the impression that the police are making no progress. They haven't said so, they tell us nothing, but we have the impression. Is it true?"

"It was true at two o'clock this morning, twelve hours ago. They may have learned something by now, but I doubt it."

"Do you think they will soon make progress? That they will soon be successful?"

"I don't know. I can only conjecture. Archie thinks that unless they have a stroke of luck the inquiry will be long and laborious, and even then may fail. I'm inclined to agree with him."

Felix nodded. "That is what we fear—Zoltan and I and others at the restaurant. It is causing a most regrettable atmosphere. A few of our most desirable patrons make jokes, but most of them do not, and some of them do not come. We do not blame them. For the maître d'hôtel and one of our chefs to assist at a dinner where a guest is served poison—that is not pleasant. If the—"

"Confound it, Felix! I have avowed my responsibility. I have apologized. Are you here for the gloomy satisfaction of reproaching me?"

"No, sir." He was shocked. "Of course not. We came to say that if the poisoner is not soon discovered, and then the affair will be forgotten, the effect on the restaurant may be serious. And if the police are making no progress that may happen so we appeal to you. We wish to engage your professional services. We know that with you there would be no question. You would solve it quickly and completely. We know it wouldn't be proper to pay you from restaurant funds, since you are the trustee, so we'll pay you with our own money. There was a meeting of the staff last night, and all will contribute, in a proper ratio. We appeal to you."

Zoltan stretched out a hand, arm's length. "We appeal to you," he said.

"Pfui," Wolfe grunted.

He had my sympathy. Not only was their matter-of-fact confidence in his prowess highly flattering, but also their appealing instead of demanding, since he had got them into it, was extremely touching. But a man with a long-standing reputation for being hard and blunt simply can't afford the softer feelings, no matter what the provocation. It called for great self-control.

Felix and Zoltan exchanged looks. "He said 'pfui,' " Zoltan told Felix.

"I heard him," Felix snapped. "I have ears."

Fritz spoke. "I wished to be present," he said, "so I could add my appeal to theirs. I offered to contribute, but they said no."

Wolfe took them in, his eyes going right to left and back again. "This is preposterous," he declared. "I said 'pfui' not in disgust but in astonishment. I am solely to blame for this mess, but you offer to pay me to clean it up. Preposterous! You should know that I have already bestirred myself. Archie?"

"Yes, sir. At least you have bestirred me."

He skipped it. "And," he told them, "your coming is opportune. Before lunch I was sitting here considering the situation, and I concluded that the only way to manage the affair with dispatch is to get the wretch to betray herself; and I conceived a plan. For it I need your cooperation. Yours, Zoltan. Your help is essential. Will you give it? I appeal to you."

Zoltan upturned his palms and raised his shoulders. "But yes! But how?"

"It is complicated. Also it will require great dexterity and aplomb. How are you on the telephone? Some people are not themselves, not entirely at ease, when they are phoning. A few are even discomfited. Are you?"

"No." He reflected. "I don't think so. No."

"If you are it won't work. The plan requires that you telephone five of those women this afternoon. You will first call Miss Iacono, tell her who you are, and ask her to meet you somewhere—in some obscure restaurant. You will say that on Tuesday evening, when you told me that you had not seen one of them return for a second plate, you were upset and flustered by what had happened, and later, when the police questioned you, you were afraid to contradict yourself and tell the truth. But now that the notoriety is harming the restaurant you feel that you may have to reveal the fact that you did see her return for a second plate, but that before—"

"But I didn't!" Zoltan cried.

"Tais-toi!" Felix snapped at him.

Wolfe resumed. "—but that before you do so you wish to discuss it with her. You will say that one reason you have kept silent is that you have been unable to believe that anyone as charming as she is could be guilty of such a crime. A parenthesis. I should have said at the beginning that you must not try to parrot my words. I am giving you only the substance; the words must be your own, those you would naturally use. You understand that?"

"Yes, sir." Zoltan's hands were clasped tight.

"So don't try to memorize my words. Your purpose is to get her to agree to meet you. She will of course assume that you intend to blackmail her, but you will not say so. You will try to give her the impression, in everything you say and in your tone of voice, that you will not demand money from her, but will expect her favors. In short, that you desire her. I can't tell you how to convey that impression; I must leave that to you. The only requisite is that she must be convinced that if she refuses to meet you, you will go at once to the police and tell them the truth."

"Then you know," Zoltan said. "Then she is guilty."

"Not at all. I haven't the slightest idea who is guilty. When you have finished with her you will phone the other four and repeat the performance—Miss Choate, Miss Annis, Miss—"

"My God, Mr. Wolfe! That's impossible!"

"Not impossible, merely difficult. You alone can do it, for they know your voice. I considered having Archie do it, imitating your voice, but it would be too risky. You said you would help, but there's no use trying it if the bare idea appalls you. Will you undertake it?"

"I don't . . . I would . . ."

"He will," Felix said. "He is like that. He only needs to swallow it. He will do it well. But I must ask, can he be expected to get them all to agree to meet him? The guilty one, yes, but the others?"

"Certainly not. There is much to discuss and arrange.

The innocent ones will react variously according to their tempers. One or more of them will probably inform the police, and I must provide for that contingency with Mr. Cramer." To Zoltan: "Since it is possible that one of the innocent ones will agree to meet you, for some unimaginable reason, you will have to give them different hours for the appointments. There are many details to settle, but that is mere routine. The key is you. You must of course rehearse, and into a telephone transmitter. There are several stations on the house phone. You will go to Archie's room and speak from there. We will listen at the other stations: Archie in the plant rooms, I in my room, Fritz in the kitchen, and Felix in here. Archie will handle the other end of the conversation; he is much better qualified than I to improvise the responses of young women.

"Do you want me to repeat the substance of what you are to say before rehearsal?"

Zoltan opened his mouth and closed it again.

"Yes," he said.

Sergeant Purley Stebbins shifted his fanny for the nth time in two hours. "She's not coming," he muttered. "It's nearly eight o'clock." His chair was about half big enough for his personal dimensions.

We were squeezed in a corner of the kitchen of John Piotti's little restaurant on Fourteenth Street between Second and Third Avenues. On the midget table between us were two notebooks, his and mine, and a small metal case. Of the three cords extending from the case, the two in front went to the earphones we had on, and the one at the back ran down the wall, through the floor, along the basement ceiling toward the front, back up through the floor, and on through a table top, where it was connected to a microphone hidden in a bowl of artificial flowers. The installation, a rush order, had cost Wolfe $191.67. Permission to have it made had cost nothing because he had once got John Piotti out of a difficulty and hadn't soaked him.

"We'll have to hang on," I said. "You never can tell with a redhead."

The exposed page of my notebook was blank, but Purley had written on his. As follows:

Helen Iacono	6:00 P.M.
Peggy Choate	7:30 P.M.
Carol Annis	9:00 P.M.
Lucy Morgan	10:30 P.M.
Nora Jaret	12:00 P.M.

It was in my head. If I had had to write it down I would certainly have made one "p.m." do.

"Anyhow," Purley said, "we know damn well who it is."

"Don't count your poisoners," I said, "before they're hatched." It was pretty feeble, but I was still short on sleep.

I hoped to heaven he was right, since otherwise the operation was a flop. So far everything had been fine. After half an hour of rehearsing, Zoltan had been wonderful. He had made the five calls from the extension in my room, and when he was through I told him his name should be in lights on a Broadway marquee. The toughest job had been getting Inspector Cramer to agree to Wolfe's terms, but he had no good answer to Wolfe's argument that if he insisted on changing the rules Zoltan wouldn't play. So Purley was in the kitchen with me, Cramer was with Wolfe in the office, prepared to stay for dinner, Zoltan was at the restaurant table with the hidden mike, and two homocide dicks, one male and one female, were at another table twenty feet away. One of the most elaborate charades Nero Wolfe had ever staged.

Purley was right when he said we knew who it was, but I was right, too—she hadn't been hatched yet. The reactions to Zoltan's calls had settled it. Helen Iacono had been indignant and after a couple of minutes had hung up on him, and had immediately phoned the district attorney's office. Peggy Choate had let him finish his spiel and then called him a liar, but she had not said definitely that she wouldn't meet him, and the D.A. or police hadn't heard from her. Carol Annis, after he had spoken his lines, had used only ten words: "Where can I meet you?" and, after

he had told her where and when: "All right, I'll be there."
Lucy Morgan had coaxed him along, trying to get him to
fill it all in on the phone, had finally said she would keep
the appointment, and then had rushed downtown and
rung our doorbell, told me her tale, demanded that I ac-
company her to the rendezvous, and insisted on seeing
Wolfe. I had to promise to go to get rid of her. Nora Jaret
had called him assorted names, from liar on up, or on
down, and had told him she had a friend listening in on an
extension, which was almost certainly a lie. Neither we
nor the law had had a peep from her.

So it was Carol Annis with the corn-silk hair, that was
plain enough, but there was no salt on her tail. If she was
really smart and really tough she might decide to sit tight
and not come, figuring that when they came at her with
Zoltan's story she would say he was either mistaken or lying, and we would be up a stump. If she was dumb and only
fairly tough she might scram. Of course they would find
her and haul her back, but if she said Zoltan was lying and
she had run because she thought she was being framed,
again we would be up a stump. But if she was both smart
and tough but not quite enough of either, she would turn
up at nine o'clock and join Zoltan. From there on it would
be up to him, but that had been rehearsed, too, and after
his performance on the phone I thought he would deliver.

At half past eight Purley said, "She's not coming," and
removed his earphone.

"I never thought she would," I said. The "she" was of
course Peggy Choate, whose hour had been 7:30. "I said
you never can tell with a redhead merely to make conversation."

Purley signaled to Piotti, who had been hovering around
most of the time, and he brought us a pot of coffee and two
fresh cups. The minutes were snails, barely moving. When
we had emptied the cups I poured more. At 8:48 Purley put
his earphone back on. At 8:56 I asked, "Shall I do a
countdown?"

"You'd clown in the hot seat," he muttered, so hoarse
that it was barely words. He always gets hoarser as the
tension grows; that's the only sign.

It was four minutes past nine when the phone brought me the sound of a chair scraping, then faintly Zoltan's voice saying good evening, and then a female voice, but I couldn't get the words.

"Not loud enough," Purley whispered hoarsely.

"Shut up." I had my pen out. "They're standing up."

There came the sound of chairs scraping, and other little sounds, and then:

Zoltan: Will you have a drink?

Carol: No, I don't want anything.

Zoltan: Won't you eat something?

Carol: I don't feel . . . Maybe I will.

Purley and I exchanged glances. That was promising. That sounded as if we might get more than conversation.

Another female voice, belonging to Mrs. Piotti: We have good Osso Buco, madame. Very good. A specialty.

Carol: No, not meat.

Zoltan: A sweet perhaps?

Carol: No.

Zoltan: It is more friendly if we eat. The spaghetti with anchovy sauce is excellent. I had some.

Carol: You had some?

I bit my lip, but he handled it fine.

Zoltan: I've been here half an hour, I wanted so much to see you. I thought I should order something, and I tried that. I might even eat another portion.

Carol: You should know good food. All right.

Mrs. Piotti: Two spaghetti anchovy. Wine? A very good Chianti?

Carol: No. Coffee.

Pause.

Zoltan: You are more lovely without a veil, but the veil is good, too. It makes me want to see behind it. Of course I—

Carol: You have seen behind it, Mr. Mahany.

Zoltan: Ah! You know my name?

Carol: It was in the paper.

Zoltan: I am not sorry that you know it, I want you to know my name, but it will be nicer if you call me Zoltan.

Carol: I might someday. It will depend. I certainly won't

call you Zoltan if you go on thinking what you said on the phone. You're mistaken, Mr. Mahany. You didn't see me go back for another plate, because I didn't. I can't believe you would tell a vicious lie about me, so I just think you're mistaken.

Mrs. Piotti, in the kitchen for the spaghetti, came to the corner to stoop and whisper into my free ear, "She's wearing a veil."

Zoltan: I am not mistaken, my dear. That is useless. I know. How could I be mistaken when the first moment I saw you I felt . . . but I will not try to tell you how I felt. If any of the others had come and taken another plate I would have stopped her, but not you. Before you I was dumb. So it is useless.

Needing only one hand for my pen, I used the free one to blow a kiss to Purley.

Carol: I see. So you're sure.

Zoltan: I am, my dear. Very sure.

Carol: But you haven't told the police.

Zoltan: Of course not.

Carol: Have you told Nero Wolfe or Archie Goodwin?

Zoltan: I have told no one. How could I tell anyone? Mr. Wolfe is sure that the one who returned for another plate is the one who killed that man, gave him poison, and Mr. Wolfe is always right. So it is terrible for me. Could I tell anyone that I know you killed a man? You? How could I? That is why I had to see you, to talk with you. If you weren't wearing that veil I could look into your beautiful eyes. I think I know what I would see there. I would see suffering and sorrow. I saw that in your eyes Tuesday evening. I know he made you suffer. I know you wouldn't kill a man unless you had to. That is why—

The voice stopped. That was understandable, since Mrs. Piotti had gone through the door with the spaghetti and coffee and had had time to reach their table. Assorted sounds came as she served them.

Purley muttered, "He's overdoing it," and I muttered back, "No. He's perfect." Piotti came over and stood looking down at my notebook. It wasn't until Mrs. Piotti was back in the kitchen that Carol's voice came.

Carol: That's why I am wearing the veil, Zoltan, because I know it's in my eyes. You're right. I had to. He did make me suffer. He ruined my life.

Zoltan: No, my dear. Your life is not ruined. No! No matter what he did. Was he . . . did he . . .

I was biting my lip again. Why didn't he give them the signal? The food had been served and presumably they were eating. He had been told that it would be pointless to try to get her to give him any details of her relations with Pyle, since they would almost certainly be lies. Why didn't he give the signal? Her voice was coming:

Carol: He promised to marry me. I'm only twenty-two years old, Zoltan. I didn't think I would ever let a man touch me again, but the way you . . . I don't know. I'm glad you know I killed him because it will be better now, to know that somebody knows. To know that *you* know. Yes, I had to kill him, I *had* to, because if I didn't I would have had to kill myself. Someday I may tell you what a fool I was, how I—Oh!

Zoltan: What? What's the matter?

Carol: My bag. I left it in my car. Out front. And I didn't lock the car. A blue Plymouth hardtop. Would you . . . I'll go . . .

Zoltan: I'll get it.

The sound came of his chair scraping, then faintly his footsteps, and then silence. But the silence was broken in ten seconds, whereas it would have taken him much longer to go for the purse and return. What broke it was a male voice saying, "I'm an officer of the law, Miss Annis," and a noise from Carol. Purley, shedding his earphone, jumped up and went, and I followed, notebook in hand.

It was quite a tableau. The male dick stood with a hand on Carol's shoulder. Carol sat stiff, her chin up, staring straight ahead. The female dick, not much older than Carol, stood facing her from across the table, holding with both hands, at breast level, a plate of spaghetti. She spoke to Purley. "She put something in it and then stuck something in her dress. I saw her in my mirror."

I moved in. After all, I was in charge, under the terms Cramer had agreed to. "Thank you, Miss Annis," I said.

"You were a help. On a signal from Zoltan they were going to start a commotion to give him an excuse to leave the table, but you saved them the trouble. I thought you'd like to know. Come on, Zoltan. All over. According to plan."

He had entered and stopped three paces off, a blue handbag under his arm. As he moved toward us Purley put out a hand. "I'll take that."

Cramer was in the red leather chair. Carol Annis was in a yellow one facing Wolfe's desk, with Purley on one side of her and his female colleague on the other. The male colleague had been sent to the laboratory with the plate of spaghetti and a small roll of paper that had been fished from inside Carol's dress. Fritz, Felix, and Zoltan were on the couch near the end of my desk.

"I will not pretend, Miss Annis," Wolfe was saying. "One reason that I persuaded Mr. Cramer to have you brought here first on your way to limbo was that I needed to appease my rancor. You had injured and humiliated not only me, but also one of my most valued friends, Fritz Brenner, and two other men whom I esteem, and I had arranged the situation that gave you your opportunity; and I wished them to witness your own humiliation, contrived by me in my presence."

"That's enough of that," Cramer growled.

Wolfe ignored him. "I admit the puerility of that reason, Miss Annis, but in candor I wanted to acknowledge it. A better reason was that I wished to ask you a few questions. You took such prodigious risks that it is hard to believe in your sanity, and it would give me no satisfaction to work vengeance on a madwoman. What would you have done if Felix's eyes had been on you when you entered with the plate of poison and went to Mr. Pyle? Or if, when you returned to the kitchen for a second plate, Zoltan had challenged you? What would you have done?"

No answer. Apparently she was holding her gaze straight at Wolfe, but from my angle it was hard to tell because she still had the veil on. Asked by Cramer to remove it, she had refused. When the female dick had extracted the roll of paper from inside Carol's dress she had asked

Cramer if she should pull the veil off and Cramer had said no. No rough stuff.

There was no question about Wolfe's gaze at her. He was forward in his chair, his palms flat on his desk. He persisted. "Will you answer me, Miss Annis?"

She wouldn't.

"Are you a lunatic, Miss Annis?"

She wasn't saying.

Wolfe's head jerked to me. "Is she deranged, Archie?"

That was unnecessary. When we're alone I don't particularly mind his insinuations that I presume to be an authority on women, but there was company present. I gave him a look and snapped, "No comment."

He returned to her. "Then that must wait. I leave to the police such matters as your procurement of the poison and your relations with Mr. Pyle, mentioning only that you cannot now deny possession of arsenic, since you used it a second time this evening. It will unquestionably be found in the spaghetti and in the roll of paper you concealed in your dress; and so, manifestly, if you are mad you are also ruthless and malevolent. You may have been intolerably provoked by Mr. Pyle, but not by Zoltan. He presented himself not as a nemesis, but as a bewitched champion. He offered his homage, making no demands, and your counteroffer was death."

"You lie," Carol said. "And he lied. He was going to lie about me. He didn't see me go back for a second plate, but he was going to say he did. And you lie. He did make demands. He threatened me."

Wolfe's brows went up. "Then you haven't been told?"

"Told what?"

"That you were overheard. That is the other question I had for you. I have no apology for contriving the trap, but you deserve to know you are in its jaws. All that you and Zoltan said was heard by two men at the other end of a wire in another room, and they recorded it—Mr. Stebbins of the police, now at your left, and Mr. Goodwin."

"You lie," she said.

"No, Miss Annis. This isn't the trap; it has already been sprung. You have it, Mr. Stebbins?"

Purley nodded. He hates to answer questions from Wolfe.

"Archie?"

"Yes, sir."

"Did Zoltan threaten her or make demands?"

"No, sir. He followed instructions."

He returned to Carol. "Now you know. I wanted to make sure of that. To finish, since you may have had a just and weighty grievance against Mr. Pyle, I would myself prefer to see you made to account for your attempt to kill Zoltan, but that is not in my discretion. In any case, my rancor is appeased, and I hold—"

"That's enough," Cramer blurted, leaving his chair. "I didn't agree to let you preach at her all night. Bring her along, Sergeant."

As Purley arose a voice came. "May I say something?" It was Fritz. Heads turned as he left the couch and moved, detouring around Zoltan's feet and Purley's bulk to get to Carol, and turning to stand looking down at her.

"On account of what Mr. Wolfe said," he told her. "He said you injured me, and that is true. It is also true that I wanted him to find you. I can't speak for Felix, and you tried to kill Zoltan and I can't speak for him, but I can speak for myself. I forgive you."

"You lie," Carol said.

GARDEN OF EVIL

by Carol Cail

Carol Cail is the author of some fourteen short stories, the majority of which have appeared in Ellery Queen's Mystery Magazine *and* Alfred Hitchcock's Mystery Magazine. *She has also published close to fifty poems in assorted places. She has no pets, is not writing a novel, and her fondest ambition is to have someone contact her about adapting one of her stories for television. She is married, has two teenage sons, and lives in Colorado.*

Leaning on the kitchen table, washing yesterday's dishes, she could see the garden waiting for her. The August sun bouncing off the parched Kentucky clay made the landscape quiver and weave. All that motion and not a breath of wind. All that warm dishwater and still her fingers would scarcely bend.

Why am I so scared of that garden, she kept wondering. Me, eighty-two years a country girl and wife. This garden is the same as the others year after year. First you stir up the sleeping dirt, then you mix seeds in it, then you guard it against weeds and rabbits, and, when the time comes, you take what's due you. What did I plant different this spring out there with all the usual peas and beans?

She knew she'd be gnawing hungry in a couple hours, and she'd have to brave the garden. She had stayed in the house three days straight living off the pantry, and now it was depleted except for a bag of sugar and one of flour. Breakfast this morning had been a slice of dry toast and two cups of tea.

The first time she'd sensed the evil in the garden had been one steamy July evening as she waded among the scrambled tomato vines looking for some supper. She had been lazy early in the season, not putting up the poles or tying the plants. Now she was paying for it, thinking about snakes and finding spiders, rot, and rabbit leavings.

99

The apparently perfect red fruit she wrapped her fingers around had a slimy underside; her hand came up dripping sour-smelling tomato entrails that she hastily wiped on the nearest plantain. An outraged grasshopper sprang at her, and her step backward crushed a cluster of green tomatoes, the seeds squirting and clinging to her legs.

She had fled to a bare space, one of the rows she'd had the energy to weed, and stood there breathing hard, taking stock.

This familiar patch of truck garden where she had spent hours of her life buzzed and hissed and rustled. She saw the ground teeming with bees and beetles and ants and worms. She felt the fire of mosquitoes and oats bugs and flies devouring her. Perspiration trickled down her spine, and she twitched around to see what had touched her. A spire of Johnson grass tapped the back of her knee, and again she jumped.

She could summon up neither humor nor reason. So she had retreated, abandoning the half-filled basket, to the sanctuary of the kitchen, where she immediately felt foolish.

That was the first time the garden had menaced her. She couldn't count how often it had happened since.

At two o'clock she sat on the front porch swing, pretending she couldn't hear the growling in her stomach. The sun would slither behind the mountain in another hour or so, and the garden would be cooler, she'd rationalized.

From the porch she could see far, or could when she was younger. The view was up, not down. She lived in a cup of land surrounded by wooded cliffs. She counted distance by the ridges, one hill to her nearest neighbor, three hills to the nearest crossroads, and so on. The closest store, where she traded her Social Security for what she couldn't grow, was five hills away.

She'd never been lonely. Not even when Calvin passed away a year ago. It had been something of a relief to have the place to herself after all those years of doing for him. Now she could sleep late if she wanted, let the housework slide. Let the weeds grow.

"Hey!"

She shaded her eyes and peered into the little wild yard. Long red hair swinging was what she picked out first.

"Hey, Granny! What you doing?" the girl yelled, climbing onto the porch.

"Donna, I swan," she welcomed, her voice coming out wobbly and hoarse from disuse. "My only kin in the whole world, and ain't you the stranger!"

"Now don't go expecting me to stay or anything. I'm just passing by on my way from California to New York. I couldn't find a job I liked out West, so now I'm going to try the East."

"What kind of work you looking for?" she asked, remembering how to sound interested. She hadn't seen Donna since Calvin's funeral, and not often before that. The child was obviously a hippie. All that hair, and, from the way she jiggled, no underwear.

"Oh, something glamorous. I studied acting at the university. Maybe you'll read about me on Broadway."

"How'd you get here?"

"A friend of mind." She paused and simpered to make clear the friend was male. "Lent me his car. It's up on the road. So I can't stay. Not long enough to let the local yokels strip it down."

The old woman plotted. "My neighbors usually fetch me in supplies every week, but this time I'm short. You go get me a few things at the store, and we'll have a nice supper and talk."

"No, I don't think so. I really need to be getting on."

"Just a bite to eat. I won't keep you overnight. It would do me good to hear what you been doing and all," she lied.

"Well—" And the right mixture of guilt and vanity made her say yes.

While Donna was gone, the old woman set the table. She knew she ought to at least sweep the floor, but she knew, too, that Donna didn't care about the place being run-down. When she inherited it, she would sell it for whatever she could get and as fast as she could get it. A clean floor wouldn't bring up the price any. Come to that, Donna didn't look too clean herself.

So she sat at the table gazing out toward the garden,
thinking how she'd tell Donna to pick extra vegetables to
ensure having leftovers. "They're just as good warmed
over, and it'll save me a heap of work," she'd say. Then
she'd watch out the window to see if the garden did anything to Donna.

Not that it had ever really done anything to *her*. But
there had been the rabbit.

That was the last time she'd worked up the spunk to go
out there. It was three days ago, in early August. The
beans and corn needed canning, but she didn't want the
job. She'd told herself, Why bother? You probably won't
live out the winter anyway.

So this was to be her usual hurried trip into the now
weed-infested garden to harvest a meal's worth. She had
started for the carrot row, holding the spade in front of her
chest like a cross warding off dark powers. The sides of her
eyes saw little movements, but if she looked directly at the
spot, nothing stirred. She'd learned it was no good to sneak
into the garden, so she plunged headlong.

She overshot the carrots, had to retrace her steps to find
them underneath a swarm of morning-glory vines. She put
the spade into a likely space and raised one foot to shove it
home. That's when she saw the rabbit.

He was in among the vines, and she knew he was dead,
but never in all her years had she seen an animal look like
this in death. He wasn't lying sideways and limp. He lay
on his back, spread-eagled, each foot entangled in morning-glory tendrils, and a bindweed wrapped around his
neck.

The spade was still out there. Probably covered by vines
now, too. She'd thought about that rabbit a lot, but she
couldn't shake off the impression of the garden watching
her and swaying around her and whispering that it had
killed him.

Of course, she knew the garden couldn't have killed the
rabbit. Though come to think, it had killed Calvin, in a
way.

He'd been out there hoeing and pruning and thinning all
day in the hot sun, just like always, early spring to late

fall, taming the wilderness and bending it to his will. When he came in for supper, he was all trembly-limbed and dizzy, too weak to eat a mouthful. Just climbing the stairs to bed was the last straw.

She'd heard him from the kitchen. There was a scrabbling on the stairwell wall and then a soft thud thud thud as he hit the three steps down from the first landing.

She didn't try to fetch anyone. She knew it was too late. She did get him to the sofa, and that's where he died sometime during the night, still wearing his garden shoes, the soles caked with dried mud.

Ashes to ashes, dust to dust . . .

The house shuddered as feet hit the front porch. Donna staggered through the door, a grocery bag in each arm. The table squeaked when she set them down.

"Here you are. Don't let me forget to give you your change."

The old woman reached into one bag and yanked back her hand as if it had been slapped.

"You, girl. What did you buy bacon for? You know I got no use for meat."

"Oh, Granny, I'm sorry. I just picked it up out of habit. You're still a vegetarian, huh?"

"A dollar and eighty-nine cents for something I'll just chuck out," she grieved.

"Well, I'll eat some. Where's your skillet?"

"No. I'll cook. You got to get some vegetables."

She gave the girl the basket and the instructions about quantity, then watched out the window as Donna sashayed into the garden, squatted down in the string-bean row, and commenced to work.

Minutes ticked by. Donna moved on to the sweet corn. After she'd wrested a dozen ears from their stalks, she stood and shucked them all. Next she started on the tomatoes. Her industry was a pleasant surprise.

The old woman walked out to the edge of the garden.

Donna glanced up. "No need to help—I'm through."

"Let's just check if any melons has come ready," she said and boldly entered.

She pretended to be inspecting muskmelons. The garden

surrounded them in perfect tranquillity. Tan earth smelling dusty sweet. Humming insect songs. Bone-warming sun. Viceroy butterflies dancing.

Donna had found the perennial bed, and she was breaking stems—gloriosa daisies, chrysanthemums, asters, scabiosa, statice. "What's the use of having posies out there where you can't enjoy them?"

Some of the fibrous stems she had to twist back and forth as if she were snapping wires, leaving the stumps bruised and shredded. A tough old aster uprooted in Donna's grip. The garden bided.

The old woman had to say it. "Sometimes—something—out here makes me afraid."

Donna went on plundering the flowers, her face peering over an armload of color. "Well, of course you must be. Alone all the time. You ought to have a dog."

"Paaah. No dog. And no cat neither. I'd be more scared of them than of being alone."

"You used to have a dog," Donna said unkindly.

She didn't answer, remembering the dog. Charlie. A 'coon hound they'd raised from a pup. A vision of Donna as a toddler, teasing Charlie till he cried. Donna's mother, looking white and sickly even then, twisting a switch off the willow tree and stinging the chubby legs. And then, years later, the foaming muzzle sinking poisoned teeth into Donna's pappy's, her son's hand. She'd mourned them both, dog and man. She could never have another son, and she wouldn't have another dog.

Donna said, "Let's go on into the house. I got to leave before it's too dark to find the way up the road."

They made the meal together. Donna was a fast, steady worker, maybe because she was in a hurry to eat and leave; she ate fast and steady, too. The old woman ate carefully, thankful that her fast had had a fortuitous ending. With each mouthful her opinion of her granddaughter improved. She had not let Donna fry the bacon, but now she said the girl must take the package with her as "a present."

"Oh, Granny, in this heat?" she laughed. "It would just spoil and smell up the car before I'm anywhere to use it."

She had a carrot stick that she waved around between bites, and, while she chewed and swallowed, she talked. "You really ought to try the bacon yourself. It's delicious. Honest. You don't know what you're missing, not eating meat."

"I'd gag. Thinking of the poor innocent animal. I haven't eaten flesh for prit' near seventy years, and I'm proud and thankful for it."

"Well, now, Granny, if you're feeling righteous about it," Donna teased, "maybe you'd feel even prouder and thankfuler if you didn't eat vegetables either. One time in psychology class the professor was telling us about how plants feel pain same as humans."

When the falling sensation passed, she said, "What do you mean? How does he know?"

"He mentioned it, is all. I guess the class had discussed it another day when I wasn't there."

Her fingers wouldn't support the fork any longer. She asked, amazed, "Didn't you wonder about it? Didn't it worry you?"

"Well, of course," Donna bristled. "But the kids said he wasn't going to test us on it, so it was okay."

The bouquet Donna had crowded into one mason jar smelled like a funeral.

"Listen, Granny, I hate to eat and run, but I just must be scooting along. Thanks for supper. I'll do all the dishes next time," she promised, laughing and winking. She didn't try to bestow a goodbye kiss, only waved and ran out.

The old woman sat staring at the dishes of leftovers. She wondered if the pain stopped once the ear of corn left the stalk, or did it go on as the husk was ripped away. Was it there while the knife severed kernels from cob, and was it there for the scalding water flood? She saw herself forking and chewing and swallowing. At last she rose and scraped out every dish into the slop bucket.

She left the kitchen as it was, hoisting herself upstairs. The first landing had always groaned. This time it froze her in her tracks.

If it is true, she thought, then life is impossible. The

house a tomb, made of tree bones. The bedstead, an oak slaughtered by her own father, holding her every night like an open coffin. Books, rugs, pictures, all, all maimed, skinned, murdered. Not just here. Everywhere.

She ground her knuckles into her eyes and moaned, "The tree was crucified first."

She went downstairs slowly, full of dread. She found a shovel in the tool shed, dug a hole by the front porch, and committed to it mason jar and all. When she'd tamped the dirt and put away the shovel, she walked to the brink of the garden.

Light was fading fast. Crickets had begun gnashing their legs. She sensed the grass blades straining beneath her shoes. The garden crouched before her.

She was trembling so hard she ached. Her voice shook loose and said, "Listen." She hugged herself to keep from flying apart. "If you can understand English," she added hesitantly.

There was no answer.

"I didn't know. I didn't! But now I do, so I won't be bothering you again. Never."

She backed away and turned and made for the house. The skin of her skull prickled with expectation.

Nothing happened.

She went inside and straight upstairs. She fell onto the bed and lay rigid, watching the ceiling disappear. Later she slept, but she didn't rest.

The old woman died the first week of September. She didn't know it because she was in bed asleep. The coroner said it was from natural causes—old age and malnutrition.

Another friend let Donna borrow his black car. When the funeral ended, Donna drove to her inheritance to meet the county's leading realtor.

The two of them strolled around the rocky, weedy yard discussing possibilities. Mr. Howard was reluctant to quote any figure till he'd felt out some potential buyers. Donna wondered if an auction wouldn't be the quickest, easiest way. They stopped at the verge of the garden.

"This place looks a lot worse than it is," Donna prompted. "Why, I was in this garden just about a month ago, and what a world of difference. Not a weed in sight. Now look at it. A jungle. Of course, if I'd realized how sick Granny was I'd have stayed right here. But she never let on she wasn't the same as always."

Donna broke a tall blade of grass to chew. She said, "Well, she *was* talking kind of funny part of the time. I guess I should have guessed from that. Do you know they say she didn't eat or drink a single thing but milk for three weeks? Milk is supposed to be the perfect food, I know, but, like the Bible says, man can't live by milk alone."

Mr. Howard opened his mouth, saw she was serious, and snapped it shut again.

"Anyway, like I was saying, the place needs cleaning up is all. Why, Mr. Howard, just clearing out this mess of overgrown truck patch would do wonders. Maybe I could borrow a riding mower before you bring anybody out to look at the property. Or better yet, I could just set fire to it. Pour kerosene on and throw in a match. Maybe I should do that to the house, too." And she laughed, so Mr. Howard laughed.

"Well, first I got to get the antiques out," she went on. "There's a man coming from Corbin this afternoon to see what's valuable and what's just old."

Mr. Howard said he must go, that he'd check around and give her a ring. He left her beside the garden.

Donna watched him picking his way past the house and out of sight up the hill. She sighed, frowned at her watch, and scuffed a sandy anthill shut with the toe of her shoe. She gazed across the tangled garden, thinking about New York. Her eyes fixed on a blur of color; they focused.

She didn't know her flowers, but this one looked like some kind of rose. Dark red and waxy-petaled, it seemed to lean toward her, begging to be picked. She measured the distance with her eyes. Two giant steps in and out—that was all it would take. She chose her foothold carefully, a grassy patch that stuck up above the weedy area.

As she took the leaping step, some taller plants brushed against her inner thighs. She teetered, steadied, reached to break the stem. The flower swayed aside, and she pinched vacant air, startled to have felt no breeze. That same split second something coiled around her left leg. Snake! her mind squealed before she looked. Her pupils contracted in horror. Her throat scraped with one scream as she fell.

The antiques dealer found her.

Since she wasn't at the house, but her car was still parked on the road, he made a search. He said he was drawn to the garden by the smell, but that was hardly possible, as she had been dead only a few hours.

There were many theories offered by the many people who discussed the event. The most widely accepted, because it seemed the most reasonable, was that the girl had been in the garden when an epileptic fit had seized her. She'd fallen down and rolled around till she was hopelessly tangled in the plants.

The coroner studied on it half a day; then he typed "accidental strangulation" on his report and went outside to groom his privet hedge.

THE SPECIALTY OF THE HOUSE

by Stanley Ellin

*"The Specialty of the House" (1948) was Stanley Ellin's
first short story, and the first of seven to win prizes in* Ellery
Queen's Mystery Magazine's *prestigious annual contests.*

*Ellin is known for his finely honed, laboriously crafted,
brilliant tales. He has three Edgars to his credit, as well as
Le Grand Prix de Littérature Policière (the latter for the
French edition of his novel,* Mirror, Mirror on the Wall*).*

*Movies and television have fed upon his novels and short
stories, including our current selection, which was presented by Alfred Hitchcock, who apparently found it tasty.*

"And this," said Laffler, "is Sbirro's." Costain saw a square
brownstone facade identical with the others that extended
from either side into the clammy darkness of the deserted
street. From the barred windows of the basement at his
feet, a glimmer of light showed behind heavy curtains.

"Lord," he observed, "it's a dismal hole, isn't it?"

"I beg you to understand," said Laffler stiffly, "that
Sbirro's is the restaurant without pretensions. Besieged
by these ghastly, neurotic times, it has refused to compromise. It is perhaps the last important establishment in this
city lit by gas jets. Here you will find the same honest fur-
nishings, the same magnificent Sheffield service, and possibly, in a far corner, the very same spider webs that were
remarked by the patrons of a half century ago!"

"A doubtful recommendation," said Costain, "and hardly sanitary."

"When you enter," Laffler continued, "you leave the in-
sanity of this year, this day, and this hour, and you find
yourself for a brief span restored in spirit, not by opulence,
but by dignity, which is the lost quality of our time."

Costain laughed uncomfortably. "You make it sound
more like a cathedral than a restaurant," he said.

In the pale reflection of the street lamp overhead, Laffler

peered at his companion's face. "I wonder," he said abruptly, "whether I have not made a mistake in extending this invitation to you."

Costain was hurt. Despite an impressive title and large salary, he was no more than clerk to this pompous little man, but he was impelled to make some display of his feelings. "If you wish," he said coldly, "I can make other plans for my evening with no trouble."

With his large, cowlike eyes turned up to Costain, the mist drifting into the ruddy, full moon of his face, Laffler seemed strangely ill at ease. Then, "No, no," he said at last, "absolutely not. It's important that you dine at Sbirro's with me." He grasped Costain's arm firmly and led the way to the wrought-iron gate of the basement. "You see, you're the sole person in my office who seems to know anything at all about good food. And on my part, knowing about Sbirro's but not having some appreciative friend to share it is like having a unique piece of art locked in a room where no one else can enjoy it."

Costain was considerably mollified by this. "I understand there are a great many people who relish that situation."

"I'm not one of that kind!" Laffler said sharply. "And having the secret of Sbirro's locked in myself for years has finally become unendurable." He fumbled at the side of the gate and from within could be heard the small, discordant jangle of an ancient pull bell. An interior door opened with a groan, and Costain found himself peering into a dark face whose only discernible feature was a row of gleaming teeth.

"Sair?" said the face.

"Mr. Laffler and a guest."

"Sair," the face said again, this time in what was clearly an invitation. It moved aside and Costain stumbled down a single step behind his host. The door and gate creaked behind him, and he stood blinking in a small foyer. It took him a moment to realize that the figure he now stared at was his own reflection in a gigantic pier glass that extended from floor to ceiling. "Atmosphere," he said under his breath and chuckled as he followed his guide to a seat.

He faced Laffler across a small table for two and peered curiously around the dining room. It was no size at all, but the half dozen guttering gas jets which provided the only illumination threw such a deceptive light that the walls flickered and faded into uncertain distance.

There were no more than eight or ten tables about, arranged to insure the maximum privacy. All were occupied, and the few waiters serving them moved with quiet efficiency. In the air was a soft clash and scrape of cutlery and a soothing murmur of talk. Costain nodded appreciatively.

Laffler breathed an audible sigh of gratification. "I knew you would share my enthusiasm," he said. "Have you noticed, by the way, that there are no women present?"

Costain raised inquiring eyebrows.

"Sbirro," said Laffler, "does not encourage members of the fair sex to enter the premises. And, I can tell you, his method is decidedly effective. I had the experience of seeing a woman get a taste of it not long ago. She sat at a table for not less than an hour waiting for service which was never forthcoming."

"Didn't she make a scene?"

"She did." Laffler smiled at the recollection. "She succeeded in annoying the customers, embarrassing her partner, and nothing more."

"And what about Mr. Sbirro?"

"He did not make an appearance. Whether he directed affairs from behind the scenes, or was not even present during the episode, I don't know. Whichever it was, he won a complete victory. The woman never reappeared nor, for that matter, did the witless gentleman who by bringing her was really the cause of the entire contretemps."

"A fair warning to all present," laughed Costain.

A waiter now appeared at the table. The chocolate-dark skin, the thin, beautifully molded nose and lips, the large liquid eyes, heavily lashed, and the silver white hair so heavy and silken that it lay on the skull like a cap, all marked him definitely as an East Indian. The man arranged the stiff table linen, filled two tumblers from a huge, cut-glass pitcher, and set them in their proper places.

"Tell me," Laffler said eagerly, "is the special being served this evening?"

The waiter smiled regretfully and showed teeth as spectacular as those of the majordomo. "I am sorry, sair. There is no special this evening."

Laffler's face fell into lines of heavy disappointment. "After waiting so long. It's been a month already, and I hoped to show my friend here . . ."

"You understand the difficulties, sair."

"Of course, of course." Laffler looked at Costain sadly and shrugged. "You see, I had in mind to introduce you to the greatest treat that Sbirro's offers, but unfortunately it isn't on the menu this evening."

The waiter said, "Do you wish to be served now, sair?" and Laffler nodded. To Costain's surprise the waiter made his way off without waiting for any instructions.

"Have you ordered in advance?" he asked.

"Ah," said Laffler, "I really should have explained. Sbirro's offers no choice whatsoever. You will eat the same meal as everyone else in this room. Tomorrow evening you would eat an entirely different meal, but again without designating a single preference."

"Very unusual," said Costain, "and certainly unsatisfactory at times. What if one doesn't have a taste for the particular dish set before him?"

"On that score," said Laffler solemnly, "you need have no fears. I give you my word that no matter how exacting your tastes, you will relish every mouthful you eat in Sbirro's."

Costain looked doubtful, and Laffler smiled. "And consider the subtle advantages of the system," he said. "When you pick up the menu of a popular restaurant, you find yourself confronted with innumerable choices. You are forced to weigh, to evaluate, to make uneasy decisions which you may instantly regret. The effect of all this is a tension which, however slight, must make for discomfort.

"And consider the mechanics of the process. Instead of a hurly-burly of sweating cooks rushing about a kitchen in a frenzy to prepare a hundred varying items, we have a chef who stands serenely alone, bringing all his talents to bear on one task, with all assurance of a complete triumph!"

"Then you have seen the kitchen?"

"Unfortunately, no," said Laffler sadly. "The picture I offer is hypothetical, made of conversational fragments I have pieced together over the years. I must admit, though, that my desire to see the functioning of the kitchen here comes very close to being my sole obsession nowadays."

"But have you mentioned this to Sbirro?"

"A dozen times. He shrugs the suggestion away."

"Isn't that a rather curious foible on his part?"

"No, no," Laffler said hastily, "a master artist is never under the compulsion of petty courtesies. Still," he sighed, "I have never given up hope."

The waiter now reappeared bearing two soup bowls, which he set in place with mathematical exactitude, and a small tureen, from which he slowly ladled a measure of clear, thin broth. Costain dipped his spoon into the broth and tasted it with some curiosity. It was delicately flavored, bland to the verge of tastelessness. Costain frowned, tentatively reached for the salt and pepper cellars, and discovered there were none on the table. He looked up, saw Laffler's eyes on him, and although unwilling to compromise with his own tastes, he hesitated to act as a damper on Laffler's enthusiasms. Therefore he smiled and indicated the broth.

"Excellent," he said.

Laffler returned his smile. "You do not find it excellent at all," he said coolly. "You find it flat and badly in need of condiments. I know this," he continued as Costain's eyebrows shot upward, "because it was my own reaction many years ago, and because like yourself I found myself reaching for salt and pepper after the first mouthful. I also learned with surprise that condiments are not available at Sbirro's.

Costain was shocked. "Not even salt?" he exclaimed.

"Not even salt. The very fact that you require it for your soup stands as evidence that your taste is unduly jaded. I am confident that you will now make the same discovery that I did: by the time you have nearly finished your soup, your desire for salt will be nonexistent."

Laffler was right; before Costain had reached the bottom of his plate, he was relishing the nuances of the broth with steadily increasing delight. Laffler thrust aside his own empty bowl and rested his elbows on the table. "Do you agree with me now?"

"To my surprise," said Costain, "I do."

As the waiter busied himself clearing the table, Laffler lowered his voice significantly. "You will find," he said, "that the absence of condiments is but one of several noteworthy characteristics which mark Sbirro's. I may as well prepare you for these. For example, no alcoholic beverages of any sort are served here, nor for that matter any beverage except clear, cold water, the first and only drink necessary for a human being."

"Outside of mother's milk," suggested Costain dryly.

"I can answer that in like vein by pointing out that the average patron of Sbirro's has passed that primal stage of his development."

Costain laughed. "Granted," he said.

"Very well. There is also a ban on the use of tobacco in any form."

"But good heavens," said Costain, "doesn't that make Sbirro's more a teetotaler's retreat than a gourmet's sanctuary?"

"I fear," said Laffler solemnly, "that you confuse the words *gourmet* and *gourmand*. The gourmand, through glutting himself, requires a wider and wider latitude of experience to stir his surfeited senses, but the very nature of the gourmet is simplicity. The ancient Greek in his coarse chiton savoring the ripe olive; the Japanese in his bare room contemplating the curve of a single flower stem—these are the true gourmets."

"But an occasional drop of brandy, or pipeful of tobacco," said Costain dubiously, "are hardly overindulgences."

"By alternating stimulant and narcotic," said Laffler, "you seesaw the delicate balance of your taste so violently that it loses its most precious quality: the appreciation of fine food. During my years as a patron of Sbirro's, I have proved this to my satisfaction."

"May I ask," said Costain, "why you regard the ban on these things as having such deep aesthetic motives? What about such mundane reasons as the high cost of a liquor license, or the possibility that patrons would object to the smell of tobacco in such confined quarters?"

Laffler shook his head violently. "If and when you meet Sbirro," he said, "you will understand at once that he is not the man to make decisions on a mundane basis. As a matter of fact, it was Sbirro himself who first made me cognizant of what you call 'aesthetic' motives."

"An amazing man," said Costain as the waiter prepared to serve the entrée.

Laffler's next words were not spoken until he had savored and swallowed a large portion of meat. "I hesitate to use superlatives," he said, "but to my way of thinking, Sbirro represents man at the apex of his civilization!"

Costain cocked an eyebrow and applied himself to his roast, which rested in a pool of stiff gravy ungarnished by green or vegetable. The thin steam rising from it carried to his nostrils a subtle, tantalizing odor which made his mouth water. He chewed a piece as slowly and thoroughly as if he were analyzing the intricacies of a Mozart symphony. The range of taste he discovered was really extraordinary, from the pungent nip of the crisp outer edge to the peculiarly flat yet soul-satisfying ooze of blood which the pressure of his jaws forced from the half-raw interior.

Upon swallowing he found himself ferociously hungry for another piece, and then another, and it was only with an effort that he prevented himself from wolfing down all his share of the meat and gravy without waiting to get the full voluptuous satisfaction from each mouthful. When he had scraped his platter clean, he realized that both he and Laffler had completed the entire course without exchanging a single word. He commented on this, and Laffler said, "Can you see any need for words in the presence of such food?"

Costain looked around at the shabby, dimly lit room, the quiet diners, with a new perception. "No," he said humbly,

"I cannot. For any doubts I had I apologize unreservedly. In all your praise of Sbirro's there was not a single word of exaggeration."

"Ah," said Laffler delightedly. "And that is only part of the story. You heard me mention the special, which unfortunately was not on the menu tonight. What you have just eaten is nothing when compared to the absolute delights of that special!"

"Good Lord!" cried Costain. "What is it? Nightingales' tongues? Filet of unicorn?"

"Neither," said Laffler. "It is lamb."

"Lamb?"

Laffler remained lost in thought for a minute. "If," he said at last, "I were to give you in my own unstinted words my opinion of this dish, you would judge me completely insane. That is how deeply the mere thought of it affects me. It is neither the fatty chop, nor the too solid leg; it is, instead, a select portion of the rarest sheep in existence and is named after the species—lamb Amirstan."

Costain knit his brows. "Amirstan?"

"A fragment of desolation almost lost on the border which separates Afghanistan and Russia. From chance remarks dropped by Sbirro, I gather it is no more than a plateau which grazes the pitiful remnants of a flock of superb sheep. Sbirro, through some means or other, obtained rights to the traffic in this flock and is, therefore, the sole restaurateur ever to have lamb Amirstan on his bill of fare. I can tell you that the appearance of this dish is a rare occurrence indeed, and luck is the only guide in determining for the clientele the exact date when it will be served."

"But surely," said Costain, "Sbirro could provide some advance knowledge of this event."

"The objection to that is simply stated," said Laffler. "There exists in this city a huge number of professional gluttons. Should advance information slip out, it is quite likely that they will, out of curiosity, become familiar with the dish and henceforth supplant the regular patrons at these tables."

"But you don't mean to say," objected Costain, "that these few people present are the only ones in the entire city, or for that matter, in the whole wide world, who know of the existence of Sbirro's!"

"Very nearly. There may be one or two regular patrons who, for some reason, are not present at the moment."

"That's incredible."

"It is done," said Laffler, the slightest shade of menace in his voice, "by every patron making it his solemn obligation to keep the secret. By accepting my invitation this evening, you automatically assume that obligation. I hope you can be trusted with it."

Costain flushed. "My position in your employ should vouch for me. I only question the wisdom of a policy which keeps such magnificent food away from so many who would enjoy it."

"Do you know the inevitable result of the policy *you* favor?" asked Laffler bitterly. "An influx of idiots who would nightly complain that they are never served roast duck with chocolate sauce. Is that picture tolerable to you?"

"No," admitted Costain, "I am forced to agree with you."

Laffler leaned back in his chair wearily and passed his hand over his eyes in an uncertain gesture. "I am a solitary man," he said quietly, "and not by choice alone. It may sound strange to you, it may border on eccentricity, but I feel to my depths that this restaurant, this warm heaven in a coldly insane world, is both family and friend to me."

And Costain, who to this moment had never viewed his companion as other than tyrannical employer or officious host, now felt an overwhelming pity twist inside his comfortably expanded stomach.

By the end of two weeks the invitations to join Laffler at Sbirro's had become something of a ritual. Every day, at a few minutes after five, Costain would step out into the office corridor and lock his cubicle behind him; he would drape his overcoat neatly over his left arm, and peer into the glass of the door to make sure his homburg was set at the proper angle. At one time he would have followed this by lighting a cigarette, but under Laffler's prodding he had decided to give abstinence a fair trial. Then he would start down the corridor, and Laffler would fall in step at his elbow, clearing his throat. "Ah, Costain. No plans for this evening, I hope."

"No," Costain would say, "I'm footloose and fancy-free," or "At your service," or something equally inane. He wondered at times whether it would not be more tactful to vary the ritual with an occasional refusal, but the glow with which Laffler received his answer, and the rough friendliness of Laffler's grip on his arm, forestalled him.

Among the treacherous crags of the business world, reflected Costain, what better way to secure your footing than friendship with one's employer. Already, a secretary close to the workings of the inner office had commented publicly on Laffler's highly favorable opinion of Costain. That was all to the good.

And the food! The incomparable food at Sbirro's! For the first time in his life, Costain, ordinarily a lean and bony man, noted with gratification that he was certainly gaining weight; within two weeks his bones had disappeared under a layer of sleek firm flesh, and here and there were even signs of incipient plumpness. It struck Costain one night, while surveying himself in his bath, that the rotund Laffler himself might have been a spare and bony man before discovering Sbirro's.

So there was obviously everything to be gained and nothing to be lost by accepting Laffler's invitations. Perhaps after testing the heralded wonders of lamb Amirstan and meeting Sbirro, who thus far had not made an appearance, a refusal or two might be in order. But certainly not until then.

That evening, two weeks to a day after his first visit to Sbirro's, Costain had both desires fulfilled: he dined on lamb Amirstan, and he met Sbirro. Both exceeded all his expectations.

When the waiter leaned over their table immediately after seating them and gravely announced, "Tonight is special, sair," Costain was shocked to find his heart pounding with expectation. On the table before him he saw Laffler's hands trembling violently. "But it isn't natural," he thought suddenly. "Two full-grown men, presumably intelligent and in the full possession of their senses, as jumpy as a pair of cats waiting to have their meat flung to them!"

"This is it!" Laffler's voice startled him so that he almost leaped from his seat. "The culinary triumph of all times! And faced by it you are embarrassed by the very emotions it distills."

"How did you know that?" Costain asked faintly.

"How? Because a decade ago I underwent your embarrassment. Add to that your air of revulsion and it's easy to see how affronted you are by the knowledge that man has not yet forgotten how to slaver over his meat."

"And these others," whispered Costain, "do they all feel the same thing?"

"Judge for yourself."

Costain looked furtively around at the nearby tables. "You are right," he finally said. "At any rate, there's comfort in numbers."

Laffler inclined his head slightly to the side. "One of the numbers," he remarked, "appears to be in for a disappointment."

Costain followed the gesture. At the table indicated a gray-haired man sat conspicuously alone, and Costain frowned at the empty chair opposite him.

"Why, yes," he recalled, "that very stout, bald man, isn't it? I believe it's the first dinner he's missed here in two weeks."

"The entire decade more likely," said Laffler sympathetically. "Rain or shine, crisis or calamity, I don't think he's missed an evening at Sbirro's since the first time I dined here. Imagine his expression when he's told that on his very first defection, lamb Amirstan was the *plat du jour.*"

Costain looked at the empty chair again with a dim discomfort. "His very first?" he murmured.

"Mr. Laffler! And friend! I am so pleased. So very, very pleased. No, do not stand; I will have a place made." Miraculously a seat appeared under the figure standing there at the table. "The lamb Amirstan will be an unqualified success, hurr? I myself have been stewing in the miserable kitchen all the day, prodding the foolish chef to do everything just so. The just so is the important part, hurr? But I see your friend does not know me. An introduction, perhaps?"

The words ran in a smooth, fluid eddy. They rippled, they purred, they hypnotized Costain so that he could do no more than stare. The mouth that uncoiled this sinuous monologue was alarmingly wide, with thin mobile lips that curled and twisted with every syllable. There was a flat nose with a straggling line of hair under it; wide-set eyes, almost Oriental in appearance, that glittered in the unsteady flare of gaslight; and long, sleek hair that swept back from high on the unwrinkled forehead—hair so pale that it might have been bleached of all color. An amazing face surely, and the sight of it tortured Costain with the conviction that it was somehow familiar. His brain twitched and prodded but could not stir up any solid recollection.

Laffler's voice jerked Costain out of his study. "Mr. Sbirro. Mr. Costain, a good friend and associate." Costain rose and shook the proffered hand. It was warm and dry, flint-hard against his palm.

"I am so very pleased, Mr. Costain. So very, very pleased," purred the voice. "You like my little establishment, hurr? You have a great treat in store, I assure you."

Laffler chuckled. "Oh, Costain's been dining here regularly for two weeks," he said. "He's by way of becoming a great admirer of yours, Sbirro."

The eyes were turned on Costain. "A very great compliment. You compliment me with your presence and I return same with my food; hurr? But the lamb Amirstan is far superior to anything of your past experience, I assure you. All the trouble of obtaining it, all the difficulty of preparation, is truly merited."

Costain strove to put aside the exasperating problem of that face. "I have wondered," he said, "why with all these difficulties you mention, you even bother to present lamb Amirstan to the public. Surely your other dishes are excellent enough to uphold your reputation."

Sbirro smiled so broadly that his face became perfectly round. "Perhaps it is a matter of the psychology, hurr? Someone discovers a wonder and must share it with others. He must fill his cup to the brim, perhaps, by observing the so evident pleasure of those who explore it with him. Or"—he shrugged—"perhaps it is just a matter of good business."

"Then in the light of all this," Costain persisted, "and considering all the conventions you have imposed on your customers, why do you open the restaurant to the public instead of operating it as a private club?"

The eyes abruptly glinted into Costain's, then turned away. "So perspicacious, hurr? Then I will tell you. Because there is more privacy in a public eating place than in the most exclusive club in existence! Here no one inquires of your affairs; no one desires to know the intimacies of your life. Here the business is eating. We are not curious about names and addresses or the reasons for the coming and going of our guests. We welcome you when you are here; we have no regrets when you are here no longer. That is the answer, hurr?"

Costain was startled by this vehemence. "I had no intention of prying," he stammered.

Sbirro ran the tip of his tongue over his thin lips. "No, no," he reassured, "you are not prying. Do not let me give you that impression. On the contrary, I invite your questions."

"Oh, come, Costain," said Laffler. "Don't let Sbirro intimidate you. I've known him for years and I guarantee that his bark is worse than his bite. Before you know it, he'll be showing you all the privileges of the house—outside of inviting you to visit his precious kitchen, of course."

"Ah," smiled Sbirro, "for that, Mr. Costain may have to wait a little while. For everything else I am at his beck and call."

Laffler slapped his hand jovially on the table. "What did I tell you!" he said. "Now let's have the truth, Sbirro. Has anyone, outside of your staff, ever stepped into the sanctum sanctorum?"

Sbirro looked up. "You see on the wall above you," he said earnestly, "the portrait of the one to whom I did the honor. A very dear friend and a patron of most long standing, he is evidence that my kitchen is not inviolate."

Costain studied the picture and started with recognition. "Why," he said excitedly, "that's the famous writer—you know the one, Laffler—he used to do such wonderful short stories and cynical bits and then suddenly took himself off and disappeared in Mexico!"

"Of course!" cried Laffler, "and to think I've been sitting under his portrait for years without even realizing it!" He turned to Sbirro. "A dear friend, you say? His disappearance must have been a blow to you."

Sbirro's face lengthened. "It was, it was, I assure you. But think of it this way, gentlemen: he was probably greater in his death than in his life, hurr? A most tragic man, he often told me that his only happy hours were spent here at this very table. Pathetic, is it not? And to think the only favor I could ever show him was to let him witness the mysteries of my kitchen, which is, when all is said and done, no more than a plain, ordinary kitchen."

"You seem very certain of his death," commented Costain. "After all, no evidence has ever turned up to substantiate it."

Sbirro contemplated the picture. "None at all," he said softly. "Remarkable, hurr?"

With the arrival of the entrée Sbirro leaped to his feet and set about serving them himself. With his eyes alight he lifted the casserole from the tray and sniffed at the fragrance from within with sensual relish. Then, taking great care not to lose a single drop of gravy, he filled two platters with chunks of dripping meat. As if exhausted by this task, he sat back in his chair, breathing heavily. "Gentlemen," he said, "to your good appetite."

Costain chewed his first mouthful with great deliberation and swallowed it. Then he looked at the empty tines of his fork with glazed eyes.

"God God!" he breathed.

"It is good, hurr? Better than you imagined?"

Costain shook his head dazedly. "It is as impossible," he

said slowly, "for the uninitiated to conceive the delights of lamb Amirstan as for mortal man to look into his own soul."

"Perhaps"—Sbirro thrust his head so close that Costain could feel the warm, fetid breath tickle his nostrils—"perhaps you have just had a glimpse into your soul, hurr?"

Costain tried to draw back slightly without giving offense. "Perhaps," he laughed, "and a gratifying picture it made: all fang and claw. But without intending any disrespect, I should hardly like to build my church on lamb *en casserole.*"

Sbirro rose and laid a hand gently on his shoulder. "So perspicacious," he said. "Sometimes when you have nothing to do, nothing, perhaps, but sit for a very little while in a dark room and think of this world—what it is and what it is going to be—then you must turn your thoughts a little to the significance of the Lamb in religion. It will be so interesting. And now"—he bowed deeply to both men—"I have held you long enough from your dinner. I was most happy" —he nodded to Costain—"and I am sure we will meet again." The teeth gleamed, the eyes glittered, and Sbirro was gone down the aisle of tables.

Costain twisted around to stare after the retreating figure. "Have I offended him in some way?" he asked.

Laffler looked up from his plate. "Offended him? He loves that kind of talk. Lamb Amirstan is a ritual with him; get him started and he'll be back at you a dozen times worse than a priest making a conversion."

Costain turned to his meal with the face still hovering before him. "Interesting man," he reflected. "Very."

It took him a month to discover the tantalizing familiarity of that face, and when he did, he laughed aloud in his bed. Why, of course! Sbirro might have sat as the model for the Cheshire cat in *Alice!*

He passed this thought on to Laffler the very next evening as they pushed their way down the street to the restaurant against a chill, blistering wind. Laffler only looked blank.

"You may be right," he said, "but I'm not a fit judge. It's a far cry back to the days when I read the book. A far cry, indeed."

As if taking up his words, a piercing howl came ringing down the street and stopped both men short in their tracks. "Someone's in trouble there," said Laffler. "Look!"

Not far from the entrance to Sbirro's two figures could be seen struggling in the near darkness. They swayed back and forth and suddenly tumbled into a writhing heap on the sidewalk. The piteous howl went up again, and Laffler, despite his girth, ran toward it at a fair speed with Costain tagging cautiously behind.

Stretched out full length on the pavement was a slender figure with the dusky complexion and white hair of one of Sbirro's servitors. His fingers were futilely plucking at the huge hands which encircled his throat, and his knees pushed weakly up at the gigantic bulk of a man who brutally bore down with his full weight.

Laffler came up panting. "Stop this!" he shouted. "What's going on here?"

The pleading eyes almost bulging from their sockets turned toward Laffler. "Help, sair. This man—drunk—"

"Drunk am I, ya dirty—" Costain saw now that the man was a sailor in a badly soiled uniform. The air around him reeked with the stench of liquor. "Pick me pocket and then call me drunk, will ya!" He dug his fingers in harder, and his victim groaned.

Laffler seized the sailor's shoulder. "Let go of him, do you hear! Let go of him at once!" he cried, and the next instant was sent careening into Costain, who staggered back under the force of the blow.

The attack on his own person sent Laffler into immediate and berserk action. Without a sound he leaped at the sailor, striking and kicking furiously at the unprotected face and flanks. Stunned at first, the man came to his feet with a rush and turned on Laffler. For a moment they stood locked together, and then as Costain joined the attack, all three went sprawling to the ground. Slowly Laffler and Costain got to their feet and looked down at the body before them.

"He's either out cold from liquor," said Costain, "or he struck his head going down. In any case, it's a job for the police."

"No, no, sair!" The waiter crawled weakly to his feet, and stood swaying. "No police, sair. Mr. Sbirro do not want such. You understand, sair." He caught hold of Costain with a pleading hand, and Costain looked at Laffler.

"Of course not," said Laffler. "We won't have to bother with the police. They'll pick him up soon enough, the murderous sot. But what in the world started all this?"

"That man, sair. He make most erratic way while walking, and with no meaning I push against him. Then he attack me, accusing me to rob him."

"As I thought." Laffler pushed the waiter gently along. "Now go on in and get yourself attended to."

The man seemed ready to burst into tears. "To you, sair, I owe my life. If there is anything I can do—"

Laffler turned into the areaway that led to Sbirro's door. "No, no, it was nothing. You go along, and if Sbirro has any questions send him to me. I'll straighten it out."

"My life, sair," were the last words they heard as the inner door closed behind them.

"There you are, Costain," said Laffler as a few minutes later he drew his chair under the table, "civilized man in all his glory. Reeking with alcohol, strangling to death some miserable innocent who came too close."

Costain made an effort to gloss over the nerve-shattering memory of the episode. "It's the neurotic cat that takes to alcohol," he said. "Surely there's a reason for that sailor's condition."

"Reason? Of course there is. Plain atavistic savagery!" Laffler swept his arm in an all-embracing gesture. "Why do we all sit here at our meat? Not only to appease physical demands, but because our atavistic selves cry for release. Think back, Costain. Do you remember that I once described Sbirro as the epitome of civilization? Can you now see why? A brilliant man, he fully understands the nature of human beings. But unlike lesser men he bends all his efforts to the satisfaction of our innate natures without resultant harm to some innocent bystander."

"When I think back on the wonders of lamb Amirstan," said Costain, "I quite understand what you're driving at. And, by the way, isn't it nearly due to appear on the bill of fare? It must have been over a month ago that it was last served."

The waiter, filling the tumblers, hesitated. "I am so sorry, sair. No special this evening."

"There's your answer," Laffler grunted, "and probably just my luck to miss out on it altogether the next time."

Costain stared at him. "Oh, come, that's impossible."

"No, blast it." Laffler drank off half his water at a gulp and the waiter immediately refilled the glass. "I'm off to South America for a surprise tour of inspection. One month, two months, Lord knows how long."

"Are things that bad down there?"

"They could be better." Laffler suddenly grinned. "Mustn't forget it takes very mundane dollars and cents to pay the tariff at Sbirro's."

"I haven't heard a word of this around the office."

"Wouldn't be a surprise tour if you had. Nobody knows about this except myself—and now you. I want to walk in on them completely unsuspected. Find out what flim-flammery they're up to down there. As far as the office is concerned, I'm off on a jaunt somewhere. Maybe recuperating in some sanatorium from my hard work. Anyhow, the business will be in good hands. Yours among them."

"Mine?" said Costain, surprised.

"When you go in tomorrow you'll find yourself in receipt of a promotion, even if I'm not there to hand it to you personally. Mind you, it has nothing to do with our friendship, either; you've done fine work, and I'm immensely grateful for it."

Costain reddened under the praise. "You don't expect to be in tomorrow. Then you're leaving tonight?"

Laffler nodded. "I've been trying to wangle some reservations. If they come through, well, this will be in the nature of a farewell celebration."

"You know," said Costain slowly, "I devoutly hope that your reservations don't come through. I believe our dinners here have come to mean more to me than I ever dared imagine."

The waiter's voice broke in. "Do you wish to be served now, sair?" and they both started.

"Of course, of course," said Laffler sharply. "I didn't realize you were waiting."

"What bothers me," he told Costain as the waiter turned away, "is the thought of the lamb Amirstan I'm bound to miss. To tell you the truth, I've already put off my departure for a week, hoping to hit a lucky night, and now I simply can't delay anymore. I do hope that when you're sitting over your share of lamb Amirstan, you'll think of me with suitable regrets."

Costain laughed. "I will indeed," he said as he turned to his dinner.

Hardly had he cleared the plate when a waiter silently reached for it. It was not their usual waiter, he observed; it was none other than the victim of the assault.

"Well," Costain said, "how do you feel now? Still under the weather?"

The waiter paid no attention to him. Instead, with the air of a man under great strain, he turned to Laffler. "Sair," he whispered. "My life. I owe it to you. I can repay you!"

Laffler looked up in amazement, then shook his head firmly. "No," he said, "I want nothing from you, understand? You have repaid me sufficiently with your thanks. Now get on with your work and let's hear no more about it."

The waiter did not stir an inch, but his voice rose slightly. "By the body and blood of your God, sair, I will help you even if you do not want! *Do not go into the kitchen, sair.* I trade you my life for yours, sair, when I speak this. Tonight or any night of your life, do not go into the kitchen at Sbirro's!"

Laffler sat back, completely dumbfounded. "Not go into the kitchen? Why shouldn't I go into the kitchen if Mr. Sbirro ever took it into his head to invite me there? What's all this about?"

A hard hand was laid on Costain's back, and another

gripped the waiter's arm. The waiter remained frozen to the spot, his lips compressed, his eyes downcast.

"What is all *what* about, gentlemen?" purred the voice. "So opportune an arrival. In time as ever, I see, to answer all the questions, hurr?"

Laffler breathed a sigh of relief. "Ah, Sbirro, thank heaven you're here. This man is saying something about my not going into your kitchen. Do you know what he means?"

The teeth showed in a broad grin. "But of course. This good man was giving you advice in all amiability. It so happens that my too emotional chef heard some rumor that I might have a guest into his precious kitchen, and he flew into a fearful rage. Such a rage, gentlemen! He even threatened to give notice on the spot, and you can understand what that should mean to Sbirro's, hurr? Fortunately, I succeeded in showing him what a signal honor it is to have an esteemed patron and true connoisseur observe him at his work firsthand, and now he is quite amenable. Quite, hurr?"

He released the waiter's arm. "You are at the wrong table," he said softly. "See that it does not happen again."

The waiter slipped off without daring to raise his eyes, and Sbirro drew a chair to the table. He seated himself and brushed his hand lightly over his hair. "Now I am afraid that the cat is out of the bag, hurr? This invitation to you, Mr. Laffler, was to be a surprise; but the surprise is gone, and all that is left is the invitation."

Laffler mopped beads of perspiration from his forehead. "Are you serious?" he said huskily. "Do you mean that we are really to witness the preparation of your food tonight?"

Sbirro drew a sharp fingernail along the tablecloth, leaving a thin, straight line printed in the linen. "Ah," he said, "I am faced with a dilemma of great proportions." He studied the line soberly. "You, Mr. Laffler, have been my guest for ten long years. But our friend here—"

Costain raised his hand in protest. "I understand perfectly. This invitation is solely to Mr. Laffler, and naturally my presence is embarrassing. As it happens, I have an early engagement for this evening and must be on my way anyhow. So you see there's no dilemma at all, really."

"No," said Laffler, "absolutely not. That wouldn't be fair at all. We've been sharing this until now, Costain, and I won't enjoy this experience half as much if you're not along. Surely Sbirro can make his conditions flexible, this one occasion."

They both looked at Sbirro, who shrugged his shoulders regretfully.

Costain rose abruptly. "I'm not going to sit here, Laffler, and spoil your great adventure. And then too," he bantered, "think of that ferocious chef waiting to get his cleaver on you. I prefer not to be at the scene. I'll just say goodbye," he went on, to cover Laffler's guilty silence, "and leave you to Sbirro. I'm sure he'll take pains to give you a good show." He held out his hand, and Laffler squeezed it painfully hard.

"You're being very decent, Costain," he said. "I hope you'll continue to dine here until we meet again. It shouldn't be too long."

Sbirro made way for Costain to pass. "I will expect you," he said. *"Au 'voir."*

Costain stopped briefly in the dim foyer to adjust his scarf and fix his homburg at the proper angle. When he turned away from the mirror, satisfied at last, he saw with a final glance that Laffler and Sbirro were already at the kitchen door, Sbirro holding the door invitingly wide with one hand while the other rested, almost tenderly, on Laffler's meaty shoulders.

LAMB TO THE SLAUGHTER

by Roald Dahl

Roald Dahl's considerable reputation in the crime fiction field rests entirely on a large number of short stories, almost all of which bristle with suspense, tension, and horror. These have been brought together in at least nine collections, including the definitive The Best of Roald Dahl *(1978). He has twice won the Edgar Award from the Mystery Writers of America. In addition, he is a noted screenwriter, having done the scripts for such diverse films as* You Only Live Twice *(1965) and* Willie Wonka and the Chocolate Factory *(1971), the latter adapted from his novel of 1964,* Charlie and the Chocolate Factory, *one of many wonderful books he has written for children.*

The room was warm and clean, the curtains drawn, the two table lamps alight—hers and the one by the empty chair opposite. On the sideboard behind her, two tall glasses, soda water, whiskey. Fresh ice cubes in the Thermos bucket.

Mary Maloney was waiting for her husband to come home from work.

Now and again she would glance up at the clock, but without anxiety, merely to please herself with the thought that each minute gone by made it nearer the time when he would come. There was a slow smiling air about her, and about everything she did. The drop of the head as she bent over her sewing was curiously tranquil. Her skin—for this was her sixth month with child—had acquired a wonderful translucent quality, the mouth was soft, and the eyes, with their new placid look, seemed larger, darker than before.

When the clock said ten minutes to five, she began to listen, and a few moments later, punctually as always, she heard the tires on the gravel outside, and the car door slamming, the footsteps passing the window, the key turning in the lock. She laid aside her sewing, stood up, and went forward to kiss him as he came in.

"Hullo, darling," she said.

"Hullo," he answered.

She took his coat and hung it in the closet. Then she walked over and made the drinks, a strongish one for him, a weak one for herself; and soon she was back again in her chair with the sewing, and he in the other, opposite, holding the tall glass with both his hands, rocking it so the ice cubes tinkled against the side.

For her, this was always a blissful time of day. She knew he didn't want to speak much until the first drink was finished, and she, on her side, was content to sit quietly, enjoying his company after the long hours alone in the house. She loved to luxuriate in the presence of this man, and to feel—almost as a sunbather feels the sun—that warm male glow that came out of him to her when they were alone together. She loved him for the way he sat loosely in a chair, for the way he came in a door, or moved slowly across the room with long strides. She loved the intent, far look in his eyes when they rested on her, the funny shape of the mouth, and especially the way he remained silent about his tiredness, sitting still with himself until the whiskey had taken some of it away.

"Tired, darling?"

"Yes," he said. "I'm tired." And as he spoke, he did an unusual thing. He lifted his glass and drained it in one swallow, although there was still half of it, at least half of it, left. She wasn't really watching him, but she knew what he had done because she heard the ice cubes falling back against the bottom of the empty glass when he lowered his arm. He paused a moment, leaning forward in the chair, then he got up and went slowly over to fetch himself another.

"I'll get it!" she cried, jumping up.

"Sit down," he said.

When he came back, she noticed that the new drink was dark amber with the quantity of whiskey in it.

"Darling, shall I get your slippers?"

"No."

She watched him as he began to sip the dark yellow drink, and she could see little oily swirls in the liquid because it was so strong.

"I think it's a shame," she said, "that when a policeman gets to be as senior as you, they keep him walking about on his feet all day long."

He didn't answer, so she bent her head again and went on with her sewing; but each time he lifted the drink to his lips, she heard the ice cubes clinking against the side of the glass.

"Darling," she said. "Would you like me to get you some cheese? I haven't made any supper because it's Thursday."

"No," he said.

"If you're too tired to eat out," she went on, "it's still not too late. There's plenty of meat and stuff in the freezer, and you can have it right here and not even move out of the chair."

Her eyes waited on him for an answer, a smile, a little nod, but he made no sign.

"Anyway," she went on, "I'll get you some cheese and crackers first."

"I don't want it," he said.

She moved uneasily in her chair, the large eyes still watching his face. "But you *must* have supper. I can easily do it here. I'd like to do it. We can have lamb chops. Or pork. Anything you want. Everything's in the freezer."

"Forget it," he said.

"But darling, you *must* eat! I'll fix it anyway, and then you can have it or not, as you like."

She stood up and placed her sewing on the table by the lamp.

"Sit down," he said. "Just for a minute, sit down."

It wasn't till then that she began to get frightened.

"Go on," he said. "Sit down."

She lowered herself back slowly into the chair, watching him all the time with those large, bewildered eyes. He had finished the second drink and was staring down into the glass, frowning.

"Listen," he said. "I've got something to tell you."

"What is it, darling? What's the matter?"

He had now become absolutely motionless, and he kept his head down so that the light from the lamp beside him fell across the upper part of his face, leaving the chin and mouth in shadow. She noticed there was a little muscle moving near the corner of his left eye.

"This is going to be a bit of a shock to you, I'm afraid," he said. "But I've thought about it a good deal and I've decided the only thing to do is tell you right away. I hope you won't blame me too much."

And he told her. It didn't take long, four or five minutes at most, and she sat very still through it all, watching him with a kind of dazed horror as he went further and further away from her with each word.

"So there it is," he added. "And I know it's kind of a bad time to be telling you, but there simply wasn't any other way. Of course I'll give you money and see you're looked after. But there needn't really be any fuss. I hope not anyway. It wouldn't be very good for my job."

Her first instinct was not to believe any of it, to reject it all. It occurred to her that perhaps he hadn't even spoken, that she herself had imagined the whole thing. Maybe, if she went about her business and acted as though she hadn't been listening, then later, when she sort of woke up again, she might find none of it had ever happened.

"I'll get supper," she managed to whisper, and this time he didn't stop her.

When she walked across the room she couldn't feel her feet touching the floor. She couldn't feel anything at all—except a slight nausea and a desire to vomit. Everything was automatic now—down the steps to the cellar, the light switch, the deep freeze, the hand inside the cabinet taking hold of the first object it met. She lifted it out, and looked at it. It was wrapped in paper, so she took off the paper and looked at it again.

A leg of lamb.

All right then, they would have lamb for supper. She carried it upstairs, holding the thin bone end of it with both her hands, and as she went through the living room, she saw him standing over by the window with his back to her, and she stopped.

"For God's sake," he said, hearing her, but not turning around. "Don't make supper for me. I'm going out."

At that point, Mary Maloney simply walked up behind him and without any pause she swung the big frozen leg of lamb high in the air and brought it down as hard as she could on the back of his head.

She might just as well have hit him with a steel club.

She stepped back a pace, waiting, and the funny thing was that he remained standing there for at least four of five seconds, gently swaying. Then he crashed to the carpet.

The violence of the crash, the noise, the small table overturning, helped bring her out of the shock. She came out slowly, feeling cold and surprised, and she stood for a while blinking at the body, still holding the ridiculous piece of meat tight with both hands.

All right, she told herself. So I've killed him.

It was extraordinary now, how clear her mind became all of a sudden. She began thinking very fast. As the wife of a detective, she knew quite well what the penalty would be. That was fine. It made no difference to her. In fact, it would be a relief. On the other hand, what about the child? What were the laws about murderers with unborn children? Did they kill them both—mother and child? Or did they wait until the tenth month? What did they do?

Mary Maloney didn't know. And she certainly wasn't prepared to take a chance.

She carried the meat into the kitchen, placed it in a pan, turned the oven on high, and shoved it inside. Then she washed her hands and ran upstairs to the bedroom. She sat down before the mirror, tidied her hair, touched up her lips and face. She tried a smile. It came out rather peculiar. She tried again.

"Hullo, Sam," she said brightly, aloud.

The voice sounded peculiar too.

"I want some potatoes please, Sam. Yes, and I think a can of peas."

That was better. Both the smile and the voice were coming out better now. She rehearsed it several times more.

Then she ran downstairs, took her coat, went out the back door, down the garden, into the street.

It wasn't six o'clock yet, and the lights were still on in the grocery shop.

"Hullo, Sam," she said brightly, smiling at the man behind the counter.

"Why, good evening, Mrs. Maloney. How're *you?*"

"I want some potatoes, please, Sam. Yes, and I think a can of peas."

The man turned and reached up behind him on the shelf for the peas.

"Patrick's decided he's tired and doesn't want to eat out tonight," she told him. "We usually go out Thursdays, you know, and now he's caught me without any vegetables in the house."

"Then how about meat, Mrs. Maloney?"

"No, I've got meat, thanks. I got a nice leg of lamb from the freezer."

"Oh."

"I don't much like cooking it frozen, Sam, but I'm taking a chance on it this time. You think it'll be all right?"

"Personally," the grocer said, "I don't believe it makes any difference. You want these Idaho potatoes?"

"Oh yes, that'll be fine. Two of those."

"Anything else?" The grocer cocked his head on one side, looking at her pleasantly. "How about afterward? What you going to give him for afterward?"

"Well—what would you suggest, Sam?"

The man glanced around his shop. "How about a nice big slice of cheesecake? I know he likes that."

"Perfect," she said. "He loves it."

And when it was all wrapped and she had paid, she put on her brightest smile and said, "Thank you, Sam. Good night."

"Good night, Mrs. Maloney. And thank *you.*"

And now, she told herself as she hurried back, all she was doing now, she was returning home to her husband and he was waiting for his supper; and she must cook it good, and make it as tasty as possible because the poor man was tired; and if, when she entered the house, she happened to find anything unusual, or tragic, or terrible, then naturally it would be a shock and she'd become frantic with grief and horror. Mind you, she wasn't *expecting* to find anything. She was just going home with the vegetables. Mrs. Patrick Maloney going home with the vegetables on Thursday evening to cook supper for her husband.

That's the way, she told herself. Do everything right and natural. Keep things absolutely natural and there'll be no need for any acting at all.

Therefore, when she entered the kitchen by the back door, she was humming a little tune to herself and smiling.

"Patrick!" she called. "How are you, darling?"

She put the parcel down on the table and went through into the living room; and when she saw him lying there on the floor with his legs doubled up and one arm twisted back underneath his body, it really was rather a shock. All the old love and longing for him welled up inside her, and she ran over to him, knelt down beside him, and began to cry her heart out. It was easy. No acting was necessary.

A few minutes later she got up and went to the phone. She knew the number of the police station, and when the man at the other end answered, she cried to him, "Quick! Come quick! Patrick's dead!"

"Who's speaking?"

"Mrs. Maloney. Mrs. Patrick Maloney."

"You mean Patrick Maloney's dead?"

"I think so," she sobbed. "He's lying on the floor and I think he's dead."

"Be right over," the man said.

The car came very quickly, and when she opened the front door, two policemen walked in. She knew them both—she knew nearly all the men at that precinct—and she fell right into Jack Noonan's arms, weeping hysterically. He put her gently into a chair, then went over to join the other one, who was called O'Malley, kneeling by the body.

"Is he dead?" she cried.

"I'm afraid he is. What happened?"

Briefly, she told her story about going out to the grocer and coming back to find him on the floor. While she was talking, crying and talking, Noonan discovered a small patch of congealed blood on the dead man's head. He showed it to O'Malley, who got up at once and hurried to the phone.

Soon, other men began to come into the house. First a doctor, then two detectives, one of whom she knew by name. Later, a police photographer arrived and took pictures, and a man who knew about fingerprints. There was a great deal of whispering and muttering beside the corpse, and the detectives kept asking her a lot of questions. But they always treated her kindly. She told her story again, this time right from the beginning, when Patrick had come in, and she was sewing, and he was tired, so tired he hadn't wanted to go out for supper. She told how she'd put the meat in the oven—"it's there now, cooking"— and how she'd slipped out to the grocer for vegetables, and come back to find him lying on the floor.

"Which grocer?" one of the detectives asked.

She told him, and he turned and whispered something to the other detective, who immediately went outside into the street.

In fifteen minutes he was back with a page of notes, and there was more whispering, and through her sobbing she heard a few of the whispered phrases—". . . acted quite normal . . . very cheerful . . . wanted to give him a good supper . . . peas . . . cheesecake . . . impossible that she . . ."

After a while, the photographer and the doctor departed and two other men came in and took the corpse away on a stretcher. Then the fingerprint man went away. The two detectives remained, and so did the two policemen. They were exceptionally nice to her, and Jack Noonan asked if she wouldn't rather go somewhere else, to her sister's house perhaps, or to his own wife, who would take care of her and put her up for the night.

No, she said. She didn't feel she could move even a yard at the moment. Would they mind awfully if she stayed just where she was until she felt better. She didn't feel too good at the moment, she really didn't.

Then hadn't she better lie down on the bed? Jack Noonan asked.

No, she said. She'd like to stay right where she was, in this chair. A little later perhaps, when she felt better, she would move.

So they left her there while they went about their business, searching the house. Occasionally one of the detectives asked her another question. Sometimes Jack Noonan spoke at her gently as he passed by. Her husband, he told her, had been killed by a blow on the back of the head administered with a heavy blunt instrument, almost certainly a large piece of metal. They were looking for the weapon. The murderer may have taken it with him, but on the other hand he may've thrown it away or hidden it somewhere on the premises.

"It's the old story," he said. "Get the weapon, and you've got the man."

Later, one of the detectives came up and sat beside her. Did she know, he asked, of anything in the house that could've been used as a weapon? Would she mind having a look around to see if anything was missing—a very big wrench, for example, or a heavy metal vase.

They didn't have any heavy metal vases, she said.

"Or a big wrench?"

She didn't think they had a big wrench. But there might be some things like that in the garage.

The search went on. She knew that there were other policemen in the garden all around the house. She could hear their footsteps on the gravel outside, and sometimes she saw the flash of a torch through a chink in the curtains. It began to get late, nearly nine, she noticed by the clock on the mantel. The four men searching the rooms seemed to be growing weary, a trifle exasperated.

"Jack," she said the next time Sergeant Noonan went by. "Would you mind giving me a drink?"

"Sure I'll give you a drink. You mean this whiskey?"

"Yes, please. But just a small one. It might make me feel better."

He handed her the glass.

"Why don't you have one yourself," she said. "You must be awfully tired. Please do. You've been very good to me."

"Well," he answered. "It's not strictly allowed, but I might take just a drop to keep me going."

One by one the others came in and were persuaded to take a little nip of whiskey. They stood around rather awkwardly with the drinks in their hands, uncomfortable in her presence, trying to say consoling things to her. Sergeant Noonan wandered into the kitchen, came out quickly, and said, "Look, Mrs. Maloney. You know that oven of yours is still on, and the meat still inside."

"Oh *dear* me!" she cried. "So it is!"

"I better turn it off for you, hadn't I?"

"Will you do that, Jack. Thank you so much."

When the sergeant returned the second time, she looked at him with her large, dark, tearful eyes. "Jack Noonan," she said.

"Yes?"

"Would you do me a small favor—you and these others?"

"We can try, Mrs. Maloney."

"Well," she said. "Here you all are, and good friends of dear Patrick's too, and helping to catch the man who killed him. You must be terrible hungry by now because it's long past your suppertime, and I know Patrick would never forgive me, God bless his soul, if I allowed you to remain in his house without offering you decent hospitality. Why don't you eat up that lamb that's in the oven. It'll be cooked just right by now."

"Wouldn't dream of it," Sergeant Noonan said.

"Please," she begged. "Please eat it. Personally I couldn't touch a thing, certainly not what's been in the house when he was here. But it's all right for you. It'd be a favor to me if you'd eat it up. Then you can go on with your work again afterward."

There was a good deal of hesitating among the four policemen, but they were clearly hungry, and in the end they were persuaded to go into the kitchen and help themselves. The woman stayed where she was, listening to them through the open door, and she could hear them speaking among themselves, their voices thick and sloppy because their mouths were full of meat.

"Have some more, Charlie?"

"No. Better not finish it."

"She *wants* us to finish it. She said so. Be doing her a favor."

"Okay, then. Give me some more."

"That's the hell of a big club the guy must've used to hit poor Patrick," one of them was saying. "The doc says his skull was smashed all to pieces just like from a sledgehammer."

"That's why it ought to be easy to find."

"Exactly what I say."

"Whoever done it, they're not going to be carrying a thing like that around with them longer than they need."

One of them belched.

"Personally, I think it's right here on the premises."

"Probably right under our very noses. What you think, Jack?"

And in the other room, Mary Maloney began to giggle.

WHEN NO MAN PURSUETH

by Isaac Asimov

*Science fact and fiction, history, Shakespeare, the Bible—
where does one start to compile a list of Dr. Asimov's literary accomplishments? His mysteries include two novels
(Murder at the ABA and A Whiff of Death) and three collections of short stories (Tales of the Black Widowers—
1974—More Tales of the Black Widowers—1976—, and The
Casebook of the Black Widowers—1980), as well as his famous science-fiction mysteries The Caves of Steel (1954),
The Naked Sun (1957), and The Robots of Dawn (1983).*

*The aforementioned Black Widowers is a genial group of
gentlemen who regularly meet for inspirational repast and
postprandial puzzles. Despite the settings of the stories, to
our knowledge only one of the Black Widowers mysteries in-
volves food.*

Thomas Trumbull scowled with only his usual ferocity and
said, "How do you justify your existence, Mr. Stellar?"

Mortimer Stellar lifted his eyebrows in surprise and
looked about the table at the six Black Widowers whose
guest he was for that evening.

"Would you repeat that?" he said.

But before Trumbull could, Henry, the club's redoubta-
ble waiter, had moved in silently to offer Stellar his
brandy, and Stellar took it with an absently murmured
"Thank you."

"It's a simple question," said Trumbull. "How do you
justify your existence?"

"I didn't know I had to," said Stellar.

"Suppose you did have to," said Trumbull. "Suppose you
were standing before God's great judgment seat."

"You sound like an editor," said Stellar, unimpressed.

And Emmanuel Rubin, host for the evening, and a fellow writer, laughed and said, "No, he doesn't, Mort. He's
ugly, but he's not ugly enough."

"You stay out of it, Manny," said Trumbull, pointing a forefinger.

"All right," said Stellar. "I'll give you an answer. I hope that, as a result of my stay on Earth, I will have left some people a little more informed about science than they would have been if I had never lived."

"How have you done that?"

"By the books and articles I write on science for the layman." Stellar's blue eyes glinted from behind his heavily black-rimmed glasses, and he added with no perceptible trace of modesty, "Which are probably the best that have ever been written."

"They're pretty good," said James Drake, the chemist, stubbing out his fifth cigarette of the evening and coughing as though to celebrate the momentary pulmonary release. "I wouldn't put you ahead of Gamow, though."

"Tastes differ," said Stellar coldly. "I would."

Mario Gonzalo said, "You don't write only about science, do you? It seems to me I read an article by you in a television weekly magazine, and that was just humor." He had propped up the caricature he had drawn of Stellar in the course of the meal. The black-rimmed glasses were prominent and so was the shoulder-length, fading brown hair, the broad grin, and the horizontal lines across the forehead.

"Good Lord," said Stellar. "Is that me?"

"It's the best Mario can do," said Rubin. "Don't shoot him."

"Let's have some order," said Trumbull testily. "Mr. Stellar, please answer the question Mario put to you. Do you write only about science?"

Geoffrey Avalon, who had been sipping gently at his brandy, said in his deep voice, which could, whenever he chose, utterly dominate the table, "Aren't we wasting time? We've all read Mr. Stellar's articles. It's impossible to avoid him. He's everywhere."

"*If* you don't mind, Jeff," said Trumbull, "it's what I'm trying to get at in a systematic way. I've seen his articles and Manny says he has written a hundred-and-something books on all sorts of subjects, and the point is why and how?"

The monthly banquet of the Black Widowers was in its concluding phase—that of the grilling of the guest. It was a process that was supposed to be conducted along the simple, ordinary lines of a judicial cross-examination but never was. The fact that it so often dissolved into chaos was a matter of deep irritation to Trumbull, the club's code expert, whose dream it was to conduct the grilling after the fashion of a drumhead court-martial.

"Let's get into that, then, Mr. Stellar," he said. "Why the hell do you write so many books on so many subjects?"

Stellar said, "Because it's good business. It pays to be unspecialized. Most writers are specialists; they've got to be. Manny Rubin is a specialist; he writes mysteries—when he bothers to write at all."

Rubin's sparse beard lifted and his eyes widened with indignation behind his thick-lensed glasses. "I happen to have published over forty books, and they're not all mysteries. I've published"—he began ticking off his fingers—"sport stories, confessions, fantasies—"

"Mostly mysteries," amended Stellar smoothly. "Me, I try not to specialize. I'll write on any subject that strikes my fancy. It makes life more interesting for me, so that I never go through a writer's block. Besides, it makes me independent of the ups and downs of fashion. If one kind of article loses popularity, what's the difference? I write others."

Roger Halsted passed his hand over the smooth balding forepart of his head and said, "But how do you do it? Do you have set hours to write in?"

"No," said Stellar. "I just write when I feel like. But I feel like all the time."

"Actually," said Rubin, "you're a compulsive writer."

"I've never denied it," said Stellar.

Gonzalo said, "But steady composition doesn't seem to be consistent with artistic inspiration. Does it just pour out of you? Do you revise at all?"

Stellar's face lowered, and for a moment he seemed to be staring at his brandy glass. He pushed it to one side and

said, "Everyone seems to worry about inspiration. You're
an artist, Mr. Gonzalo. If you waited for inspiration, you'd
starve."

"Sometimes I starve even when I don't," said Gonzalo.

"I just write," said Stellar, a bit impatiently. "It's not so
difficult to do that. I have a simple, straightforward,
unornamented style, so that I don't have to waste time on
clever phrases. I present my ideas in a clear and orderly
way because I have a clear and orderly mind. Most of all, I
have security. I know I'm going to sell what I write, and
so I don't agonize over every sentence, worrying about
whether the editor will like it."

"You didn't always know you would sell what you
wrote," said Rubin. "I assume there was a time when you
were a beginner and got rejection slips like everyone else."

"That's right. And in those days writing took a lot longer and was a lot harder. But that was thirty years ago.
I've been literarily secure for a long time."

Drake twitched his neat gray mustache and said, "Do
you really sell everything you write now? Without exception?"

Stellar said, "Just about everything, but not always
first crack out of the box. Sometimes I get a request for revision and, if it's a reasonable request, I revise, and if it's
unreasonable, I don't. And once in a while—at least once a
year, I think—I get an outright rejection." He shrugged.
"It's part of the freelance game. It can't be helped."

"What happens to something that's rejected, or that you
won't revise?" asked Trumbull.

"I try it somewhere else. One editor might like what another editor doesn't. If I can't sell it anywhere I put it
aside; a new market might open up; I might get a request
for something that the rejected article can fill."

"Don't you feel that's like selling damaged goods?" said
Avalon.

"No, not at all," said Stellar. "A rejection doesn't necessarily mean an article is bad. It just means that one particular editor found it unsuitable. Another editor might find
it suitable."

Avalon's lawyer mind saw an opening. He said, "By that

reasoning, it follows that if an editor likes, buys, and publishes one of your articles, that is no necessary proof that the article is any good."

"None at all, in any one case," said Stellar, "but if it happens over and over again, the evidence in your favor mounts up."

Gonzalo said, "What happens if *everyone* rejects an article?"

Stellar said, "That hardly ever happens, but if I get tired of submitting a piece, chances are I cannibalize it. Sooner or later I'll write something on a subject that's close to it, and then I incorporate parts of the rejected article into a new piece. I don't waste *anything*."

"Then everything you write sees print, one way or another. Is that right?" And Gonzalo shook his head slightly, in obvious admiration.

"That's about right." But then Stellar frowned. "Except, of course," he said, "when you deal with an idiot editor who buys something and then doesn't publish it."

Rubin said, "Oh, have you run into one of those things? The magazine folded?"

"No, it's flourishing. Haven't I ever told you about this?"

"Not as far as I remember."

"I'm talking about Bercovich. Did you ever sell anything to him?"

"Joel Bercovich?"

"Are there likely to be two editors with that last name? Of *course,* Joel Bercovich."

"Well, sure. He used to edit *Mystery Story* magazine some years ago. I sold him a few items. I still have lunch with him occasionally. He's not in mysteries any more."

"I know he isn't. He's editing *Way of Life* magazine. One of those fancy new slick jobs that appeal to the would-be affluent."

"Hold it. *Hold it!*" cried out Trumbull. "This thing's degenerating. Let's go back to the questioning."

"Now wait," said Stellar, waving his hand at Trumbull in clear annoyance. "I've been asked a question as to whether everything I write sees print and I want to answer that, because it brings up something I'm pretty sore about and would like to get off my chest."

"I think he's within his rights there, Tom," said Avalon.

"Well, go head, then," said Trumbull discontentedly, "but don't take forever."

Stellar nodded with a sort of grieved impatience and said, "I met Bercovich at some formal party. I don't even remember the occasion for it, or very much who was involved. But I remember Bercovich because we did some business as a result. I was there with Gladys, my wife, and Bercovich was there with his wife and there were maybe eight other couples. It was an elaborate thing.

"In fact, it was very elaborate, and deadly. It was formal. It wasn't black tie; they stopped short of that; but it was formal. The serving was slow; the food was bad; the conversation was constipated. I hated it. —Listen, Manny, what do you think of Bercovich?"

Rubin shrugged. "He's an editor. That limits his good points, but I've known worse. He's not an idiot."

"He isn't? Well, I must admit that at the time he seemed all right. I had vaguely heard of him, but he knew me, of course."

"Oh, of course," said Rubin, twirling his empty brandy glass.

"Well, he did," said Stellar indignantly. "It's the whole point of the story that he knew me, or he wouldn't have asked me for an article. He came up to me after dinner and told me that he read my stuff and that he admired it, and I nodded and smiled. Then he said, 'What do you think of the evening?'

"I said cautiously, 'Oh well, sort of slow,' because for all I knew he was the hostess's lover and I didn't want to be needlessly offensive.

"And he said, 'I think it's a bomb. It's too formal, and that doesn't fit the American scene these days.' Then he went on to say, 'Look, I'm editor of a new magazine, *Way of Life,* and I wonder if you couldn't write us an article on formality. If you could give us, say, twenty-five hundred to three thousand words, that would be fine. You could have a free hand and take any approach you want, but be light-hearted.'

"Well, it sounded interesting and I said so, and we discussed price a little, and I said I would try and he asked if I could have it in his office within three weeks, and I said maybe. He seemed very anxious."

Rubin said, "When was all this?"

"Just about two years ago."

"Uh-huh. That was about when the magazine started. I look at it occasionally. Very pretentious and not worth the money. I didn't see your article, though."

Stellar snorted. "Naturally you haven't."

"Don't tell me you didn't write it," said Gonzalo.

"Of course I wrote it. I had it in Bercovich's office within a week. It was a very easy article to do, and it was good. It was lightly satirical and included several examples of stupid formality at which I could fire my shots. In fact, I even described a dinner like the one we had."

"And he rejected it?" asked Gonzalo.

Stellar glared at Gonzalo. "He didn't reject it. I had a check in my hands within another week."

"Well then," said Trumbull impatiently, "what's all this about?"

"He never printed it," shouted Stellar. "That idiot has been sitting on it ever since, for nearly two years. He hasn't published it; he hasn't even scheduled it."

"So what," said Gonzalo, "as long as he's paid for it?"

Stellar glared again. "You don't suppose a one-time sale is all I'm after, do you? I can usually count on reprints here and there for additional money. And then I publish collections of my articles; and I can't include that one until it's published."

"Surely," said Avalon, "the money involved is not very important."

"No," admitted Stellar, "but it's not utterly unimportant either. Besides, I don't understand why the delay. He was in a hurry for it. When I brought it in he slavered. He said, 'Good, good. I'll be able to get an artist on it right away, and there'll be time to do some strong illustrations.'

And then nothing happened. You would think he didn't like it; but if he didn't like it, why did he buy it?"

Halsted held up his coffee cup for a refill, and Henry took care of it. Halsted said, "Maybe he only bought it to buy your goodwill, so to speak, and make sure you would write other articles for him, even though the one you wrote wasn't quite good enough."

Stellar said, "Oh no. . . . Oh no. . . . Manny, tell these innocents that other editors don't do that. They never have the budget to buy bad articles in order to buy goodwill. Besides, if a writer turns out bad articles you don't want his goodwill. And what's more, you don't earn goodwill by buying an article and burying it."

Trumbull said, "All right, Mr. Stellar. We listened to your story and you'll note I didn't interrupt you. Now, why did you tell it to us?"

"Because I'm tired of brooding over it. Maybe one of *you* can figure it out. Why doesn't he publish it? —Manny, you said you used to sell him. Did he ever hold up anything of yours?"

"No," said Manny, after a judicious pause. "I can't recall that he did. —Of course, he's had a bad time."

"What kind of a bad time?"

"This dinner took place two years ago, you said, so that was his first wife you met him with. She was an older woman, wasn't she, Mort?"

Stellar said, "I don't remember her. That was the only time we ever met."

"If it was his second wife, you'd remember. She's about thirty and very good-looking. His first wife died about a year and a half ago. She'd been ill a long time, it turned out, though she'd done her best to hide it and I never knew, for instance. She had a heart attack and it broke him up. He went through quite a period there."

"Oh! Well, I didn't know about that. But even so, he's married again, right?"

"Sometime last year, yes."

"And she's a good-looking person and he's consoled. Right?"

"The last time I saw him, about a month ago—just in passing—he looked all right."

"Well then," said Stellar, "why is he still holding out?"

Avalon said thoughtfully, "Have you explained to Mr. Bercovich the advantages of having your article published?"

Stellar said, "He *knows* the advantages. He's an editor."

"Well then," said Avalon, just as thoughtfully, "it may be that on second reading he found some serious flaws and feels it is not publishable as it stands. Perhaps he's embarrassed at having bought it and doesn't know how to approach you."

Stellar laughed but without humor. "Editors don't get embarrassed and they're not afraid to approach you. If he found something wrong on second reading, he'd have called me and asked for a revision. I've been asked for revisions many times."

"Do you revise when they ask for it?" said Gonzalo.

"I told you. . . . Sometimes, when it sounds reasonable," said Stellar.

James Drake nodded as though that were the answer he would have expected and said, "And this editor never asked for any revision at all?"

"No," said Stellar explosively, and then almost at once he added, "Well, once! One time when I called him to ask if it were scheduled—I was getting pretty edgy about it by then—he asked if it would be all right if he cut it a little, because it seemed diffuse in spots. I asked where the hell it was diffuse in spots, because I knew it wasn't, and he was vague and I was just peeved enough to say, no, I didn't want a word touched. He could print it as it was or he could send it back to me."

"And he didn't send it back to you, I suppose," said Drake.

"No, he didn't. Damn it, I offered to *buy* it back. I said, 'Send it back, Joel, and I'll return the money.' And he said, 'Oh, come, Mort, that's not necessary. I'm glad to have it in my inventory even if I don't use it right away.' Damn fool. What good does it do either him or me to have it in his inventory?"

"Maybe he's lost it," said Halsted, "and doesn't want to admit it."

"There's no reason not to admit it," said Stellar. "I've got a carbon; two carbons, in fact. Even if I wanted to keep the carbons—and they come in handy when it's book time—it's no problem these days to get copies made."

There was a silence around the table, and then Stellar's brow furrowed and he said, "You know, he did ask once if I had a carbon copy, I don't remember when. It was one of the more recent times I called him. He said, 'By the way, Mort, do you have a carbon copy?'—just like that, 'By the way,' as if it were an afterthought. I remember thinking he was an idiot; does he expect a man of my experience *not* to have a carbon copy? I had the notion, then, that he was getting around to saying he had mislaid the manuscript, but he never said a word of the kind. I said that I had a carbon copy, and he let the subject drop."

"Seems to me," said Trumbull, "that all this isn't worth the trouble you're taking."

"Well, it isn't," said Stellar, "but the thing bothers me. I keep careful files of my articles; I've got to; and this one has been in the 'to be published' file for so long I can recognize the card by the fact that its edges are dark from handling. It's a sort of irritation. —Now why did he ask me if I had a carbon copy? If he'd lost the manuscript, why not say so? And if he hadn't lost it, why ask about the carbon?"

Henry, who had been standing at the sideboard, as was his custom after the dinner had been served and the dishes cleared away, said, "May I make a suggestion, gentlemen?"

Trumbull said, "Good Lord, Henry, don't tell me that this nonsense means something to you?"

Henry said, "No, Mr. Trumbull, I'm afraid I no more understand what it's all about than anyone else in the room. It merely strikes me as a possibility that Mr. Bercovich may have been prepared to tell Mr. Stellar that the manuscript was mislaid—but perhaps only if Mr. Stellar had said that he had no carbon. It might have been the fact that Mr. Stellar *did* have a carbon that made it useless to lose, or possibly, destroy the manuscript."

"Destroy it?" said Stellar in high-pitched indignation.

"Suppose we consider what would happen if he published the manuscript, sir," said Henry.

"It would appear in print," said Stellar, "and people would read it. That's what I *want* to happen."

"And if Mr. Bercovich rejected it?"

"Then I would have sold it somewhere else, damn it, and it would still have appeared in print and people would have read it."

"And if he returned it to you now, either because you refused revision or because you bought it back, then again you would sell it somewhere else and it would appear in print and be read."

"Damn right."

"But suppose, Mr. Stellar, the editor bought the article as he did and does *not* publish it. Can you sell it elsewhere?"

"Of course not. It's not mine to sell. *Way of Life* has bought first serial rights, which means they have the full and sole right to publish it before any other use is made of it. Until they publish it, or until they formally relinquish the right to do so, I can't sell it anywhere."

"In that case, Mr. Stellar, does it not seem to you that the only conceivable way in which Mr. Bercovich can keep the article from being generally read is to do exactly as he has done?"

"Are you trying to tell me, Henry," said Stellar, with naked incredulity in his voice, "that he doesn't want it read? Then why the hell did he ask me to write it?"

Henry said, "He asked you to write *an* article, sir. He did not know the exact article you would write till he saw it. Isn't it possible that, once he read the article you *did* in actual fact write, he realized that he didn't want it read and therefore took the only action possible to keep it unpublished, perhaps forever unpublished? He probably did not expect you to be the kind of writer who would hound an editor over such a matter."

Stellar spread out his hands, palms upward, and looked about at the faces of the Black Widowers in a kind of semi-humorous exasperation. "I never heard of anything so ridiculous."

Avalon said, "Mr. Stellar, you don't know Henry as we do. If this is his opinion, I suggest you take it seriously."

"But why should Joel want to destroy the thing or bury it? It's a perfectly harmless article."

Henry said, "I merely advance a possible explanation for what has gone on for two years."

"But yours is not an explanation that explains, Henry. It doesn't explain *why* he wants the article to be left unread."

"You had said, sir, that he asked for permission to cut the article a little and you refused. If you had agreed, he would perhaps have changed it so as to render it really innocuous and then he would have published it."

"But what did he want cut?"

"I'm afraid I can't say, Mr. Stellar, but I gather that *he* wanted to do the cutting. That may have been in order not to call your attention to the precise passage he wanted altered."

Stellar said, "But if he made the cuts himself, I'd still see what he had done once the article appeared."

Henry said, "Would you be likely to read the article once published and compare it sentence by sentence with the original manuscript, sir?"

"No," admitted Stellar reluctantly.

"And even if you did, sir, there might be a number of small changes and you would have no reason to suppose that one change was more significant than the others."

Stellar said, "You know, this is a more peculiar mystery than the first, Henry. What could I have said to bother him?"

"I cannot say, Mr. Stellar," said Henry.

Avalon cleared his throat in his best lawyer-like fashion and said, "It is rather a pity, Mr. Stellar, that you didn't bring the carbon copy of your manuscript with you. You could have read it to us and perhaps we could then spot the critical passage. At the very least, I'm sure we would have been entertained."

Stellar said, "Who thought this sort of thing would come up?"

Gonzalo said eagerly, "If your wife is at home, Mr. Stellar, we might call her and have her read the article to Henry on the phone. The club could afford the charge."

Henry seemed to be lost in thought. Now he said slowly, as though the thinking had surfaced but was still a private colloquy he was holding with himself, "Surely it couldn't be anything impersonal. If the tenets of good taste had been broken, if the policy of the magazine had been violated, he would have seen that at once and asked for specific changes. Even if he had bought it after a hasty reading and then discovered these impersonal errors afterward, there would have been no reason to hesitate to ask for specific changes, surely. Could it be that some superior officer in the publishing firm had vetoed the article and Mr. Bercovich is embarrassed to tell you that?"

"No," said Stellar. "An editor who isn't given a free hand by the front office is very likely to quit. And even if Bercovich didn't have the guts to do that he would be only too glad to use upstairs interference as an excuse to return the manuscript. He certainly wouldn't just hold onto it."

"Then," said Henry, "it must be something personal; something that has meaning to him, an embarrassing meaning, a horrifying meaning."

"There's nothing of the kind in it," insisted Stellar.

"Perhaps there is no significance in the passage to you or to anyone else, but only to Mr. Bercovich."

"In that case," interrupted Drake, "why should Bercovich care?"

"Perhaps," said Henry, "because, if attention were called to it, it would *come* to have significance. That is why he dared not even tell Mr. Stellar what passage he wanted cut."

"You keep inventing perhapses," muttered Stellar. "I just don't believe it."

Gonzalo said abruptly, "*I* believe it. Henry has been right before, and I don't hear anyone suggesting any other theory to account for the fact that the article isn't being published."

Stellar said, "But we're talking about nothing. What is the mysterious passage that is bothering Joel?"

Henry said, "Perhaps you can recall some personal reference, since that is what we suspect it would have to be. Did you not say that included in your article was an account of a dinner rather like the one that had inspired Mr. Bercovich to ask for the article in the first place?"

"Aha," said Gonzalo, *"got* it! You described the dinner too accurately, old boy, and the editor was afraid that the host would recognize it and be offended. Maybe the host is an old and valued friend of the publisher and would get the editor fired if the article appeared."

Stellar said, with no effort to hide his contempt, "In the first place, I'm an old hand at this. I don't write anything either actionable or embarrassing. I assure you I masked that dinner so that no one could reasonably speak of a resemblance. I changed every major characteristic of the dinner and I used no names. —Besides, if I had slipped and made the damned thing too real, why shouldn't he tell me? That sort of thing I would change in a shot."

Henry said, "It might be something more personal still. He and his wife were at the dinner. What was it you said about them?"

"Nothing!" said Stellar. "Do you suppose I would make use of the editor to whom I was submitting the article? Give me that much credit. I didn't refer to him under any name or any guise; didn't refer to anything he said or did at all."

"Or anything about his wife either, sir?" asked Henry.

"Or about his wife—well, wait, she may have inspired one small exchange in the article, but of course I didn't name her, describe her, or anything of the sort. It was entirely insignificant."

Avalon said, "Nevertheless, that may be it. The memory was too poignant. She had died and he just couldn't publish an article that reminded him of—of—"

Stellar said, "If you're about to finish that sentence with 'the dear departed,' I walk out. That's tripe, Mr. Avalon. With all respect—no, without too damn much respect— that's tripe. Why wouldn't he ask me to take out a sentence or two if it aroused too keen a memory? I would do it."

Avalon said, "Just because I phrase the matter in sentimental fashion, Mr. Stellar, doesn't mean it can't have significance all the same. His failure to mention it to you might be the result of a certain shame. In our culture, such things as sorrow over lost love are made fun of. *You've* just made fun of it. Yet it can be very real."

Stellar said, "Manny Rubin said she died about a year and a half ago. That means at least half a year after I wrote the article. Time enough to have it printed by then, considering his anxiety to have me meet an instant deadline. And it's been a year and a half since he's married a beautiful woman. —Come on, how long does one sorrow over a lost love after one has found another?"

"It might help," said Henry, "if Mr. Stellar could tell us the passage in question."

"Yes," said Gonzalo, "call your wife and have her read it to Henry."

"I don't have to," said Stellar, who had only with difficulty withdrawn the wounded stare he had been directing at Avalon. "I read the damn thing again a couple of weeks ago—about the fifth time—and I have it reasonably fresh in my mind. What it amounts to is this: we had been served the roast at a kind of snail's pace, and I was waiting for others to be served before beginning. A few weren't quite that formal and were eating. Finally I broke down and salted it and was going to eat when I noticed that Mrs. Bercovich, who was on my right, had still not been served. I looked surprised, and she said she had a special request and it was delayed in getting to her, and I offered her my plate, and she said, 'No, thank you, it's been salted.' I told that passage, without names, just so I could get across my funny line, which I remember exactly. It went, 'She was the only one at the table who objected to the salt; the rest of us objected to the meat. In fact, several of us scraped off the salt, then ate it in a marked manner.' "

No one laughed at the funny line. Trumbull went to the trouble of simulating nausea.

Halsted said, "I certainly don't see any great sentimental value in that."

"I should say not," said Stellar, "and that's every last mention of her, without name or description, and none of Joel himself."

Henry said, "Yet Mr. Rubin said that the first Mrs. Bercovich died of a heart attack, which is rather a catchall reference to circulatory disorders in general. She may well have had seriously high blood pressure and have been put on a low-salt diet."

"Which is why she refused Stellar's salted meat," said Gonzalo. *"Right!"*

"And why she was waiting for a special dish," said Henry. "And this is something to which Mr. Bercovich desperately wants no attention drawn. Mr. Rubin said Mrs. Bercovich had done her best to hide her condition. Perhaps few people knew she was on a low-salt diet."

Stellar said, "Why should Joel care if they know?"

"I must introduce another perhaps, sir. Perhaps Mr. Bercovich, weary of waiting and, perhaps, already attracted to the woman who is now his second wife, took advantage of the situation. He may have salted her food surreptitiously, or, if she used salt substitute, he may have replaced it, at least in part, with ordinary salt—"

"And killed her, you mean?" interrupted Avalon.

Henry shook his head. "Who can tell? She might have died at the same moment anyway. He, however, may feel he contributed to the death and may now be in panic lest anyone find out. The mere mention of a woman refusing salt at that table may, in his eyes, be a shrieking out of his guilt—"

Stellar said, "But I didn't name her, Henry. There's no way of telling who she was. And even if somehow one were to find out that it was she, how could anyone suspect anything out of the way?"

"You are perfectly right, Mr. Stellar," said Henry. "The only reason we have come to suspect Mr. Bercovich now is because of his peculiar behavior with respect to the article and not to anything in the article itself. —But, you know, we have biblical authority to the effect that the wicked flee when no man pursueth."

Stellar paused a moment in thought, then said, "All this may be, but it's not getting my article published." He pulled out a black address book, turned to the B's, then looked at his watch. "I've called him at his home before, and it isn't ten yet."

Avalon raised his hand in an impressive stop sign. "One moment, Mr. Stellar. I trust you are not going to tell your editor about what we've said here. It is all strictly confidential, in the first place, and it would be slander, in the second. You would not be able to support it, and you may get yourself into serious trouble."

Stellar said impatiently, "I wish all of you would take it for granted that an experienced writer is aware of what libel and slander are. —Is there a telephone handy, Henry?"

"Yes, sir," said Henry. "I can bring one to the table. —May I also suggest caution?"

"Don't worry," said Stellar as he dialed. He waited a moment, then, "Hello, Mrs. Bercovich? This is Mort Stellar, one of the writers for your husband's magazine. May I speak to Joel? —Oh, sure, I'll wait." He did not look up from the telephone as he waited. "Hello, Joel, sorry to call you at home, but I've been going over the piece on formality. You don't have it scheduled, do you? —Well, all right, I didn't feel like waiting on this because I didn't want to weaken. You can shorten it if you want. —Oh, sure, that's all right. —No, Joel, just a minute, no. I don't want you to do it. I've got some things I *want* cut out, and maybe that will satisfy you. —For instance, that time I have about eating the salt instead of the meat isn't funny, now that I think of it. —Yes, that's right. Suppose I cut out that part about the woman refusing the salted meat. Will you publish it if I cut that out?"

There was a pause at this moment, and now Stellar looked up at the others, grinning. Then he said, "All right, Joel. —Sure I can do it. How about eleven A.M.? —Okay, see you then."

Stellar looked complacent. "It hit him right between the eyes. He repeated the line to me. You can't tell me that he remembered that passage, in an article he bought two years ago, right off the top of his head, unless it had special meaning to him. I'll bet you're right after all, Henry. —Well, I'll cut it. The important thing is that I'll get my article into print."

Avalon frowned and said with heavy dignity, "I should say that, from the standpoint of public morality, the really important thing is that a man may have tried to kill his wife and may even have actually done so and will get away with it."

Trumbull said, "Don't get virtuously aggrieved, Jeff. If Henry is right, then there's no way of proving that he did anything, or that if he did tamper with the salt it actually contributed to her death, so what is there to do? In fact, what do we have to do? The really important thing is that Stellar has done it all. He's given the man two years of agony, first by writing the article and then by being constantly after him to publish it."

Henry said, "The really important thing, sir, may be that Mr. Bercovich will, as a result of all this, be discouraged from attempting similar experiments in the future. After all, he has a second wife now, and he may grow tired of her too."

THE TWO BOTTLES OF RELISH

by Lord Dunsany

Edward John Moreton Drax Plunkett, eighteenth Baron Dunsany, managed to cram his writing career into a life of genteel pursuits, including traveling, hunting, and cricket. Fantasy and mystery are often combined in his plays and short stories.

Perhaps his best-known tale is the classic "The Two Bottles of Relish" (1934), which appeared in the anthology Powers of Darkness: A Collection of Uneasy Tales.

Smithers is my name. I'm what you might call a small man and in a small way of business. I travel for Num-numo, a relish for meats and savories—the world-famous relish, I ought to say. It's really quite good, no deleterious acids in it, and does not affect the heart; so it is quite easy to push. I wouldn't have got the job if it weren't. But I hope some day to get something that's harder to push, as of course the harder they are to push, the better the pay. At present I can just make my way, with nothing at all over; but then I live in a very expensive flat. It happened like this, and that brings me to my story. And it isn't the story you'd expect from a small man like me, yet there's nobody else to tell it. Those that know anything of it besides me are all for hushing it up. Well, I was looking for a room to live in in London when first I got my job. It had to be in London, to be central; and I went to a block of buildings, very gloomy, they looked, and saw the man that ran them and asked him for what I wanted. Flats, they called them; just a bedroom and a sort of a cupboard. Well, he was showing a man round at the time who was a gent, in fact more than that, so he didn't take much notice of me—the man that ran all those flats didn't, I mean. So I just ran behind for a bit, seeing all sorts of rooms and waiting till I could be shown my class of thing. We came to a very nice flat, a sitting room, bedroom, and bathroom, and a sort of little place that they called a hall. And that's how I came to know Linley. He was the bloke that was being shown round.

"Bit expensive," he said.

And the man that ran the flats turned away to the window and picked his teeth. It's funny how much you can show by a simple thing like that. What he meant to say was that he'd hundreds of flats like that, and thousands of people looking for them, and he didn't care who had them or whether they all went on looking. There was no mistaking him, somehow. And yet he never said a word, only looked away out of the window and picked his teeth. And I ventured to speak to Mr. Linley then; and I said, "How about it, sir, if I paid half, and shared it? I wouldn't be in the way, and I'm out all day, and whatever you said would go, and really I wouldn't be no more in your way than a cat."

You may be surprised at my doing it; and you'll be much more surprised at him accepting it—at least, you would if you knew me, just a small man in a small way of business. And yet I could see at once that he was taking to me more than he was taking to the man at the window.

"But there's only one bedroom," he said.

"I could make up my bed easy in that little room there," I said.

"The hall," said the man, looking round from the window without taking his toothpick out.

"And I'd have the bed out of the way and hid in the cupboard by any hour you like," I said.

He looked thoughtful, and the other man looked out over London; and in the end, do you know, he accepted.

"Friend of yours?" said the flat man.

"Yes," answered Mr. Linley.

It was really very nice of him.

I'll tell you why I did it. Able to afford it? Of course not. But I heard him tell the flat man that he had just come down from Oxford and wanted to live for a few months in London. It turned out he wanted just to be comfortable and do nothing for a bit while he looked things over and chose a job, or probably just as long as he could afford it. Well, I said to myself, what's the Oxford manner worth in business, especially a business like mine? Why, simply everything you've got. If I picked up only a quarter of it from this Mr. Linley I'd be able to double my sales, and that would soon mean I'd be given something a lot harder to push, with perhaps treble the pay. Worth it every time. And you can make a quarter of an education go twice as far again, if you're careful with it. I mean you don't have to quote the whole of the *Inferno* to show that you've read Milton; half a line may do it.

Well, about the story I have to tell. And you mightn't think that a little man like me could make you shudder. Well, I soon forgot about the Oxford manner when we settled down in our flat. I forgot it in the sheer wonder of the man himself. He had a mind like an acrobat's body, like a bird's body. It didn't want education. You didn't notice whether he was educated or not. Ideas were always leaping up in him, things you'd never have thought of. And not only that, but if any ideas were about, he'd sort of catch them. Time and again I've found him knowing just what I was going to say. Not thought reading, but what they call intuition. I used to try to learn a bit about chess, just to take my thoughts off Num-numo in the evening, when I'd done with it. But problems I never could do. Yet he'd come along and glance at my problem and say, "You probably move that piece first," and I'd say, "But where?" and he'd say. "Oh, one of those three squares." And I'd say, "But it will be taken on all of them." And the piece a queen all the time, mind you. And he'd say, "Yes, it's doing no good there: you're probably meant to lose it."

And, do you know, he'd be right.

You see, he'd been following out what the other man had been thinking. That's what he'd been doing.

Well, one day there was that ghastly murder at Unge. I don't know if you remember it. But Steeger had gone down to live with a girl in a bungalow on the North Downs, and that was the first we had heard of him.

The girl had £200, and he got every penny of it, and she utterly disappeared. And Scotland Yard couldn't find her.

Well, I'd happened to read that Steeger had bought two

bottles of Num-numo; for the Otherthorpe police had found
out everything about him, except what he did with the
girl; and that of course attracted my attention, or I should
have never thought again about the case or said a word of
it to Linley. Num-numo was always on my mind, as I always spent every day pushing it, and that kept me from
forgetting the other thing. And so one day I said to Linley,
"I wonder with all that knack you have for seeing through
a chess problem, and thinking of one thing and another,
that you don't have a go at that Otherthorpe mystery. It's
a problem as much as chess," I said.

"There's not the mystery in ten murders that there is in
one game of chess," he answered.

"It's beaten Scotland Yard," I said.

"Has it?" he asked.

"Knocked them endwise," I said.

"It shouldn't have done that," he said. And almost immediately after he said, "What are the facts?"

We were both sitting at supper, and I told him the facts,
as I had them straight from the papers. She was a pretty
blonde, she was small, she was called Nancy Elth, she had
£200, they lived at the bungalow for five days. After that
he stayed there for another fortnight, but nobody ever saw
her alive again. Steeger said she had gone to South America, but later said he had never said South America, but
South Africa. None of her money remained in the bank
where she had kept it, and Steeger was shown to have
come by at least £150 just at that time. Then Steeger
turned out to be a vegetarian, getting all his food from the
greengrocer, and that made the constable in the village of
Unge suspicious of him, for a vegetarian was something
new to the constable. He watched Steeger after that, and
it's well he did, for there was nothing that Scotland Yard
asked him that he couldn't tell them about him, except of
course the one thing. And he told the police at Otherthorpe
five or six miles away, and they came and took a hand at it
too. They were able to say for one thing that he never went
outside the bungalow and its tidy garden ever since she
disappeared. You see, the more they watched him the more
suspicious they got, as you naturally do if you're watching

a man; so that very soon they were watching every move he made, but if it hadn't been for his being a vegetarian they'd never have started to suspect him, and there wouldn't have been enough evidence even for Linley. Not that they found out anything much against him, except that £150 dropping in from nowhere, and it was Scotland Yard that found that, not the police of Otherthorpe. No, what the constable of Unge found out was about the larch trees, and that beat Scotland Yard utterly, and beat Linley up to the very last, and of course it beat me. There were ten larch trees in the bit of a garden, and he'd made some sort of an arrangement with the landlord, Steeger had, before he took the bungalow, by which he could do what he liked with the larch trees. And then from about the time that little Nancy Elth must have died he cut every one of them down. Three times a day he went at it for nearly a week, and when they were all down he cut them all up into logs no more than two foot long and laid them all in neat heaps. You never saw such work. And what for? To give an excuse for the ax was one theory. But the excuse was bigger than the ax; it took him a fortnight, hard work every day. And he could have killed a little thing like Nancy Elth without an ax, and cut her up too. Another theory was that he wanted firewood, to make away with the body. But he never used it. He left it all standing there in those neat stacks. It fairly beat everybody.

Well, those are the facts I told Linley. Oh yes, and he bought a big butcher's knife. Funny thing, they all do. And yet it isn't so funny after all; if you've got to cut a woman up, you've got to cut her up; and you can't do that without a knife. Then, there were some negative facts. He hadn't burned her. Only had a fire in the small stove now and then, and only used it for cooking. They got on to that pretty smartly, the Unge constable did, and the men that were lending him a hand from Otherthorpe. There were some little woody places lying round, shaws, they call them in that part of the country, the country people do, and they could climb a tree handy and unobserved and get a sniff at the smoke in almost any direction it might be blowing. They did that now and then, and there was no smell of flesh burning, just ordinary cooking. Pretty smart of the Otherthorpe police that was, though of course it didn't help to hang Steeger. Then later on the Scotland Yard men went down and got another fact—negative, but narrowing things down all the while. And that was that the chalk under the bungalow and under the little garden had none of it been disturbed. And he'd never been outside it since Nancy disappeared. Oh yes, and he had a big file besides the knife. But there was no sign of any ground bones found on the file, or any blood on the knife. He'd washed them, of course. I told all that to Linley.

Now I ought to warn you before I go any further. I am a small man myself, and you probably don't expect anything horrible from me. But I ought to warn you this man was a murderer, or at any rate somebody was; the woman had been made away with, a nice pretty little girl too, and the man that had done that wasn't necessarily going to stop at things you might think he'd stop at. With the mind to do a thing like that, and with the long thin shadow of the rope to drive him further, you can't say what he'll stop at. Murder tales seem nice things sometimes for a lady to sit and read all by herself by the fire. But murder isn't a nice thing, and when a murderer's desperate and trying to hide his tracks he isn't even as nice as he was before. I'll ask you to bear that in mind. Well, I've warned you.

So I says to Linley, "And what do you make of it?"

"Drains?" said Linley.

"No," I says, "you're wrong there. Scotland Yard has been into that. And the Otherthorpe people before them. They've had a look in the drains, such as they are, a little thing running into a cesspool beyond the garden; and nothing has gone down it—nothing that oughtn't to have, I mean."

He made one or two other suggestions, but Scotland Yard had been before him in every case. That's really the crab of my story, if you'll excuse the expression. You want a man who sets out to be a detective to take his magnifying glass and go down to the spot; to go to the spot before everything; and then to measure the footmarks and pick up the clues and find the knife that the police have overlooked.

But Linley never even went near the place, and he hadn't got a magnifying glass, not as I ever saw, and Scotland Yard were before him every time.

In fact they had more clues than anybody could make head or tail of. Every kind of clue to show that he'd murdered the poor little girl; every kind of clue to show that he hadn't disposed of the body; and yet the body wasn't there. It wasn't in South America either, and not much more likely in South Africa. And all the time, mind you, that enormous bunch of chopped larchwood, a clue that was staring everyone in the face and leading nowhere. No, we didn't seem to want any more clues, and Linley never went near the place. The trouble was to deal with the clues we'd got. I was completely mystified; so was Scotland Yard; and Linley seemed to be getting no forwarder; and all the while the mystery was hanging on me. I mean if it were not for the trifle I'd chanced to remember, and if it were not for one chance word I said to Linley, that mystery would have gone the way of all the other mysteries that men have made nothing of, a darkness, a little patch of night in history.

Well, the fact was Linley didn't take much interest in it at first, but I was so absolutely sure that he could do it that I kept him to the idea. "You can do chess problems," I said.

"That's ten times harder," he said, sticking to his point.

"Then why don't you do this?" I said.

"Then go and take a look at the board for me," said Linley.

That was his way of talking. We'd been a fortnight together, and I knew it by now. He meant to go down to the bungalow at Unge. I know you'll say why didn't he go himself; but the plain truth of it is that if he'd been tearing about the countryside he'd never have been thinking, whereas sitting there in his chair by the fire in our flat there was no limit to the ground he could cover, if you follow my meaning. So down I went by train next day, and got out at Unge station. And there were the North Downs rising up before me, somehow like music.

"It's up there, isn't it?" I said to the porter.

"That's right," he said. "Up there by the lane; and mind

to turn to your right when you get to the old yew tree, a very big tree, you can't mistake it, and then . . ." and he told me the way so that I couldn't go wrong. I found them all like that, very nice and helpful. You see, it was Unge's day at last. Everyone had heard of Unge now; you could have got a letter there any time just then without putting the county or post town; and this was what Unge had to show. I daresay if you tried to find Unge now . . . well, anyway, they were making hay while the sun shone.

Well, there the hill was, going up into sunlight, going up like a song. You don't want to hear about the spring, and all the may rioting, and the color that came down over everything later on in the day, and all those birds; but I thought, "What a nice place to bring a girl to." And then when I thought that he'd killed her there, well, I'm only a small man, as I said, but when I thought of her on that hill with all the birds singing, I said to myself, "Wouldn't it be odd if it turned out to be me after all that got that man killed, if he did murder her." So I soon found my way up to the bungalow and began prying about, looking over the hedge into the garden. And I didn't find much, and I found nothing at all that the police hadn't found already, but there were those heaps of larch logs staring me in the face and looking very queer.

I did a lot of thinking, leaning against the hedge, breathing the smell of the may, and looking over the top of it at the larch logs, and the neat little bungalow the other side of the garden. Lots of theories I thought of, till I came to the best thought of all; and that was that if I left the thinking to Linley, with his Oxford-and-Cambridge education, and only brought him the facts, as he had told me, I should be doing more good in my way than if I tried to do any big thinking. I forgot to tell you that I had gone to Scotland Yard in the morning. Well, there wasn't really much to tell. What they asked me was what I wanted. And, not having an answer exactly ready, I didn't find out very much from them. But it was quite different at Unge; everyone was most obliging; it was their day there, as I said. The constable let me go indoors, so long as I didn't touch anything, and he gave me a look at the garden from the inside.

And I saw the stumps of the ten larch trees, and I noticed one thing that Linley said was very observant of me, not that it turned out to be any use, but anyway I was doing my best: I noticed that the stumps had been all chopped anyhow. And from that I thought that the man that did it didn't know much about chopping. The constable said that was a deduction. So then I said that the ax was blunt when he used it; and that certainly made the constable think, though he didn't actually say I was right this time. Did I tell you that Steeger never went outdoors, except to the little garden to chop wood, ever since Nancy disappeared? I think I did. Well, it was perfectly true. They'd watched him night and day, one or another of them, and the Unge constable told me that himself. That limited things a good deal. The only thing I didn't like about it was that I felt Linley ought to have found all that out instead of ordinary policemen, and I felt that he could have too. There'd have been romance in a story like that. And they'd never have done it if the news hadn't gone round that the man was a vegetarian and only dealt at the greengrocer's. Likely as not even that was only started out of pique by the butcher. It's queer what little things may trip a man up. Best to keep straight is my motto. But perhaps I'm straying a bit away from my story. I should like to do that forever—forget that it ever was; but I can't.

Well, I picked up all sorts of information; clues, I suppose I should call it in a story like this, though they none of them seemed to lead anywhere. For instance, I found out everything he ever bought at the village, I could even tell you the kind of salt he bought, quite plain with no phosphates in it, that they sometimes put in to make it tidy. And then he got ice from the fishmonger's, and plenty of vegetables, as I said, from the greengrocer, Mergin & Sons. And I had a bit of a talk over it all with the constable. Slugger, he said his name was. I wondered why he hadn't come in and searched the place as soon as the girl was missing. "Well, you can't do that," he said. "And besides, we didn't suspect at once, not about the girl, that is. We only suspected there was something wrong about him on account of him being a vegetarian. He stayed a good fortnight after

the last that was seen of her. And then we slipped in like a
knife. But, you see, no one had been inquiring about her,
there was no warrant out."

"And what did you find?" I asked Slugger, "when you
went in?"

"Just a big file," he said, "and the knife and the ax that
he must have got to chop her up with."

"But he got the ax to chop trees with," I said.

"Well, yes," he said, but rather grudgingly.

"And what did he chop them for?" I asked.

"Well, of course, my superiors has theories about that,"
he said, "that they mightn't tell to everybody."

You see, it was those logs that were beating them.

"But did he cut her up at all?" I asked.

"Well, he said that she was going to South America," he
answered. Which was really very fair-minded of him.

I don't remember now much else that he told me. Steeger left the plates and dishes all washed up and very neat,
he said.

Well, I brought all this back to Linley, going up by the
train that started just about sunset. I'd like to tell you
about the late spring evening, so calm over that grim bungalow, closing in with a glory all round it as though it were
blessing it; but you'll want to hear of the murder. Well, I
told Linley everything, though much of it didn't seem to
me to be worth the telling. The trouble was that the moment I began to leave anything out, he'd know it, and
make me drag it in. "You can't tell what may be vital,"
he'd say. "A tin tack swept away by a housemaid might
hang a man."

All very well, but be consistent, even if you are educated
at Eton and Harrow, and whenever I mentioned Num-
numo, which after all was the beginning of the whole
story, because he wouldn't have heard of it if it hadn't been
for me, and my noticing that Steeger had bought two bottles of it, why then he said that things like that were triv-
ial and we should keep to the main issues. I naturally
talked a bit about Num-numo, because only that day I had
pushed close on fifty bottles of it in Unge. A murder certainly stimulates people's minds, and Steeger's two bottles

gave me an opportunity that only a fool could have failed
to make something of. But of course all that was nothing at
all to Linley.

You can't see a man's thoughts, and you can't look into
his mind, so that all the most exciting things in the world
can never be told of. But what I think happened all that
evening with Linley, while I talked to him before supper,
and all through supper, and sitting smoking afterward in
front of our fire, was that his thoughts were stuck at a barrier there was no getting over. And the barrier wasn't the
difficulty of finding ways and means by which Steeger
might have made away with the body, but the impossibil-
ity of finding why he chopped those masses of wood every
day for a fortnight, and paid, as I'd just found out, £25 to
his landlord to be allowed to do it. That's what was beating
Linley. As for the ways by which Steeger might have hidden the body, it seemed to me that every way was blocked
by the police. If you said he buried it, they said the chalk
was undisturbed; if you said he carried it away, they said
he never left the place; if you said he burned it, they said
no smell of burning was ever noticed when the smoke blew
low, and when it didn't they climbed trees after it. I'd
taken to Linley wonderfully, and I didn't have to be educated to see there was something big in a mind like his, and I
thought that he could have done it. When I saw the police
getting in before him like that, and no way that I could see
of getting past them, I felt real sorry.

Did anyone come to the house, he asked me once or
twice. Did anyone take anything away from it? But we
couldn't account for it that way. Then perhaps I made
some suggestion that was no good, or perhaps I started
talking of Num-numo again, and he interrupted me rather
sharply.

"But what would you do, Smithers?" he said. "What
would you do yourself?"

"If I'd murdered poor Nancy Elth?" I asked.

"Yes," he said.

"I can't ever imagine doing such a thing," I told him.

He sighed at that, as though it were something against
me.

"I suppose I should never be a detective," I said. And he just shook his head.

Then he looked broodingly into the fire for what seemed an hour. And then he shook his head again. We both went to bed after that.

I shall remember the next day all my life. I was till evening, as usual, pushing Num-numo. And we sat down to supper about nine. You couldn't get things cooked at those flats, so of course we had it cold. And Linley began with a salad. I can see it now, every bit of it. Well, I was still a bit full of what I'd done in Unge, pushing Num-numo. Only a fool, I know, would have been unable to push it there; but still, I *had* pushed it; and about fifty bottles, forty-eight to be exact, are something in a small village, whatever the circumstances. So I was talking about it a bit; and then all of a sudden I realized that Num-numo was nothing to Linley, and I pulled myself up with a jerk. It was really very kind of him; do you know what he did? He must have known at once why I stopped talking, and he just stretched out a hand and said, "Would you give me a little of your Num-numo for my salad?"

I was so touched I nearly gave it him. But of course you don't take Num-numo with salad. Only for meats and savories. That's on the bottle.

So I just said to him, "Only for meats and savories." Though I don't know what savories are. Never had any.

I never saw a man's face go like that before.

He seemed still for a whole minute. And nothing speaking about him but that expression. Like a man that's seen a ghost, one is tempted to write. But it wasn't really at all. I'll tell you what he looked like. Like a man that's seen something that no one has ever looked at before, something he thought couldn't be.

And then he said in a voice that was all quite changed, more low and gentle and quiet, it seemed, "No good for vegetables, eh?"

"Not a bit," I said.

And at that he gave a kind of sob in his throat. I hadn't thought he could feel things like that. Of course I didn't know what it was all about; but, whatever it was, I thought all that sort of thing would have been knocked out of him at Eton and Harrow, an educated man like that. There were no tears in his eyes, but he was feeling something horribly.

And then he began to speak with big spaces between his words, saying, "A man might make a mistake, perhaps, and use Num-numo with vegetables."

"Not twice," I said. What else could I say?

And he repeated that after me as though I had told of the end of the world, and adding an awful emphasis to my words, till they seemed all clammy with some frightful significance, and shaking his head as he said it.

Then he was quite silent.

"What is it?" I asked.

"Smithers," he said.

"Yes," I said.

"Smithers," said he.

And I said, "Well?"

"Look here, Smithers," he said, "you must phone down to the grocer at Unge and find out from him this."

"Yes?" I said.

"Whether Steeger bought those two bottles, as I expect he did, on the same day, and not a few days apart. He couldn't have done that."

I waited to see if any more was coming, and then I ran out and did what I was told. It took me some time, being after nine o'clock, and only then with the help of the police. About six days apart, they said; and so I came back and told Linley. He looked up at me so hopefully when I came in, but I saw that it was the wrong answer by his eyes.

You can't take things to heart like that without being ill, and when he didn't speak I said, "What you want is a good brandy, and go to bed early."

And he said, "No. I must see someone from Scotland Yard. Phone round to them. Say here at once."

But I said, "I can't get an inspector from Scotland Yard to call on us at this hour."

His eyes were all lit up. He was all there, all right.

"Then tell them," he said, "they'll never find Nancy Elth. Tell one of them to come here, and I'll tell him why."

And he added, I think only for me, "They must watch Steeger, till one day they get him over something else."

And, do you know, he came. Inspector Ulton; he came himself.

While we were waiting I tried to talk to Linley. Partly curiosity, I admit. But I didn't want to leave him to those thoughts of his, brooding away by the fire. I tried to ask him what it was all about. But he wouldn't tell me. "Murder is horrible" is all he would say. "And as a man covers his tracks up it only gets worse."

He wouldn't tell me. "There are tales," he said, "that one never wants to hear."

That's true enough. I wish I'd never heard this one. I never did, actually. But I guessed it from Linley's last words to Inspector Ulton, the only ones that I overheard. And perhaps this is the point at which to stop reading my story, so that you don't guess it too; even if you think you want murder stories. For don't you rather want a murder story with a bit of a romantic twist, and not a story about real foul murder? Well, just as you like.

In came Inspector Ulton, and Linley shook hands in silence, and pointed the way to his bedroom; and they went in there and talked in low voices, and I never heard a word.

A fairly hearty-looking man was the inspector when they went into that room.

They walked through our sitting room in silence when they came out, and together they went into the hall, and there I heard the only words they said to each other. It was the inspector that first broke that silence.

"But why," he said, "did he cut down the trees?"

"Solely," said Linley, "in order to get an appetite."

THE THEFT OF THE USED TEABAG

by Edward D. Hoch

Author of hundreds of short stories, published under pseudonyms as well as his real name, Edward Hoch is a master of the series detective. Among his creations are Simon Ark, a two-thousand-year-old supernatural detective; Rand, a British cipher expert (now retired); and Nick Velvet, a thief who, for a tasty fee, will steal almost anything without value—even a used teabag.

It was Gloria who brought him the assignment, on one of their infrequent Florida vacations. "She told me she knew I lived with Nick Velvet and she wants to hire you. For your usual fee, no special favors."

Nick roused himself from the sand and turned over. He'd been getting too much sun anyway. "Tell me again who this woman is."

"Her name is Mildred Fargo—I went to high school with her. I haven't seen her in twenty years, but we've kept in touch, and as long as I was down here for the week I phoned her and suggested we have lunch. Anyway, she knows about you and she needs to have something stolen. She'll pay you twenty-five thousand dollars."

"I'm supposed to be on vacation," Nick complained. "We tried to get away on the boat for a few days and got involved in that soap business. Now we come to Florida and you involve me in something else!"

"She's an old friend, Nicky."

He sighed and stared up at the cloudless sky. "What does she want stolen?"

"A used teabag," Gloria answered distastefully. "It sounds right up your alley."

Nick thought about that. Finally he said, "Well, it's

173

something different anyway. I guess I'd like to meet a woman who wants me to steal a used teabag."

"I knew you would. She's invited us for dinner tonight. You'll like Mildred, I promise."

"What does she do for a living?"

"She was married to a bartender a long time ago. I may be wrong, but I have a feeling that now she smuggles dope."

Dinner with Mildred Fargo was to be at the Landsmen's Club overlooking Biscayne Bay. Gloria and Nick arrived early at the private club, and he passed the time while they waited reading the notices on the members' bulletin board. There was the telephone number of the Birdwatchers' Hotline and a notice of typing services available to members, along with the traditional listing of members in arrears on their dues. He decided it was not a club for him.

"Here they are," Gloria said. This was the first he'd heard of "they," and he turned to see a tall slim man with a gray mustache and thinning gray hair, accompanied by a strikingly beautiful woman whose long blond hair swept over the shoulders of her clinging black dress. If she'd gone to high school with Gloria, Nick knew she had to be nearly forty, but she might easily have passed for ten years younger.

"You must be Nick Velvet." She held out a delicate hand. "I've heard so much about you from Gloria."

"All good, I hope," Nick murmured.

She smiled and turned to her partner. "This is Seymour Bentley, a good friend of mine. Seymour, Nick Velvet and Gloria." They shook hands all around and Mildred added, "Seymour is a member here. The dues are too rich for my blood."

"Landsmen was an all-male club until last year," Bentley explained, leading them into the dining room. "We still have very few women members—mainly widows of deceased members."

Their table was by the window, overlooking the bay. In the early evening light they could see a regatta of yachts under way, their tall sails forming an irregular line across the water. "Do you sail?" Mildred Fargo asked Nick.

"Gloria and I manage to get out a few times each summer."

"We were up to Cape Cod last month," Gloria added.

"I could go for that myself," Bentley said. "Not as much as Millie, though. She's forever racing high-speed motorboats between here and the Bahamas."

"Really?" Nick said. "I'd think that would be a bit dangerous. We're getting into the hurricane season, to say nothing of the drug smugglers. From what I read that's getting to be a real problem." Gloria nudged him under the table with her foot, but Mildred Fargo didn't change her expression.

"The Coast Guard looks after us,'" she said simply and opened the menu.

Dinner was elegant and expensive, but Seymour Bentley waved away Nick's offer of money as dessert was being served. "You're my guests." He had ordered tea while the others had coffee—and Nick began to understand why Mildred Fargo had arranged for them to have dinner with him.

As they lingered over after-dinner drinks and Bentley excused himself, Gloria said, "Tell him about it now, Mildred."

Millie turned and smiled at Nick. "As you see, Seymour takes tea after dinner. He dines here almost every evening when he's in town. I want you to steal the used teabag from his plate tomorrow."

"I see."

"Gloria tells me that would be no problem for you."

"No problem at all, but I'm sure you could bribe a waiter to do the same thing for five dollars. Why pay me twenty-five thousand?"

"This is a private club, Mr. Velvet, and the employees are quite loyal to the membership. I could never do what you suggest, and I warn you in advance that your efforts in that direction would not only meet with failure but would warn Seymour to be on his guard."

Nick saw Bentley returning from across the room. "All right," he said quickly. "Tomorrow night."

"Are we about ready to go?" Seymour Bentley asked as he returned. "I have something I'd like to show you all."

Nick and Gloria left their car in the club parking lot and went with Bentley in his long white Continental. Nick sat behind Mildred Fargo during the short ride. Gloria had been right about his liking her. However she earned her money, she was a very pretty lady.

"Here it is," Bentley announced, turning off into a parking spot by the water's edge. They were at a small private marina, one of several that dotted the shoreline along this stretch of Biscayne Bay.

"You've got a new boat!" Mildred exclaimed. She ran from the car along the pier to the sleek cabin cruiser Bentley had indicated. "Oh, Seymour—it's beautiful! When can I go out on it?"

"Whenever you want. How about tomorrow?"

Her face fell. "You know I'm off to the Bahamas tomorrow. How about next Monday?"

He smiled at her disappointment. "Monday it is. I'll phone you over the weekend."

"Can we go aboard now?" she asked.

"No—" He glanced apologetically at Nick and Gloria. "I'd show you around, but my time's a bit short. Maybe some other time."

"We'll be going back home this weekend," Nick said. "But I can see she's a beauty. I wish you luck with her."

"Thank you, sir."

Seymour drove them back to the club parking lot, where he and Mildred parted with a friendly kiss. When it developed she'd be taking a taxi home Nick offered her a ride, realizing this was probably what she'd planned.

Settling into the back seat of his rented car she asked, "Well, what did you think of him?"

"Handsome," Nick said. "Personable. I imagine he's a good yachtsman."

"Are you deeply involved with him?" Gloria asked.

"Not really," Millie said. "Why do you ask?"

"Because by hiring Nick you're obviously double-crossing him in some manner. Or setting him up for something."

"By hiring Nick I'm protecting myself, that's all."

"What does he use that boat for?" Nick asked her, though he suspected he knew the answer.

"It's better if you don't know too much," she replied. "All I want is that teabag tomorrow, after he uses it."

"Will he be dining alone?"

"I have no way of knowing, though I suspect not. No doubt he'll be with some business associate, or even another woman."

"That doesn't bother you? Do you want a report on it?"

She shook her head. "No, all I want is the teabag. I'll give you your money when you deliver it. In cash, of course."

"You'll be in the Bahamas tomorrow?" Nick asked.

"I'm flying over to pick up a boat a friend borrowed. I'll be bringing it back sometime during the night."

Nick and Gloria exchanged glances. "I see," Nick said. "Then I should deliver the teabag to you on Friday. Where should we meet?"

She jotted some numbers on a slip of paper from her notebook. "Call me at this number Friday morning—any time after nine. I should be back by then."

As they pulled up in front of the gleaming white condominium where Mildred lived, Gloria ventured a suggestion to her old friend. "Be careful, Mildred. Don't get in too deep."

Millie squeezed Gloria's hand and slipped out of the car without a reply.

The following morning over breakfast on the patio of their hotel, Gloria asked Nick, "Why do you think she wants it stolen?"

He shrugged. "Someone is gradually poisoning Bentley with the nightly teabags and she wants proof of it. Or someone is smuggling uncut diamonds to him in the bags and she wants to intercept them. It could be anything. I'll probably know when I get the bag."

"Nothing ever surprises you, does it, Nicky?"

"Not much," he admitted. "Losing a fee once in a while—that's always a surprise." He'd been thinking about Mildred Fargo, as he did about each new client, weighing her motives, speculating about her ability and willingness to pay on delivery. "You said you thought she was smuggling dope. How come?"

Gloria toyed with her coffee cup. "I don't know. Maybe it's just the way she dresses and acts. And that's a beautiful condo she's got. The papers are full of stories about the south Florida drug traffic. She must get her money from somewhere, and that seems likely to me."

"Perhaps she has a wealthy lover."

"She wouldn't be fooling around with Seymour Bentley if she did. And he's certainly not supporting her. He wouldn't even trust her on his new boat last night."

Nick nodded. "They seemed more like friendly rivals than lovers, and her hiring me to steal the teabag strengthens that feeling."

"How are you going to do it?" she asked.

He smiled at her. "By misdirection," he said. . . .

That evening, as the parking lot at the Landsmen's Club began to fill up, Nick parked his rented car in the special employees' area and walked quickly to the back door. He entered through a locker room adjoining the kitchen and immediately encountered a bearded man in white, who seemed to be one of the cooks. "I'm the new waiter," Nick said.

The bearded man scowled at him. "New waiter? Who hired you?"

"The manager, Mr.—"

"Jennings?" the cook supplied helpfully. "I guess he's still around. You know where his office is?"

Nick nodded and went out through the swinging doors to the dining room, careful to keep his face turned away from the table Seymour Bentley had occupied the night before. But when he did steal a look he saw the table was empty. Had all his plans been for nothing?

He lingered a few minutes at the bulletin board, rereading the same notices he'd seen the previous evening. Finally he strolled over to the registration desk by the door.

"Could you tell me if Mr. Bentley has reserved a table for this evening?" he asked the young woman on duty.

As he spoke, a middle-aged man with dark curly hair entered through the outside door. He heard Nick's question and paused on the steps.

"I'm Graham Jennings, the manager," he said. "What's your business with Mr. Bentley?"

The question took Nick off guard. "I was supposed to meet him here for dinner."

Jennings let out his breath in a sort of sigh. "Then I have some bad news for you. Seymour Bentley's new boat caught fire at sea and sank a few hours ago. We're afraid he might have gone down with it."

Nick telephoned Mildred Fargo promptly at nine the following morning. "I suppose you've seen the newspapers," he said.

"Yes. Can you come over?"

"I'm on my way."

As he prepared to leave, Gloria asked if she should come along.

"Maybe I'd better go alone," Nick told her. "I can't imagine what she wants now, but I can see we're out twenty-five grand. I can't steal a used teabag from a dead man."

"Have they recovered the body?"

"According to the papers, no. But the boat was seen to be on fire, and they found pieces of the superstructure floating in the water. A Coast Guard vessel was nearby at the time but no rescues were made."

"Do you think someone killed him, Nicky?"

"I don't know, and whatever happened I don't want to get involved. But I'll see what Millie has to say."

Mildred Fargo had a great deal to say. She met Nick at the door of her condominium and ushered him inside.

"I don't believe he's dead," she announced at once. "It's some sort of trick."

"How could that be?" Nick asked innocently. "The newspaper account says there was a Coast Guard cutter nearby at the time."

"Exactly! That's why it happened—I'm sure of it!" She sat down and fumbled for a cigarette. He could see that she was far more nervous than on their previous meeting. "I think I'm going to have to take you into my confidence, Nick," she said. "I hope I can trust you. Gloria said I could."

Nick smiled. "I think we're both on the same side of the law. That makes for a certain amount of trust."

"Then Gloria knows how I make my living?"

"Only a suspicion. In south Florida, frequent boat trips between the mainland and the Bahamas do suggest drugs."

She nodded. "I suppose it's obvious. I've been into it for three years now, buying marijuana in Jamaica and bringing it into the country, usually in two-thousand-pound lots. We fly it from Kingston to one of the islands in the Bahamas and then bring it the rest of the way in high-speed motorboats, landing in the marshes along the southern part of Biscayne Bay."

"The Coast Guard must know," Nick commented.

"Of course they know. But knowing it and proving it are two different things. I've never been caught with a load yet. My boats are custom-made with hiding places they'd never find in a hundred years."

"And Seymour Bentley?"

"He's in the business. You might call it a friendly rivalry. That's why he took me down to see his new boat the other night."

"He operates the same way you do?"

"Pretty much. We're always one jump ahead of the Coast Guard, and they've stopped him a half dozen times without finding a trace of drugs. Once they even sent a skin diver down to examine the hull of his yacht, but he found nothing. I think I'm good, but Seymour's a magician when it comes to hiding the stuff. If the Coast Guard was approaching to board him yesterday he may have scuttled the boat and escaped somehow."

"Well, at any rate there's no chance to steal the teabag now."

"Maybe there is," Millie said. She leaned forward intently. "Only this time from a man named Marc Watson."

"What makes these teabags so important?" Nick asked.

"You must trust me it's nothing of value, Nick. Gloria told me about your scruples. All I can say is that when I dined with Seymour at Landsmen's he often slipped the used teabag into his handkerchief and pocketed it when he thought I wasn't looking. Once I noticed Marc Watson doing the same thing. I want to know why, that's all."

"You must have some important suspicions. That's a great deal of money just to satisfy your curiosity."

"Of course I have suspicions. I believe some members of the Landsmen's Club are using it as a front for narcotics smuggling on a massive scale. Despite the name, they're mainly yachtsmen. They make frequent trips between here and the islands. Jennings, the club manager, may have enlisted them in a scheme to get rich quick."

But Nick still had his doubts. "It seems to me that most of the Landsmen members are wealthy enough already. Why should they get involved in something like this and risk arrest?"

"Sometimes people like Seymour aren't as rich as they seem. And many of the Landsmen members gained their wealth through drugs in the first place."

"Surely the police—"

"The police and the Coast Guard are overworked. Every day they have drugs by the ton coming into south Florida by sea and by air. They manage to stop just a small part of it." She rose and walked to a desk across the room and returned with a sheet of paper on which were written the names of Bentley and Watson. Bentley's name was followed by a half dozen recent dates, Watson's by just one.

"You're really serious about this," Nick commented.

"Of course I'm serious—and I hope that for twenty-five thousand you are too. Look at these dates. Each of them indicates a lunch or a dinner at which I observed either Seymour Bentley or Marc Watson putting a used teabag into his pocket. And on each occasion the man took his boat out the following day. I checked."

"It's still summer," Nick pointed out. "I'd expect people

are out with their boats every day if they can spare the time. I know I would be if I lived here."

"No, these were long trips. Overnight trips—most likely across to the islands. You Northerners don't seem to realize that the closest of the Bahamas is much nearer to Florida than Cuba—not ninety miles away. It's less than sixty miles from Miami to Bimini and only about seventy from Palm Beach to the western tip of Grand Bahama Island. High-speed boats can make the journey in under two hours."

"You don't need to convince me," Nick assured her. "Okay, I'll try for Marc Watson's teabag. Does he dine at the Landsmen's Club every night?"

She thought about it. "No, only once a week or so. But if I'm right about Seymour and the whole operation they'll need someone to take his place until he reappears—if he reappears. Watson has a good fast boat to make the crossing. If I had to bet on it, I'd say the odds are he'll be dining at Landsmen's tonight."

Mildred Fargo would have won her bet.

After studying several photographs of Marc Watson, Nick had no trouble picking him out as he entered the Landsmen's Club shortly after seven o'clock in the company of a lovely young woman with curly red hair and a figure that turned the head of every man in the club lobby. Nick had again entered through the employees' door. Since Watson had never seen him, stealing the used teabag would present no problem at all.

Donning one of the white jackets the busboys wore, Nick made a quick trip through the dining room, picking up a tray of dirty glasses. He was careful to avoid the real busboys. When one waiter passed him and asked, "You new here?" he merely grunted.

He watched from a distance as Marc Watson and the red-headed woman finished their dinner, then moved in close in order to hear the stocky man order his tea.

"Two coffees, please," Watson told the waiter.

Nick felt as if the floor had dropped out from under him.

Before he could react, a passing waiter said to him, "You workin' here or what? If you're workin', grab a tray."

Nick obeyed and hurried out to the kitchen. He couldn't risk more than one more trip to the dining room. Most of the other busboys were Cuban, and sooner or later his appearance would attract attention. But he had to see Watson drinking that coffee.

He tried it one more time, reaching the table just as the waiter was setting down two cups. "The chef thought you might prefer tea this evening, sir. He says it's your favorite blend."

"Fine," Watson said.

Nick retreated to the kitchen area, where trays of dirty dishes were waiting to be unloaded into the dishwasher. He spotted a used teabag on one saucer and quickly put it in his pocket.

Back in the dining room he waited until the time was exactly right, then moved in to Marc Watson's table to collect the cups and saucers. "Just a minute!" Watson barked. "We're not finished yet!"

"Sorry, sir," Nick fumbled and moved away.

He retreated to the kitchen with Watson's teabag in his pocket. Making the switch of teabags had been easy, and with luck Watson wouldn't find anything amiss until he inspected the other teabag at his leisure later that evening.

Nick didn't stop to remove his white jacket. He cut quickly through the kitchen and was on his way out the back door when he ran into a familiar figure.

"Well, well," Seymour Bentley said. "Who have we here? It's Millie's friend Nick Velvet, isn't it? And wearing a busboy's jacket."

"I thought you were dead," Nick said lamely.

"I got lucky—which is more than you seem to have done."

His right hand slid inside his jacket and Nick didn't wait for anything else. His fist flew at Bentley's jaw in a single solid blow. Caught off guard, the taller man toppled backward and went down. Nick sprinted to his car. As he started the engine he heard a shout, but he stepped on the gas pedal and didn't look back. If Seymour Bentley had a gun, he chose not to fire it.

Nick announced himself over the downstairs speaker in Mildred Fargo's condominium and waited for her to buzz him in. Upstairs, he found her waiting at her open door when he stepped off the elevator. She was clad in a trailing white lounging robe.

"Did you get it?" she asked.

"Right here." He slipped the handkerchief from his pocket and unwrapped the still damp teabag.

She smiled down at it, then took a thick envelope from the desk and placed it on the cocktail table. "That's your money. Now let's see what we've got."

Very carefully she sliced open the bag with a razor blade and dumped the tea leaves onto a paper towel. "There should be something—" Her voice trailed off as she separated the leaves with the edge of the razor.

"What is it?"

"There's nothing here but tea leaves! Are you certain you stole the right bag?"

"It's right from Marc Watson's saucer. He ordered coffee at first but the waiter brought him tea. It has to be the bag you want."

"I'm not paying twenty-five thousand dollars for some *tea leaves!*" Her hand moved toward the envelope, but Nick was a split second faster.

"I'm hired to steal worthless things, and that's what I did. Now that you've got it, if it really is worthless that's your problem."

"Gloria said you could be trusted."

"That's true. But I'm not running a charity."

"But—"

"By the way, you were right about Seymour Bentley being alive. I met him as I was leaving the club. He tried to pull a gun on me and I slugged him."

"You what?"

"I had no choice. He was coming in the employees' entrance as I was going out."

"That's odd. Why should he come in the back way?"

"To avoid being seen, I suppose. Maybe he still wants people to think he's dead. Everyone except Graham Jennings, that is—assuming he was on his way to see Jennings."

She looked down dispiritedly at the tea again. "Do you have any ideas about this?"

"I'm not paid for ideas, only for stealing."

"Damn you," she muttered.

"If there's nothing in the teabag itself," Nick ventured, "what about that little pasteboard attached to it?"

"That's just the brand name—" She stopped suddenly, staring at the square label between her fingers. "You may be right. Something could be written here in invisible ink. But how can we tell?"

"Heat might bring it out. Or—"

"Tea!" The thought came to them both simultaneously. Nick had stolen the bag before Marc Watson had had an opportunity to dip the label into his cup.

Millie quickly heated some water and dropped in a teabag of her own. When the tea was strong enough Nick plunged the little pasteboard square into it. They held their breath and studied it, and as they watched some tiny printing appeared along one edge.

"Jarret's Cove," Nick read. "Does that mean anything to you?"

She nodded. "It's down the bay a bit. A perfect place to unload narcotics. But this doesn't say when."

"You told me Bentley and Watson always took their boats out the following day. A trip across to the Bahamas and back would make it late tomorrow sometime. Probably after dark."

"There are dozens of coves and capes and islands where they might land. That's why it's so hard to catch them."

Nick glanced at her oddly and said, "I think I'd better take my money and go."

"I—"

"If you're working with the police I don't want to know about it. And if you're planning to hijack the shipment I want to know about it even less."

"All right," she said. "Thank you for what you've done."

He slid the envelope into his pocket, went for the door, and opened it. And got his next surprise.

Seymour Bentley was standing outside with another man Nick had never seen before. Both of them were holding guns. Bentley smiled and pointed his pistol at Nick's chest. "We were just about to knock," he said.

A few minutes later Nick and Mildred were seated side by side, their wrists tied behind their backs, and Seymour Bentley was holding the stolen teabag. "She's a detective, you know," he told Nick. "They've been trying to get me for years, but they never quite succeed."

"I didn't realize the law could afford my fees," Nick said.

"The government keeps a special fund, financed by the sale of cars, boats, and planes they seize from drug runners. Isn't that right, Millie?"

She tossed her head. "You seem to know all the answers, Seymour."

He turned to the man at his side. "Can we get them out to the car without being seen, Otto?"

"Sure." Otto was a burly man of few words.

"Would you mind telling me how you worked that trick with the burning boat?" Mildred asked. Nick thought she might be stalling for time.

"I built a false superstructure of plywood over the real one. It changed the whole silhouette of the yacht, made it look like a different vessel completely. That's why I wouldn't let you board her the other night. But you tipped off the Coast Guard anyway, and they were waiting when I sailed out the next morning on my way to Bimini. I set off a smoke generator, and under cover of the smoke screen we dismantled the plywood superstructure, set it on fire, and tossed it overboard. By the time the smoke cleared we were a mile away, appearing to be a different boat entirely. The Coast Guard thought we sank."

"But where do you hide the drugs? Why don't they ever find them when they do stop you?"

"Let's get moving," Otto said.

Bentley agreed. "On your feet, both of you. I'll answer

your question before we kill you, Millie," he added. "I wouldn't want you to die in ignorance."

Otto draped their raincoats over their shoulders so that their bound wrists couldn't be seen and led them down to a parked car. Seymour followed along, reminding them there was a gun pointed at them through his jacket pocket.

"I'm sorry I got you into this," Mildred told Nick. "Gloria will never forgive me."

"It's part of the business," he said.

"I don't much like ending up as one more body in the Miami drug wars. I should have known after you had your run-in with Seymour that he'd come for me right away."

Bentley crowded into the back seat with them and Otto drove. They were silent much of the way, driving south on roads little traveled by night. "This is the way to Jarret's Cove," Mildred said.

"That's right," Seymour said. "I told Jennings that invisible writing was unnecessarily melodramatic, but he wanted to avoid any direct contact between himself and the boat skippers."

"So the Landsmen's Club is merely a front for narcotics smuggling."

"No, no—it's quite legitimate. Jennings simply recruited some of us with fast boats and a yen for ready cash."

They turned onto a dirt road that ran east toward the bay. There were marshes all around them now, and in the darkness Nick could see nothing but the swampy vegetation that lined the road, caught briefly in the car's headlights as they sped along. Then "We're here," Otto announced suddenly and stopped the car.

Bentley prodded Nick with the gun. "Out," he said.

During the journey Nick had managed to free his hands from the bonds, but he kept them behind his back. Bentley kept Millie and Nick covered while Otto opened the trunk and took out an automatic rifle. "They're going to kill us now," Millie said under her breath.

Nick couldn't risk waiting any longer. He leaped at Otto, trying to grab the rifle and swing it around at Bentley. It should have been a simple maneuver, but the weapon was coated with Cosmoline and it slipped from his grasp, falling to the road. As he and Otto both grabbed for it Bentley fired two quick shots in their direction. Nick dove for the reeds and Otto retrieved the weapon, spraying a burst of bullets into the swamp.

"We still have the girl!" Seymour shouted. "If you bring the police she'll be the first one to die!"

Nick lay very still, the muddy water soaking his clothes. He wondered why they didn't come after him, but then he heard Otto chuckle and say, "Come on—leave him to the alligators."

After a time, when Nick was sure they'd moved on, he started crawling toward the road. The car was still there but he didn't go near it. There was no way to turn it around on the narrow road, even if he could start it, without attracting gunfire.

But with him missing they might keep Mildred alive as a hostage, at least until they finished the run to the islands and back. And as long as she was alive he had a chance of rescuing her.

Not with the police, though. Bentley had meant it when he said she'd be the first to die.

Nick spent the next two hours trudging along the dirt road back to civilization, now and then dodging into the swamp when a car's headlights appeared. He couldn't risk stopping anyone for help on this road, which led only to Jarret's Cove.

Finally, on the main highway a truck driver picked him up and took him to an all-night lunch counter, where he found a telephone. The second call he made was to Gloria back at the hotel. After he assured her he was all right he instructed her to telephone the police at six in the morning, just before sunrise, and tell them to come to Jarret's Cove. Allowing for the time it would take them, he figured he couldn't wait any later than that.

It was after five by the time he made his way back to the Cove, walking quite openly down the road toward a few spots of light he could see glowing near the shore. It was Otto who spotted him first, though there were some twenty men nearby moving bales and boxes. The big man lifted his automatic rifle as if to fire, but Nick raised his hands and said, "Take me to Seymour Bentley."

Otto gave his customary chuckle. "Had enough of the alligators, eh? All right, come on—but no tricks."

Bentley was on board his yacht, chatting in the dull predawn glow with Marc Watson. There was another craft anchored nearby Nick assumed belonged to Watson. He wondered which of them would be making the next run across to the islands.

"I recognize him!" Watson said as Otto led Nick up to them. "He was a busboy at the club!"

"Right," Bentley said. "He stole the teabag for Millie."

"Where is she?" Nick asked.

"At the bottom of the bay."

"I don't believe that—you wouldn't have killed her while there was a chance I'd come back here with the police," Nick bluffed.

"I'm here!" a voice called from inside the cabin. "I'm all right!"

Bentley smiled. "It matters little. Now you'll both be at the bottom of the bay together. Tie his hands, Otto, and do a good job this time."

The eastern sky was glowing now, and Nick noted that the sun would be rising soon. They'd be leaving then, in one yacht or two, and there'd no longer be a reason to keep witnesses alive. "One more trip across?" Nick asked with a smile. "A big one this time?"

"The biggest," Seymour agreed. "Both boats loaded. Once we get back here with it we'll be able to retire for life."

Suddenly there was a shout from the road. "Car coming!"

"The police!" Watson gasped. "He called the police!"

Bentley sprang into action. "Prepare to cast off."

But even as he spoke two small boats rounded the point and headed into Jarret's Cove. Nick could see others in the distance. A man came running up. "There must be five or six cars on the road now, parked every which way! They got us blocked in!"

"And more boats!" Watson shouted, pointing out to sea. He turned to Bentley. "Tell the men to start firing!"

But Seymour Bentley had lifted a pair of binoculars to his eyes. "They don't seem to be armed," he said. "They're just watching."

"Watching?"

"Through binoculars. One has a telescope. They're scanning the shoreline."

"Then dump Velvet and the girl overboard and let's make a run for it!"

Bentley shook his head. "Those boats could radio the Coast Guard before we even clear the cove."

Nick stole a look at his watch. It was just after six, and in the distance he could hear the familiar thump of a helicopter motor. It came into view then, and he smiled. Gloria hadn't quite waited till six o'clock to make her call.

With the road blocked by cars and the cove rapidly filling with boats, Bentley and the others had no way out. Some of them took to the swamps, but the others surrendered without firing a shot when the Coast Guard and federal agents moved in. Nick told Mildred Fargo about it as he untied her.

"I simply called the Birdwatchers' Hotline—the phone number I'd noticed on the club bulletin board a couple of times. I got somebody out of bed and told him I was calling for Marc Watson, and that Watson had sighted a rare Glaucous Gull a thousand miles south of its natural habitat, in Jarret's Cove. I knew the word would bring out some birdwatchers, but I hardly expected such an overflow crowd. The police would have just caused a lot of shooting. This way, Bentley and Watson didn't know what to do."

Mildred rubbed her wrists. "You're quite a guy, Nick. I guess you're worth that twenty-five thousand, one way or another."

"And you *are* with the police?"

"Justice Department. I'm sorry I had to deceive Gloria all this time. We've been trying to get something on Bentley for years. But I suppose even now we'll never know for sure where he hid the narcotics on all those trips across."

Nick smiled. "I said earlier I'd try to steal the teabag through misdirection. That was what Bentley and the others have been using all this time—misdirection! The Coast Guard could never find narcotics on his trips back because there were no narcotics. The rumors that he smuggled narcotics were probably started by Bentley himself."

"What do you mean?"

"It was on the trip *out* from Florida that he used the smoke-screen trick and pretended to burn the boat! It was on the trips out, not back, that he had something to fear. When I grabbed for Otto's rifle earlier it was coated with Cosmoline, freshly unpacked. They weren't smuggling drugs into Florida—they were smuggling guns out of Florida, to those Caribbean islands."

THE REFUGEES

By T. S. Stribling

The late (1881–1965) T. S. Stribling was one of the rare writers of the pulp era who successfully crossed over and became famous for his "serious" fiction. He is best known to general audiences as the winner of the 1933 Pulitzer Prize for Literature for his novel The Store, *one of a trilogy of books about a family in Tennessee. He was an important regional and social writer in the mold of Faulkner, with a deep concern for the prejudices blacks suffered in the segregated South. As a mystery writer he is best known for his marvelous stories of his detective Henry Poggioli, which can be found in* Best Dr. Poggioli Stories *(1975), works that in addition to being entertaining, also cast light on human nature.*

Herr Karel Heinsius, police inspector of Curaçao, Dutch West Indies, sat glancing first at the passenger list of the incoming Dutch steamer *Vollendam* and then through his window at the storm signal flying from the customhouse staff. And the inspector saw a sardonic fitness in the fact that the barometer should fall on precisely the forenoon when the noted—not to use the vile but more exact term "notorious"—Cesar Pompalone, deposed dictator of Venezuela, landed in the harbor of Willemstad.

Half an hour after the "Magnificent" Pompalone came ashore, one of Heinsius's men telephoned that the ex-dictator had lodged in the Hotel Saragossa in Otrabanda, and Heinsius instructed his informant to remain at the hotel until the refugee president shipped north.

Inspector Heinsius hoped, but did not expect, that this incident would end his relations with the Magnificent Pompalone. It was the inspector's duty to see that the ex-dictator did ship north. Deposed presidents flying out of Venezuela are a fairly ordinary phenomenon in the West Indies; and there is an informal international agreement among the powers that own these islands that once a dictator leaves Venezuela he must not be allowed to return. All the rest of the world is open to the fugitive's business or pleasure, but not Venezuela. His native land he must never see again.

The reason for this harsh and apparently unjust mandate is simple. All those powers that own West Indian islands also possess large commercial interests in Venezuela. The flight of a dictator means the end of a revolution and more stable business conditions, but the return of an ex-dictator marks the beginning of a new revolt and a new series of financial disturbances. Therefore, by this informal agreement, the road of dictators out of Venezuela is devoted exclusively to one-way traffic.

Not until the following day did the Magnificent Pompalone obtrude himself again on Herr Heinsius's attention. The inspector was eating breakfast, which occurs in Curaçao from twelve to one o'clock, when the telephone called the inspector to come at once to the Hotel Saragossa in Otrabanda.

The officer immediately imagined a clash between his agent and the Venezuelan. He hurried into his motor and then down the white street between the gaily painted Dutch houses of Willemstad. As he drove he pondered what he would do with the Magnificent Pompalone: put him in the *cuartel* there in Willemstad, ship him north, willy-nilly, to New York, where the American Secret Service would keep him safely away from Venezuela, transport him to London? Back of this pondering he knew that he would ship his man on the first steamer out, no matter where it sailed. Still, of course, the fellow had certain selective rights.

A few minutes later the inspector was motoring across the long pontoon bridge that connects Otrabanda on one side of the sea canal to Willemstad on the other. At a pier a hundred yards away lay the *Vollendam*, disgorging her hold of Dutch products to be reshipped to South and Central American ports. On the rising wind came the smell of shipping and the tang of the sea. Inspector Heinsius thought ruefully that his two storms were rising together.

The Hotel Saragossa in Otrabanda is a large hostelry, brightly painted in reds and greens. This building, and indeed the whole Dutch city, gives the impression of having been constructed out of big, gay toy blocks for overgrown children.

Around the entrance of the hotel was a rabble of dirty enough Negroes who had been attracted to the place by that nose for the exciting and the uncanny which the West Indian Negro possesses to a degree.

As the motor drove up the hotel physician, Dr. van Maasdyk, appeared on the piazza and made a gesture of relief at seeing the inspector. Heinsius jumped out and ran up the steps, speculating what trouble his man had had with the Venezuelan. The sight of such a crowd suggested a fight.

"Has anything happened to Barneveldt?" he asked the physician quickly.

"Not to Barneveldt, to Señor Grillet, the proprietor."

Heinsius was surprised.

"What's the matter with Grillet?"

"He is dead," said van Maasdyk, with excited brevity. "Has been dead for an hour at least. We found him a few minutes ago."

"There was no fight, no disturbances?" queried the inspector, trying to orient his ideas to this new phase of things.

"Nothing of the sort. He was found in his study. I gave the body a cursory examination and was about to pronounce it heart failure, but—" He hesitated.

"But what, Herr Doctor?"

"Well, there was a peculiar twist to our old friend's death—but you will see. We left the body sitting at the table exactly as we found it. I thought—"

The two men were now entering the lobby of the Hotel Saragossa, where a number of guests of half a dozen different nationalities were assembled. The doctor and the officer were too close to the group to continue their remarks.

Barneveldt, the inspector's man, had corralled the entire hotel in the lobby, and the guests were talking in a low babel about the proprietor's sudden death. An American was saying in an aggrieved tone:

"It's a shame we can't go in and look at the body. I paid my three bucks a day here, and they told me it included everything."

From the upper story came the sound of a woman's weeping. Somebody in the crowd whispered:

"There's the inspector now."

A glance over the lobby showed Heinsius the squarely built form and aggressive olive face of a man who he knew instantly must be the Magnificent Pompalone.

Renewed suspicion, entirely unfounded now, floated through the inspector's head, that if any foul play had been dealt to Señor Grillet somehow this Venezuelan was at the bottom of it. He wondered for an instant what possible connection there could be between the flying president of Venezuela and a simple tavern keeper in Curaçao. The next moment he said above the subdued excitement of the guests, first in English, then in Spanish:

"Gentlemen, señores, may I request that none of you leave the hotel until I finish my investigations. Her Majesty's government will appreciate this courtesy."

He bowed to the lobby in general; a number of citizens bowed in return. The American grumbled sotto voce:

"Courtesy! If we try to go out we'll get pinched."

On the second floor the inspector and the doctor were met by Hortensia Grillet, daughter of the deceased man, a tall, olive-tinted girl who showed clearly her Latin extraction, although she wore the usual apron and cap of the Dutch. As a last Dutch touch, the girl had a dustrag in her hand.

"Which room, Hortensia?" asked van Maasdyk, for the doors opening into the upper hallway were confusing.

Hortensia, still sobbing, pointed to a door and then turned away in a renewed burst of grief. The physician murmured some word of consolation to the girl and the two men entered the study.

Instead of any ghastly effect such as Herr Heinsius had anticipated, the proprietor of the Saragossa Hotel might have been asleep in his study with his head leaning over

on his arms on his greenheart table, save that he sat too
still. Around the walls of the room ranged bookcases of the
same cool-colored hardwood. On the floor were rare Peruvian llama-wool blankets used as rugs.

The inspector stood looking about the library from the
doorway.

"You mentioned something unusual, Herr Doctor, something that aroused your suspicions."

Dr. van Maasdyk moved silently across the Peruvian
rugs and touched a yellowed photograph which lay at the
hand of the dead man.

"It's this. I'd like you to look at it."

Herr Heinsius came over and regarded it attentively. It
was the picture of a young and extremely pretty Latin-
American woman, and the photographer's signature bore
the address of Caracas. Written in a fine old hand in faded
letters was the name: "Ana Sixto y Carrera, 1902."

A resemblance between the woman in the picture and
the girl he had seen weeping in the hall caused the inspector to remark:

"That must have been Grillet's wife, Hortensia's mother."

"Undoubtedly," agreed the doctor. "Now, look here!
This is why I telephoned you."

He turned the picture over and showed on its back in the
same faded letters: "Account of *12 de agosto,* 1906." And
immediately beneath this in fresh blue ink was the entry:
"Account settled *5 de enero,* 1925."

Beside the photograph, where it had dropped from Señor
Grillet's fingers, lay a fountain pen making a little blue
spot on the blotter where its point touched.

The two men stood looking at each other thoughtfully in
the presence of the dead man. This entry, the last he had
ever made in life, held its faint suggestion of mystery and
bygone drama.

"If it hadn't been for that," explained the doctor, "I
should have attributed his death to heart failure without
hesitation."

Heinsius nodded.

"There is nothing about the appearance of the body that suggests an unnatural death?"

"Nothing at all. His end evidently came as peacefully as sleep. But the photograph suggests that he realized his end had come."

"Nineteen hundred and six—that was only a year or two before Señor Grillet came to Curaçao and bought this hotel, was it not?"

Van Maasdyk smoothed his whiskers.

"He came here, I believe, about nineteen hundred and five or six. Hortensia, I remember, was about three years old, for I attended her during an attack of fever."

"Sixto y Carrera," repeated the inspector. "That must have been this woman's name after her marriage with some man by the name of Sixto; then Grillet's removal from Caracas to this island—Let me talk to Hortensia, Doctor."

The two men reentered the hallway and found the girl still sobbing, and wiping her eyes with the back of her wrist to avoid getting the dustcloth in her face.

"Fräulein," began the inspector, "have you any memory of your early life—where you were and what you did as a child?"

"I have always lived here, Herr Inspector."

"Do you remember your mother?"

"She died when I was born, Herr Inspector. This—this leaves me all alone." And the girl began sobbing afresh.

The two men glanced at each other, and the inspector changed the direction of his queries.

"Have you been in this upper story all morning, Hortensia?"

"Coming and going, mynheer."

"Was your father up here too?"

"He came and went as usual, mynheer."

"Did he seem in good health?"

"He was never any other way, Herr Heinsius; in fact, he seemed more lively than usual this morning. I mean more in a rush, more excited—"

The girl burst out weeping again as she talked of her father.

"There, there, Hortensia. I remember when my own father died—"

"Oh, Herr Inspector!" sobbed Hortensia. "You had nothing on your heart. Just an hour before my poor father died, I—I quarreled with him! Oh, if I had only known, Herr Heinsius! I can't endure it! I can never tell him how sorry I am!"

"Poor child, I am sure it amounted to nothing."

"But—but it was the first time he ever spoke sharply to me in all my life! He was carrying breakfast to the room of Señor Pompalone and Señor Afanador."

"What did you quarrel about, my poor Hortensia?"

"The wine. He had been down in the cellar after some very fine wine. He said they were going to have a rare breakfast together."

The inspector's attention veered a little from his sympathy to the story the girl was telling.

"They? Who, Hortensia? Señor Pompalone and Señor Afanador?"

"They and my father. He meant to eat with them; they were countrymen of his. And he was coming up the stairs with three bottles of rare old wine, and I took them, meaning to rub the cobwebs from them, when my father cried out, '*Caramba*, Hortensia, you are as stupid as the Dutch! Don't you realize that cobwebs grace a wine bottle as pearls did the neck of your beautiful mother?' But I said, 'Father, it is so dirty!' And he said, 'Attend to your rooms, and let me alone!' "

Inspector Heinsius was now engrossed in the girl's narrative.

"So your father went on and ate with his guests?"

"Yes, mynheer, he always showed honor to any of his own countrymen."

"I see. Will you please show us the room these men occupied, Hortensia?"

The girl was a little unwilling.

"I haven't cleaned away the breakfast things yet, Herr Heinsius."

"That's all right. I've seen breakfast things before; just show us the room."

A little farther down the hall the girl opened a door and displayed an unmade room, with the leavings of a breakfast on a little center table. Evidently it had been, as Hortensia suggested, a rather finer breakfast than usual. On the plates were the remains of a sea-turtle steak, broiled flying fish, a salad of alligator pears, three bottles of wine, some grafted mangoes from Trinidad, and the inevitable wineglasses, coffee cups, and tiny liqueur glasses of Curaçao.

The inspector glanced around and saw the salver on which the things had been brought. He picked it up and began rearranging the dishes on it.

"May I ask you to open that window screen a moment, Herr Doctor?" he requested.

"*Caramba*, you're not going to dump all this out the window!" cried the medico.

"I'll set it out of the way a moment while we look around."

The doctor swung open the screen and the inspector placed the tray on the windowsill inside the bars. Then he went to the door again and called the girl. When she appeared with her red eyes he asked in a lowered tone:

"Hortensia, when your father brought in this breakfast did he and his guests eat immediately?"

"Yes, mynheer," gasped the girl, about to weep again.

The inspector frowned thoughtfully.

"You are sure your father remained in this room from the very moment he brought in the tray till the meal was eaten?"

The girl evidently tried to remember, then said doubtfully, "I—I think he did." Then she exclaimed, "Oh, look, the screen's open; the room will get full of flies!"

"Yes, I opened it. And your father was not called out?"

"Yes, he was," recalled Hortensia, still looking at the open screen. "Our Negro boy, Zubio, came up and wanted a special wine for one of the Americans downstairs; Father had to go down and get it for him."

"So your father left this tray in this room and went back to get wine for the American; then he came back up and had his breakfast?"

"Yes, mynheer."

"Very well; thank you, Hortensia."

Heinsius turned back to the window, followed by the physician. Here the officer stood looking over the tray of leavings. A butterfly was unfurling its tube into the liqueur glass while a swarm of flies was already at the fish and fruit. A bumblebee buzzed away at the men's approach. In one wineglass and on the neck of one bottle lay half a dozen dead houseflies, two or three bees, and one of those curiously marked "89" butterflies which are found in the West Indies.

The inspector studied these dead insects and nodded; then he said to van Maasdyk with a certain professional pride in his voice:

"You see, Doctor, this is a rude but fairly effective test for poison. No doubt Cesar Pompalone dropped something in his host's bottle when he left the room for a moment."

Dr. van Maasdyk stared at the inspector.

"But, Herr Heinsius—Pompalone, the ex-dictator of Venezuela—what could he have against a poor tavern keeper in Curaçao?"

The inspector lifted his hands.

"I should hazard that Hortensia's mother was not Señor Grillet's wife. The photograph suggests it—the name on the photograph was Sixto. But that's a mere guess; the trial jury will have to search out the motive if they want any. I don't. I'll go down and arrest the two men. You can bring this wineglass and bottle as evidence."

Van Maasdyk moved in the tray, closed the screen, picked up the glass and bottle, and followed the inspector downstairs.

"We'll have to keep this from Hortensia as long as we can, Heinsius," he cautioned; "at least until after the shock of her father's death."

A little later the two men came down the stairs into the lobby under the inquiring glances of the guests of the hotel. The murmuring conversation which had been going on ceased, and the group in the lobby tried to read the officer's conclusion in his face. So pronounced was this scrutiny that the inspector, who was by nature a courteous

man, lifted his hand to the group, then descended into
their midst and walked over to the powerful and pictur-
esque figure of the Magnificent Pompalone, who stood
somewhat withdrawn from the other patrons of the establishment. He spoke in an undertone:

"Pardon me, Señor Pompalone, but may I ask you to
come with me for a moment to my office in Leidenstraat. I
would like to ask you some questions."

The refugee president looked intently at the officer.

"Couldn't you ask your questions here, Herr Inspector?"
he inquired in English.

"I might. Didn't Señor Grillet take breakfast with you
in your room about two hours ago?"

"He did."

"I have the wine left in his bottle and glass. I have evidence that suggests it has been poisoned. Until we can
prove that the wine is harmless, or that you personally did
not tamper with it, I will have to hold you under arrest
pending the investigation of the death of Señor Grillet."

The ex-dictator straightened and stared in cold astonishment, first at the inspector and then around the lobby, until his eyes rested on his traveling companion, Señor
Afanador.

"Herr Inspector," he asked, "do you consider it possible
that I, a fugitive from my own country, would be so mad as
to further complicate my already harassed flight by com-
mitting a murder in the first safe port I reached?"

The crowd gathered around officer and prisoner at this
remarkable charge and declaration.

"But, Señor Pompalone, I found poisoned wine left on
your breakfast table, where Grillet had eaten."

"Then I ask would I have been so childish as to keep the
remains of the poison in my room? I am not a child. Besides, what motive would I have to murder the first man
who took me in?"

"I can't go into your motive here, Señor Pompalone."

"Cá! Then you have discovered a motive!"

"I suspect one. It has something to do with a woman,
with a Señora Sixto." The inspector peered at the ex-
dictator sharply.

"A Señor Sixto?" repeated the Venezuelan with an uninformed expression.

He stood ruminating on the name, "Sixto—Sixto," which apparently yielded him nothing at all. Again he glanced at his companion, Afanador. Then he said:

"You must realize, Herr Inspector, I am here in Curaçao on an important mission. I must frame my defense as quickly as possible. May I have a sample of the poisoned wine?"

Van Maasdyk instantly poured a little into the glass and offered it to the dictator.

"Now will someone bring me a piece of shell?—conch, oyster, any sort of shell."

Heinsius motioned to his man, Barneveldt, who left the lobby and in a few moments returned with a piece of abalone. The dictator dipped the shell into the wine several times, watching the reaction closely. Presently the pearly tint of the nacre turned a cream color, which later strengthened into a yellow.

"Señores," he said, looking at the yellowed shell, "this is a test I have made at frequent intervals during my presidency of Venezuela. In fact, as president of my country I formed the habit of feeding to a cat or dog a little of all the food I meant to eat, and then awaiting results. This poison I could not test in that manner because it can be so timed that it will have no effect from one to twenty-four hours, and then it will act instantly and fatally. This is a poison obtained from the Orinocan Indians, and is called *Las Ojos de la Culebra.*"

"Are you admitting your guilt?" asked the inspector.

"Not at all, Herr Inspector—establishing my innocence. I have had so many attempts made on my life I feel this was also directed at me and went astray."

"Who do you think it was, Señor Pompalone?" inquired the inspector.

"I have a theory which I prefer not to state openly, but I would like to make a request of this group of *caballeros.*"

He turned toward the lobby.

"Certainly, anything you please."

"Gentlemen," said the ex-dictator, lifting his voice a trifle, "as you see, I am about to be placed under arrest here in Curaçao, and will not be free to construct my own defense. Now, when travelers are dispersed, which will be within a day or two, my defense will be impossible to make, for naturally someone in this hotel used this poison. So, if it is to be done at all it must be done at once. Now I ask, if there is any criminologist, secret-service man, or trained investigator in any line in this hotel, would he oblige a fellow traveler by aiding him in freeing himself? I would greatly appreciate it and would reward him well."

"Why don't you hire a lawyer here in the city?" suggested the inspector.

"Because I don't want a man who can quibble over evidence. I want an investigator who can produce absolute evidence."

The group of travelers stared at this strange request. Presently one of the Americans said:

"I'll have a shot at it, Mr. Pompalone. I'm a great reader of detective stories. I think I know the methods by which—"

The ex-dictator glanced at the fellow.

"What is your profession?"

"I am a commercial traveler. I sell soap."

"You sell soap in the West Indies?"

"That's my occupation," repeated the salesman a little curtly.

"Then I am afraid you lack the reasoning faculty if you are trying to sell soap in the West Indies. Is there anyone else?"

There was a cavalier humor about this which gained the sympathy of the crowd. Another man, a smallish dark-eyed gentleman of a certain academic appearance, spoke up from the group.

"If you are really innocent, Señor Pompalone," he stated crisply, "I can demonstrate that scientifically in about thirty minutes, but if you are not really innocent I would do you more harm than good."

"That's splendid, splendid, if you can make good your word. Are you a criminologist, señor?"

"No, I am an instructor in psychology. My name is Poggioli."

"Are you from an Italian university?"

"No, I am an American of Italian parentage. I teach at Ohio State University. I am taking my sabbatical year. To get back to my proof of your innocence, I can demonstrate it very simply."

"How do you do it?"

"By giving you scopolamine and simply asking you the question, 'Did you poison Señor Grillet?' If you did you will say so; if you did not you will say you did not. The drug deadens all sense of caution."

The inspector spoke up.

"We don't know any such drug as that in our criminal practice here in Curaçao."

"I am aware of that," said Poggioli with the slight acerbity of a college instructor toward a forward undergraduate. "I am simply explaining a method of finding out the truth almost instantly. I do not know of any court in any country which uses it now."

"Mr. Poggioli," inquired the inspector courteously, "would you expect me to turn a prisoner loose on evidence no court on earth would accept?"

"Wouldn't you prefer to loose an innocent man, even in an unconventional manner, than to see him go to jail for life, or perhaps to the gallows?"

Here the Magnificent Pompalone smilingly interrupted the colloquy.

"Gentlemen, allow me a word. It is true I did not poison Señor Grillet, nor do I know anything at all about him. However, I have innumerable other things in my mind which I would not expose for my fortune or my life. So, if my freedom depended upon my taking this new drug and telling all I know, I would go very cheerfully to the gallows instead."

The psychologist hesitated a moment and then with a little bow said:

"I suppose, then, you don't care for my assistance?"

"On the contrary, I will be glad indeed to enlist you in my behalf, but work on the facts, not on my sense of caution. Also, I would like Inspector Heinsius to place me in my room here in the hotel under guard, and allow this gentleman, Mr. Poggioli, the privilege of consulting with me at any time he sees fit."

Heinsius considered a moment and then agreed. He called his man, Barneveldt, then motioned to the dictator's traveling companion, Señor Afanador, and these three men, together with the American psychologist, went up the stairs to the dictator's suite of rooms. As they went up the American in the lobby growled out:

"Hybrid American! He won't be no good—highbrow, hasn't got any practical sense."

On the second floor Señor Afanador and the Magnificent Pompalone went into their separate apartments, and the dictator nodded for the inspector and the psychologist to follow him. When the door was closed the ex-president turned suddenly from the suave self-possession to flushed and swollen anger.

"Señores," he whipped out with that effect of hissing common to excited Latin Americans, "I know the man who committed this outrage." He shook a finger toward Señor Afanador's room. "That traitor! That serpent! That crawling *Pizanista!*"

"But, señor," interrupted the psychologist, "what grounds have you for your charges?"

"Isn't Grillet dead? I had nothing to do with it, so Afanador must have done it!"

"But if he is a traitor and a *Pizanista*, what motive had he in killing Señor Grillet and not you, Señor Pompalone?"

"*Cá*, there's the subtlety of it, Señor Poggioli!" exclaimed the dictator tensely. "I am worth more to the *Pizanista* alive in prison than dead. As long as I live there will be no other leader of my cause, but once I am dead"—the Magnificent Pompalone made a gesture—"some other patriot will spring up!"

He stood staring at the two men with black eyes protruding in rage.

"All I ask of you, Señor Poggioli, is to prove to Herr Inspector that this vile and perfidious wretch, Afanador, my secretary, sold out to my enemies and tried to betray me!"

"But, Señor Pompalone—"

"Señor Poggioli, this is not a debatable question! That is the solution! Now you prove it!"

"But I was going to say," persisted the psychologist, "this doesn't take into account the photograph of the Señora Sixto which Herr Heinsius mentioned, and the strange entry which Señor Grillet made on the back of the picture as he was dying."

The ex-president frowned, snapped his fingers.

"I have it. He timed the poison. He knew when Señor Grillet would expire. So he slipped into the señor's room, found a picture—any picture of a woman—made this entry to give it an appearance of mystery, to involve me in an imaginary intrigue. To show that he chose completely at random, he didn't even select a woman anyone knew—a Señora Sixto. Who is Señora Sixto? Nobody knows. Why, his plot is puerile! It's elementary!"

Inspector Heinsius stood with a skeptical look on his broad Dutch face.

"It seems to me, Señor President, it is not simple at all. It's rather too farfetched to be true. I can't imagine a man working out such minutiae to his crime."

"Herr Heinsius," interposed Poggioli, "I ask you not to discard my client's theory merely because it is foreign to your Northern temperament. What sounds farfetched to a Hollander may be a most natural procedure to a Latin. Not that I agree with Señor Pompalone, but I recognize his hypothesis as tenable."

The inspector gave a faint shrug.

"I see you are a man of learning, Herr Professor, but I have had twenty-four years of experience as an inspector, and I have found that when a woman comes into a murder she is a real woman, and not just a picture."

"This may be the one exception. Now I suggest that we go to Señor Afanador and hear his version of the tragedy."

The Magnificent made a movement forward.

"No, let him alone, señores. He will prejudice you against me!"

"But we must hear what he says, Señor President," explained the inspector.

"Then be prepared for the most outrageous fabrications," warned the dictator. "He will stick at nothing! I don't doubt he will swear to you that he saw me place the poison in the bottle with my own hands!"

"That will be difficult proof to offset," observed the inspector.

"Dios in cielo, it will be!" sibilated the dictator, making a furious gesture. "To be laid by the heels by such a scurvy liar; a cur; a worm, a foul maggot of a spy! *Cá!"*

He broke into a rasping laugh and made a great sardonic gesture toward the door.

"Go! Go listen to him as if he were a man!"

The two Northerners went out of the room, moved in spite of themselves by the Venezuelan's melodramatics. In the hallway they passed Barneveldt on guard, and a moment later entered the apartment of Señor Afanador.

At first glance Poggioli received a little shock, for the room appeared empty. But the next moment he was reassured, and somewhat disgusted, to see the secretary pressed as closely as possible against the door communicating between his own and the dictator's room. Afanador had his ear to the crack of the door. His face was colorless, and his black eyes rolled as he listened intently to his chief.

When he saw the psychologist and the inspector, instead of exhibiting shame, he drew a breath of relief and came toward them panting, as if after some great exertion.

"Señores," he said in a whisper, getting out a handkerchief and dabbing his brow, "I know that His Excellency, the president of Venezuela, suspects me in this matter, does he not?"

Heinsius nodded briefly, moved by a distaste for the man.

"He does, Señor Afanador."

The secretary stretched out a hand that trembled.

"Ole! señores, I—" He glanced with widened eyes at the door communicating between his own room and Señor Pompalone's. "Is that lock strong?" he whispered.

"Certainly," tossed out the inspector. "It's an old Dutch

lock. It would hold an ox. Nobody can get through it without a key."

Afanador breathed a little more easily.

"That's good, that's very good!" He smiled wryly. "Señores, you do not require a guard to keep me in this room."

The inspector's contempt for a coward got the better of
his voice.

"Señor Afanador," he sneered, "I suppose you are prepared to say that you saw Señor Pompalone drop the
poison in the wine bottle?"

"Caramba!" cried the secretary, coming out of his ague
of fear in his surprise and denial. "I am prepared to say
nothing of the sort! His Excellency, the president, is as innocent of that murder as a saint in heaven! It is as shocking and mysterious to him as it is to me."

The psychologist stared at this direct denial of what he
had expected to hear. Then he observed that the secretary
made this statement in a loud tone. He went immediately
to the fellow and asked under his breath:

"Is that your real opinion, Señor Afanador?"

"Sí, sí, señor," nodded the fellow earnestly, now speaking in an undertone himself. "I know His Excellency, the
president, had nothing whatever to do with the poisoning."

Heinsius stared in puzzled contempt.

"Then why are you shivering and shaking and asking
about that lock, if you are going to stand by your employer
like a man?"

The fellow's face, which had resumed a little color, went
sickly again.

"Because His Excellency suspects me, señores," he
whispered. "Do you know, up until now he has had nine
private secretaries? They are—" He waggled a finger and
pulled down his lips dolefully. "One after the other they
fell under his suspicion; some for one reason, some for another. No doubt many of them were innocent, as I am,
but"—he shrugged miserably and spread his hands—"His
Excellency cannot risk anything. He is so much more valuable than we. Perhaps we are innocent, well—we die for
our country. We are patriots! I have heard His Excellency

explain it many times. We are all patriots—I am the tenth patriot."

Señor Afanador moistened his dry mouth with his tongue.

The psychologist was moved to an equivocal sympathy and disgust. There was more than a hint in this of the old Incan caste which caused those Indians to lay down their lives in unquestioning self-sacrifice for their rulers. He recalled that much of the Venezuelan blood is of Indian origin.

Herr Heinsius muttered a contemptuous oath under his breath.

"Help us clear the matter up, Afanador," suggested Poggioli. "If you can show another murderer, he will no longer suspect you. What is your idea about the poisoning of the wine?"

"Do you know who did it?" questioned the inspector bluntly.

"I don't know who did it, but I know when it was done."

Heinsius gave a snort.

"That isn't a very difficult problem. It was done when Señor Grillet went to his cellar, naturally."

"Ye-es," admitted the secretary, a little taken aback. "But I can be even more exact than that. It was done when His Excellency and I walked with Señor Grillet down the hallway to the head of the staircase."

"Did all three of you leave the room together?" inquired the inspector in astonishment.

"*Ciertamente*, señor!" ejaculated Afanador. "We had paid for our rooms. In a way we were the hosts of Señor Grillet, and you do not imagine we would allow a guest to walk out of our room unaccompanied! We are Venezuelan *caballeros*, señores, always. We went with him. When we returned I observed that someone had entered during our absence and had moved the wine bottles."

"How long did you stay out of your room?"

"For ten or fifteen minutes, señores. Neither of us had seen Curaçao before, and we stood at the window looking out on the canal and the houses."

"And who do you think came in and tampered with your

wine?" interrupted Heinsius, a little more credulous of the story.

Afanador spread his hands.

"Señores, this may sound impossible to you, but I believe some spy, one of the *Pizanistas,* followed us here from La Guayra, slipped into our room at that unfortunate moment when His Excellency and I were out, and poisoned our wine."

Heinsius shrugged in the awkward manner of a Dutchman in Curaçao.

"Moonshine, Poggioli; every tale they concoct fizzles into moonshine at last. I don't see that we need to go any further with this investigation. Pompalone poisoned Grillet over an old affair with a woman, and that ends it."

"Just a moment, Inspector—Señor Afanador, have you any theory why this supposed spy did not poison all three of the bottles, and be sure of killing Pompalone?"

"That would have cast suspicion on some fourth person, and he himself might have got apprehended. No, the logical thing was to kill one man; the other two would certainly be arrested and held prisoners, while the actual poisoner would be free of any suspicion at all."

The inspector laughed.

"Señor Afanador, you have concocted the flimsiest story of all—a third mysterious Venezuelan unseen, unknown, floating into your room and poisoning your wine in a fifteen-minute interval. That would make good fiction, but poor testimony before a court of law."

The secretary flushed, lifted his right hand.

"Señores, calling on Him Who reads my heart, I swear to you somebody tampered with our bottles while His Excellency and I were out. There is no doubt about that. They were moved. I know they were moved!"

"Well, anyway," returned the inspector ironically, "I don't suspect you of the crime, Señor Afanador, and I don't believe the court will, either. You can rest easy on that point."

The psychologist had just an opposite thought in his mind.

"But, señores!" cried the secretary, "I would give my life

a thousand times for His Excellency. He alone can save my poor country, my poor Venezuela!"

The inspector turned on his heel in disgust and walked out of the room. When Poggioli followed and closed the door Heinsius reiterated:

"There is no use pursuing their investigations. Their suspicions chase around and around, like a puppy after its tail."

The psychologist stood stroking his jaw and looking at Barneveldt.

"I think someone did enter their room during their absence, Herr Heinsius," he said.

The inspector stared.

"Surely Afanador hasn't converted you to the theory of the imaginary spy!"

"No, but still I think somebody did."

"Who could it have been?"

"Well, everybody was downstairs at breakfast except these two men and the girl Hortensia."

The inspector, who was staring down the stairway, stopped and stared at his companion with the color draining from his sunburned face.

"*Gott im Himmel,* Herr Professor! What are you saying? Not that my poor crushed little Hortensia murdered her own father!"

The American lifted a hand.

"Don't let your feelings enter into this problem, Herr Heinsius. I know she is your friend; that you feel almost like a father to her. But she herself told you that she had quarreled with her father about the wine bottles."

"*Ach,* yes, but it was only a little quarrel. She only wanted to wipe the cobwebs off the bottles, Herr Poggioli."

"That is true, but she is an only child and probably a spoiled one. And then she is of Venezuelan blood, fiery and rash. Perhaps she committed this mad act in a moment of fury. Now look at her; her grief is uncontrollable."

"Why, that's scandalous, outrageous, an infernal explanation; that innocent child, that bereaved daughter. She is as innocent as a saint in paradise!"

"I certainly hope so," returned Poggioli warmly. "But in

solving a problem, Herr Heinsius, it is our duty to pursue every line of evidence. You don't object to my talking for a moment with the Señorita Hortensia, do you?"

"No, no, not at all. I will go after her. I am sure you will find her—as you have found all the other witnesses—quite innocent." And with a faintly ironic bow Inspector Heinsius set out up the hallway to find the Señorita Hortensia Grillet. Poggioli entered his client's room to await the return of the Dutchman with the girl.

The psychologist found the ex-dictator standing by the barred window of his room in a bellicose attitude, with his shoulders thrown back and his head down, staring at the shipping along the canal as if it were the enemy's works, which he meant presently to charge.

As the American entered Pompalone turned and said: "I suppose Señor Afanador testified against me in every detail?"

"No," returned the psychologist, "quite the contrary." And he told what Afanador really had said, and how he had expressed a desire to give his life for Pompalone's freedom.

The Magnificent Pompalone broke into the account with a gesture.

"Don't you see the subtlety of this viper?" he cried. "He has concocted a perfectly unbelievable tale to cast a darker suspicion on me. A second *Pizanista* on my trail! Excuse me, Señor Poggioli. One is quite enough for me, and he is that scurvy cur, Afanador!"

"But, Señor Pompalone, is it a fact that you and Señor Afanador accompanied Señor Grillet to the head of the steps this morning and remained at the window for several minutes before returning to your rooms?"

"Certainly, that is the truth," snapped the dictator. "But Afanador simply seized that fact to hang a long cock-and-bull story on it. No, nobody entered our room in our absence. Who was there on the second story to do it? It's his treachery!"

The psychologist saw it was impossible to discuss the secretary's theory, and he turned impatiently to the door, wondering what was detaining Herr Heinsius and the

Señorita Hortensia. He stepped outside again and saw the inspector standing at some distance down the hallway with a pleased expression on his broad brown face.

"What are you waiting on?" called Poggioli impatiently.

The inspector winked silently in reply.

The psychologist's patience was of academic brevity. He advanced sharply on the officer.

"What is it? What's the matter?"

"Nothing at all," returned the Dutchman in the best of spirits. "I've thought of a little plan to trick this scoundrelly Venezuelan."

"You have? How have you done it?"

The Dutchman studied the psychologist a moment.

"You won't warn your client? You won't give me away?"

"No!" snapped the American. "If he is guilty, I am as keen to see him hanged as you are!"

"So—I told Hortensia to put on her mother's clothes."

"What was that for?"

"You know how much like the photograph Hortensia is. Perhaps when Pompalone sees the girl he will be shocked into a restoration of his memory."

The psychologist was moved with the first touch of admiration he had felt for the Dutchman.

"By George, Heinsius!" he whispered warmly. "Capital! Splendid! I'll give you an 'A' on that!"

"Thanks! Thanks!" whispered the inspector, gratified. Both men now stood looking eagerly up the hall for Hortensia.

Three minutes later a door opened and Hortensia Grillet came out. At the sight of her a little thrill moved even the pulse of the psychologist. The girl wore a black dress with a band of mourning purple at her bosom. Her dust cap was gone and her dark hair was piled high after the stately fashion of a Venezuelan señorita. About her neck hung a string of matched pearls.

The two men stared at the transformation. Almost as an afterthought in the wake of her loveliness, Poggioli recalled what he had meant to ask the girl.

"Señorita," he began a little awkwardly, "I have a question to ask you. This morning when your father went to his wine cellar, did you see Señor Pompalone and Señor Afanador come from their room and stand looking out of the hall window at the canal?"

"*Sí*, señor." The girl nodded faintly, questioning the American with large eyes.

"And may I ask, señorita, if you or any other person entered their breakfast room while they were out?"

"I did, señor," breathed Hortensia.

"And what did you do in there, señorita?" queried the psychologist, studying her face intently.

"Señor, I—I—one of the wine bottles was so cobwebby, señor, I could not endure to see it set before Venezuelan *caballeros*. So I slipped in and wiped it clean. But I am sorry now, señor, I disobeyed my poor father's last wish."

She was about to cry again.

"Well, don't feel so badly about it, Hortensia—that was all you did, cleaned a bottle?"

"*Sí*, señor."

The psychologist stood nodding gently.

"That shows Afanador was right in this respect, Herr Heinsius. Someone did enter their room in their absence."

"I hope I did nothing wrong," exclaimed the girl in alarm.

"Nothing at all," assured Heinsius. "Just a little question between me and Herr Professor. Now I want you to come with me and repeat what you have just told me to Señor Pompalone."

"That is a very simple thing, señores," agreed the girl in a low tone. "I will tell it to anyone."

The three passed the sentry, Barneveldt, and went into the dictator's room.

The Magnificent Pompalone had flung himself down on a sofa. As the group entered he looked up, saw Hortensia, and sprang to his feet with the swiftest change of expression.

"Maria in heaven!" he exclaimed in amazement. "Is this the exquisite Ana Carrera again? Has my good angel so blessed me?"

The girl was bewildered at his words and his emotion.

"Señor Pompalone, Ana Carrera was my mother."

"Your mother!"

"*Sí*, señor."

"Is it possible! Why, señorita, you are her very flesh and spirit; the same look, the same soft music of her speech—"

The girl flushed a trifle.

"My mother died when I was born, señor."

"Pobrecita!"

The Magnificent Pompalone crossed himself, then went to her and, with the utmost gentleness, lifted and pressed her small work-hardened fingers to his lips.

"Poor little dove, left all alone in the world."

Hortensia caught a breath that lifted her bosom and her pearls.

"Sí, señor, my mother and father are both gone now."

The dictator touched the jewels with delicate fingers.

"Olé! señorita, these were Ana's pearls. I remember how long I was collecting them from Margarita Island. The divers—"

"Oh, señor, did you gather these pearls for my mother?"

"And I could swear they were about her neck this moment!"

"Am I indeed like her?"

"As two orchids from one stem!"

"Was she as tall as I?"

"To my shoulder, both of you."

"And her hair so black?"

"It was like a silken summer night with jeweled combs for constellations."

The girl stretched her hands toward the dictator.

"Mi madrecita! My poor little mother!"

She began to weep once more.

Neither the inspector nor the psychologist was so hardened as to break into the girl's eager questioning about her lost mother. The two Northern men stepped quietly out of the room and left Hortensia and her informant to their causerie.

Outside, Inspector Heinsius drew a long breath.

"So-o!" he breathed, without any triumph in his voice. "It was as I expected. He forgot himself, gave himself completely away over a woman. Herr Professor, these Latins are incomprehensible beings—so subtle, so simple, so complex, yet so easily entangled; so like fiends out of hell and yet so lovable." He sighed, and then added quite irrelevantly: "*Ach,* I'm glad I didn't marry one, anyway."

Then he said that his work was over, that he would go back to his office, send men back to arrest the dictator and throw him in jail.

The psychologist was depressed over the interview upstairs. He asked the inspector to keep the dictator under guard in the hotel that afternoon and give him time to think over the whole problem.

"Come back and take dinner with me here this evening," he suggested, "and I will tell you the result of my analysis."

The Dutchman shrugged, awkwardly but finally.

"There can be but one result, Herr Professor."

"I am afraid so," agreed the American. "And yet Señor Pompalone wears every aspect of innocence."

"Except of course that he has practically confessed his crime," grunted the inspector, and shrugged.

Mr. Poggioli accompanied his friend to the door of the hostelry and watched him shoulder his way through the half gale that was sweeping along the street. The wind, driving in from the sea, felt moist, and the sunshine that struggled through the vaporous air might have been English sunlight instead of the usual diamond brilliance of Curaçao.

As the psychologist turned back into the lobby a group of the guests watched him, and the American salesman called baldly:

"Poggioli, what did you find out—did the greaser kill him?"

"I don't know," returned the psychologist heavily, and hurried upstairs.

The salesman winked at the silent group.

"Highbrow, no practical sense. Now if I had that case—"

In the upper story the American asked Barneveldt where Señorita Grillet had gone.

"To her room, mynheer," answered the guard.

The psychologist was vaguely disappointed. He had an inclination to question Hortensia a little further. He hardly knew along what line. Her father, her mother, perhaps. But he would not disturb her in her room.

He moved on, his mood tuned to the gray tragedy, thinking over its conflicting details. His steps carried him into the private library where Señor Grillet's body was by now laid out for burial.

The psychologist walked over to the greenheart table, picked up and looked at the photograph with its two enigmatic annotations on its back. He read them silently, "Account of 12 *de agosto*, 1906. Account settled 5 *de enero*, 1925."

Poggioli wondered if the dead man, lying under the white sheet on the cane settee, had stolen Pompalone's wife or betrothed on that August day in 1906.

After all its permutations, the riddle had come back to the inspector's simple solution—"When there is a woman in a murder case," the Dutchman had said, "my twenty-four years' experience tells me she is a real one and not a photograph."

And so it had proved.

But there was a snarl somewhere in the burden of proof. It did not seem to Poggioli that the Magnificent Pompalone was a man who would murder by strategy. He could not imagine the dictator slipping poison into a wine bottle. Afanador would have done that.

He began reviewing the dictator's case against his secretary. This, also, was too nebulous, too fantastic.

The psychologist's mind went over other details of the tragedy—the accidental, the irrelevant details: the murdered man's anger with his daughter for wanting to clean the bottles, her disobedience in slipping into the room and dusting them after his injunction, the girl's eagerness to hear about her mother, of whom, evidently, her father never spoke. Naturally, he would not.

And still, the Magnificent Pompalone seemed to hold no bitterness against Ana Sixto y Carrera. This, too, seemed not quite in keeping with his temperament. In fact, the only suggestion of the dictator's innocence was psychological. What would a jury of hard-headed Curaçaoan Dutch make of a defense founded on psychology?

The wind was piping now an eerie threnody about the eaves of the big hotel. The dead man, done to death by some mysterious assailant, lay on the long wicker couch with the sheet drawn to his chin. On the table, beside the photograph of the woman, lay the contents of the dead man's pockets: a small penknife, a few pieces of Netherland money, a ring of keys—noncommittal relics beside the faded photograph.

Then it occurred to Poggioli that this woman had not come to Curaçao with the tavern keeper. According to van Maasdyk, Herr Heinsius had said, Señor Grillet arrived in Curaçao accompanied only by his baby girl, Hortensia. The psychologist could not piece together these details of the tragedy. As he sat listening to the wind and the far-off resurgence of the sea he had a feeling as if he were working with some jigsaw puzzle. A number of pieces seemed to fit, but he felt they were wrongly placed, yet he almost dared not undo the few articulating sections for fear he would never make even an approach to a pattern again.

In an effort to relieve his mind of these incongruities, he opened one of the bookcases and selected two or three volumes. They were all old-fashioned romances of revenge, *The Corsican Brothers, Vendetta, The Count Balderschino.* Apparently the whole library was of this tenor.

It struck the investigator that Señor Grillet had been fearing this very fate, and that explained the mystery of the last notation on the portrait. He had expiated his abduction of Pompalone's wife or mistress. His account had been settled with his life. Now he lay in the darkening library, the sheet drawn up to his chin, with a rising storm wailing his requiem.

After all, the Magnificent Pompalone had done this man to death. It was somehow out of character, but Pompalone was even more Latin than the American-Italian who was trying to understand his crime; and an individual of one race is always more or less out of character to a man of another.

From the the lower story there floated the three notes of

the dinner gong, repeated over and over. Even if the storm brewed and men were murdered, travelers had to eat. The psychologist got up and went below.

In the lobby the American found Herr Heinsius awaiting him. The two men went together to the dining room, which already was full. They took a small table in the corner of the room. The Negro, Zubio, brought them water and the menu card. The inspector looked over the good Dutch dishes with pleased eyes.

"Suppose we do not discuss our problem until after we eat, Herr Professor," suggested Heinsius, with a Dutchman's respect for a good meal.

"We don't have to," said the psychologist. "I have come to a decision."

The inspector glanced up keenly.

"You have?"

"Yes, I agree with you."

"*Ach,*" exclaimed the inspector, with a falling of the face. "I am sorry to hear it, Herr Professor; I had hoped somehow you would fasten the murder somewhere else than on Herr Pompalone, but, of course, the facts remain facts."

Zubio approached with the soup.

"Let us think no more about it until after we have dined."

He began swathing himself with a huge napkin while his mild eyes shone at the clear green turtle soup.

Over the big dining room the other guests were eating in accordance with their national manners. An Englishman was diligently using his knife and fork, holding one in each hand without ever laying down either implement. It gave him a certain rushed appearance. A German pinched each piece of bread on a plate before he selected his roll. An Italian made a sucking sound as he inhaled the spaghetti from his plate. All were mutually bad-mannered, each to the other. The American soap salesman drummed his knife on the table and called to Zubio:

"Here, nigger, come here, you!"

As Zubio approached, the soap seller began in an offended tone:

"Do you call this stuff wine?" He tapped his bottle.

Zubio bobbed.

"Yas, suh, dat—dat's whut I calls it, *senyo.*"

"Well, I call it ditch water! Have you got anything a man can drink?"

"*Sí, senyo.*"

"Something old and prime?"

"*Sí, sí, senyo.*"

The American flipped out a coin.

"Go bring me some of the oldest and best you've got in this joint."

"Yah, yessuh, *sí, oui, m'sieu,*" he bobbed in polyglot, moved by the money.

Zubio hurried away, and presently Poggioli heard him calling in his thick, blurred tones in the lobby:

"Señorita! Oh, señorita, come down! *Un Americano* wants the best wine, the oldest wine—"

Poggioli cursed the salesman for disturbing the grief-stricken girl over a glass of wine.

There was more long-distance conversation, which the psychologist could not understand. After a while the señorita came into the dining room and approached the salesman.

"Señor," she said in a low tone, "nobody but Father knew much about the wine. He always attended to it himself. I don't know which is the best or the worst."

"Bring me the oldest," ordered the American roundly, "and here is a five for yourself."

But the girl hurried away, leaving him holding the bill in his fingers. She said to Zubio:

"I think you will find the key to the wine cellar among Father's things on the library table upstairs."

Then she hurried from the room.

Poggioli condemned the salesman again, looking across the tables at him; then with a swerve in his thoughts he began pondering on what the girl had just said: her father always had kept the key to the wine cellar. For some reason he recalled once more that Señor Grillet had quarreled with his daughter that morning over cleaning the dusty bottles. Both of these little points were odd—Grillet's an-

ger at the girl for offering to polish a bottle, and the fact
that she had slipped in and cleaned it anyway.

It seemed to Poggioli that these pieces of the grim jigsaw
puzzle suddenly fitted together perfectly. There was something exciting about it. It cast a vague light over the whole
tragic occurrence. He tried to think out a fuller connection.

A cat, which probably haunted the dining room, rubbed
against his ankle and disturbed the delicate skein of his
thoughts. He tried to kick the animal under his chair. A
moment later Zubio entered with a single, very cobwebby
bottle of amber liquid borne aloft on a silver tray. The
black carried it to the drummer's table and began opening
it with elaborate ceremony.

As he was pouring the liquid into the American's glass a
sudden impulse seized the psychologist. He swooped down,
picked up the cat at his feet, and the next moment sprang
up and strode toward the salesman's table.

"Just a moment," he called in a low, urgent tone. "Wait,
put that glass down, sir! Let me test it before you drink it!"

The soap salesman stared at Poggioli in amazement and
irritation.

"Where the hell do you come in?"

"I don't know exactly. I have an idea, an impression.
Give me a spoonful of that wine. I believe it's dangerous!"

The American stared with glass uplifted, but he did not
drink. He got his spoon and dipped into the liquid. The psychologist produced the cat with a certain effect of legerde-
main.

"Pour some down its throat. I'll hold its mouth open!"

Came a chorus of ejaculations and grunts from the other
tables. Inspector Heinsius hurried to Poggioli's side. The
cat mewed and scratched, but the wine was poured into its
mouth. After a moment of watching the psychologist com-
manded:

"Another spoonful."

"Aw, you're kiddin' me," cried the salesman, growing
red in the face.

"You try it, Inspector," directed Poggioli briefly.

The inspector reached for the spoon. As he tried to pour
more wine in the cat's mouth he ejaculated:

"Ach! The creature's dead!"

The soap salesman turned cotton-colored.

"Dead! How come it's dead? What killed it?"

Excited comments went up throughout the room. Came a movement of guests toward the table. Inspector Heinsius was amazed.

"Herr Professor, how did you know? Why did you suspect?"

"Come out of the crowd," directed the psychologist. "We can't talk here."

The inspector ordered Zubio to retain the poisoned wine as evidence, and the two men went into the lobby; but the lobby was instantly filled from the dining room. The inspector and the psychologist passed on out the door into the night together. A gale laden with spume whipped them as they entered the canal side.

"Come to my office on the Leidenstratt!" shouted the inspector above the wind. "We can talk there."

In the dim street light the psychologist wagged a nervous negative finger.

"Let's stay out a while. I'm jumpy. I've been indoors too much today."

"Let's turn up this street where it's quieter."

The two turned down a side street, and went holding each other's arms in the occasional gusts that swept the narrow thoroughfare. After they had walked some distance the inspector came back to the point they had been discussing.

"Why did you suspect that bottle of wine was poisoned? It came straight from the cellar."

"The thing that set me off," said Poggioli, lifting his voice, "was the fact that the bottle was cobwebby and dusty, exactly like the one Señor Grillet had served to the men upstairs. Added to that was a complex of associated ideas touching Grillet's quarrel with his daughter. As a matter of fact, Herr Heinsius, what we call our reason is never the fatally sure, mathematical progression we fancy it is. If you will examine reason in the making you will find it a very cloudy process, a kind of blind jumping among hypotheses. When it finally hits the right one, it then proceeds to build a logical bridge from its point of departure to its goal, and it imagines it has crossed on that bridge, but it has not. The bridge was flung out afterward."

The inspector laughed briefly.

"That's all right how you did it, Herr Professor. I am neither an undergraduate nor a fellow in psychology. Why should Grillet poison himself? Why should Zubio infallibly have brought up another poisoned bottle out of a cellar of good wine? Why—"

"Here, take a question at a time," cried the psychologist. "The Negro brought up a poisoned bottle because he picked out the oldest one in the cellar, according to the order of the soap salesman."

"Why should the oldest be poisoned?"

"Because Señor Grillet brought a case of poisoned wine with him from Venezuela when he came to Curaçao some twenty years ago."

"You don't mean," cried the inspector, "you thought of all these things when you leaped up and ran to the American!"

"No. I received what the vulgar call a 'hunch.' Now when we analyze 'hunches' we find they are composed of an instinctive correlation of facts which have not yet reached the surface of consciousness—"

"That's all right about hunches, but why did Grillet bring poisoned wine with him from Caracas twenty years ago?"

"Because the Magnificent Pompalone had stolen his wife. You see, we approached the problem with a reversed theory. We worked on the idea that Pompalone had a grievance against Señor Sixto, alias Grillet, and murdered him for it. In reality, Sixto had a grievance against Pompalone.

"If we had paused to consider feminine nature we might have known that a man like Grillet could never have alienated the wife of a man like Pompalone. On the contrary, what could be more natural than the dictator of Venezuela seizing on the wife of some humble fellow and possessing her. These dictators have a high-handed way with them."

The inspector nodded in the darkness.

"That hangs together all right, Herr Professor, and then what happened?"

"Then Grillet, or Sixto, took his infant daughter, Hortensia, and a case of poisoned wine and emigrated from Venezuela to Curaçao, and here set up the finest hostelry in the city."

"Perhaps he had been a tavern keeper in Caracas?"

"I doubt it. I feel sure Señor Sixto studied out his complete revenge on the Magnificent Pompalone twenty years ago. He reasoned Pompalone would be deposed eventually; that he would fly for sanctuary to Curaçao, which is the nearest free port to Venezuela. He knew the Magnificent would lodge in the finest hostelry in the city. Therefore, to accomplish his revenge, he must possess that finest hotel, together with his case of poisoned wine."

The inspector nodded, impressed by the psychologist's extraordinary analysis. "Sixto accomplished his purpose," he said. "His meals were a delight, and his rooms as sweet as the sea air itself. Even his daughter, a native Venezuelan, was cleanlier than we Dutch."

"That was all built up, waiting for one man to enter his door and die. That man was the Magnificent Pompalone. And here is the irony of it, Herr Inspector, the satire that sometimes makes me believe in the old pagan gods who laughed at the antics of mankind. The very carefulness with which Señor Sixto trained his daughter led to his own death."

Heinsius listened interrogatively.

"When Hortensia, who could endure nothing dirty or dusty, cleaned the cobwebs off the wine bottle in the breakfast room, she killed her own father."

"How did she do that?" cried the officer in amazement.

"When Señor Sixto carried the breakfast with the poisoned wine to his guests, naturally he was tremendously excited. The vengeance of twenty years was about to be consummated. He meant to hand the Magnificent Pompalone the oldest, dustiest, and cobwebbiest bottle on the platter with a pretty speech such as all Venezuelans know how to make, and poison him.

"When he met Hortensia on the upper floor she wanted to clean the poisoned bottle. That was his mark, the cobwebs. It unstrung him. He reprimanded her severely and told her to go about her work. Then he was called down to the wine cellar, for naturally he never allowed anyone to enter that dangerous place except himself. His guests accompanied him to the stairs. Hortensia, annoyed by the dust, as he had trained her to be, saw her opportunity to slip in and clean the worst of the bottles, the poisoned one. When Sixto returned with the excitement of murder upon him, he did not observe the change. He gave his enemy the dustiest bottle, and drank his own bane. Herr Heinsius, if it were in our power to exchange our earthiness for the high divan of the gods, if we could look down on this tragedy—this romantic, revengeful man, after twenty years of waiting and hating and planning, then sitting before his enemy and drinking his own poison, all through mere excess of training his child—Herr Heinsius, I think we, too, would have been moved, as were the Olympian gods, to enormous laughter."

The inspector was somehow dismayed at his companion's fantasy. He said uneasily: "But naturally we don't believe in the old pagan gods anymore."

"Oh, no, certainly not," agreed the psychologist. "But they really do explain life more accurately than our modern theology, don't you think? Sometimes it seems to me that men have a reverse theory of the gods, just as you and I had of the murder. Suppose men assumed that the gods were inimical or satiric toward them instead of friendly, how many of the perplexities of life that would explain!"

"Well—I'm a good churchman myself," said Heinsius.

"Oh, so am I," agreed the American.

The two walked on with a feeling of spiritual disjunction at this little quirk in their conversation. Poggioli regretted he had mentioned his whimsy.

The two had walked out past the houses now onto a little pleasure beach, which was quite deserted in the gale. A string of pale electric lights along the water's edge showed the curves of the incoming waves, which marched in endless procession from the dark Caribbean. Spindrift blew in past the lights in torn veils, and its last mist beat gratefully on the faces of the two companions. Poggioli continued musing over the ironic death of the hotel keeper and the odd triumph of Pompalone. There was a moral planlessness, an anarchy about it. The line of a poem recurred to his mind: "Perpetual strife amid confused alarms." That was life—perpetual strife.

Here the inspector touched the scientist's arm and pointed out to sea.

"There's a brave soul out there," he called above the surf.

Poggioli looked and saw a red-and-green signal burning in the darkness.

"Fishermen?" queried Poggioli in a friendly tone.

"Natives in a jack boat, I suppose. They brave any sea."

The inspector had begun a description of jack boats—solid logs with the bottom hewn out—when he was interrupted by two figures silhouetted against the row of watery beach lights. A large man and a slight one were hurrying toward the surf.

The psychologist and the inspector watched them curiously, when at a certain resolute bearing of the larger man the inspector gasped suddenly:

"Mein Gott! That's the Magnificent Pompalone!" And he dashed down the strand after the dictator.

Poggioli set out after him, running.

"Let him go, Herr Inspector!" shouted the American. "He hasn't committed any crime in this country!"

"Gott im Himmel, but he mustn't go back! That's worse than a crime! It's against business!"

The police inspector jerked out a pistol as he ran and shouted against the blast:

"Stop! Halt! I'll shoot!"

But at that moment the two figures dashed across the last shining foot of sand and plunged headlong into the curve of an incoming wave.

The inspector fired four shots into the surf, then with an oath turned his fire on the signal lights at sea. But perhaps the tossed sailors never knew that a man on shore was firing at them. After some fifteen minutes the signal lights blinked out.

As the two men turned back to the hotel the psychologist said frankly:

"Heinsius, I'm glad he's gone. He was a very devil, no doubt, but there was something likable, something rather splendid about the fellow."

"You mean he was Pompalone the Magnificent—"

At this moment a figure dashed out of the side street, shouting—a huge, mouthy Negroid shout as if the fiends were after him:

"Herr Inspectuh! Senyo Inspectuh! Mistuh Inspectuh!"

Both men stared in the new direction and saw the white-eyed figure of Zubio appear against the night.

"He's coming to tell us they're gone!" said the Dutchman.

Zubio made for the two.

"Herr Inspectuh!" he gasped. "Come to the hotel, *pronto!* Quick!"

"I know they are gone, Zubio."

"Gone! Gone! No! Poor Senyo Afanador, someone has struck a dagger to his heart!"

Heinsius swayed in the gale.

"What! Afanador murdered! *Mein Gott!* I saw him that moment. Where was Barneveldt?"

"Sitting by the door where you put him, Herr Inspectuh. Somebody opened the doors on the inside between all the rooms, somebody with a key; and now Señorita Hortensia is gone, run away, mad, perhaps."

Simultaneously the two men whirled and stared out into the black, incoming surf. They could see nothing at all.

On the following day, immediately after the funeral of Señores Grillet and Afanador, the Hotel Saragossa was closed and the windows and doors boarded up.

RECIPE FOR A HAPPY MARRIAGE

by Nedra Tyre

Nedra Tyre is a Virginia-based mystery writer whose care-fully crafted short stories have graced the pages of Ellery Queen's Mystery Magazine *since 1955, and richly deserve collection. She has also written some half-dozen mystery novels, including* Hall of Death *(1960) and* Twice So Fair *(1971). Her fiction frequently reflects her experiences as a social worker, and her characters are always vivid and convincing.*

Today is just not my day.

And it's not even noon.

Maybe it will take a turn for the better.

Anyway, it's foolish to be upset.

That girl from the *Bulletin* who came to interview me a little while ago was nice enough. I just wasn't expecting her. And I surely wasn't expecting Eliza McIntyre to trip into my bedroom early this morning and set her roses down on my bedside table with such an air about her as if I'd broken my foot for the one and only purpose of having her arrive at seven thirty to bring me a bouquet. She's been coming often enough since I broke my foot, but never before eleven or twelve in the morning.

That young woman from the *Bulletin* sat right down, and before she even smoothed her skirt or crossed her legs she looked straight at me and asked if I had a recipe for a happy marriage. I think she should at least have started off by saying it was a nice day or asking how I felt, especially as it was perfectly obvious that I had a broken foot.

I told her that I certainly didn't have any recipe for a happy marriage, but I'd like to know why I was being asked, and she said it was almost St. Valentine's Day and she had been assigned to write a feature article on love,

228

and since I must know more about love than anybody else in town she and her editor thought that my opinions should have a prominent place in the article.

Her explanation put me more out of sorts than her question. But whatever else I may or may not be I'm a good-natured woman. I suppose it was my broken foot that made me feel irritable.

At that very moment Eliza's giggle came way up the back stairwell from the kitchen, and it was followed by my husband's laughter, and I heard dishes rattle and pans clank, and all that added fire to my irritability.

The one thing I can't abide, never have been able to stand, is to have somebody in my kitchen. Stay out of my kitchen and my pantry, that's my motto. People always seem to think they're putting things back in the right place, but they never do. How well I remember Aunt Mary Ellen saying she just wanted to make us a cup of tea and to cut some slices of lemon to go with it. I could have made that tea as well as she did, but she wouldn't let me. I couldn't tell a bit of difference between her tea and mine, yet she put my favorite paring knife some place or other and it didn't turn up until eight months later, underneath a stack of cheese graters. That was a good twenty years ago and poor Aunt Mary Ellen has been in her grave for ten, and yet I still think about that paring knife and get uneasy when someone is in my kitchen.

Well, that young woman leaned forward and had an equally dumbfounding question. She asked me just which husband I had now.

I don't look at things—at husbands—like that. So I didn't answer her. I was too aghast. And then again from the kitchen came the sound of Eliza's giggle and Lewis's whoop.

I've known Eliza Moore, now Eliza McIntyre, all my life. In school she was two grades ahead of me from the very beginning, but the way she tells it now she was three grades behind me; but those school records are somewhere, however yellowed and crumbled they may be, and there's no need for Eliza to try to pretend she's younger than I am when she's two years older. Not that it matters. I just don't want her in my kitchen.

That young woman was mistaking my silence. She leaned close as if I were either deaf or a very young child who hadn't paid attention. How many times have you been married? she asked in a very loud voice.

When she put it like that, how could I answer her? Husbands aren't like teacups. I can't count them off and gloat over them the way Cousin Lutie used to stand in front of her china cabinets, saying she had so many of this pattern and so many of that.

For goodness sake, I had them one at a time, a husband at a time, and perfectly legally. They all just died on me. I couldn't stay the hand of fate. I was always a sod widow—there weren't any grass widows in our family. As Mama said, it runs in our family to be with our husbands till death us do part. The way that girl put her question, it sounded as if I had a whole bunch of husbands at one time like a line of chorus men in a musical show.

I didn't know how to answer her. I lay back on my pillows with not a word to say, as if the cat had run off with my tongue.

It's sheer accident that I ever married to begin with. I didn't want to. Not that I had anything against marriage or had anything else special to do. But Mama talked me into it. Baby, she said, other women look down on women who don't marry. Besides, you don't have any particular talent and Aunt Sallie Mae, for all her talk, may not leave you a penny. I don't think she ever forgave me for not naming you after her, and all her hinting about leaving you her money may just be her spiteful way of getting back at me.

Besides, Mama said, the way she's held on to her money, even if she did leave it to you, there would be so many strings attached you'd have to have a corps of Philadelphia lawyers to read the fine print before you could withdraw as much as a twenty-five-cent piece. If I were you, baby, Mama said, I'd go and get married. If you don't marry you won't get invited any place except as a last resort, when they need somebody at the last minute to keep from having thirteen at table. And it's nice to have somebody to open the door for you and carry your packages. A husband can be handy.

So I married Ray.

Well, Ray and I hadn't been married six months when along came Mama with a handkerchief in her hand and dabbing at her eyes. Baby, she said, the wife is always the last one to know. I've just got to tell you what everyone is talking about. I know how good you are and how lacking in suspicion, but the whole town is buzzing. It's Ray and Marjorie Brown.

Ray was nice and I was fond of him. He called me Lucyhoney, exactly as if it were one word. Sometimes for short he called me Lucyhon. He didn't have much stamina or backbone—how could he when he was the only child and spoiled rotten by his mother and grandma and three maiden aunts?

Baby, Mama said, and her tears had dried and she was now using her handkerchief to fan herself with, don't you be gullible. I can't stand for you to be mistreated or betrayed. Should I go to the rector and tell him to talk to Ray and point out where his duty lies? Or should I ask your uncle Jonathan to talk to Ray man-to-man?

I said, Mama, it's nobody's fault but my own. For heaven's sake let Ray do what he wants to do. He doesn't need anyone to tell him when he can come and go and what persons he can see. It's his house and he's paying the bills. Besides, his taking up with Marjorie Brown is no discredit to me—she's a lot prettier than I am. I think it's romantic and spunky of Ray. Why, Marjorie Brown is a married woman. Her husband might shoot Ray.

I don't know exactly what it was that cooled Ray down. He was back penitent and sheep-eyed, begging forgiveness. I'm proud of you, Ray, I said. Why, until you married me you were so timid you wouldn't have said boo to a goose, and here you've been having an illicit affair. I think it's grand. Marjorie Brown's husband might have horsewhipped you.

Ray grinned and said, I really have picked me a wife.

And he never looked at another woman again as long as he lived. Which unfortunately wasn't very long.

I got to thinking about him feeling guilty and apologizing to me, when I was the one to blame—I hadn't done enough for him, and I wanted to do something real nice for him, so I thought of that cake recipe. Except we called it a receipt. It had been in the family for years—centuries, you might say, solemnly handed down from mother to daughter, time out of mind.

And so when that girl asked me whether I had a recipe for a happy marriage I didn't give the receipt a thought. Besides, I'm sure she didn't mean an actual recipe, but some kind of formula like let the husband know he's boss, or some such foolishness.

Anyway, there I was feeling penitent about not giving Ray the attention he should have had so that he was bored enough by me to go out and risk his life at the hands of Marjorie Brown's jealous husband.

So I thought, well, it's the hardest receipt I've ever studied and has more ingredients than I've ever heard of, but it's the least I can do for Ray. So I went here and there to the grocery stores, to drugstores, to apothecaries, to people who said, good Lord, no, we don't carry that but if you've got to have it try so-and-so, who turned out to be somebody way out in the country that looked at me as if I asked for the element that would turn base metal into gold and finally came back with a little packet and a foolish question as to what on earth I needed that for.

Then I came on back home and began grinding and pounding and mixing and baking and sitting in the kitchen waiting for the mixture to rise. When it was done it was the prettiest thing I had ever baked.

I served it for dessert that night.

Ray began to eat the cake and to savor it and to say extravagant things to me, and when he finished the first slice he said, Lucyhon, may I have another piece, a big one, please.

Why, Ray, it's all yours to eat as you like, I said.

After a while he pushed the plate away and looked at me with a wonderful expression of gratitude on his face and he said, Oh, Lucyhoney, I could die happy. And as far as I know he did.

When I tapped on his door the next morning to give him his first cup of coffee and open the shutters and turn on his bathwater he was dead, and there was the sweetest smile on his face.

But that young woman was still looking at me while I had been reminiscing, and she was fluttering her notes and wetting her lips with her tongue like a speaker with lots of things to say. And she sort of bawled out at me as if I were an entire audience whose attention had strayed: Do you think that the way to a man's heart is through his stomach?

Excuse me, young lady, I wanted to say, but I never heard of Cleopatra saying to Mark Antony or any of the others she favored, Here, won't you taste some of my potato salad, and I may be wrong because my reading of history is skimpy, but it sounds a little unlikely that Madame de Pompadour ever whispered into the ear of Louis XV, I've baked the nicest casserole for you.

My not answering put the girl off, and I felt that I ought to apologize, yet I couldn't bring myself around to it.

She glanced at her notes to the next question, and was almost beet-red from embarrassment when she asked: Did the financial situation of your husbands ever have anything to do with your marrying them?

I didn't even open my mouth. I was as silent as the tomb. Her questions kept getting more and more irrelevant. And I was getting more stupefied as her eyes kept running up and down her list of questions.

She tried another one: What do you think is the best way to get a husband?

Now that's a question I have never asked myself and about which I have nothing to offer anybody in a St. Valentine's Day article or elsewhere. I have never gone out to *get* a husband. I haven't ever, as that old-fashioned expression has it, set my cap for anybody.

Take Lewis, who is this minute in the kitchen giggling with Eliza McIntyre. I certainly did not set out to get him. It was some months after Alton—no, Edward—had died, and people were trying to cheer me up, not that I needed any cheering up. I mean, after all the losses I've sustained

I've become philosophical. But my cousin Wanda's grandson had an exhibition of paintings. The poor deluded boy isn't talented, not a bit. All the same I bought two of his paintings, which are downstairs in the hall closet, shut off from all eyes.

Anyway, at the opening of the exhibition there was Lewis, looking all forlorn. He had come because the boy was a distant cousin of his dead wife. Lewis leaped up from a bench when he got a glimpse of me and said, Why, Lucy, I haven't seen you in donkey's years, and we stood there talking while everybody was going ooh and aah over the boy's paintings, and Lewis said he was hungry and I asked him to come on home with me and have a bite to eat.

I fixed a quick supper and Lewis ate like a starving man, and then we sat in the back parlor and talked about this and that, and about midnight he said, Lucy, I don't want to leave. This is the nicest feeling I've ever had, being here with you. I don't mean to be disrespectful to the dead, but there wasn't any love lost between Ramona and me. I'd like to stay on here forever.

Well, after that—after a man's revealed his innermost thoughts to you—you can't just show him the door. Besides, I couldn't put him out because it was beginning to snow, and in a little while the snow turned to sleet. He might have fallen and broken his neck going down the front steps, and I'd have had that on my conscience the rest of my life.

Lewis, I said, it seems foolish at this stage of the game for me to worry about my reputation, but thank heaven Cousin Alice came down from Washington for the exhibition and is staying with me, and she can chaperon us until we can make things perfectly legal and aboveboard.

That's how it happened.

You don't plan things like that, I wanted to tell the girl. They happen in spite of you. So it's silly of you to ask me what the best way is to get a husband.

My silence hadn't bothered her a bit. She sort of closed one eye like somebody about to take aim with a rifle and asked: Exactly how many times have you been married?

Well, she had backed up. She was repeating herself.

That was practically the same question she had asked me earlier. It had been put a little differently this time, that was all.

I certainly had no intention of telling her the truth, which was that I wasn't exactly sure myself. Sometimes my husbands become a little blurred and blended. Sometimes I have to sit down with pencil and paper and figure it out.

Anyhow, that's certainly no way to look at husbands—the exact number or the exact sequence.

My husbands were an exceptional bunch of men, if I do say so. And fine-looking, too. Even Art, who had a harelip. And they were all good providers. Rich and didn't mind spending their money—not like some rich people. Not that I needed money. Because Aunt Sallie Mae, for all Mama's suspicions, left me hers, and there was nothing spiteful about her stipulations. I could have the money when, as, and how I wanted it.

Anyway, I never have cared about money or what it could buy for me.

There's nothing much I can spend it on for myself. Jewelry doesn't suit me. My fingers are short and stubby and my hands are square—no need to call attention to them by wearing rings. Besides, rings bother me. I like to cook and rings get in the way. Necklaces choke me and earrings pinch. As for fur coats, mink or chinchilla or just plain squirrel—well, I don't like the idea of anything that has lived ending up draped around me.

So money personally means little to me. But it's nice to pass along. Nothing gives me greater pleasure, and there's not a husband of mine who hasn't ended up without having a clinic or a college library or a hospital wing or a research laboratory or something of the sort founded in his honor and named after him. Sometimes I've had to rob Peter to pay Paul. I mean, some of them have left more than others, and once in a while I've had to take some of what one left me to pay on the endowment for another. But it all evened itself out.

Except for Buster. There was certainly a nice surplus where Buster was concerned. He lived the shortest time and left me the most money of any of my husbands. For every month I lived with him I inherited a million dollars. Five.

My silent reminiscing like that wasn't helping the girl with her St. Valentine's Day article. If I had been in anybody's house and the hostess was as taciturn as I was, I'd have excused myself and reached for the knob of the front door.

But, if anything, that young lady became even more impertinent.

Have you had a favorite among your husbands? she asked and her tongue flicked out like a snake's.

I was silent even when my husbands asked that question. Sometimes they would show a little jealousy for their predecessors and make unkind remarks. But naturally I did everything in my power to reassure whoever made a disparaging remark about another.

All my husbands have been fine men, I would say in such a case, but I do believe you're the finest of the lot. I said it whether I really thought so or not.

But I had nothing at all to say to that girl on the subject.

Yet if I ever got to the point of being forced to rank my husbands, I guess Luther would be very nearly at the bottom of the list. He was the only teetotaler in the bunch. I hadn't noticed how he felt about drink until after we were married—that's when things you've overlooked during courtship can confront you like a slap in the face. Luther would squirm when wine was served to guests during a meal, and his eyes looked up prayerfully toward heaven when anybody took a second glass. At least he restrained himself to the extent of not saying any word of reproach to a guest, but Mama said she always expected him to hand around some of those tracts that warn against the pitfalls that lie in wait for drunkards.

Poor man. He was run over by a beer truck.

The irony of it, Mama said. There's a lesson in it for us all. And it was broad daylight, she said, shaking her head, not even dark, so that we can't comfort ourselves that Luther didn't know what hit him.

Not long after Luther's unfortunate accident Matthew

appeared—on tiptoe, you might say. He was awfully short
and always stretched himself to look taller. He was terri-
bly apologetic about his height. I'd ask you to marry me,
Lucy, he said, but all your husbands have been over six
feet tall. Height didn't enter into it, I told him, and it
wasn't very long before Matthew and I were married.

He seemed to walk on tiptoe and I scrunched down, and
still there was an awful gap between us, and he would go
on about Napoleon almost conquering the world in spite of
being short. I started wearing low-heeled shoes and walking hunched over, and Mama said, For God's sake, Baby,
you can push tact too far. You never were beautiful but
you had an air about you and no reigning queen ever had a
more elegant walk, and here you are slumping. Your aunt
Francine was married to a midget, as you well know, but
there wasn't any of this bending down and hunching over.
She let him be his height and he let her be hers. So stop
this foolishness.

But I couldn't. I still tried literally to meet Matthew
more than halfway. And I had this feeling—well, why
shouldn't I have it, seeing as how they had all died on me—
that Matthew wasn't long for this world, and it was my
duty to make him feel as important and as tall as I possibly
could during the little time that was left to him.

Matthew died happy. I have every reason to believe it.
But then, as Mama said, they all died happy.

Never again, Mama, I said. Never again. I feel like Typhoid Mary or somebody who brings doom on men's heads.

Never is a long time, Mama said.

And she was right. I married Hugh.

I think it was Hugh.

Two things I was proud of and am proud of. I never spoke
a harsh word to any one of my husbands and I never did
call one of them by another's name, and that took a lot of
doing because after a while they just all sort of melted together in my mind.

After every loss, Homer was the greatest solace and comfort to me. Until he retired last year Homer was the medical examiner, and he was a childhood friend, though I
never saw him except in his line of duty, you might say.

It's the law here, and perhaps elsewhere, that if anyone dies unattended or from causes that aren't obvious, the medical examiner must be informed.

The first few times I had to call Homer I was chagrined. I felt apologetic, a little like calling the doctor up in the middle of the night when, however much the pain may be troubling you, you're afraid it's a false alarm and the doctor will hold it against you for disturbing his sleep.

But Homer always was jovial when I called him. I guess that's not the right word. Homer was reassuring, not jovial. Anytime, Lucy, anytime at all, he would say when I began to apologize for having to call him.

I think it was right after Sam died. Or was it Carl? It could have been George. Anyway, Homer was there reassuring me as always, and then this look of sorrow or regret clouded his features. It's a damned pity, Lucy, he said, you can't work me in somewhere or other. You weren't the prettiest little girl in the third grade, or the smartest, but damned if from the beginning there hasn't been something about you. I remember, he said, that when we were in the fourth grade I got so worked up over you that I didn't pass a single subject but arithmetic and had to take the whole term over. Of course you were promoted, so for the rest of my life you've been just out of my reach.

Why, Homer, I said, that's the sweetest thing anybody has ever said to me.

I had it in the back of my mind once the funeral was over and everything was on an even keel again that I'd ask Homer over for supper one night. But it seemed so calculating, as if I was raking him up on that sweet remark he had made about wishing I had worked him in somewhere among my husbands. So I decided against it.

Instead I married Beau Green.

There they go laughing again—Eliza and Lewis down in the kitchen. *My* kitchen.

It's funny that Eliza has turned up in my kitchen, acting very much at home, when she's the one and only person in this town I never have felt very friendly toward—at least, not since word got to me that she had said I snatched Beau Green right from under her nose.

That wasn't a nice thing for her to say. Besides, there wasn't a word of truth in it. I'd like to see the man that can be snatched from under anybody's nose unless he wanted to be.

Eliza was surely welcome to Beau Green if she had wanted him and if he had wanted her.

Why, I'd planned to take a trip around the world, already had my tickets and reservations, and had to put it off for good because Beau wouldn't budge any farther away from home than to go to Green River—named for his family—to fish. I really wanted to take that cruise—had my heart especially set on seeing the Taj Mahal by moonlight—but Beau kept on saying if I didn't marry him he would do something desperate, which I took to mean he'd kill himself or take to drink. So I canceled all those reservations and turned in all those tickets and married him.

Well, Eliza would certainly have been welcome to Beau.

I've already emphasized that I don't like to rank my husbands, but in many ways Beau was the least satisfactory one I ever had. It was his nature to be a killjoy—he had no sense of the joy of living, and once he set his mind on something he went ahead with it, no matter if it pleased anybody else or not.

He knew good and well I didn't care for jewelry. But my preference didn't matter to Beau Green, not one bit. Here he came with this package and I opened it. I tried to muster all my politeness when I saw that it was a diamond. Darling, I said, you're sweet to give me a present, but this is a little bit big, isn't it?

It's thirty-seven carats, he said.

I felt like I ought to take it around on a sofa pillow instead of wearing it, but I did wear it twice and felt as conspicuous and as much of a showoff as if I'd been waving a peacock fan around and about.

It was and is my habit when I get upset with someone to go to my room and write my grievances down and get myself back in a good humor, just as I'm doing now because of that girl's questions; but sometimes it seemed like there wasn't enough paper in the world on which to write down my complaints against Beau.

Then I would blame myself. Beau was just being Beau. Like all God's creatures he was behaving the way he was made, and I felt so guilty that I decided I ought to do something for him to show I really loved and respected him, as deep in my heart I did.

So I decided to make him a cake by that elaborate recipe that had been in our family nobody is sure for how long. I took all one day to do the shopping for it. The next day I got up at five and stayed in the kitchen until late afternoon.

Well, Beau was a bit peckish when it came to eating the cake. Yet he had the sweetest tooth of any of my husbands.

Listen, darling, I said when he was mulish about eating it, I made this special for you—it's taken the best part of two days. I smiled at him and asked wouldn't he please at least taste it to please me. Really, I was put out when I thought of all the work that had gone into it. For one terrible second I wished it were a custard pie and I could throw it right in his face, like in one of those old Keystone comedies; and then I remembered that we were sworn to cherish each other, so I just put one arm around his shoulder and with my free hand I pushed the cake a little closer and said, Belle wants Beau to eat at least one small bite. Belle was a foolish pet name he sometimes called me because he thought it was clever for him to be Beau and for me to be Belle.

He looked sheepish and picked up his fork and I knew he was trying to please me, the way I had tried to please him by wearing that thirty-seven-carat diamond twice.

Goodness, Belle, he said, when he swallowed his first mouthful, this is delicious.

Now, darling, you be careful, I said. That cake is rich.

Best thing I ever ate, he said, and groped around on the plate for the crumbs, and I said, Darling, wouldn't you like a little coffee to wash it down?

He didn't answer, just sat there smiling. Then after a little he said he was feeling numb. I can't feel a thing in my feet, he said. I ran for the rubbing alcohol and pulled off his shoes and socks and started rubbing his feet, and there was a sort of spasm and his toes curled under, but nothing affected that smile on his face.

Homer, I said a little later—because of course I had to telephone him about Beau's death—what on earth is it? Could it be something he's eaten? And Homer said, What do you mean, something he's eaten? Of course not. You set the best table in the county. You're famous for your cooking. It couldn't be anything he's eaten. Don't be foolish, Lucy. He began to pat me on the shoulder and he had said, I read a book about guilt and loss and it said the bereaved often hold themselves responsible for the deaths of their beloved ones. But I thought you had better sense than that, Lucy.

Homer was a little bit harsh with me that time.

Julius Babb settled Beau's estate. Beau left you a tidy sum, all right, he said, and I wanted to say right back at him but didn't: not as tidy as most of the others left me.

Right then that young woman from the *Bulletin* repeated her last question.

Have you had a favorite among your husbands? Her tone was that of a prosecuting attorney and had nothing to do with a reporter interested in writing about love for St. Valentine's Day.

I had had enough of her and her questions. I dragged myself up to a sitting position in the bed. Listen here, young lady, I said. It looks as if I've gotten off on the wrong foot with you—and then we both laughed at the pun I had made.

The laughter put us both in a good humor and then I tried to explain that I had an unexpected caller downstairs who needed some attention, and that I really was willing to cooperate on the St. Valentine's Day article, but all those questions at first hearing had sort of stunned me. It was like taking an examination and finding all the questions a surprise. I told her if she would leave her list with me I'd mull over it, and she could come back tomorrow and I'd be prepared with my answers and be a little more presentable than I was now, wearing a rumpled wrapper and with my hair uncombed.

Well, she was as sweet as apple pie and handed over the list of questions and said she hoped that ten o'clock tomorrow morning would be fine; and I said, Yes, it would.

There goes Eliza's laugh again. It's more of a caw than a laugh. I shouldn't think that. But it's been such a strange day, with that young reporter being here and Eliza showing up so early.

Come to think of it, Eliza has done very well for herself, as far as marrying goes. That reporter should ask Eliza some of those questions.

Mama was a charitable woman all her life and she lived to be eighty-nine, but Eliza always rubbed Mama's skin the wrong way. To tell the truth, Eliza rubbed the skin of all the women in this town the wrong way. It's not right, Baby, Mama said, when other women have skimped and saved and cut corners all their lives and then when they're in their last sickness here comes Eliza getting her foot in the door just because she's a trained nurse. Then the next thing you hear, Eliza has married the widower and gets in one fell swoop what it took the dead wife a lifetime to accumulate.

That wasn't the most generous way in the world for Mama to put it, but I've heard it put much harsher by others. Mrs. Perkerson across the street, for one. Eliza is like a vulture, Mrs. Perkerson said. First she watches the wives die, then she marries, and then she watches the husbands die. Pretty soon it's widow's weeds for Eliza and a nice-sized bank account, not to mention some of the most valuable real estate in town.

Why, Mrs. Perkerson said the last time I saw her, I know that Lois Eubanks McIntyre is turning in her grave thinking of Eliza inheriting that big estate, with gardens copied after the Villa d'Este. And they tell you nursing is hard work.

I hadn't seen Eliza in some time. We were friendly enough, but not real friends, never had been, and I was especially hurt after hearing what she said about me taking Beau Green away from her. But we would stop and chat when we bumped into each other downtown, and then back off smiling and saying we must get together. But nothing ever came of it.

And then three weeks ago Eliza telephoned and I thought for sure somebody was dead. But, no, she was as sweet as magnolia blossoms and cooing as if we saw each other every day, and she invited me to come by that afternoon for a cup of tea or a glass of sherry. I asked her if there was anything special, and she said she didn't think there had to be any special reason for old friends to meet, but, yes, there was something special. She wanted me to see her gardens—of course they weren't her gardens, except by default, they were Lois Eubanks McIntyre's gardens—which she had opened for the Church Guild Benefit Tour and I hadn't come. So she wanted me to see them that afternoon.

It was all so sudden that she caught me off guard. I didn't want to go and there wasn't any reason for me to go, but for the life of me I couldn't think of an excuse not to go. And so I went.

The gardens really were beautiful, and I'm crazy about flowers.

Eliza gave me a personally guided tour. There were lots of paths and steep steps and unexpected turnings, and I was so delighted by the flowers that I foolishly didn't pay attention to my footing. I wasn't used to walking on so much gravel or going up and down uneven stone steps and Eliza didn't give me any warning.

Then all of a sudden, it was the strangest feeling, not as if I'd fallen but as if I'd been pushed, and there Eliza was leaning over me saying she could never forgive herself for not telling me about the broken step, and I was to lie right there and not move until the doctor could come, and what a pity it was that what she had wanted to be a treat for me had turned into a tragedy. Which was making a whole lot more out of it than need be because it was only a broken foot—not that it hasn't been inconvenient.

But Eliza has been fluttering around for three weeks saying that I should sue her as she carried liability insurance, and anyway it was lucky she was a nurse and could see that I got devoted attention. I don't need a nurse, but she has insisted on coming every day, and on some days several times; she seems to be popping in and out of the house like a cuckoo clock.

I had better get on with that reporter's questions.

Do you have a recipe for a happy marriage?

I've already told her I don't, and of course there's no such thing as a recipe for a happy marriage; but I could tell her this practice I have of working through my grievances and dissatisfactions by writing down what bothers me and then tearing up what I've written. For all I know it might work for somebody else, too.

I didn't hear Eliza coming up the stairs. It startled me when I looked up and saw her at my bedside. What if she discovered I was writing about her? What if she grabbed the notebook out of my hands and started to read it? There isn't a thing I could do to stop her.

But she just smiled and asked if I was ready for lunch and she hoped I'd worked up a good appetite. How on earth she thinks I could have worked up an appetite by lying in bed I don't know, but that's Eliza for you, and all she had fixed was canned soup and it wasn't hot.

All I wanted was just to blot everything out—that girl's questions, Eliza's presence in my home, my broken foot.

I would have thought that I couldn't have gone to sleep in a thousand years. But I was so drowsy that I couldn't even close the notebook, much less hide it under the covers.

I don't know what woke me up. It was pitch-dark, but dark comes so soon these winter days you can't tell whether it's early dark or midnight.

I felt refreshed after my long nap and equal to anything. I was ready to answer any question on that girl's list.

The notebook was still open beside me and I thought that if Eliza had been in here and had seen what I had written about her it served her right.

Then from the kitchen rose a wonderful smell and there was a lot of noise downstairs. Suddenly the back stairway and hall were flooded with light, and then Eliza and Lewis were at my door and they were grinning and saying they had a surprise for me. Then Lewis turned and picked up something from a table in the hall and brought it proudly toward me. I couldn't tell what it was. It was red and heart-shaped and had something white on top. At first I thought it might be a hat, and then I groped for my distance glasses, but even with them on I still couldn't tell what Lewis was carrying.

Lewis held out the tray. It's a St. Valentine's Day cake, he said, and Eliza said, we iced it and decorated it for you; then Lewis tilted it gently and I saw L U C Y in wobbly letters spread all across the top.

I don't usually eat sweets. So their labor of love was lost on me. Then I thought how kind it was that they had gone to all that trouble, and I forgave them for messing up my kitchen and meddling with my recipes—or maybe they had just used a mix. Anyway, I felt I had to show my appreciation, and it certainly wouldn't kill me to eat some of their cake.

They watched me with such pride and delight as I ate the cake that I took a second piece. When I had finished they said it would be best for me to rest, and I asked them to take the cake and eat what they wanted, then wrap it in foil.

And now the whole house is quiet.

I never felt better in my life. I'm smiling a great big contented smile. It must look exactly like that last sweet smile on all my husbands' faces—except Luther, who was run over by a beer truck.

I feel wonderful and so relaxed.

But I can hardly hold this pencil.

Goodness, it's

f
  a
   l
    l
     i
      n
       g

THE DEADLY EGG

by Janwillem van de Wetering

In 1971, when he was forty-one, Janwillem van de Wetering was to write about his experiences in a Buddhist monastery. With the appearance of the autobiographical The Empty Mirror, *his writing career was launched.*

Two years later, while reading Simenon he thought, "I could do that!" Tapping into his experience in the Amsterdam Special Constabulary, he began his internationally successful series of "cop books," as he calls them, about Sergeant de Gier and Adjutant Grijpstra. The first four or five plots came at once to him.

He produces a novel a year, writing in English and Dutch.

The siren of the tiny dented Volkswagen shrieked forlornly between the naked trees of the Amsterdam Forest, the city's largest park, set on its southern edge: several square miles of willows, poplars, and wild growing alders, surrounding ponds and lining paths. The paths were restricted to pedestrians and cyclists, but the Volkswagen had ignored the many No Entry signs, quite legally, for the vehicle belonged to the Municipal Police and more especially to its Criminal Investigation Department, or the Murder Brigade. Even so it looked lost, and its howl seemed defensive.

It was Easter Sunday and it rained, and the car's two occupants, Detective Adjutant Grijpstra and Detective Sergeant de Gier, sat hunched in their overcoats, watching the squeaky rusted wipers trying to deal with the steady drizzle. The car should have been junked some years before, but the adjutant had lost the form that would have done away with his aging transport, lost it on purpose and with the sergeant's consent. They had grown fond of the Volkswagen, of its shabbiness and its ability to melt away in traffic.

But they weren't fond of the car now. The heater didn't work, it was cold, and it was early. Not yet nine o'clock on a Sunday is early, especially when the Sunday is Easter. Technically they were both off-duty, but they had been telephoned out of warm beds by headquarters' radio room. A dead man dangling from a branch in the forest; please, would they care to have a look at the dead man?

Grijpstra's stubby index finger silenced the siren. They had followed several miles of winding paths so far and hadn't come across anything alive except tall blue herons, fishing in the ponds and moats and flapping away slowly when the car came too close for their comfort.

"You know who reported the corpse? I wasn't awake when the radio room talked to me."

De Gier had been smoking silently. His handsome head with the perfect curls turned obediently to face his superior. "Yes, a gentleman jogger. He said he jogged right into the body's feet. Gave him a start. He ran all the way to the nearest telephone booth, phoned headquarters, then headquarters phoned us, and that's why we are here, I suppose. I am a little asleep myself—we are here, aren't we?"

They could hear another siren, and another. Two limousines came roaring toward the Volkswagen, and Grijpstra cursed and made the little car turn off the path and slide into a soggy lawn; they could feel its wheel sink into the mud.

The limousines stopped and men poured out of them; the men pushed the Volkswagen back on the path.

"Morning, Adjutant, morning, Sergeant. Where is the corpse?"

"Shouldn't you know too?"

"No, Adjutant," several men said simultaneously, "but we thought maybe you know. All we know is that the corpse is in the Amsterdam Forest and that this is the Amsterdam Forest."

Grijpstra addressed the sergeant. "You know?"

De Gier's well modulated baritone chanted the instructions. "Turn right after the big pond, right again, then left. Or the other way round. I think I have it right, we should be close."

The three cars drove about for a few minutes more until they were waved down by a man dressed in what seemed to be long blue underwear. The jogger ran ahead, bouncing energetically, and led them to their destination. The men from the limousines brought out their boxes and suitcases, then cameras clicked and a video recorder hummed. The corpse hung on and the two detectives watched it hang.

"Neat," Grijpstra said, "very neat. Don't you think it is neat?"

The sergeant grunted.

"Here. Brought a folding campstool and some nice new rope, made a perfect noose, slipped it around his neck, kicked the stool. Anything suspicious, gentlemen?"

The men from the limousines said there was not. They had found footprints—the prints of the corpse's boots. There were no other prints, except the jogger's. The jogger's statement was taken, he was thanked and sent on his sporting way. A police ambulance arrived and the corpse was cut loose, examined by doctor and detectives, and carried off. The detectives saluted the corpse quietly by inclining their heads.

"In his sixties," the sergeant said, "well dressed in old but expensive clothes. Clean shirt. Tie. Short gray beard, clipped. Man who took care of himself. A faint smell of liquor—he must have had a few to give him courage. Absolutely nothing in his pockets. I looked in the collar of his shirt—no laundry mark. He went to some trouble to be nameless. Maybe something will turn up when they strip him at the mortuary; we should phone in an hour's time."

Grijpstra looked hopeful. "Suicide?"

"I would think so. Came here by himself, no traces of anybody else. No signs of a struggle. The man knew what he wanted to do, and did it, all by himself. But he didn't leave a note; that wasn't very thoughtful."

"Right," Grijpstra said, "time for breakfast, Sergeant! We'll have it at the airport—that's close and convenient. We can show our police cards and get through the customs barrier; the restaurant on the far side is better than the coffee shop on the near side."

De Gier activated the radio when they got back to the car.

"Male corpse, balding but with short gray beard. Dentures. Blue eyes. Sixty-odd years old. Three-piece blue suit, elegant dark gray overcoat, no hat. No identification."

"Thank you," the radio said.

"Looks very much like suicide. Do you have any missing persons of that description in your files?"

"No, not so far."

"We'll be off for breakfast and will call in again on our way back."

"Echrem," the radio said sadly, "there's something else. Sorry."

De Gier stared at a duck waddling across the path and trailing seven furry ducklings. He began to mumble. Adjutant Grijpstra mumbled with him. The mumbled four-letter words interspersed with mild curses formed a background for the radio's well-articulated message. They were given an address on the other side of the city. "The lady was poisoned, presumably by a chocolate Easter egg. The ambulance that answered the distress call just radioed in. They are taking her to hospital. The ambulance driver thought the poison was either parathion, something used in agriculture, or arsenic. His assistant is pumping out the patient's stomach. She is in a bad way but not dead yet."

Grijpstra grabbed the microphone from de Gier's limp hand. "So if the lady is on her way to hospital who is left in the house you want us to go to?"

"Her husband, man by the name of Moozen, a lawyer, I believe."

"What hospital is Mrs. Moozen being taken to?"

"The Wilhelmina."

"And you have no one else on call? Sergeant de Gier and I are supposed to be off-duty for Easter, you know!"

"No," the radio's female voice said, "no, Adjutant. We never have much crime on Easter day, especially not in the morning. There are only two detectives on duty and they are out on a case too—some boys have derailed a streetcar with matches."

"Right," Grijpstra said coldly, "we are on our way."

The old Volkswagen made an effort to jump away, protesting feebly. De Gier was still muttering but had stopped cursing. "Streetcar? Matches?"

"Yes. They take an empty cartridge, fill it with matchheads, then close the open end with a hammer. Very simple. All you have to do is insert the cartridge into the streetcar's rail and when the old tram comes clanging along, the sudden impact makes the cartridge explode. If you use two or three cartridges the explosion may be strong enough to lift the wheel out of the rail. Didn't you ever try that? I used to do it as a boy. The only problem was to get the cartridges. We had to sneak around on the rifle range with the chance of getting shot at."

"No," de Gier said. "Pity. Never thought of it, and it sounds like a good game."

He looked out of the window. The car had left the park and was racing toward the city's center through long empty avenues. There was no life in the huge apartment buildings lining the old city—nobody had bothered to get up yet. Ten o'clock and the citizenry wasn't even considering the possibility of slouching into the kitchen for a first cup of coffee.

But one man had bothered to get up early and had strolled into the park, carrying his folding chair and a piece of rope to break off the painful course of his life, once and for all. An elderly man in good but old clothes. De Gier saw the man's beard again, a nicely cared-for growth. The police doctor had said that he hadn't been dead long. A man alone in the night that would have led him to Easter, a man by himself in a deserted park, testing the strength of his rope, fitting his head into the noose, kicking the campstool.

"Bah!" he said aloud.

Grijpstra had steered the car through a red light and was turning the wheel.

"What's that?"

"Nothing. Just bah."

"Bah is right," Grijpstra said.

They found the house, a bungalow, on the luxurious extreme north side of the city. Spring was trying to revive the small lawn and a magnolia tree was in hesitant bloom. Bright yellow crocuses set off the path. Grijpstra looked at the crocuses. He didn't seem pleased.

"Crocuses," de Gier said, "very nice. Jolly little flowers."

"No. Unimaginative plants, manufactured, not grown. Computer plants. They make the bulbs in a machine and program them to look stupid. Go ahead, Sergeant, press the bell."

"Really?" the sergeant asked.

Grijpstra's jowls sagged. "Yes. They are like mass-manufactured cheese, tasteless; cheese is probably made with the same machines."

"Cheese," de Gier said moistly, "there's nothing wrong with cheese either, apart from not having any right now. Breakfast has slipped by, you know." He glanced at his watch.

They read the nameplate while the bell rang. *H. F. Moozen, Attorney at Law.* The door opened. A man in a housecoat made out of brightly striped towel material said good morning. The detectives showed their identifications. The man nodded and stepped back. A pleasant man, still young, thirty years or a bit more. The ideal model for an ad in a ladies' magazine. A background man, showing off a modern house, or a mini-car, or expensive furniture. The sort of man ladies would like to have around. Quiet, secure, mildly good-looking. Not a passionate man, but lawyers seldom are. Lawyers practice detachment; they identify with their clients, but only up to a point.

"You won't take long, I hope," Mr. Moozen said. "I wanted to go with the ambulance, but the driver said you were on the way, and that I wouldn't be of any help if I stayed with my wife."

"Was your wife conscious when she left here, sir?"

"Barely. She couldn't speak."

"She ate an egg, a chocolate egg?"

"Yes. I don't care for chocolate myself. It was a gift, we thought, from friends. I had to let the dog out early this morning, an hour ago, and there was an Easter bunny sit-

ting on the path. He held an egg wrapped up in silver paper. I took him in, woke up my wife, and showed the bunny
to her, and she took the egg and ate it, then became ill. I
telephoned for the ambulance and they came almost immediately. I would like to go to the hospital now."

"Come in our car, sir. Can I see the bunny?"

Mr. Moozen took off the housecoat and put on a jacket.
He opened the door leading to the kitchen and a small dog
jumped around the detectives, yapping greetings. The
bunny stood on the kitchen counter; it was almost a foot
high. Grijpstra tapped its back with his knuckles; it
sounded solid.

"Hey," de Gier said. He turned the bunny around and
showed it to Grijpstra.

"Brwah!" Grijpstra said.

The rabbit's toothless mouth gaped. The beast's eyes
were close together and deeply sunk into the skull. Its ears
stood up aggressively. The bunny leered at them, its torso
crouched; the paws that had held the deadly egg seemed
ready to punch.

"It's roaring," de Gier said. "See? A roaring rabbit.
Easter bunnies are supposed to smile."

"Shall we go?" Mr. Moozen asked.

They used the siren, and the trip to the hospital didn't
take ten minutes. The city was still quiet. But there
proved to be no hurry. An energetic, bright young nurse
led them to a waiting room. Mrs. Moozen was being
worked on; her condition was still critical. The nurse
would let them know if there was any change.

"Can we smoke?" Grijpstra asked.

"If you must." The nurse smiled coldly, appraised de
Gier's tall, wide-shouldered body with a possessive femi-
nist glance, swung her hips, and turned to the door.

"Any coffee?"

"There's a machine in the hall. Don't smoke in the hall,
please."

There were several posters in the waiting room. A picture of a cigarette pointing to a skull with crossed bones. A
picture of a happy child biting into an apple. A picture of a
drunken driver (bubbles surrounding his head proved he

was drunk) followed by an ambulance. The caption read:
"Not *if* you have an accident, but *when* you have an accident."

De Gier fetched coffee and Grijpstra offered cigars. Mr.
Moozen said he didn't smoke.

"Well," Grijpstra said patiently and puffed out a ragged
dark cloud, "now who would want to poison your wife, sir?
Has there been any recent trouble in her life?"

The question hung in the small white room while Moozen thought. The detectives waited. De Gier stared at the floor, Grijpstra observed the ceiling. A full minute passed.

"Yes," Mr. Moozen said, "some trouble. With me. We contemplated a divorce."

"I see."

"But then we decided to stay together. The trouble passed."

"Any particular reason why you considered a divorce, sir?"

"My wife had a lover." Mr. Moozen's words were clipped and precise.

"Had," de Gier said. "The affair came to an end?"

"Yes. We had some problems with our central heating, something the mechanics couldn't fix. An engineer came out and my wife fell in love with him. She told me—she doesn't like to be secretive. They met each other in motels for a while."

"You were upset?"

"Yes. It was a serious affair. The engineer's wife is a mental patient; he divorced her and was awarded custody of his two children. I thought he was looking for a new wife. My wife has no children of her own—we have been married some six years and would like to have children. My wife and the engineer seemed well matched. I waited a month and then told her to make up her mind—either him or me, not both, I couldn't stand it."

"And she chose you?"

"Yes."

"Do you know the engineer?"

A vague pained smile floated briefly on Moozen's face.
"Not personally. We did meet once and discussed central

heating systems. Any further contact with him was through my wife."

"And when did all this happen, sir?"

"Recently. She only made her decision a week ago. I don't think she has met him since. She told me it was all over."

"His name and address, please, sir."

De Gier closed his notebook and got up. "Shall we go, Adjutant?"

Grijpstra sighed and got up too. They shook hands with Moozen and wished him luck. Grijpstra stopped at the desk. The nurse wasn't helpful, but Grijpstra insisted and de Gier smiled and eventually they were taken to a doctor who accompanied them to the next floor. Mrs. Moozen seemed comfortable. Her arms were stretched out on the blanket. The face was calm. The detectives were led out of the room again.

"Bad," the doctor said. "Parathion is a strong poison. Her stomach is ripped to shreds. We'll have to operate and remove part of it, but I think she will live. The silly woman ate the whole egg, a normal-size egg. Perhaps she was still too sleepy to notice the taste."

"Her husband is downstairs. Perhaps you should call him up, especially if you think she will live." Grijpstra sounded concerned. He probably was, de Gier thought. He felt concerned himself. The woman was beautiful, with a finely curved nose, very thin in the bridge, and large eyes and a soft and sensitive mouth. He looked at her long delicate hands.

"Husbands," the doctor said. "Prime suspects in my experience. Husbands are supposed to love their wives, but usually they don't. It's the same the other way around. Marriage seems to breed violence—it's one of the impossible situations we humans have to put up with."

Grijpstra's pale blue eyes twinkled. "Are you married, Doctor?"

The doctor grinned back. "Very. Oh, yes."

"A long time?"

"Long enough."

Grijpstra's grin faded. "So am I. Too long. But poison is nasty. Thank you, Doctor."

There wasn't much conversation in the car when they drove to the engineer's address. The city's streets had filled up. People were stirring about on the sidewalks and cars crowded each other, honking occasionally. The engineer lived in a block of apartments, and Grijpstra switched off the engine and lit another small black cigar.

"A family drama. What do you think, Sergeant?"

"I don't think. But that rabbit was most extraordinary. Not bought in a shop. A specially made rabbit, and well made, not by an amateur."

"Are we looking for a sculptor? Some arty person? Would Mr. Moozen or the engineer be an artist in his spare time? How does one make a chocolate rabbit, anyway?"

De Gier tried to stretch, but didn't succeed in his cramped quarters. He yawned instead. "You make a mold, I suppose, out of plaster of Paris or something, and then you pour hot chocolate into the mold and wait for it to harden. That rabbit was solid chocolate, several kilos of it. Our artistic friend went to a lot of trouble."

"A baker? A pastry man?"

"Or an engineer—engineers design forms sometimes, I believe. Let's meet this lover man."

The engineer was a small nimble man with a shock of black hair and dark lively eyes, a nervous man, nervous in a pleasant childlike manner. De Gier remembered that Mrs. Moozen was a small woman too. They were ushered into a four-room apartment. They had to be careful not to step on a large number of toys, spread about evenly. Two little boys played on the floor; the eldest ran out of the room to fetch his Easter present to show it to the uncles. It was a basketful of eggs, homemade, out of chocolate. The other boy came to show his basket, identical but a size smaller.

"My sister and I made them last night," the engineer said. "She came to live here after my wife left and she looks after the kids, but she is spending the Easter weekend with my parents in the country. We couldn't go because Tom here had measles, hadn't you, Tom?"

"Yes," Tom said. "Big measles. Little Klaas here hasn't had them yet."

Klaas looked sorry. Grijpstra took a plastic truck off a chair and sat down heavily after having looked at the engineer, who waved him on. "Please, make yourself at home." De Gier had found himself a chair too and was rolling a cigarette. The engineer provided coffee and shooed the children into another room.

"Any trouble?"

"Yes," Grijpstra said. "I am afraid we usually bring trouble. A Mrs. Moozen has been taken to hospital. An attempt was made on her life. I believe you are acquainted with Mrs. Moozen?"

"Ann," the engineer said. "My God! Is she all right?"

De Gier had stopped rolling his cigarette. He was watching the man carefully; his large brown eyes gleamed, but not with pleasure or anticipation. The sergeant felt sorrow, a feeling that often accompanied his intrusions into the private lives of his fellow citizens. He shifted, and the automatic pistol in his shoulder holster nuzzled into his armpit. He impatiently pushed the weapon back. This was no time to be reminded that he carried death with him, legal death.

"What happened?" the engineer was asking. "Did anybody hurt her?"

"A question," Grijpstra said gently. "A question first, sir. You said your sister and you were making chocolate Easter eggs last night. Did you happen to make any bunnies too?"

The engineer sucked noisily on his cigarette. Grijpstra repeated his question.

"Bunnies? Yes, or no. We tried, but it was too much for us. The eggs were easy—my sister is good at that. We have a pudding form for a bunny, but all we could manage was a pudding. It is still in the kitchen, a surprise for the kids later on today. Chocolate pudding—they like it."

"Can we see the kitchen, please?"

The engineer didn't get up. "My God," he said again, "so she was poisoned, was she? How horrible! Where is she now?"

"In the hospital, sir."

"Bad?"

Grijpstra nodded. "The doctor said she will live. Some sort of pesticide was mixed into chocolate, which she ate."

The engineer got up; he seemed dazed. They found the kitchen. Leftover chocolate mix was still on the counter. Grijpstra brought out an envelope and scooped some of the hardened chips into it.

"Do you know that Ann and I had an affair?"

"Yes, sir."

"Were you told that she finished the affair, that she decided to stay with her husband?"

"Yes, sir."

The engineer was tidying up the counter mechanically. "I see. So I could be a suspect. Tried to get at her out of spite or something. But I am not a spiteful man. You wouldn't know that. I don't mind being a suspect, but I would like to see Ann. She is in the hospital, you said. What hospital?"

"The Wilhelmina, sir."

"Can't leave the kids here, can I? Maybe the neighbors will take them for an hour or so . . . yes. I'll go and see Ann. This is terrible."

Grijpstra marched to the front door with de Gier trailing behind him. "Don't move from the house today if you please, sir, not until we telephone or come again. We'll try and be as quick as we can."

"Nice chap," de Gier said when the car found its parking place in the vast courtyard of headquarters. "That engineer, I mean. I rather liked Mr. Moozen too, and Mrs. Moozen is a lovely lady. Now what?"

"Go back to the Moozen house, Sergeant, and get a sample of the roaring bunny. Bring it to the laboratory together with this envelope. If they check we have a heavy point against the engineer."

De Gier restarted the engine. "Maybe he is not so nice, eh? He could have driven his wife crazy and now he tries to murder his girlfriend, his ex-girlfriend. Lovely Ann Moozen, who dared to stand him up. Could be, do you think so?"

Grijpstra leaned his bulk against the car and addressed

his words to the emptiness of the yard. "No. But that could
be the obvious solution. He was distressed, genuinely distressed, I would say. If he hadn't been and if he hadn't had
those kids in the house, I might have brought him in for
further questioning."

"And Mr. Moozen?"

"Could be. Maybe he didn't find the bunny on the garden path; maybe he put it there, or maybe he had it ready
in the cupboard and brought it to his wandering wife. He is
a lawyer—lawyers can be devious at times. True?"

De Gier said, "Yes, yes, yes . . ." and kept on saying so
until Grijpstra squeezed the elbow sticking out of the car's
window. "You are saying *yes*, but you don't sound convinced."

"I thought Moozen was suffering too."

"Murderers usually suffer, don't they?"

De Gier started his "Yes, yes," and Grijpstra marched
off.

They met an hour later, in the canteen in headquarters.
They munched rolls stuffed with sliced liver and roast beef
and muttered diligently at each other.

"So it is the same chocolate?"

"Yes, but that doesn't mean much. One of the lab's assis-
tants has a father who owns a pastry shop. He said that
there are only three mixes on the market and our stuff is
the most popular make. No, not much of a clue there."

"So?"

"We may have a full case on our hands. We should go
back to Mr. Moozen, I think, and find out about friends and
relatives. Perhaps his wife had other lovers, or jealous lady
friends."

"Why her?"

Grijpstra munched on. "Hmm?"

"Why *her?*" de Gier repeated. "Why not him?"

Grijpstra swallowed. "Him? What about him?"

De Gier reached for the plate, but Grijpstra restrained
the sergeant's hand. "Wait, you are hard to understand
when you have your mouth full. What about him?"

De Gier looked at the roll. Grijpstra picked it up and ate
it.

"Him," de Gier said unhappily. "He found the bunny on the garden path, the ferocious bunny holding the pernicious egg. A gift, how nice. But he doesn't eat chocolate, so he runs inside and shows the gift to his wife and his wife grabs the egg and eats it. She may have thought *he* was giving it to her, she was still half asleep. Maybe she noticed the taste, but she ate on to please her husband. She became ill at once and he telephoned for an ambulance. Now, if he had wanted to kill her he might have waited an hour or so, to give the poison a chance to do its job. But he grabbed his phone, fortunately. What I am trying to say is, the egg may have been intended for him, from an enemy who didn't even know Moozen had a wife, who didn't care about killing the wife."

"Ah," Grijpstra said, and swallowed the last of the roll. "Could be. We'll ask Mr. Moozen about the enemies. But not just now. There is the dead man we found in the park—a message came in while you were away. A missing person has been reported and the description fits our corpse. According to the radio room a woman phoned to say that a man who is renting a room in her house has been behaving strangely lately and has now disappeared. She traced him to the corner bar, where he spent last evening until two a.m., when they closed.

"He was a little drunk, according to the barkeeper, but not blind drunk. She always takes him tea in the morning, but this morning he wasn't there and the bed was still made. But she does think he's been home, for she heard the front door at a little after two a.m., opening and closing twice. He probably fetched the rope and his campstool then."

"And the man was fairly old and has a short gray beard?"

"Right."

"So we go and see the landlady. I'll get a photograph—they took dozens this morning and they should be developed by now. Was anything found in his clothes?"

"Nothing." Grijpstra looked guiltily at the empty plate. "Want another roll?"

"You ate it."

"That's true, and the canteen is out of rolls; we got the last batch. Never mind, Sergeant. Let's go out and do some work. Work will take your mind off food."

"That's him," the landlady with the plastic curlers said. Her glasses had slipped to the tip of her blunt nose while she studied the photograph. "Oh, how horrible! His tongue is sticking out. Poor Mr. Marchant, is he dead?"

"Yes, ma'am."

"For shame, and such a nice gentleman. He has been staying here for nearly five years now and he was always so polite."

Grijpstra tried to look away from the glaring pink curlers pointing at his forehead from the woman's thinning hair.

"Did he have any troubles, ma'am? Anything that may have led him to take his own life?"

The curlers bobbed frantically. "Yes. Money troubles. Nothing to pay the taxman with. He always paid the rent, but he hadn't been paying his taxes. And his business wasn't doing well. He has a shop in the next street; he makes things—ornaments he calls them, out of brass. But there was some trouble with the neighbors. Too much noise, and something about the zoning too; this is a residential area now, they say. The neighbors wanted him to move, but he had nowhere to move to, and he was getting nasty letters, lawyers' letters. He would have had to close down, and he had to make money to pay the taxman. It was driving him crazy. I could hear him walk around in his room at night, round and round, until I had to switch off my hearing aid."

"Thank you, ma'am."

"He was alone," the woman said and shuffled with them to the door. "All alone, like me. And he was always so nice." She was crying.

"Happy Easter," de Gier said, and opened the Volkswagen's door for the adjutant.

"The same to you. Bacl to Mr. Moozen again—we *are* driving about this morning. I could use some coffee again. Maybe Mr. Moozen will oblige."

"He won't be so happy either. We aren't making anybody happy today," the sergeant said and tried to put the Volkswagen into first gear. The gear slipped and the car took off in second.

They found Mr. Moozen in his garden. It had begun to rain again, but the lawyer didn't seem to notice that he was getting wet. He was staring at the bright yellow crocuses, touching them with his foot. He had trampled a few of them into the grass.

"How is your wife, sir?"

"Conscious and in pain. The doctors think they can save her, but she will have to be on a stringent diet for years and she'll be very weak for months. I won't have her back for a while."

Grijpstra coughed. "We visited your wife's, ah, previous lover, sir." The word "previous" came out awkwardly, and he coughed again to take away the bad taste.

"Did you arrest him?"

"No, sir."

"Any strong reasons to suspect the man?"

"Are you a criminal lawyer, sir?"

Moozen kicked the last surviving crocus, turned on his heels, and led his visitors into the house. "No, I specialize in civil cases. Sometimes I do divorces, but I don't have enough experience to point a finger in this personal case. Divorce is a messy business, but with a little tact and patience reason usually prevails. To try and poison somebody is unreasonable behavior. I can't visualize Ann provoking that type of action—she is a gentle woman, sensuous but gentle. If she did break her relationship with the engineer she would have done it diplomatically."

"He seemed upset, sir, genuinely upset."

"Quite. I had hoped as much. So where are we now?"

"With you, sir. Do *you* have any enemies? Anybody who hated you so badly that he wanted you to die a grotesque death, handed to you by a roaring rabbit? You did find the rabbit on the garden path this morning, didn't you, sir?"

Moozen pointed. "Yes, out there, sitting in between the crocuses, leering and, as you say, roaring. Giving me the egg."

"Now, which demented mind might have thought of

shaping that apparition, sir? Are you dealing with any particularly unpleasant cases at this moment? Any cases that have a badly twisted undercurrent? Is anyone blaming you for something bad that is happening to them?"

Moozen brushed his hair with both hands. "No. I am working on a bad case having to do with a truckdriver who got involved in a complicated accident; his truck caught fire and it was loaded with expensive cargo. Both his legs were crushed. His firm is suing the firm that owned the other truck. A lot of money in claims is involved and the parties are becoming impatient, with me mostly. The case is dragging on and on. But if they kill me the case will become even more complicated, with no hope of settlement in sight."

"Anything else, sir?"

"The usual. I collect bad debts, so sometimes I have to get nasty. I write threatening letters, sometimes I telephone people or even visit them. I act tough—it's got to be done in my profession. Usually they pay, but they don't like me for bothering them."

"Any pastry shops?"

"I beg your pardon?"

"Pastry shops," Grijpstra said, "people who make and sell confectionery. That rabbit was a work of art in a way, made by a professional. Are you suing anybody who would have the ability to create the roaring rabbit?"

"Ornaments!" de Gier shouted. His shout tore at the quiet room. Moozen and Grijpstra looked up, startled.

"Ornaments! Brass ornaments. Ornaments are made from molds. We've got to check his shop."

"Whose shop?" Grijpstra frowned irritably. "Keep your voice down, Sergeant. What shop? What ornaments?"

"Marchant!" de Gier shouted. "Marchant's shop."

"Marchant?" Moozen was shouting too. "Where did you get that name? *Emil* Marchant?"

Grijpstra's cigar fell on the carpet. He tried to pick it up and it burned his hand, sparks finding their way into the carpet's strands. He stamped them out roughly.

"You know a Mr. Marchant, sir?" de Gier asked quietly.

"No, I haven't met him. But I have written several letters to a man named Emil Marchant. On behalf of clients who are hindered by the noise he makes in his shop. He works with brass, and it isn't only the noise, but there seems to be a stink as well. My clients want him to move out and are prepared to take him to court if necessary. Mr. Marchant telephoned me a few times, pleading for mercy. He said he owed money to the tax department and wanted time to make the money, that he would move out later; but my clients have lost patience. I didn't give in to him—in fact, I just pushed harder. He will have to go to court next week, and he is sure to lose out."

"Do you know what line of business he is in, sir?"

"Doorknobs, I believe, and knockers for doors, in the shape of lions' heads—that sort of thing. And weathervanes. He told me on the phone. All handmade. He is a craftsman."

Grijpstra got up. "We'll be on our way, sir. We found Mr. Marchant this morning, dead, hanging from a tree in the Amsterdam Forest. He probably hanged himself around seven a.m., and at some time before he must have delivered the rabbit and its egg. According to his landlady he has been behaving strangely lately. He must have blamed you for his troubles and tried to take his revenge. He didn't mean to kill your wife, he meant to kill you. He didn't know that you don't eat chocolate and he probably didn't even know you were married. We'll check further and make a report. The rabbit's mold is probably still in his shop, and if not we'll find traces of the chocolate. We'll have the rabbit checked for fingerprints. It won't be difficult to come up with irrefutable proof. If we do, we'll let you know, sir, a little later today. I am very sorry all this has happened."

"Nothing ever happens in Amsterdam," de Gier said as he yanked the door of the Volkswagen open, "and when it does it all fits in immediately."

But Grijpstra didn't agree.

"We would never have solved the case, or rather *I* wouldn't have, if you hadn't thought of the rabbit as an ornament."

"No, Grijpstra, we would have found Marchant's name in Moozen's files."

The adjutant shook his heavy grizzled head. "No, we wouldn't have checked the files. If he had kept on saying that he wasn't working on any bad cases I wouldn't have pursued that line of thought. I'd have reverted to trying to find an enemy of his wife. We might have worked for weeks and called in all sorts of help and wasted everybody's time. You are clever, Sergeant."

De Gier was studying a redheaded girl waiting for a streetcar.

"Am I?"

"Yes. But not as clever as I am," Grijpstra said and grinned. "You work for me. I personally selected you as my assistant. You are a tool in my expert hands."

De Gier winked at the redheaded girl and the girl smiled back. The traffic had jammed up ahead and the car was blocked. De Gier opened his door.

"Hey! Where are you going?"

"It's a holiday, Adjutant, and you can drive this wreck for a change. I am going home. That girl is waiting for a streetcar that goes to my side of the city. Maybe she hasn't had lunch yet. I am going to invite her to go to a Chinese restaurant."

"But we have reports to make, and we've got to check out Marchant's shop; it'll be locked, we have to find the key in his room, and we have to telephone the engineer to let him off the hook."

"I am taking the streetcar," de Gier said. "You do all that. You ate my roll."

THE NORWEGIAN APPLE MYSTERY

by James Holding

James Holding is a retired advertising executive whose numerous short stories for the mystery magazines usually feature series characters. These include his "Ellery Queen" tales, in which the late writer-editor appears in the form of King Danforth and Martin Leroy, two writers whose character is named Leroy King. The present selection is part of this series. A second group of stories stars Manuel Andradas, a hit man for organized crime in Brazil, one of the most unusual protagonists in crime fiction. Finally, his "Hal Johnson" stories concern a detective who "reacquires" stolen library books! All of these series would make outstanding books. Holding has also written many juvenile novels for a variety of American and British publishers.

Two hours after the stewardess found Angela Cameron lying dead in her bed in Cabin A-12, the news was all over the ship. That was pretty good going, even allowing for the fact that rumor is commonly conceded to fly faster on a ship at sea than anywhere else.

Most of the cruise passengers, of course, after forty-five days afloat, were eager for something besides shore excursions and shopping triumphs to gossip about; they seized this tidbit avidly, chewed it over, and passed it on to their neighbors with unusual celerity. Sunning themselves idly in the gaily striped deck chairs of the Norwegian cruise ship *Valhalla* as she plowed through the South China Sea toward Hong Kong, they chattered about Miss Cameron's death like a flock of hungry sparrows that suddenly discovers a slice of bread on the snow.

Despite the animation with which the passengers discussed the event, however, a general feeling of regret and even sadness spread with the news. For Angela Cameron

265

had not only been vivacious, intelligent, pretty, and liber-
ally endowed with sex appeal, she had actually been as
well liked by the women passengers as by the men—which
is saying a great deal for an attractive young woman traveling alone on a luxury cruise around the world.

The Danforths and the Leroys were sitting in the after
Promenade Bar, having a pre-luncheon gimlet, when they
were first apprised of the fact that there had been a death
on board. As the bar steward leaned forward to deposit a
dish of salted nuts on their table, he said to King Danforth
in a solemn undertone, "Too bad about Miss Cameron,
sir."

Helen Leroy, who was blond, vital, and fast off the mark,
spoke up before Danforth could say anything. "Miss Cameron?" she asked of the steward. "What about her,
Eric?"

"I'm sorry, madam," the Norwegian bar steward said in
his stiff English, "I thought you might have heard. Miss
Cameron is dead. Edith, her stewardess, found her this
morning. She died while reading in bed."

"Oh, dear, what a shame!" Carol Danforth said with instant sympathy. "She was such a lovely person. And how
awful for Edith. What was it, Eric? Did Miss Cameron
have a heart attack?"

"No, madam," Eric said. "She choked to death on a bite
of apple."

King Danforth and Martin Leroy exchanged glances.
Death was no stranger to them. Indeed, they made a living
from it. Under the pseudonym of Leroy King, the two men
operated with fabulous success as a writing team specializ-
ing in stories of murder, mystery, and crime. Several dozen
best-selling novels, scores of short stories, numerous television and movie scripts about murder had made them
world-famous. And here, on a cruise with their wives to get
away from it all, the bar steward was saying—it might
well have leaped directly from the page of one of their own
mysteries—"No, madam. She choked to death on a bite of
apple."

Pressed by Helen and Carol, Eric gave them details. It
was obvious that the story had swept through the ship's

crew like a brushfire in the Hollywood hills. Miss Cameron usually had breakfast in her cabin. So Edith, her steward-ess, unless warned away by a "Do Not Disturb" sign on the door of A-12, would normally enter Miss Cameron's cabin at ten o'clock, using her passkey, wake the lady, and take her breakfast order.

This morning, however, Miss Cameron had not awak-ened, nor did she need breakfast. Edith had found her clad in her nightgown, propped up against the pillows on her bed, a book fallen from one hand and a half-eaten apple from the other, her face dreadfully discolored and dis-torted, and her flesh beginning to turn cold. The reading lamp was still burning.

Although Miss Cameron was quite obviously past help, Edith had put through a hurry call for the ship's doctor. He was able only to confirm that poor Miss Cameron was in-deed dead, and to point out the cause: a large fragment of the apple she had been eating was wedged tightly in her throat.

When the bar steward left them to their gimlets, Dan-forth wriggled his lanky frame in his chair, ran a hand over his crew cut, and said a trifle sheepishly, "I am not callous and unfeeling about things like this. But I couldn't help feeling that 'she choked to death on a bite of apple' would fit very well into one of our stories, Mart."

"I had the same thought," Leroy said, grinning. His dark eyes, short wide face, and compact body suggested In-dian impassivity, but he denied it with every word and movement. "It was almost like being home again, working on a plot."

"Whoa!" Helen Leroy said. "This is a vacation, remember? No plotting, no murder gimmicks, no looking for criminals to fit into stories—that was the agreement. Right?"

"Right," Carol Danforth agreed emphatically. She was short and dark, like her husband's partner, with a brisk way of speaking. "So forget about it, boys. Miss Cameron died a perfectly natural accidental death—to coin a contra-diction in terms. Let her alone."

"But what a starting point for a mystery!" Her hus-band's eyes kindled.

"The first thing we'd have to postulate," Martin picked him up instantly, "is that the girl did *not* die a perfectly natural accidental death, as Carol insists, but was murdered."

"Of course," Danforth said. "That's where the challenge lies. In figuring out how this perfectly natural accidental death could be made to appear that way by a murderer."

"And how he murdered her, and where, and why."

"Exactly."

"And who he was."

Their wives saw with resignation that the two incurable story plotters had the bit in their teeth and were not to be headed. So rather than nag, and mellowed, moreover, by the gimlets they were drinking, they sighed and entered into the discussion.

"Before you apply your keen analytical brains to the solving of this murder that doesn't exist," Carol Danforth said, "do you realize that there are approximately seven hundred and fifty *suspects* aboard this ship? Four hundred crew members and three hundred and fifty passengers? Isn't that a few too many for even two geniuses like you to sift successfully?"

"Not at all," her husband said. "Motive. Surely all those people wouldn't have a motive for killing an attractive girl like Miss Cameron?"

"Not likely," Leroy agreed, "unless everybody on board found out Miss Cameron was a typhoid carrier, or fatally radioactive, or something like that."

Danforth shook his head. "Farfetched. Very few people would commit murder as a public service, even under such circumstances. No, it's got to be something more credible than that."

Helen Leroy said, "Well, I'm no writer, thank goodness, but if you want to be logical about it, *I'd* suggest that for one minute of respectful silence you turn your brilliant deductive powers on Miss Cameron's exceptionally fine figure."

King Danforth patted her hand and leaned back to sip at his gimlet thoughtfully. "Now we're getting somewhere, my sweet. A sex killing. That's more like it. This girl was very beautiful and, if you'll pardon a vulgarism, sensationally stacked. Suppose somebody made a pass at her, was ruthlessly repulsed, and killed her out of sexual frustration?"

"Hear, hear," Helen Leroy said. She was watching through the bar window the lazily lifting swells of blue sea that carried small antimacassars of lacy foam on their crests. "I'm getting bored with all the supposing. Doesn't that water look good enough to swim in?"

"Speaking of swimming," Danforth murmured, "The girl, Miss Cameron, was quite a fine swimmer herself. I have seen her churning back and forth in the ship's indoor swimming pool on occasion."

"In a bathing suit?" Leroy inquired.

"Of course."

"Then you're in a position to speak with authority on her figure, King. Was it enough to make a man commit murder?"

"It was," Danforth said appreciatively.

"This is the first I knew you'd been sneaking down to the pool to watch Angela Cameron do the Australian crawl!" Carol Danforth said sharply. "Luring husbands to swimming pools! No wonder she got herself murdered!"

"If you will be guided by my long experience as a plotter," Martin Leroy said hastily, "let us for the moment drop the motive and settle a few questions about method. She choked on an apple, remember."

"Easy," Danforth replied. "She was strangled first. The bite of apple was merely shoved down her throat by her murderer and wedged there for the doctor to find—so he would think exactly what he did think."

"Ah, but the bar steward said nothing about marks on the lady's throat that might indicate a manual strangling."

"The murderer didn't choke her with his hands. He garroted her."

"Impossible. A garrote cord would leave a plainly visible mark."

"Who said anything about a cord? The murderer used something soft to choke her—like a bed sheet or a bath towel."

"A bed sheet!" Helen Leroy laughed. "You men!"

"That would narrow down the suspects, though," Leroy grinned. "It ought to eliminate all the women aboard."

"Be serious," Danforth said with a frown. "This is a problem levity will not solve."

"All right. Where are we? We've got a resisting Miss Cameron strangled by a murderer, hypothetically male, using, say, a bath towel. Where do we go from there?"

"To lunch," Carol Danforth said grimly. "I'm starved."

"Don't anybody order an apple for dessert," Danforth said.

Their table was in the *Valhalla's* forward dining room, familiarly called the Runic Room. As they seated themselves for luncheon, they could tell from the buzz of conversation enlivening the usually sedate dining saloon that Miss Cameron's death was being discussed all about them. But adhering to their long-established rule that no business be discussed during meals—long-established by the wives—the Danforths and the Leroys talked about yesterday's shore trip to Bangkok, where they had been privileged to see the breathtaking temples, towers, and *cheddis* of that holy city.

The cruise ship had anchored at dawn off the mouth of the Menam River, unable to enter because of the extensive sandbar that effectively blocks the entrance to oceangoing ships. A huge flat-bottomed barge, handled by Chinese seamen, had chugged majestically out to the *Valhalla* from shore, taken aboard almost all the *Valhalla's* passengers, ferried them triumphantly over the sandbar, and three hours later disembarked them at the wharves of Bangkok, twenty-five miles up the river. The full day of sight-seeing in hundred degree heat that ensued had been wearying, but worth it, they all agreed. It had been midnight when they climbed exhausted into their beds.

"That trip was rough enough to kill any but a hardened tourist," Leroy said. "I've never seen Helen so pooped as last night when we got back to the ship."

At this point Danforth broke their rule. He had been thinking about Miss Cameron reading in bed. "Everybody who took that trip to Bangkok was completely beat last night," he said. "And that makes me think Miss Cameron wouldn't have been reading in bed after she got back on the ship. She'd have been sleeping, brother—worn out like the rest of us."

"So?"

"So she must have been reading in her bunk this *morning*. Woke up early, say, couldn't get back to sleep, picked up a book, turned on her reading light, felt the pangs of hunger stir, reached for an apple, and took a bite. How's that?"

"That's fine, Monsieur Dupin, but where does it get us?" Leroy was saying when Jackson Powell, Thos. Cook's shore excursion manager on the ship, came by their table on his way out of the dining room. He stopped for a moment.

"It's too bad about Miss Cameron, isn't it?" he asked. "Especially when she missed seeing Bangkok. She thought that would be the high spot of the cruise for her."

"What do you mean, she missed it?" Danforth exclaimed. "Wasn't she ashore yesterday with the rest of us?"

Powell shook his head. "She had a reservation for the shore trip, but she didn't go. I checked the list myself, and she wasn't there." He gazed morosely at the goat's cheese Leroy was applying to a cracker. "She'll never see Bangkok now," he said profoundly and walked away.

When they left the Runic Room, Leroy grinned self-consciously. "Go on up to our regular deck chairs, will you? I'll join you on the sun deck."

"Where are you going, Martin?" Helen Leroy demanded.

"Got a small errand to attend to in the aft dining room."

"That's where Miss Cameron's table was," his wife said. "You can't fool me. Why don't you forget it, darling?"

"Just a notion I want to ask about. See you in the sun, kids." And Leroy took off.

When he dropped into his chair on the sun deck five minutes later, Leroy was beaming. "I talked to her table steward. She didn't show up for any of her meals yesterday—or for dinner the night before!"

"Probably ate in her cabin," Carol Danforth said. "Can't we talk about *anything* else?"

But Danforth was muttering, "There's a way to find out." He left them, hurried down the starboard sun-deck corridor to the elevator, and got off at A-deck; he and Carol occupied stateroom A-20. He went to his cabin, let himself in, and rang for Edith, the stewardess.

She knocked on the door a few seconds later. "Come in, Edith," he said. She was a lovely statuesque Norwegian girl with auburn hair and an incredible snow-and-roses complexion. Her eyes were a bit puffy and red, Danforth noticed. "Sorry about Miss Cameron," he said sympathetically. "It must have been hard for you, finding her like that."

"It was not good," Edith said, making the "good" sound like "goot."

"Tell me, Edith. I hear Miss Cameron was not on the shore trip to Bangkok yesterday with us. And she didn't eat in the dining room yesterday or the night before. Was she in her cabin all that time?"

The stewardess looked puzzled. "There is the 'Do Not Disturb' sign on her door all yesterday," she said, "and evening before. So I do not disturb her for dinner, breakfast, or luncheon. That is how I am told, when there is the sign 'Do Not Disturb.' Let her alone, yes?"

He raised his eyebrows. "So she stayed in her cabin all that time, even when she was supposed to be on a shore excursion to Bangkok?"

"Not all the time," Edith corrected. "At five o'clock in the afternoon, yesterday, I use my key and enter Miss Cameron's cabin. I am worried. I have not seen her since the afternoon before yesterday."

"And?"

"She is not in A-12. Nobody is there."

"Oh. And the bed, was it made up? Had it been slept in?"

"It is made up, although I have not made it up since morning before yesterday."

Danforth said, "She probably made it up herself yesterday. Slept so late she hated to bother you, maybe. Was her door locked when you went in yesterday?"

She nodded.

"And how about this morning when you—er—discovered her?"

"Not locked," the young stewardess said, obviously picturing in her memory how it had been. "Her door key is on the dressing table beside the fruit tray."

"And was the 'Do Not Disturb' sign gone from her door?"

"Yes."

"Did you touch her when you found her this morning?"

"Yes. Her arm when I shake her." Edith shuddered. "She is getting—she is getting . . ."

"Cold?"

Silently, she nodded.

"But still a little warm, too?"

"Still a little warm. But more colder. Colder than warm."

Danforth said, "Thanks, Edith. Mr. Leroy and I write stories about things like this, you know? We're always interested in how such things happen. And we liked Miss Cameron very much."

"She was nice," Edith said, and left quickly.

Helen, Carol, and Martin were waiting for Danforth in their sun-deck chairs when he returned, but not with any noticeable eagerness, because all three of them had dropped off into the well-fed, sun-induced post-luncheon nap that overcame most of the passengers regularly every afternoon. King was hurt. "Hey!" he said loudly, sitting down in his deck chair.

They awoke with a simultaneous start.

Helen Leroy yawned. "You're back, King. Wish you'd stayed longer. I could have milked another half hour out of that nap."

"Listen—" Danforth began eagerly.

"Oh, shut up, darling," Carol Danforth said. "We're all exhausted. Go away somewhere else and plot your plans, or vice versa. Helen and I have had it."

"Not me!" said Leroy. "What's the good word from your recent investigation, King? You've been interviewing Edith, I assume."

"You assume right. Miss Cameron spent yesterday and the evening before in some mysterious limbo, Mart. She was not ashore in Bangkok. She was not in the dining room for any meals, as you yourself confirmed. And she was not in her cabin!"

"Not in her cabin?" his partner repeated, astonished.

"Edith says no. A 'Do Not Disturb' sign was up all day yesterday and the evening before. But Edith looked in at five yesterday. No Angela."

"What do you know!" Leroy breathed. "Now there's a nice complication."

"It's nice complications that make the yarn," Danforth said sententiously. "So where was she?"

"With the murderer," Leroy suggested. "Shacked up in *his* cabin while she repulsed his advances."

"Huh-uh. All the able-bodied men among the passengers were in Bangkok."

"The crew. It was obviously a member of the crew. *They* didn't go to Bangkok."

"True. They didn't."

They sat thinking in silence, watching the faint black stream of cinders from the *Valhalla*'s single stack go streaming away to port in the light breeze. Then Danforth said calmly, as though there had been no hiatus since his last remark. "The girl was murdered the day *before* yesterday. That would explain everything."

"The day before yesterday!" Leroy protested. "Impossible! The bar steward distinctly told us that Angela Cameron was just getting cold when Edith found her this morning. *Beginning* to get cold, I believe Eric said. They don't stay warm for thirty-six hours, mastermind!"

"Yes, that is a problem. In Edith's own words, Miss Cameron had still a little warm, but more colder."

Silence once more.

Leroy suddenly said. "The average rate of body-cooling is more or less one degree per hour, depending on the surrounding temperature and moisture."

Danforth looked at him respectfully. "You're quoting," he said. "But from what?"

"The *Encyclopaedia Britannica*, I think. Or is it our own

The Swedish Match Mystery? I don't remember. But I read it somewhere."

"So where," Danforth queried, "could a dead girl be stashed on this ship where the surrounding temperature and moisture might retard the cooling of her body?"

"The refrigerator," Helen Leroy said drowsily.

"Not the refrigerator, bright girl," her husband's partner denied. "That's where she is *now*. We want just the opposite effect."

Leroy had a faraway look in his eyes. "Friends," he announced, "I believe I've come up with the answer."

"Which is? And don't be so darn smug!" his wife exhorted him.

"Why, the natural, the obvious, the only possible place."

Danforth said, "Don't tell me. Let me guess. The steam room down on D-deck beside the swimming pool."

"Bingo! The steam room, of course. Where else?"

"Of course!"

Again silence descended upon the plotters.

This one lasted longer. But eventually Danforth broke it. "Say. The steam room is right off the swimming pool, next to the massage room. Miss Cameron was a regular swimmer in the pool each afternoon. In that very revealing suit. Somebody down there fell for her, but hard. Right?"

"You ought to know," his wife said.

"Somebody who saw her in that suit so frequently that he simply couldn't go on resisting his baser impulses. So the day before yesterday . . ."

"Hold it, King, hold it." The interruption was Leroy's. "You keep trying to put the finger on somebody for this fictitious crime. I say we've got to work out how it *happened* first. Explain to me, if you please, the bit about the steam room. I've been in it. I've steamed myself like a soft-shell clam with sinus trouble. I've lost six pounds in that room. But where could anybody hide a grown-up girl's body in that Spartan chamber?"

"Close your eyes, Mart," Danforth chortled. "Conjure up a picture of that steam room. It's got open-framework wooden benches in it, like bleacher seats in a ball park, for the customers to sit or recline on while steaming themselves thin. Correct?"

"Correct."

"Now think about the space *behind* those benches."

"Got it."

"Do you see?"

Leroy opened his eyes. "You're right. There's a space behind the benches about a foot and a half wide, backed by the wall of the steam room. And the back wall is solid. A body dropped in there would be hidden."

"Exactly."

"Hidden from the customers, unless somebody happened to climb to the top row and look straight down the back."

"And the steam room wasn't used by more than a dozen people yesterday, remember. Most of us were ashore in Bangkok."

"Right!"

"So there's where the murderer kept Angela Cameron," Danforth said, "between the time he killed her and early this morning."

"When *did* he kill her, swami?" Carol asked, in spite of herself.

"The probabilities seem fairly clear. What time does the indoor pool close?"

"Six o'clock?"

"And Miss Cameron liked to do her swimming late in the afternoon, as I observed. Therefore, she probably went for her usual swim about five thirty, day before yesterday. She swam until the pool closed. By then she was doubtless the only person left down there, aside from the staff. When she went into the ladies' dressing room to take off her wet suit and put on her robe—that's when it happened. The murderer, who had been waiting for just this opportunity, tried for his home run and got thrown out at first. That's when he killed her, to keep her from screaming the ship down or reporting him to the captain."

Leroy picked it up. "And then he put her in the steam room. The intense heat and moisture in there retarded, as you so delicately phrased it, the cooling of her body until the killer could get it back up to her cabin early this morning."

"Just a moment." Danforth raised a magisterial hand. "Why would he want to *delay* having her body found for a whole day?"

"Sheer terror of discovery, I should think," Carol said, now in it all the way.

"Perhaps he hoped to obscure the time of her death by allowing the mad confusion of the Bangkok shore excursion to intervene," Helen said.

"There could have been any number of reasons. The important thing is," Leroy said, "the killer stashes Angela behind the steam-room benches, then casually goes up to A-deck and drapes a 'Do Not Disturb' sign on her cabin door."

"He knows her cabin is A-12 from the tag on her door key."

"Yes. And he hangs out the sign to stall, to give him time to think, to plan."

"Check. But how does he get her body up to her cabin again, early this morning?"

"Maybe in a hamper of dirty towels from the swimming pool? The body covered up by laundry?"

"Perfect. He folds her body into a wheeled hamper, covers her with some soiled towels from the dressing rooms, and wheels her up to her cabin—pretending he's collecting laundry. And with no one stirring except crew members so early in the morning, he'd find it easy to wheel the cart right into her cabin at the proper moment. And out again, later."

"Not a very original method of body transport. But it could work."

"Of course it could work. Let's see, now. Edith said the door was locked yesterday afternoon when she went in and saw that Angela was missing. But it was not locked this morning when she discovered the body. What about that?" Danforth waited for suggestions.

Helen came through. "She had her room key with her when she went down to swim, naturally. So the murderer simply used her own key to get into A-12 when he took the body back."

"Very good. And why wasn't A-12 locked this morning when Edith discovered the body?"

Leroy said, "Because the killer had no way of locking the door after him when he left her cabin! They're not snap locks. And he had to leave her key *inside* the room because that's where it would naturally be when Miss Cameron was in her room. He couldn't take a chance that a missing key might arouse suspicion."

"Not bad," Danforth said. "That could be it."

Leroy sighed wistfully. "We could make an interesting story out of this, King, if we gave it the proper treatment. I particularly like the bath towel touch. Victim strangled with bath towel, then concealed under same when wheeled to stateroom in laundry cart."

"And then," Danforth went on ignoring him, "what happens? He's in her cabin now, with the body-laden cart. I say he dresses Miss Cameron in her nightie, puts her into bed, props her up, turns on the reading lamp, arranges a book near one hand, the apple near the other—and then scrams."

"Having first bitten a piece out of the apple and wedged it far down her throat." Leroy nodded. "I like it, King, I like it."

"So who's going to suspect murder? It's an accident. Anyway, the killer comes out of A-12 with his cart and goes about his normal business, which is obviously merely the taking of some soiled towels to the ship's laundry."

"The stairway down to the laundry is on A-deck, aft," Leroy said. "That fits."

"And poor Miss Cameron is found this morning at ten, dead in her bed, having choked to death on a bite of apple sometime during the night or early this morning. The victim of what my dear wife calls a perfectly natural accidental death." Danforth leaned back and lit a cigarette. "There we are. No holes in *that* fabric."

"But . . ." said Helen Leroy.

"Are there buts?" King Danforth asked. "Do you mean there are loose ends?"

"One," she said succinctly. "Who's the man who couldn't resist his baser impulses when he saw Miss Cameron in a bathing suit?"

Danforth laughed. "You do have a point there," he said. "What do you think, Mart?"

"I am at an extreme disadvantage in this area of speculation," Leroy said. "I am not a swimmer." He slanted a look at Danforth. "I am not even drawn to swimming pools by sensational chassis, either singular or plural. In fact, I have never been down to D-deck for anything except a steam bath and massage. But if I were to pick out a member of the crew who could have fallen for Miss Cameron's charms at the swimming pool and killed her when he was denied them, I am in favor of the Neanderthal blond Viking type with the rabbit's teeth who's employed to pull you out of the pool if you start to drown. Isn't his name Nils?"

"The very fellow I was thinking of," Danforth agreed. "And he'd have ready access to the towels, too."

"And the laundry cart," Helen Leroy said. "But I know Nils quite well. He's sweet."

"Perhaps your chassis is not sensational enough to arouse the beast in him," her husband started to say, but thought better of it.

"Well, children," Danforth said, "if fact were as strange as Leroy King's fiction, which it unfortunately ain't, that's the way poor Angela Cameron would have got hers."

"Face it," Leroy sighed. "Miss Cameron just had the bad luck to choke to death on her apple. And to be quite fair to Nils, the lad at the swimming pool, I'd say that if he went to an orthodontist and got those outboard teeth of his brought into line, he'd be better-looking, more appealing, and more gentle than either gentleman in this present company."

"That," Carol Danforth said heartily, "is fact, not fiction!"

At dinner they were in high spirits and ordered a bottle of champagne. "To celebrate," Leroy said, "our solution of The Norwegian Apple Mystery."

They had stingers on the rocks in the ballroom after dinner while playing bingo games, which were always won by other passengers. Then they danced until midnight to the excellent music of the all-Scandinavian jazz band.

And when they finally descended to their cabins on A-deck to turn in, they were pleasantly aware of the fact that despite its tragic result for one of their fellow passengers, the day had been stimulating.

To get to their staterooms from the elevator, they had to pass the door of Cabin A-12, recently occupied by the late Miss Angela Cameron. As they approached it, the door to A-12 opened and Edith, their stewardess, stepped out into the corridor, carrying a fruit tray. She bobbed her auburn head at them and started to pass. Danforth put out his hand and restrained her.

"Hi, Edith," he said. "Something more happening in A-12?"

"No, Mr. Danforth," she said. "I am cleaning up Miss Cameron's stateroom, packing her things. To take off the ship with her when we arrive Hong Kong. It is now all finished. Her parents radio to have her cremated in Hong Kong, and send ashes home on airplane."

"Poor thing," Helen Leroy said, suddenly feeling very guilty. But then she looked at the dish of fruit that Edith was taking from A-12 to dispose of in her service pantry.

Leroy was looking at it, too. He reached out and took an apple from the tray. "Is this the apple Miss Cameron was eating when she choked?"

Edith nodded.

"Look at that," Leroy whispered.

He held out the apple.

The flesh of the apple had turned brown where someone had taken a single large bite out of it.

The tooth marks showed clearly along the top edges of the bite. They could not possibly have been made by the small even teeth of Angela Cameron. Unmistakably they had been carved into the fruit by two very large, protruding front teeth.

GIDEON AND THE
CHESTNUT VENDOR

by J.J. Marric (John Creasey)

John Creasey was so prolific he wrote under twenty-eight pseudonyms and left a backlog of unpublished manuscripts at the time of his death in 1973. With more than six hundred published books to his credit, he was probably the most prolific mystery writer in the English language.

J. J. Marric was his best-known nom de plume, and he used it for his stories about George Gideon, of the London police.

Old Ben Fairley had sold fresh roasted chestnuts for more winters than he could remember. As a matter of fact, he remembered very little of his seventy-odd years, for he had always lived almost entirely in the present, whether it was good or bad. Each summer he went out on the road, calling on those farms where he could find temporary employment planting or hoeing or fruit picking. Each winter he came "home," to the rooming house near London's Covent Garden, where he stored his barrow and brazier, bought his chestnuts at wholesale, and roasted them.

Old Ben's pitch was near Leicester Square.

His chestnuts were always fleshy and white, brought all the way from sun-drenched Italy, and old Ben was as fussy as a chef while splitting them and turning them and keeping them hot.

The fire in the brazier also kept him warm.

Many people knew him, passing his barrow with a smile or a nod, sometimes pausing to hand him a shilling or a two-shilling piece, usually "forgetting" to take their bag of chestnuts. Some, on the other hand, liked chestnuts, and were not embarrassed to skin and eat them as they pounded London's hard pavements.

Among these was George Gideon, Commander of the

Criminal Investigation Department of New Scotland
Yard. From time to time, often late at night after the thea-
ter crowds had left and London was quiet and empty, Gideon would stroll around the square mile which included all
Soho as well as Piccadilly Circus and Leicester Square, almost as if he owned the ground he walked on. Certainly he
loved it. The sight of his solid massive figure, his square
chin thrust forward, his broad forehead wrinkled under
iron-gray hair, was familiar to newsdealer and pavement
artist, taxi driver and night-club tout, peddler and policeman.

On cold nights Gideon would stop at old Ben's chestnut
barrow, pay his shillings, take a soft appetizing nut, and
pop it hot and whole into his mouth.

"Must have a palate like a piece of iron," old Ben would
say. Or: "You're the only man I know who can open those
nuts without burning his fingers. How do you do it, Mr.
Gideon?"

"I get a tough skin catching bad men," Gideon would answer invariably.

They would both laugh, and Gideon would stay for a few
moments, talking to old Ben, tossing the husks onto the
fire and watching them blaze.

One night, only half an hour after he had left the chestnut vendor, a taxi drew up close to old Ben's barrow. Ben
watched first one, then two, three, four youths scramble
out, and sensed some kind of trouble. Almost at once another taxi screeched to a halt at the far side of the street.
This time old Ben was too busy to count how many men got
out; he had grabbed the handles of his barrow and started
to move off.

He did not get far.

Suddenly one of the youths pushed him aside. As old Ben
staggered, another snatched at the barrow and a third began to pluck the chestnuts from their wire container. Angry now as much as frightened, old Ben shouted a protest.

More youths rushed up, and passersby stopped in alarm
as the two groups fought. In the struggle someone pushed
against the brazier and tipped it over. As old Ben ran forward to save his chestnuts, red-hot coals glowed like trac-

ers through the air, striking against his outstretched hands.

He screamed with pain.

A police whistle shrilled out.

In five minutes old Ben Fairley, groaning and only half conscious, was being rushed to the hospital. The two opposing gangs had disappeared, and the hot coals, scattered across the pavement, were dying.

Gideon heard of this in the middle of his briefing session at New Scotland Yard at about half past ten the next morning. It was mentioned almost in passing by a Superintendent Lloyd, who was in charge of the police attempt to curtail the activities of the teenage gangs in Soho.

"I could understand if they had a purpose," Lloyd was saying. He was big, earnest, and Welsh. "But they fight just for the sake of fighting. Razor blades and brass knuckles were used again last night, George."

Gideon looked bleak. "Did you catch any of them?"

"No. They were gone before our chaps arrived. The swine don't care what damage they do or whether they injure anybody. This time an old chestnut seller was badly burned when they knocked over his brazier."

Gideon stiffened. "Chestnut seller? Where was his pitch?"

"Just past the National Portrait Gallery, near Leicester Square," the superintendent answered.

Gideon pressed a bell on his desk, and when his assistant came in he said quickly, "A chestnut seller was burned last night near Leicester Square. Find out what his name was, where he is, and how he's doing."

"Right," said the assistant, a tall, lean, bony man named Lemaitre.

"Do you know the fellow?" asked the Welshman.

"If it's the man I think it is, I've known him for thirty years," said Gideon. "Have you put in your report yet?"

"It's being typed out now."

"See that I get a copy," Gideon ordered.

Very soon he learned that it was indeed Ben Fairley, that old Ben was comfortable, but that for a man of his age the shock might have grave consequences.

"His hands are burned so badly that he won't roast any more chestnuts for some time," Lemaitre reported. "He can see visitors, though."

"Have we got a man with him?"

"Lloyd didn't ask for one," Lemaitre said defensively. "It isn't as if he were involved in any particular crime. Just these young hooligans fighting among themselves."

Gideon grunted.

He studied the brief report, prepared as routine, as well as two statements from eyewitnesses, which also said very little. Armed with these, Gideon went to have a word with old Ben at the Charing Cross Hospital. He had never seen the man washed and shaved before. Both of Ben's hands were heavily bandaged, and he looked tired and worn; but his eyes were bright in his lined face, and his frail voice held a note of anger.

"Just rushed at me, they did, and *I'd* never done them any harm. Never even seen them before in my life!"

"We'll get them, Ben," said Gideon, and he meant to. "Tell me a little more, will you?"

"There's nothing more to tell," said old Ben. "One lot came up in one taxi and the other lot came up in another. Just rushed at me, they did."

"How did you burn your hands?" asked Gideon.

Ben looked at him as if wondering how an intelligent man could ask such a question.

"Trying to save my chestnuts, of course. They were my capital, Mr. Gideon—I needed them if I was going to stay in business."

"I'll see that you stay in business," promised Gideon. "Now, Ben, what happened after that? The report says there were no chestnuts left in the basket."

"The so-and-sos grabbed them," said Ben, anger making his voice hoarse. "Fancy stealing a few bobs' worth of chestnuts from an old man! How mean can you get?"

"Don't you worry about it," said Gideon soothingly. "Just tell me this. How many chestnuts did you have?"

"About five pounds—in weight, I mean. That would be including those the young lady gave me. But Mr. Gideon—"

"Young lady?" interrupted Gideon sharply. "What young lady? And when did she give you the chestnuts?"

"Yesterday afternoon, Mr. Gideon. She came out of one of those new apartment houses at the back of Oxford Street. I've seen her several times as I've pushed my barrow past there—it's on my route to the pitch, see. 'Hello, dad,' she says, 'I've got something for you.' Then she hands me a great big bag of chestnuts. Beauties, they were—otherwise I wouldn't have sold them," added Ben virtuously.

Gideon leaned forward. "Now, Ben, think hard. Are you quite sure about all this?"

" 'Course I'm sure!" cried Ben. "A bit of all right, she is, with long blond hair hanging down her back. Funny thing, life, ain't it, Mr. Gideon? In the afternoon someone gives me chestnuts—in the evening someone pinches 'em, and my own with 'em."

Gideon was looking thoughtful. "One of the new apartment houses behind Oxford Street," he murmured to himself. "Blond. Hmm." Slowly he got to his feet. "Yes, it's a funny life, Ben. But you take it easy. When you're well, I'll see you get all you need to start up in business again."

Leaving the hospital, Gideon hurried back to New Scotland Yard, and as soon as he reached his office he sent for Superintendent Lloyd.

"Any lead on those lads in the fight last night?" Gideon asked.

"No, Commander. Two of our chaps saw them, but they weren't the usual Soho troublemakers. That's the problem—it's contagious. What fun they got out of snatching a few chestnuts, heaven only knows."

"Check with N.E. Division on Dicey Gamble and find out if he still lives in one of the new apartment houses behind Oxford Street," said Gideon. "And find out what color his wife's hair is—she used to bleach it," he added thoughtfully.

Lloyd looked up sharply.

"Dicey? I saw him only last week, and he's still living in that flat—must cost him a fortune. His wife's a blonde."

"A bit of all right?" inquired Gideon. "With the long hair?"

"You've got her to a T," said Lloyd. "Why she ever married that thieving slob I'll never know. What's on your mind about Dicey?"

Dicey Gamble was the leader of a small group of smash-and-grab raiders who specialized in robbing jewelry shops. He had already been to prison once, and some of his "boys" were still inside, but he could always find others to join him.

"Call it a long shot," replied Gideon. "Tell N.E. Division to find out if any of his gang bought any chestnuts recently. If necessary, check every grocer in the district. Get a move on, there's no time to lose."

The superintendent hurried out, and within an hour he was on the telephone to Gideon.

"You were right, sir! One of Dicey Gamble's boys bought two pounds of chestnuts yesterday morning."

"Good! Get all the help you need and raid Dicey's apartment straightaway," Gideon ordered. "I'm just going home. Phone me there and let me know what happens."

He wished, as he so often did, that he could take an active part in what was to follow; in this, at least, he envied his subordinates, who had the stimulus and excitement of physical action.

At seven o'clock that evening the police from N.E. Division and from the Yard arrived at Dicey Gamble's apartment.

Panic showed in Dicey's eyes when the Yard men appeared at his door, but the panic was quickly veiled.

"I've got nothing here, Super," he insisted. "You can search the place, but you won't find anything."

Lloyd looked at him squarely. "You won't get away with that old chestnut, Dicey."

The color drained from Dicey's face. Lloyd pushed past him and walked through the apartment, stopping short when he came to the kitchen. The table was covered with a sheet of newspaper, and on the newspaper was a pile of chestnuts. Dicey had obviously been in the process of cutting each nut in two—several had already been halved.

In eight of the halves, buried inside the hard nuts, were diamonds.

"There's nothing new in this game," Gideon explained to Lloyd. "I once knew a thief who split a hazelnut in two, put a diamond inside, and stuck the shell together. The gangs that attacked old Ben obviously weren't in it for the sheer fun—so they were in it for the chestnuts. Add to that the fact that old Ben was given chestnuts by a woman who lived in the same house as one of our cleverest jewel thieves, and it all started to make sense."

"I'll say it made sense," agreed Lloyd. "Dicey and his mob had these hot diamonds and hid them in the chestnuts. One of the boys dumped them at Dicey's flat, on instructions. But Dicey was out, and as neither he nor his wife eat chestnuts, wifey gave them to old Ben."

"Everyone says she's a bit of all right," murmured Gideon.

Later that day, as he sat with old Ben at the Charing Cross Hospital, Gideon finished the story.

"As soon as Dicey discovered what his wife had done, he got his mob together for a raid on your barrow to get back the chestnuts—but in getting word to his boys, another gang learned what had happened and reached you first. Dicey's lot caught up with them. Simple, Ben, wasn't it?"

Old Ben gave a slow, pleased smile. Perhaps when he next roasted chestnuts he would dream of a fortune in diamonds.

THE SAME OLD GRIND

by Bill Pronzini

The multitalented Bill Pronzini has been entertaining mystery and suspense readers since the mid-1960s. His novels featuring "the nameless detective" are particularly popular, and are to some extent autobiographical, since "Nameless," like his creator, is Italian, likes beer, and owns a large collection of pulp magazines. Pronzini's large number of excellent short stories are only now beginning to be collected. He has also written extensively on the mystery field, and his Gun in Cheek, *a masterful study of the genre through its worst works, is certain to become a landmark book. In addition, he has found time to edit and co-edit some of the best mystery anthologies extant.*

There were no customers in the Vienna Delicatessen when Mitchell came in at two on a Thursday afternoon. But that wasn't anything unusual. He'd been going there a couple of times a week since he'd discovered the place two months ago, and he hadn't seen more than a dozen people shopping there in all that time.

It wasn't much of a place. Just a little hole-in-the-wall deli tucked down at the end of a side street, in an old neighborhood that was sliding downhill. Which was exactly the opposite of what he himself was doing, Mitchell thought. He was heading *uphill*—out of the slums he'd been raised in and into this section of the city for a few months, until he had enough money and enough connections, and then uptown where the living was easy and you drank champagne instead of cheap bourbon and ate in fancy restaurants instead of dusty old delis.

But he had to admit that he got a boot out of coming to the Vienna Delicatessen. For one thing, the food was good and didn't cost much. And for another the owner, Giftholz, amused him. Giftholz was a frail old bird who talked with an accent and said a lot of humorous things because he didn't understand half of what you rapped to him about. He was from Austria or someplace like that, been in this country for thirty years, but damned if he didn't talk like he'd just come off the boat.

What Giftholz was doing right now was standing behind the deli counter and staring off into space. Daydreaming about Austria, maybe. Or about the customers he wished he had. He didn't hear Mitchell open the door, but as soon as the little bell overhead started tinkling, he swung around and smiled in a sad, hopeful way that always made Mitchell think of an old mutt waiting for somebody to throw him a bone.

"Mr. Mitchell, good afternoon."

Mitchell shut the door and went over to the counter. "How's it going, Giftholz."

"It goes," Giftholz said sadly. "But not so well."

"The same old grind, huh?"

"Same old grind?"

"Sure. Day in, day out. Rutsville, you dig?"

"Dig?" Giftholz said. He blinked like he was confused and smoothed his hands over the front of his clean white apron. "What will you have today, Mr. Mitchell?"

"The usual. Sausage hero and an order of cole slaw. Might as well lay a brew on me too."

"Lay a brew?"

Mitchell grinned. "Beer, Giftholz. I want a beer."

"Ah. One beer, one sausage hero, one cole slaw. Yes."

Giftholz got busy. He didn't move too fast—hell, he was so frail he'd probably keel over if he *tried* to move fast—but that was all right. He knew what he was doing and he did it right: lots of meat on the sandwich, lots of slaw. You had to give him that.

Mitchell watched him for a time. Then he said, "Tell me something, Giftholz. How do you hang in like this?"

"Please?"

"Hang in," Mitchell said. "Stay in business. You don't have many customers and your prices are already dirt cheap."

"I charge what is fair."

"Yeah, right. But you can't make any bread that way."

"Bread?" Giftholz said. "No, my bread is purchased from the bakery on Union Avenue."

Mitchell got a laugh out of that. "I mean money, Giftholz. You can't make any *money.*"

"Ah. Yes, it is sometimes difficult."

"So how do you pay the bills? You got a little something going on the side?"

"Something going?"

"A sideline. A little numbers action, maybe?"

"No, I have no sideline."

"Come on, everybody's got some kind of scam. I mean, it's a dog-eat-dog world, right? Everybody's got to make ends meet any way he can."

"That is true," Giftholz said. "But I have no scam. I do not even know the word."

Mitchell shook his head. Giftholz probably *didn't* have a scam; it figured that way. One of these old-fashioned merchant types who were dead honest. And poor as hell because they didn't believe in screwing their customers and grabbing a little gravy where they could. But still, the way things were these days, how did he stand up to the grind? Even with his cheap prices, he couldn't compete with the big chain outfits in the neighborhood that had specials and drawings and gave away stamps; and he had to pay higher and higher wholesale prices himself for the stuff he sold. Yet here he was, still in business. Mitchell just couldn't figure out how guys like him did it.

Giftholz finished making the sandwich, put it on a paper plate, laid a big cup of slaw beside it, opened a beer from his small refrigerator, and put everything down on the counter. He was smiling as he did it—a kind of proud smile, like he'd done something fine.

"It is two dollars, please, Mr. Mitchell."

Two dollars. Man. The same meal would have cost him four or five at one of the places uptown. Mitchell shook his head again, reached into his pocket, and flipped his wallet out.

When he opened it and fingered through the thick roll of bills inside, Giftholz's eyes got round. Probably because he'd never seen more than fifty bucks at one time in his life. Hell, Mitchell thought, give him a thrill. He opened the wallet wider and waved it under Giftholz's nose.

"That's what real money looks like, Giftholz," he said. "Five bills here, five hundred aces. And plenty more where that came from."

"Where did you earn so much money, Mr. Mitchell?"

Mitchell laughed. "I got a few connections, that's how. I do little jobs for people and they pay me big money."

"Little jobs?"

"You don't want me to tell you what they are. They're private jobs, if you get my drift."

"Ah," Giftholz said, and nodded slowly. "Yes, I see."

Mitchell laughed again and took a bite of his hero. Damned good. Giftholz made the best sandwiches in the city, all right. How could you *figure* a guy like him?

He ate standing up at the counter; there was one little table against the back wall, but from here he could watch Giftholz putter around in slow motion. Nobody else came into the deli; he would have been surprised if somebody had. When he finished the last of the hero and the last of the beer, he belched in satisfaction and wiped his hands on a napkin. Giftholz came over to take the paper plate away; then he reached under the counter and came up with a bowl of mints and a small tray of toothpicks.

"Please," he said.

"Free mints? Since when, Giftholz?"

"It is because you are a good customer."

It is because I gave you a three-buck tip, Mitchell thought. He grinned at Giftholz, helped himself to a handful of mints, and dropped them into his coat pocket. Then he took a toothpick and worked at a piece of sausage that was stuck between two of his teeth.

Giftholz said, "You would do me a small favor, Mr. Mitchell?"

"Favor? Depends on what it is."

"Come with me into the kitchen for a moment."

"What for?"

"There is something I would show you."

"Like what?"

"It is something of interest. Please, it will only take a short time."

Mitchell finished excavating his teeth, tucked the toothpick into a corner of his mouth, and shrugged. What the hell, he might as well humor the old guy. He had time; he didn't have any more little jobs to do today. And there wouldn't be any gambling or lady action until tonight.

"Sure," he said. "Why not."

"Good," Giftholz said. *"Wunderbar."*

He gestured for Mitchell to come around behind the counter and then doddered through a door into the kitchen. When Mitchell went through after him he didn't see anything particularly interesting. Just a lot of kitchen equipment, a butcher's block table, a couple of cases of beer, and some kind of large contraption in the far corner.

"So what do you want to show me?" he asked.

"Nothing," Giftholz said.

"Huh?"

"Really I would ask you a question."

"What question?"

"If you speak German."

"German? You putting me on?"

"Putting you on?"

For some reason Mitchell was beginning to feel short of breath. "Listen," he said, "what do you want to know a thing like that for?"

"It is because of my name. If you were to speak German, you see, you would understand what it means in English translation."

Short of breath and a little dizzy, too. He blinked a couple of times and ran a hand over his face. "What do I care what your damned name means."

"You should care, Mr. Mitchell," Giftholz said. "It means 'poison wood.'"

"Poison—?" Mitchell's mouth dropped open, and the toothpick fell out of it and fluttered to the floor. He stared at it stupidly for a second.

Poison wood.

Then he stopped feeling dizzy and short of breath; he

stopped feeling anything. He didn't even feel the floor when he fell over and hit it with his face.

Giftholz stood looking down at the body. Too bad, he thought sadly. Ah, but then, Mr. Mitchell had been a *Strolch*, a hoodlum; such men were not to be mourned. And as he had said himself in his curious idiom, it was a dog-eat-dog world today. Everything cost so much; everything was so difficult for a man of honesty. One truly did have to make ends meet any way one could.

He bent and felt for a pulse. But of course there was none. The poison paralyzed the muscles of the heart and brought certain death within minutes. It also, as he well knew, became neutralized in the body after a short period of time, leaving no toxic traces.

Giftholz picked up the special toothpick from the floor, carried it over to the garbage pail. After which he returned and took Mr. Mitchell's wallet and put it away inside the apron.

One had to make ends meet any way one could. Such a perfect phrase that was. But there was another of Mr. Mitchell's many phrases which still puzzled him. The same old grind. It was *not* the same old grind; it had not been the same old grind for some time.

No doubt Mr. Mitchell meant something else, Giftholz decided.

And began to laboriously drag the body toward the gleaming sausage grinder in the far corner.

DOGSBODY

by Francis M. Nevins, Jr.

Francis M. Nevins, Jr. is a leading authority in at least three fields: he is a nationally known expert on copyright law, a subject he teaches at Washington University Law School; a highly regarded authority on American popular culture, particularly film and television; and a prominent Edgar Award-winning critic of mystery fiction, best known for his Royal Bloodline: Ellery Queen, Author and Detective *(1974), and more recently responsible for the long-overdue revival of the work of Cornell Woolrich. In addition, he has found time to write several mystery novels and a considerable number of short stories, several like the present selection, featuring Milo Turner, professional con man and solver of crimes committed by others.*

The Oakshade Inn had been touted to me as the most restful place to stay in Barhaven, and during the first three nights of my visit to that drowsy and affluent community I had no cause to dispute the assessment. Floorboards buffed to high gloss, homey maple furniture, bright chintz curtains, view of lush meadows from my second-floor window, fine classical music from the local university's radio station, breakfasts in the hotel dining room that were a trencherman's delight, and a scam that was progressing fantastically. No con man with a taste for the finer things could have asked for more.

Until that fourth night when the phone jolted me awake.

I sprang bolt upright and groped for the night table. The digital clock beside the phone proclaimed the time to be 1:14 A.M. I found the receiver and jammed one end to my ear. "Yes?" I spoke into the mouthpiece, fighting to make the word come out calm.

"Fritz!" replied an all-too-familiar voice, low and menacing like the growl of a German shepherd on guard duty.

"Get your pants on and wait downstairs for a prowl car to pick you up. You've got four minutes."

For an awful moment I was convinced he'd tumbled to the scam and was arresting me over the phone. Then my brain came into gear and I exchanged a few sentences with my caller, hung up and dived for the clothes closet. Fully dressed and with my Vandyke brushed, I had all of ten seconds to wait in the dim empty lounge of the inn until the black-and-white braked in front of the picture window, the domelight whirling bloodily.

The scam had been going velvet-smooth till now. In fact, the only sour note in the orchestration was that Chief Knauf, for some private reason, kept calling me Fritz. My actual *nom de scam* this time was Horst—to be complete, Professor Doktor Horst Gerstad, formerly criminological consultant to the national police of the Federal Republic of Germany, currently president of Gerstad Security Systems, a corporation which analyzed and improved on existing security arrangements for businesses that were uptight about crime.

Professor Gerstad was one of my favorite identities and one of my most lucrative. The close-cropped military brush cut, the little Vandyke, the accent honed to a fine edge by hours of listening to tapes of Henry Kissinger's press conferences, all added up to the quintessence of a walking Teutonic efficiency machine.

I would present myself at a likely corporate headquarters, speak to its top management, learn its security arrangements, punch a few simple holes in them, and offer to lease the corporation my own comprehensive security system, which of course had as much real existence as a hippogriff. If the corporation didn't agree, I could always recoup my losses by selling the information I'd picked up to a potential thief.

I had come to Barhaven to make my pitch at the university, and it was in the office of its president, Herbert J. Stockford, A.B., M.A., D.Ed., that I had chanced to meet Stockford's brother-in-law, the chief of the Barhaven police.

E. W. Knaup preferred to be called Duke—I gathered because the E. stood for Elmer or Ethelbert or something equally unmacho. He was a short, tubby, gravel-voiced, genially pushy specimen, and he had a blind spot wide enough to drive a semi through. He was a gun nut. No man or woman who encountered him, however casually, could escape one of his monologues on weaponry. One might glance at the sky and remark that it looked like rain, and Knaup would say, "If you want to see a rain of lead, buddy, try the VC-70 Heckler and Koch automatic pistol. Nineteen shots, double action, comes with a stock you can use for a holster *and* which you can attach to the pistol and turn it into a submachine gun. Brip brip brip, brip brip brip! Love those three-shot bursts."

The chief's personal police cruiser sported a rear-window sticker attesting to his life membership in the National Rifle Association, three separate anti-gun control stickers, a God Bless America tag, a Support Your Local Police tag, and a flag decal. No ambiguity about ol' Duke's sympathies.

After that first meeting in Stockford's office I hadn't expected to see Knaup again, but the very next day, a little before noon, while I was in a conference room on the third floor of the university administration building, poring learnedly over security plans with the chief and deputy chief of the school force, he came striding into the room in full uniform, the polished butt of his Colt Python protruding from his buttoned-down leather holster.

"Fritz!" he barked, like an actor trying out for the voice of the Lord in a De Mille movie.

I looked curiously around the room to see if any of the security guards happened to be named Fritz. Nobody even looked up.

"No, *you*, dummy," he growled at me. That was the way he spoke to people he liked. "We're lunching."

"May I point out that my name is not Fritz?" I said in my most unruffled Kissinger tone.

"We in the law enforcement community eat Mex food for lunch. I hope you like tacos, Fritz," he said, and led me out by the elbow.

Over the guacamole salad at Panchito's he explained his

sudden interest in me. "Now here's what it is, Fritz." He wolfed down great gobs of guacamole on taco chips between sentences. "As head honcho of the college, my brother-in-law Herbie Stockford is the one who has to decide about this security package of yours." Chomp crunch. "Only he doesn't know enough about security to hit the dirt when a Remington High Standard Model 10 goes off at him, so he's asked me to sort of help him make a decision." Crunch chomp. "Those retired village constables he uses for campus security aren't much better than Herbie, so he's relying on the only pro in town." Crunch crunch. "Me." Burp.

So I repeated my well-rehearsed pitch to the Duke, being careful to throw in as many gun references as I dared. And before we had demolished our *quesodillas* he had unsubtly switched the subject to weaponry. "What kind of contacts you got in Charter Arms, or Ruger, or Dan Wesson? I've got a little proposition for you."

When I modestly lied that my connections with several of the firms he'd mentioned were at moderately high levels of management, his eyes brightened. "We in the law enforcement community appreciate the work of the arms manufacturers," he said. "And now that we're getting a lot of federal money from LEAA, we'd like to show our appreciation by placing some big orders. Like maybe a gross of M-16 or Armalite 180 rifles, a few dozen folding stock shotguns, all the Glaser Safety Slugs we can lay our mitts on. Say, if I get some of the chiefs in the neighboring towns to come in with me on a shopping list, you think you can get us, say, a thirty percent discount on a two-hundred-thousand-dollar order?"

He wasn't so crude as to make it explicit that his recommendation to his brother-in-law depended on my help in fixing him up with an arsenal, but I got the message loud and clear and assured him of my fullest cooperation. And that was how things stood between me and the gun-loving chief when, thirty-six hours later, the black-and-white whisked me through the sleeping streets of Barhaven to I knew not what destination.

* * *

We skirted the edge of the university grounds and swung north into the low foothills which sheltered the hundred-thousand-dollar homes. The black-and-white made a sharp turn into a private lane and then into the driveway of a fieldstone and redwood showplace halfway up the slope. Half of the house's windows were lit, and floodlights blazed across the broad lawn.

Duke Knaup strode tubbily into the path of the black-and-white and thrust out his palm like a crossing guard. The cop behind the wheel slammed the brakes, and I emerged from the rear with what dignity I could muster. Behind the chief shuffled a slim balding man in silk dressing gown and slippers whom I recognized as none other than President Stockford of Barhaven University. His face looked ghastly, as if his best friend had turned into a cheese Danish before his eyes. Without a word they led me across fifty yards of grass still wet from the early-evening storm to the foot of a stately old elm. The body of a large reddish-yellow dog lay beside the trunk.

"Someone poisoned the poor mutt," Knaup muttered. "Can't tell what was used—lab will give me a report in the morning. About an hour ago Herbie heard the dog whining and came out to investigate and found him lying here. Looks like he'd crawled under the tree to die."

A short dumpy woman in a blue wrapper trotted out of the house to join us. "My sister, Mrs. Stockford. This is Dr. Fritz Gerstad, a visiting criminologist," Knaup introduced us.

"Oh, are you going to help my brother find the—the animal who did this to Thor?" she demanded as we shook hands.

"It is possible I can be of assistance?" I murmured, wondering what the hell I was doing here and how best to stay in character.

"Tell Fritz what you told me about the dog's routine after dark," Knaup directed his brother-in-law.

"He was a trained guard dog," Stockford replied dully. "We let him out every night at sundown and he'd roam the grounds. We haven't had a burglary here since we got him three years ago."

"And have you had a burglary tonight?" I asked.

"No, nothing," Mrs. Stockford said. "I've just finished checking to see if anything is missing."

"Someone probably threw a poisoned meat patty onto the lawn to get rid of Thor," her husband added, "but he hasn't come back yet to break in."

"He'd probably wait till the wee hours before he came back," Knaup pointed out. "But with all the lights on and cops around the house, he won't show now. I'll assign a car to stand by the rest of the night just in case."

"Do I assume correctly, sir, that neither you nor Mrs. Stockford observed any strange automobiles on the private road this evening?"

"The storm was quite heavy up here for a while," the shaken president replied. "We couldn't see as far as the road during that period. That was probably when he came by and threw out the poisoned meat."

Chief Knaup clawed at my arm. "Come over here with me, Fritz." He led me across the squishy grass to a rose arbor behind the house. "Want to explain why I sent for you," he whispered. "You see, I don't believe Thor was killed by somebody who was out to burglarize the house. I think whoever did it wanted to kill the dog and that was all."

"A crazed dog poisoner in Barhaven?" I clucked mildly, trying to suggest his theory was ridiculous without actually insulting the man.

"It makes sense if you know the background," Knaup went on. "Thor was trained as a killer, the kind of dog they use for night security in big empty stores. When the college was going through the anti-war riots six years ago, Herbie hired an outfit that trains these dogs to let some of them run loose at night in the administration building and the ROTC building and some other vulnerable spots. A few long-haired kids broke into the ROTC building one night with a can of paint to put peace symbols on the walls. Couple of them got chewed up pretty bad by the dogs. Caused a big stink, the school went on strike for two days, and Herbie had to cancel the contract for the dogs. When the outfit went bust three years ago he bought one of those same dogs for his personal protection."

"Thor was one of the dogs involved in the incident in the ROTC building?"

"That's right. Half Irish wolfhound and half Pyrenean bearhound. Weight about one ten, a shade bigger than a full-grown German shepherd, and a hell of a lot meaner."

"I'm sure he was an excellent guard dog," I murmured, "but I fail to see why you wish to involve me in the matter." And, like a tyro swimmer who suddenly realizes he's drifted two miles out from the beach, I was becoming distinctly queasy.

"Herbie loved that dog like a son," Knaup explained, "and I owe him a lot of favors, like my job, for instance. He wants me to pull out all the stops to nail whoever poisoned Thor. Trouble is, if I give the case any more than routine attention, the papers will stomp all over me about misusing police resources. I can do without that grief."

I knew exactly what he meant, having taken the trouble to read the back issues of the Barhaven newspapers before I had made my appearance. Last year Knaup had come close to being removed from office over a little matter of assigning three patrolmen, while on duty, to paint his house and oil his gun collection. "That's why you're here, Fritz. You're going to be my dogicide squad for a while. Let's see how good a criminologist you really are."

I do not shy away from new experiences, but this one made me fight hard to repress a shudder. Very few con men have found themselves drafted into the police force while on a scam. I was far from enthusiastic but saw no way to extricate myself short of blowing town. I made an instant decision and held out my hand to Knaup gravely. "So be it," I pronounced as we shook. "Although I wish it explicitly understood that my success will guarantee a favorable recommendation by you of my security system."

Duke Knaup stuck thoughtful fingers under his chin. "I don't know if you have a saying for it in sauerkrautland, Fritz, but here in America, you scratch my back and I'll scratch yours."

* * *

It occurred to me, as the black-and-white sped me back to the Oakshade Inn, that there were two dogsbodies in this case. I was the second. The old English word *dogsbody,* meaning an insignificant underling, a lackey, fitted my present situation like pantyhose. Even worse, I had become a detective in spite of myself. But I had had enough experience putting myself in the shoes of the authorities to make me believe I could pull the thing off—with a large dose of luck.

It was too late to start on the case tonight, so I decided that tomorrow morning I would visit the college administration building, get the names of the students whom Thor had maimed six years ago, and then try to learn if they or anyone close to them still lived in Barhaven. And if someone in that category happened also to have access to the college chem lab, we might have our poisoner before the next nightfall.

The mellow sunlight of Friday morning was drenching my room when the phone exploded again. The digital clock read 7:12, and I was not yet in any mood to face the day. I made a kind of glunking noise into the mouthpiece.

"Fritz!" Even half awake it did not take me three guesses to identify my caller. "Get your rear end down to the station, *mach schnell.* All hell's broke loose!"

Thirty minutes later I stumbled out of a cab into the city hall and down a marble staircase to the basement, which was the police headquarters. I informed the fat asthmatic desk sergeant that Chief Knaup was expecting me, but before the sergeant could pick up the interoffice phone, a door flew open behind me and there he stood, posing with his hand on his holster for all the world like a short pudgy version of Randolph Scott playing marshal of Tombstone.

"Get in here!" he roared, and stalked ahead of me through the detective squad room and into his own office.

"Read this, and that, and this one." He tossed a stack of police reports across his desk at me. "We've been getting calls all night. Some nut's been driving around the county making war on the dog population of the area!"

On a first reading of the reports I almost agreed with the

sputtering chief. Our devotee of the spiked hamburger had cut himself a wide swath last night.

Winston, age five, Boston bull terrier, property of Mr. and Mrs. Horace Burgess of Newcomb Heights, found dead in the service pantry of the Burgess home at 6:00 A.M.

El Toro, French poodle, age two, owned by Miss Lucretia Runcible of Barhaven, found dead in its basket in the kitchen when Miss Runcible woke up hungry at 3:25 A.M. and went to the refrigerator for some yogurt.

Cincinnatus, mutt, age seven, belonging to Professor Featherstone of the classics department at the college, found dead behind the professor's front door at 1:30 A.M. when the professor returned home from the annual banquet of the Lucullus Club.

Including Thor, a total of seven canines had been transported overnight to that Big Kennel in the Sky, four within the Barhaven city limits and three in outlying communities.

"Has it been confirmed that the cause of death in each case was poison?"

"Only in the first three so far," Knaup told me. "County lab's been working all night on it. The others will prove out the same. This is a pattern, Fritz."

"Perhaps not the pattern you thought," I murmured, and shuffled through the police reports again. "Observe the addresses of the late dogs' masters and mistresses. Five seem to be private homes, but Miss Runcible is 243 Westview, Apartment 18-D, and Mr. Henry Wampler is 4576 North Wood Avenue, Apartment 907. Does this suggest anything to you?"

Before the chief could figure out what to say, his phone buzzed and he made a grab for it. "Knaup," he barked. "Yeah, Sergeant, I . . . *What?* . . . No, no, I'll go out on this one myself." He slammed down the phone and groped for his visored cap. "Let's go, Fritz."

"Dogsbody Number Eight?" I inquired.

"Catsbody Number One," he snarled. "Our nutcake's started zapping the cat population too!"

* * *

Knaup drove us in his own cruiser, the one with all the gun stickers on the bumper. Ten minutes out of town we turned in between a pair of stone pillars and onto another one of those private drives. The cruiser splashed through a mud puddle in a depression of the road, then sped along clean smooth macadam until the drive ended in a parking circle at the side of a huge Victorian stone monstrosity of a mansion.

"Who is the owner of this establishment?" I asked as Knaup rang the symphonic chime beside the front door.

"Used to be Franklin Bagnell, the big steel manufacturer. He died five or six years ago."

"Ah, yes, I remember seeing him on television—when he visited the Federal Republic of Germany, of course." I had almost blown my scam with that careless remark. I did remember seeing old Bagnell several times on TV newscasts, a cadaverous old reactionary who was forever ranting about Communist-inspired legal restraints on the American businessman. When he was upset a muscle in his cheek would twitch—a Bagnell family trait, I remembered having read in the news magazine.

"Ever since the old man died," Knaup continued, "the lawyers have been fighting in court over who owns the house and the money. For all practical purposes the dog owns it, I guess."

Before I could ask him to clarify that last enigmatic remark, the door was inched open and a trim, tired-looking young lady in a pink pantsuit inspected us, made a lightning deduction from the chief's uniform that he was fuzz, and threw the door wide. "Hey, Mama!" she bellowed into the depths of the house. "Cops here!"

A gray, fiftyish woman descended the oak staircase to meet us in the foyer, where she stood under a huge oil portrait of skeletal old Bagnell and threw out her hands to the Duke. "Oh, Chief Knaup, it's so good of you to come. It's not many high officials who would come in person when a cat is murdered."

"We in the law enforcement community love cats deeply," Knaup orated. "Oh, this is Dr. Gerstad, the famous criminologist. Fritz, may I present Madge Slocum, the caretaker here, and her daughter Lila. What happened to the cat, honey?"

Her mother answered for her, sniffing back the hint of a tear. "I just don't know what happened, Chief Knaup. I put Kikimora's supper out for her at 5:45 yesterday evening the way I always do, and then I whistled for Barnaby to come in from the yard for *his* supper, and around then it started raining, and Lila and I ate at 6:30. We watched TV together and went to bed early and I found poor Kiki when I came down this morning to get her and Barnaby breakfast. She was lying in her little cat box so stiff and still I knew something was wrong with her, so I picked her up and listened for her little heartbeat, and she was dead."

"Is Barnaby your husband, madam?" I asked the sorrowing caretaker.

"He gets better care than a lot of husbands I know," Lila answered pertly. "He's the dog that more or less owns the place."

I took a casual stroll the length of the hallway to a parquet-floored conservatory at the back of the house. A riot of potted plants, hanging ferns, and crawling greenery almost suffocated me. I looked out the rear window on broad landscaped terraces stretching for a few hundred yards, dotted with bright flower beds. A large gray dog of indeterminate breed was romping in the middle distance, chasing a rabbit or something. Barnaby seemed a hell of a lot more carefree than most rich people of my acquaintance.

"It's the cat we're interested in, remember?" Knaup snaked an arm through the plant life and plucked me out of the conversatory, leading me through a side corridor and a butler's pantry into a barnlike kitchen and over to a wicker basket heaped with fluffy little pillows, where the eighth victim lay. Kikimora was a broad-headed white Maltese with a black notch down the middle of her forehead.

"The cat was merely a personal pet of Mrs. Slocum, I take it?" I asked Knaup. "And the care of the dog is her job, like the care of the house?"

"You got it. Old Bagnell picked up Barnaby about five

years before he died. Just a mutt, but the old man grew to
love him a lot more than he loved the couple of relatives he
had left. So he put most of his money in a fund to care for
the dog as long as the dog lived. Honorary trust, it's called.
Dog's got the run of the house and grounds, eats better
than a lot of people, vet comes out to look it over twice a
week. The Slocum women's pay, the taxes on the property,
everything gets paid out of the trust as long as Barnaby's
alive."

"And when he dies?" I murmured.

"The property and money get divided among seven or
eight charities and those two relatives. Second or third
cousins, I think. Morton Godfrey, a lawyer in California,
and a young kid named George Bagnell. They're the ones
who started the lawsuit to knock out the will on the idea
the old man was bananas. It's been in the courts for
years."

I paced back and forth across the spotless kitchen floor.
The extent to which I'd become my own fictitious creation
was beginning to frighten me, but with a wild sense of excitement I realized that I might be on the brink of actually
solving this case. "But why should the cat have died?" I
mumbled half to myself. "Everything else I can account
for, but not the cat."

"Fritz, what the hell are you muttering about?"

"Last night you believed that Thor was the intended victim of someone who drove near the Stockford house and
threw a poisoned meat patty for him to eat. The rash of
dog deaths during the night established that animosity
against Thor was not the motive. But you still believed
that the killer was a person who spent yesterday evening driving through the area dropping poisoned meat on
lawns. This cannot be so. I remind you that at least two of
the dogs lived in high-rise apartments. Where do they
roam? How does our killer deposit the meat in front of
them? You have misconceived the technique of the crimes."

"Now wait a minute, Fritz," Knaup objected, banging
on the door of the walk-in meat keeper for emphasis. "Why
couldn't the cat over there have picked up something with

the poison in it yesterday? It could have been out in the grass playing with Barnaby all evening for all you know."

"We drove through a mud puddle," I reminded the chief, "just inside the private drive leading here. The macadam between that puddle and this house was clean and unmarked until your own car traversed it. You will recall that it rained heavily last evening. No automobile crossed the puddle between its formation and this morning. This is at least circumstantial evidence that there is no madman driving around your community with poisoned meat. Kikimora was poisoned here in the house. And the seven dead dogs were poisoned in their respective homes also."

Something like understanding was beginning to dawn over the chief's dumpy face. "I submit that it was the food their masters served them that was poisoned," I went on. "It is the only hypothesis that explains everything. Well, almost everything—everything but the cat. You must call your brother-in-law at the university and ask him where he purchases dog food. Then you must call each of the other owners and ask the same question. I predict you will receive the same answer. Go." I pointed to the phone extension hanging on the kitchen wall next to a memo board. To give orders to a police chief in his own bailiwick tickled my soul.

Knaup pressed touch-tone buttons, got the university switchboard, and asked for President Stockford's office. "Yeah, Herbie, he wants me to ask you. Where did you buy Thor's chow? . . . Fourfooted Gourmet, huh? Okay, Herbie, buzz you later."

He hung up and turned to me. "Herbie fed the dog a special-quality ground chuck he bought at The Fourfooted Gourmet. That's a specialty shop we have in town—finest cuts of meat and other goodies specially prepared for pets. It's where all the pet pamperers go."

"Then that is the place where the poison was mixed with the dog food," I insisted. "Call your office, have your sergeant phone each of the others, and ask them the same question you put to Mr. Stockford, then report back to you. Meanwhile I must deal with the problem of the cat."

Knaup whirled back to the phone while I went through

the swinging doors in and out of the butler's pantry and down the long hallway into the drawing room, where the Slocum women waited. They sat on matching armchairs upholstered in rich blue velvet, talking together in hushed tones.

"Excuse me, ladies." I stepped in front of them and executed a slight bow. "Where do you purchase Barnaby's meals?"

Madge Slocum stared up at me with a look of puzzlement behind her shell-rimmed glasses. "Why, what a strange question! Well, you know, Barnaby is not what you'd call an aristocrat among dogs. He was just a stray that Mr. Bagnell found as a puppy and grew extremely attached to. After Mr. Bagnell's death I tried to get Barnaby to eat the finest foods available but he would always turn up his nose, so ever since I've just served him canned dog food I get at the supermarket."

"And where do you obtain the food for your cat?" I continued.

This time Lila Slocum did the honors. "That's a funny story too. Like Mama said, she tried to get Barnaby to eat fancy food. There's a special grade of ground chuck she bought for him but he wouldn't eat the stuff. But Kiki went crazy over it, so ever since then we bought the ground chuck for her."

"Every Thursday afternoon I did my weekly shopping for Kiki," her mother added helpfully.

"Did you follow this procedure yesterday as well?" I inquired. Both women indicated that they had.

I didn't need to ask the next question, but I asked it anyway. "And the name of the establishment where you procured these culinary delights?"

"It's called The Fourfooted Gourmet," Lila said.

"Thank you." I practically clicked my heels at them Prussian-style, and wheeled back out to the kitchen, where Knaup was just hanging up the phone. "Sarge made four of those calls so far. You were right, by damn! They all bought that special ground chuck at The Fourfooted Gourmet."

"As did Mrs. Slocum for her cat," I reported. "The pattern is now clear. Someone poisoned the food at its source. And the rest of a week's supply is sitting in that meat keeper at this moment, and no doubt in the refrigerators of every other bereaved pet owner in this case. Call headquarters and send men out to collect the meat at once. Then let us pay a visit to these canine caterers."

We rocketed back through the mud puddle and roared onto the state highway back to town. Knaup drove with one hand on the wheel and the other on the butt of the Colt Python in its holster. We turned into the main business district in the center of Barhaven and pulled up short in the middle of a tiny parking lot next to a low tan-brick building. "That's the place," Knaup said.

"Is it permitted to park this way?" I asked. Every slot along the sides of the lot seemed to be taken, and he was blocking at least a dozen cars the way he was positioned.

"Man, I'm the law in this town, anything I do is permitted. Let's go."

And as casually as two dog owners about to pick up their pets' dinners, we stepped into the premises of The Four-footed Gourmet. A bell over the door tinkled as we walked in. The establishment looked more like a real-estate office than a food store. Pickled-pine paneling, Muzak box bracketed to the wall near the ceiling, imitation-brick tile on the floor, an occasional poster of a dog or cat carefully posed to look irresistibly cuddly.

Behind a gold-flecked Formica counter at the far end of the shop there was a long line of refrigerator cabinets. A pale and very thin young man in a white apron, with hair the color of cooked noodles, was weighing meat in a scale for a customer. "What's your pleasure, gentlemen?" he began as he looked at us.

And then he registered Knaup's uniform, and a muscle in his cheek began to twitch. I studied his cadaverous face more closely, compared it with a painted face I had seen this morning, and made one of the rashest statements of my career.

"This is Mr. George Bagnell," I announced, turning to Knaup, "the animal poisoner."

And instantly the place was a madhouse. George flung the package of meat at us, scored a direct hit on Knaup's face, and sprang through a doorway to the rear. Dripping with meat juice, Knaup vaulted the counter and clawed for his gun, shouting, "Police, halt!" as he and I ran through the rear storage area and out a side door into the parking lot.

George was gunning a blue Pinto out of the lot and smashed head-on into Knaup's cruiser. He flew out the door of the Pinto and started sprinting toward the street. Knaup snapped a shot at him, aiming low for his leg. He missed George but hit the right front tire of his own cruiser.

George was almost out of the long narrow lot when suddenly a two-tone convertible sped into the area with a fat blond woman in the front seat and a huge German shepherd in the rear. The kid had to swerve out of the car's way in a split second. He slammed against the wall as Knaup fired again, and the dog leaped out of the car and dived for George as if the kid were a cat.

The fat woman floored her brakes and screeched, "Oh, my God! Down, Schnitzel, down!" and waddled out of the convertible just as Knaup was ramming his Python into the small of George's back and motioning him to assume the frisking position against the wall.

Knaup had to radio for another car to come and haul the prisoner away. While we were waiting for the nearest service station to send someone over to change the flat on Knaup's cruiser, I explained the rest of my conclusions to him.

"As long as Barnaby lived, Bagnell's cousins profited nothing. George Bagnell came to Barhaven for the express purpose of killing the dog. He probably shadowed Mrs. Slocum on her shopping trips, observed her weekly visits to The Fourfooted Gourmet for ground chuck, and reasonably but wrongly assumed that the food was for the dog.

"He proceeded to obtain a job at the shop and some poison elsewhere and waited his chance to impregnate a supply of the special ground chuck with the poison just prior to one of Mrs. Slocum's Thursday visits. Altogether a foolish and wasteful plan, and one that betrayed its perpetrator's inexperience. Any other dog owner who picked Thursday to shop would find his animal dead too, but I suppose George was not displeased by that. The more dead dogs, the less it would appear that one particular dog was the target.

"And remember that you must arrange for announcements in the newspapers and radio and television that all patrons of The Fourfooted Gourmet must bring their meat in at once for analysis. We want no more dead animals."

"I know it was the twitch that told you the kid was a Bagnell," the chief asked, "but why couldn't he have been Morton Godfrey, the other cousin?"

Actually, of course, he could have been, and I had taken a fifty-fifty chance, but it wouldn't do to let Knaup know that.

"Being an attorney," I rationalized sagely, "Morton Godfrey would depend on his suit contesting the will, simply because if he should win, the entire Bagnell estate would pass by the law of intestacy, with the charities taking nothing and the two cousins everything. Would he have been so foolish as to try to kill the dog for a small share of the estate when by lawful means he stood to gain so much more? No, it was clearly not a legal mind that conceived these crimes."

"Sharp thinking, Fritz." Knaup clapped me on the shoulder. "And you can bet on it I'll make sure old Herbie signs that contract with your company for security services. Uhhh—provided you put through that little side deal we talked about?"

I looked at the hapless chief, with his uniform dripping meat juice and his tire flattened by his own well-placed slug, and struggled to keep from laughing aloud as I shook his hand again. "We in the criminological community," I assured him, "support a well-armed police force."